The House That Turns Black in the Rain

The House That Turns Black in the Rain

A.T. Martin

ISBN: Softcover 978-1-4363-2501-1

This book was printed in the United States of America.

To order additional copies of this book, contact:
Xlibris Corporation
1-888-795-4274
www.Xlibris.com
Orders@Xlibris.com
36659

The House That Turns Black in the Rain, though a work of fiction, is written to reflect the style and manner of the nineteenth century. Conforming to modern sensibilities, positions, and tastes would violate the novel's authenticity.

Translations by Shaun Folan.

"That there house is a queer thing. There's somethin' dark in the way she looks at you. She's like Ireland. They live from death those two. Can you ne'er set the two of 'em right? And so, know that that house was born from the very stones themselves, for there rests your answer."

Chapter 1

1860

Spring came wet that year. So wet that I feared our stone house, which was grey when dry and black when drenched, would never turn grey again. It was the sort of rain that kept coming and coming, with those little spells misting down in between, just enough wet to keep you dripping. It was the sort of rain that kept you inside.

My brother and I had spent the morning doing our lessons in the library, and we were now performing the slow, one hour of private study that was required of us each day except Sunday. It was only Friday. Our tutor was going away that night to attend her mother's birthday in Dublin. She was to be gone until Monday evening, and for us that meant a jubilous three days of freedom.

I was beginning to forget about what the sun looked like. I squinted into the desk lamp's glow, as one would do out-of-doors when the sky was shining brightly, just to see if my eyes could still do it. A bit of figuring came across me then, and I wondered that if the sun was a vain creature, then it could well have designed all the rain up for its own ends. How many of us thought of the sun on a grand afternoon? Everybody would say, "what a fine day that was," but who said, "how fine the sun looked on that afternoon"? Now the sun, being a haughty fellow, was losing all his rightful commendations to the day, which wasn't even a real thing. The sun wanted to show all those ungrateful that he, and not the day, was the cause of it all. So, he had now gone away and had brought out all those rain clouds to show his displeasure until somebody would figure it all out. Well, I had been thinking about the sun, and I wouldn't have minded to see his bright shadow make a day fine again. I wanted to test this theory with Peader and Daniel. Old Peader was our gardener, and Daniel was our groom.

With that new thought in my head and the terribly wonderful days of nothing opening wide before me, I couldn't bring myself to study geography, even if we were using Father's not ready-made Italian globe. I rested my head in my hand and stared at the walls of dark oak bookcases. The bookcases were built into the walls, which were also dark, brown, and oak. The floors were laid in the same wood and stained a now-faded chocolate. Even the military rows of volumes were bound in various shades of dark-tinted leather. They had the smell of oldness that wanted to make you sneeze.

The only lightness in the room came from the aged white plaster ceiling. I stared sleepily at the pocked and worn bookcases and at the dark cracks in the once perfectly matched joints. My schoolbook lay open before me, blathering on silently about the geography of Italy. My brother scratched something into his notebook, and unless there was a part of Italy that looked like a grazing cow, he didn't seem to be doing much studying either.

"You know Mrs. Hutcheson's new baby?" I said, blindly flipping through the pages of the geography book.

"The ugly one brought round last week?" Sheridan dropped his scratching and looked at me.

"Aye"—I nodded—"old Peader said it's a sheoque and that's why it's so ugly."

"What's a shee-oque?"

"Peader says it's one of the wee folk that comes and takes away children, or switches the baby in the cradle with a wiry-looking thousand-year-old fairy left in the child's place. They always want the boy children because they can use the human to fight in all o' their fairy wars. He says the sheoques live under the earth in mounds and forts all over Ireland. They're beautiful to look at, he says, and their fine-blooded steeds have golden bridles and are shod with silver."

"Ah"—he shook his black hair—"you could be driven to believe something like that when you look at that Hutcheson baby. But I would say he's been switched with at least a two-thousand-year-old fairy. It would take that long to get that ugly."

My brother was blessed with a most remarkable tongue for a ten-year-old. Despite that gift, he was of the sort that wasn't so keen on the supernatural. He judged such things to hold little interest for realists, who were concerned only with the workings of this world. I think he was just afraid of fairies and such.

"I think you believe it?" I leaned back in the heavy wooden chair.

"No, I don't. I'm just playin'."

"But," I continued, "how do you know what's real and what isn't."

"I believe in what I can see." He pointed to his eyes. "I don't follow those yarns o' Peader's, that is, until I see a ghost and a fairy of any species for myself."

"I only said I enjoyed those stories, I never said I believed, but I don't have the proof to doubt 'em either." I shut the geography book. "But just because you haven't seen a thing doesn't mean that ya can't feel confident in that thing's reality either."

He shrugged.

"Do you believe that there's an India?" I asked Sheridan.

"Sure I do." He looked surprised and combed his fingers through his fine black hair again. He was getting anxious. "You know I do; Mother's been to India with Father. You know they have, as well."

I nodded my head. "Did you go with them?"

Sheridan's blue eyes started from his face. "You're fierce cheeky, Anne"—he shook his thin finger at me—"you know I didn't." He looked like a little version of my father.

"So," I said, "you've not been to India then."

"No, I've ne'er been to India," he said, shaking his head.

"Now," I said, "seein' as you Sheridan O'Hayden, who has ne'er been to India, can you answer me by agreein' that this country lies to the right of the Arabian Sea?"

"I can." He nodded, causing the rich black hair to fall over his cheeks.

"But you've ne'er been there, you said so yourself!"

"Everybody knows where India is; and besides, I've got a brass elephant from Ma, a silver cup from Da, and they both come from India."

"Sure they did," I said. "And how do you know that Ma and Da weren't makin' it up? Maybe those things come from Africa?"

"Well, trash man, they weren't makin' it up!" To my pleasure, his calmness was growing ever more short-lived.

"Well, how do you know they weren't? The point I'm making is how do you know that there is an India?" I raised a hand to shut him up. "You know because Ma and Da and other people have told you that there is. You've never been to the place yourself, but you believed in it being there because you took another's words for fact. Isn't that so?"

"Well." He was humoring me.

"Well," I copied him, "go ahead and shrivel your face. I'd say it would be a pretty ignorant soul that only believed in the things that he saw himself. And a disagreeable one at that," I continued, "doubting everyone else's words without a hard fact to lay upon those doubts." Now that was a sweet payback for Mr. Fierce Cheeky himself. He sat on the bench like the standing stone in Mr. Father of the Ugly Baby Hutcheson's field. You knew you got the best of Sheridan in a scrap when he didn't answer you back.

"Well, if that's the way you're gonna be when there's three days of freedom stretchin' themselves before us, you're a shame to yourself!" I rose from the chair. "I'm goin' out, rain or no rain."

"All right, I'll follow ya." He shut his book. "I've got to change these shoes though. I can't get any mud on 'em, or I'll be killed. Hey! Where're ya gonna be?" he shouted after me.

"I'm gonna be in the stables." I opened the library door and started down the hall, calling behind me, "I've got somethin' to ask Peader and Daniel!"

I ran through the stable yard, holding back the sides of my dress as I went. The rain was spilling down as it had promised to do earlier in the morning. It was a good time to test my sun theory on Peader as I found him cleaning the horse tack with young Daniel. Most of the workers called him young Daniel. My brother and I did when we were talking to adults even though Dan was four years older than me and five years older than

Sheridan. Dan was fifteen and good at talking over theories. Dan was good at talking over anything.

"Good mornin', Ms. Anne." Peader always called me Ms. Anne. He nodded his dark copper head, where there was not a grey hair to be found despite his fifty-eight years. He had seen four decades before I had even been born. I found that remarkable. "You look as though you're keepin' as damp as the rest of us."

"I have, Peader." I walked into the humid tack room, which was so satisfyingly full of the fragrances of leather and of straw bedding and of the clean horses next door.

"I'm sick of readin' and sittin'." I leaned gloomily against a travelling trunk. "I'm sick of house things, and I'm sick of doin' lessons. But I haven't got any lessons now because Ms. Farrell's goin' away. She's upstairs packin' her things and—"

"That woman's still packin'?! God save her!" Peader interrupted with disbelief. "You'd think she was sailin' for China." He shook his head, and a laugh moved his thin, wide shoulders.

"And my mother's helpin' her now. Sheridan's gone to change his shoes 'cause he doesn't want to get the good ones ruined again. Father warned him that he doesn't"—I mimicked—"want to pay the shoemaker's wages in their entirety." I shrugged. "So, there's nobody around."

"Ahh, silence and nobody around aren't terribly sorry things. You ought to spend some time with this one." Daniel leaned over a saddle and tipped his tussled brown head toward the gardener. "Oh, it's all day with his mutterin's; that're enough to make the trees pull loose and walk away for the relief." Dan began to ape the complaints of his cleaning partner, "That sky has designs on movin' the sea onto the land drop by drop. It's movin' the sea onto the land." He squinted toward the ceiling and pointed a finger toward the sky. The boy looked like a Raphael painting. Dan turned his eyes to me, "and he calls me the soft one?!" He tapped his forehead. I raised my eyes with polite sympathy.

"I knew you when you'd not a voice to your lips!" Peader accused. "And to think of what improper words I'm hearin' from you now is somethin' I would never have figured."

Daniel smiled boldly.

"I was figurin' about a thing myself," I added. It was a grand show to see those two argue, but I wasn't up to it just then. "Don't you think it was the sun that brought all the wet because he's jealous that no one's been praisin' him for the grand days?"

"Now there's a thought." The boy walked over and nudged his older friend. "I'm not the only one around here thinkin' great things."

"Well"—Peader turned toward the boy—"while you're thinkin', go and have the big carriage made seaworthy." He rubbed some soap on a tack-cleaning cloth. "Déan deifir! Go and make quick work of it too!" You would know that Peader was agitated when he spoke in Irish, and his partner looked amused.

Daniel Whelan smiled as he looked at me and added, "See how nice the water makes that place look." We gazed at the house through the window. "There she is, shinin' like black marble with all the wet on her."

Peader turned slowly and shook out his drying rag. "You are near to makin' me sick with that kind of honeyed talk? You'll come to no good by it, none of that sort do, fearin' honest work."

I walked closer to the two of them, biting the smile off my lips. I sat on the stool next to Peader. Daniel feigned bewilderment while snatching a damp walnut hair from his forehead.

"The poet in a golden clime was born with golden stars above, dowered with the hate of hate, the scorn of scorn, the love of love." The groom lifted his shoulders and smiled forlornly. "Lord Tennyson." He sent Peader a sidelong gaze.

The old gardener couldn't choke back a laugh as he smacked his partner with the tail of the cloth.

"My mother says that Dan's a Ro-mantic," I picked up a stirrup and rubbed the shine back into it.

"See!" The boy pointed a stirrup leather at Peader. "There's a wise woman."

"Why would you want to be a Ro-man-tic?" Peader jeered at the groom.

"It's a good way to be," Dan nipped back. "I see the beauty in things." He observed with proud airs.

"Ro-mantics like nature," I teased. "But you didn't see the beauty when that spider sat upon your leg last Thursday."

"Whose side are you on?" Daniel demanded. "I ne'er thought o' you as a turnabout. Sure I see the beauty in things *when* there's beauty to be seen." He pointed a reproachful finger at me.

"All beasts are fair, boy, even if they don't suit your eyes. They're all God's creation, and they suit His." Peader put the saddle back on the form.

"Thank you, St. Francis. You speak the truth," Dan bowed reverently.

"I'll be hearin' confessions behind the henhouse." Peader straightened his neckcloth and peered out the window. "Ah, look now, the rain's stopped. That was a fast shower."

"Fish are the most religious animals," Daniel corrected, oblivious to the man's last remark.

"For those who are the most sinful"—Peader raised his blue eyes—"confessions will be taken by the pond. Mind don't step into the water, boy; the fish are so sensitive to wayward behavior and hypocrites that they might be pressed to jump out. First, I've to plant some geraniums before the rain comes again. Is anybody gonna help?"

"Speakin' of sin"—Dan's keen expression fell onto me—"I'll bet your Sheridan will be appearin' now that the clouds are goin'."

"Am I talkin' to the air?" Peader addressed an empty stall.

"He probably will, after he's changed his shoes," I said half-interested. "Although mother was talkin' about her lacemakin' today, and if she catches him, he'll be chasin' thread." I grinned deviously. "Oh!" I jumped from the stool. "Dan, do you think Mrs. Hutcheson's new baby was stolen by the fairies?"

"Ah, now don't be goin' around sayin' that," Peader groaned, "or I'll get all the blame for startin' it and puttin' it in your head."

"I'm not," I corrected. "I'm just askin' Dan, keepin' it between us. Sheridan doesn't believe it."

Peader smiled and shrugged. "Ah, you heard that right enough!"

"My aunt once said that she knew of a woman whose boy was switched with a fairy." Daniel stopped his cleaning.

"What happened?" I asked.

"I don't know. She never told me the rest. Although I heard that if you touch the fairy-switched child with a hot poker, the fairy leaps away hollerin', and the real baby's put back."

"That sounds like an awful thing," I squirmed; and I rarely squirmed over anything.

"Well, I suppose"—Daniel walked over to sit on the trunk—"that you're actually burnin' the fairy and not the real child who's away with the other fairies at the time."

"See here." Peader rolled up his left sleeve to reveal the squarish remnants of an old burn.

Dan's eyes widened, and my own answered his.

"Terrible thing," Peader looked at the brand. "Got it last year tryin' to shoe ol' Mr. Hewson's plowin' mare." He let down the sleeve. "Now, there's enough of the talk of the good people and Mrs. Hutcheson's new one; although"—he said offhandedly—"that child was probably switched. I've ne'er seen a one like that," he grimaced. "*Anois*, the day's not gonna wait for us. Whose gonna help me with those geraniums?"

"I'll help"—I straightened—"I'm dyin' to go out. If Sheridan comes, will ya tell him I'm out, Dan?"

"I will." The boy rose slowly from the trunk. "I've got to finish here," he added stiffly before reaching for another bridle.

Chapter 2

By that Friday morning the rains had stopped, but the sun still did not allow the earth the favor of his presence. Peader and I were no farther than the front path when we saw the small gig rolling over the pebbly approach. From the front of the house, you could see that it was Niamh in the traces although she was more brown than dapple white. The grey mare's legs were slapped with dirt, and the shining black collar had turned a gritty brown. My father had a cool, damp trip down the road from Dublin. I watched the mare's feet crush lazily but steadily over the gravel. As Niamh came to a stop, she caught the bit in her teeth and wrenched an extra length of rein from my father's hand. Peader scratched her soaking neck as he loosened the girth, and she sighed to him how relieved she was to be home.

"Good day, sir," Peader said, holding the blowing mare's head. "Trip's gone well, I hope."

"Well as well could be." My father leaned on the gig's door, his large, sharp stare scraped over the narrow man. He was cheerful despite the tears of water that dripped from his hat's brim.

"How has my Anne been keeping?" He turned his small, angular face to mine.

"She's been keepin' as wet as the rest of us . . . yourself included, sir," Peader revealed to my father.

"I didn't have to sit for lessons today," I said brightly as I walked to the carriage's side. "It's tonight that Ms. Farrell's leavin' for Dublin for her mother's birthday?"

My father nodded, and a spot of water tumbled off the brim of his hat.

"Now there's a woman who earns her shilling, wouldn't you say, Peader?" My father teased.

"I don't know how she does it, sir." The gardener closed his eyes in mock sympathy. I gave him a narrow glance.

"We didn't have to sit for lessons"—I continued snubbing their play—"as long as we read our history for an hour after breakfast. I read my geography instead," I said diligently. "And she said that was all right. Sheridan's still inside, and mother's helpin' Ms. Farrell with her packing."

"Now there's the girl, Anne, you sit and do what Ms. Farrell asks of you, and you'll never regret it. There are some out there less fortunate that can't have a chance for good schooling. It's a privilege to learn, and you should always remember that. No one can take what is gathered in your head, and that is the one wise saying that ever came out of my own father's fathomless mouth," he looked back and turned his penetrating eyes toward Peader, who smiled knowingly.

My father had a novel accent to his speech. It came across as an altered cadence of the talk of an Englishman who had spent rather too much time in Dublin. And the most remarkable part of the situation was that my father, who had gone to India and the exotic East, had never been to England for more than a month, and only twice at that.

"What are the two of you going off to do now?" He looked at me, removing the hat from his equally sodden hair, which fell past his collar like long black threads.

"We're off to plant geraniums," I answered directly.

"Before you're off then, I want to show you these." And he reached beneath the gig's seat and pulled an oilskin off from something resting on the floor. He straightened back up on the seat and presented me with two brown packages.

"It's a good thing that I had that sheet lying in the gig, or that wrapping would be as wet as me." He pointed at the gifts in my arms. "It was dry in Dublin when I set off this morning. I wasn't thirty minutes down the road to Wicklow when the sky started tearing open. I had to pull beneath a tree for a bit. There's one of those for you, Anne, and one for your brother."

From the shape and hardness of the wrapped objects, I guessed that they were books. Not just any books, but Dublin-bought books, and they were better than any you could buy in Bray. They were the same titles of course, but the city books just read better. It was like eating baker's bread from Dublin and baker's bread from the Main Street. They were the same, but the ones from the city were always better just because they were made in Dublin.

Dan had heard the gig drive up, and he had heard the talking, which brought him out from the stables.

"Good mornin', sir." He gave my father a courteous and retiring welcome for which he received a proper nod for an answer.

"The mare's been asking for you." My father gestured toward the dirt-covered Niamh.

"Well, she's got me now, sir. She'll get a proper lookin' after." Daniel scratched her dappled forehead, and the mare nibbled his coat sleeve. Peader released her head and moved to the gig's door.

"How did the deal go, sir?"

"Here"—my father thrust some papers at the man—"is our future pay."

"McKennit took the fall barley, Mícheál?" Peader searched the letter.

"The whole dusty lot of it and the *next* fall's too, if it's suitable. Here's the contract." He stepped to the gardener's shoulder and flipped to the second sheet.

"Now there's a neat-thinkin' businessman," Peader confirmed.

My hands were aching from holding the packages, and my head was dreaming away with the dull talk. I hoped I wouldn't start sounding like that when I got older. As I stood, I mused over the one consolation that Sheridan already spoke like that now, and he was only ten. Daniel spoke light and wonderful; he was fifteen and was almost a man. I would pray then that one was born with such notions as one was given the color of their hair. I could continue to hope so anyway.

My father reached back into the gig, and after a bit of rummaging, flourished a hard text in Daniel's direction. "Your friend," he said, "Thackeray."

Dan released Niamh's head and nodded thanks as he took the book from the tired man, and then headed to the stable, gift in hand and Niamh in tow. The gig rattled over the noisy pebbles. My father smiled and then shared a handshake with Peader.

"Well, I'll be goin' now, Mícheál, to put in those geraniums." The voice came as melancholy as dust. "I don't want to meet the rain."

"Do you go about your business, man"—he released his old friend's hand—"I don't want to hold you a half-moment more. This has been the most unpredictable stretch of weather." He pressed the water from the brim of his hat. "And most of all, I won't be leaving my fine lily of a wife for not a minute more of pining in that stone tomb I have got to house her in." My father spoke queer and sickly. "Has she asked for her husband, Peader?" He squinted.

"Ah, sir," Peader snickered, "not a moment's passed that she hasn't." He tilted his head like a corncrake.

I couldn't hold back a confused groan.

"No, she's not asked for you a t'all father." They both turned to look at me. "She was so busy. She's been getting ready for the photographing. With all the odd weather, the sun could come out at any moment, and she's to be ready for it when it does. We took some plates in the soft grey light, and none of 'em came out satisfactory at all." My father raised his eyes as if I was saying the most curious things in the world, and so I kept on going.

"On Wednesday, after the pictures, Lady Plunkett came callin', and she wanted to know if mother was wantin' to ride out with her if the rain held for a bit. The ground wasn't too soft for the hunt she said, that was what her husband found. Thursday, they went out, and you wouldn't believe it father, but mother brought Paddy out; and he jumped the stream in the back of Old Connaught House without shyin' once, and you know how he'd hardly cross a puddle before. She's been trainin' him, so." My father seemed to be somewhat stunned, as I have found adults were want to do when the conversation got complicated, and so I stopped explaining why my mother hadn't pined for him. I was going to tell him that I missed him so he'd feel better, but I blushed thinking of it, and I couldn't find anything else to say. "But your grey tomcat missed you. He was in your study every day to see if you'd come. It wasn't for mice he was searchin', I'm sure of it." I smiled. My father only raised his eyes.

"Ah, aren't you glad I talked you into takin' that little one out o' Mrs. O'Toole's calico's litter." Peader nodded. "Well then, you can count me and the cat for waitin' your return. I was hopin' you'd be back so I could ask you for the trap. Your old aunt sent her man 'round to see if I could bring her to town to get some things she's ordered at The Mart, and it wouldn't have been right to put her in the car." He rubbed his waistcoat.

"No, that wouldn't be right, Peader. I thank you for pining for me then, I think. And as to your motive, you may have the trap, of course."

"I did miss you too, Father. And not for wantin' the trap." Peader's confession had scouted a safe path for my awkward admission.

"Everyone should have such a daughter." He placed his hand on my shoulder. "You will excuse me now, Peader. I don't want to be keeping those geraniums from you." My father shook his coat.

The older man smiled. I followed my father toward the house with the packages digging unmercifully into my numbed arms.

"I'll be putting in those plants," the voice came, now more melancholic than dust. "If I start right off"—Peader lifted up his watch—"I might still have time to take some dinner. Ah, but there's so many o' them, I doubt I'll have the time at all."

I stopped my walking and twisted around slowly. My father stopped when he no longer felt me trailing behind. I turned to him with a sheepish gaze. He placed the dripping hat back over his limp black hair, and a chill ran across me as I watched the uncomfortable act.

"You give me those packages, Anne; I'll take them with me. You'd better help Peader get those plants in as you promised, in case the rain starts again."

I handed the gifts back over. "Would you tell Sheridan the rain's stopped. He was changin' his shoes, but he's not come out since."

My father smiled. "I will, and I'll tell him you're off with Peader. We'll save these packages till after the evening; that'll be the right time for them then."

Now there was a cover that would not tell you the nature of the book. To the watcher from behind, my father moved with a languid and delicate stride, his hands unfashionably thrust into the trouser pockets. He was two months over thirty-three, but to anyone unfamiliar, he seemed the unguarded schoolboy with his coat's skirt flowing freely, and the packages stuffed beneath his arm. If any man looked—and that is only looked—the free-willed rover, the untrainable rake, it was Mícheál O'Hayden of Carrickduff.

Despite the great stretch between ages, counties, and convictions, sturdy partnerships grew here like the barley in the backfields. We weren't living in Eden, and we weren't living in a bad penny novel. Sometimes you had to wait for the sun to change humors. There were the regularly passing storms of disagreement, the dark veils, but I remember many more days being cloudless and fair. I am enough of a cynic to say that recollections have a way of filtering out a lot of storms and replacing the holes with agreeable clouds, but I do know that there was one day that could never be brightened. I know that there are things too terrible to happen, and they come to you as do the clouds of the spring.

I was born here in 1849 in that grey stone house that turned black in the rain. That house had you in its keeping. It knew how it wanted you to act, and it knew how to get it from you. My father said that we owned it in name and deed only, for the house was the true master. It had an eerie way of drawing people to it, as if it was after setting matters straight. It was the sort of place that you could never leave, and if you did go, you left in body only, for your mind was still held there. The Irish name for it is Carrickduff, the English is Black Rock house.

Carrickduff was built in 1735 by a distiller named Arthur Crawford. And that was all we knew of him, save that he was an Englishman, and that he had spent a great deal of money upon its construction. He had the place built of a pleasing and closely cut stone with the blocks having a smooth face on them. In daylight, the house was a common silver grey, but after days of soaking rain, it was almost as black as boot polish. However, the place was small for such as the likes of eighteenth century Mr. Crawfords, but I suppose one had to lessen costs somewhere.

Carrickduff held his soul. That was on his headstone. And it was a building block that had been saved for that purpose during her construction all those years ago. I loved it out of all in the graveyard. It was the stone that turned black in the rain.

There was a thought held about those low rolling fields that the departed Mr. Crawford was the reason behind Carrickduff's effortless holding over people. And I don't think that he would have minded having the O'Haydens under his nose since there was and is an unusual manner of gentry in Bray. Bray was known for the actions of her free-minded and evenhanded landlords, and for their fair treatment of the tenantry even though it was beyond my ability to know the cause of such things. That was one of the reasons why my family had been so agreeably received into that house on the hill.

If you are familiar with the delicate past of my country, you will know that Irishmen like us and our guardians had rarely met over amiable terms. My town is bordered on the east by a stretch of pebbly beaches and rolling sea cliffs. If you were to cross the Irish Sea, you would be set down on the homeland of Mr. Arthur Crawford, in the country of England. Now Her Majesty Queen Victoria's land and my land of Ireland are like wine and butter, no matter how hard you stirred those things, the two would never blend together. Peader had said that you couldn't expect to raise a strawberry under the bows of an oak tree. The little vine would grow, and he would send out his leaves, but that big oak would be hovering above him, choking out the sun and stealing all the rain. That strawberry would grow, but he would never fruit. England was the stifling oak, Peader said, and Ireland the straining strawberry. Peader said he got the idea after reading Swift. I never thought of strawberries the same way again, anyway. I wondered if Mr. Crawford liked strawberries. One thing was sure though, there wasn't any intentional stifling going on at Carrickduff.

Chapter 3

I picked a trowel from out of the potting shed, and I ran off to catch Peader. He wasn't a hard man to find, as he was usually singing as he worked. I liked to hear him playing the melodies with no music but his own voice. The Irish songs were the best even though I could not follow the half-foreign words. They made me think of the wind and the hills of wild gorse and the shore in a storm. Those songs sounded to your ears as natural as the rain that sent a chill through you with the first drops on your head.

I found Peader behind the hedge of the small formal garden, digging holes in the wet dirt for the young geraniums. Their toothed, dark-veined leaves always reminded me of dragon's scales. There were a few in the waiting green crowd already sporting their five-petaled flowers that looked like purple-blushed briar roses. I took two clay pots, I sat down next to him, and he kept on singing as I made my own set of holes.

"Did my grandfather make this garden?" I interrupted his singing.

"Those hedges there"—he pointed behind us—"are over ninety years put in. There's some older too. But it was your grandfather who straightened up the inside though. That was in 1825. There's nothing harder than settin' a wild, left-alone garden right."

"He said the house had been abandoned all those years ago."

"Aye, and he picked Carrickduff and the acres with it for hardly over one thousand pounds." He lowered a plant into one of the holes and eased the muddy ground around its base. "The early owners, Arthur Crawford and his kin, had her for o'er ninety years, but it wasn't a Crawford that brought the place to ruin."

"I thought the place was abandoned?" I asked. The revelations from my friend lit my curiosity. Mother said that I was like Father's cat, but I couldn't decide whether that was a desirable or a bad way to be.

"It was abandoned, girl." Peader struck his trowel into the earth. He seemed bothered to talk, and I thought that strange, indeed. "I don't know the small parts of the business," he muttered. "But you see, there were three daughters to that marriage, and one son. The eldest girl wed a Belfast linen man and off she went. The youngest was given to a fine family in Tipperary, whose name I can't remember. It was the middle girl that married a local man; and they returned to Carrickduff—where her brother and his wife stayed—as she was terribly fond of her birth home. All o' them are gone now, of course. And so it was known then that the wife of the brother bore four children, one son, and three girls again. All those girls went off with their marriages; but the son, the youngest, stayed. He and his wife brought six children into the world, two boys and four girls. All the boys died in childhood. It was as if the house was bent on not gettin' an heir." He shrugged. "The four daughters went off, save for the last one. She went for the London season, and she didn't return alone. She was courtin' an Englishman. And good it was that they wed swiftly for her parents were both dead within years of the ceremony. Her husband became the master of the house, as there were no sons; and a sorry day it was when his hand was placed o'er Carrickduff. And I heard it said that on the day the bride's father died, the rain began to fall. The sky shed its tears day after day, and the house turned as black as writer's ink. And ever since, at each hard and lastin' rain, she again goes black as soot." He looked at me. "Well, that's what was said, anyway."

"I am sure she went black before then, Peader." I didn't believe in curses. I sat down upon an edging stone.

"Aye, Ms. Anne, I'm sure that she did too." He brushed his cheek, leaving a powdering of dirt behind.

I had known that Carrickduff had flourished under Arthur and his descendants. It wasn't until that Crawford daughter married a Richard Cosgrove from across the Irish Sea that the house and the name of the family that was her master for one century, came down with her as if they were bound in fate. Indeed, I knew very little about the house's disastrous fall. There seemed to be a legend circling about the circumstances. And part of that legend involved the closed mouths of the local people. Even Peader stalled before speaking of it, and he could find a story in a chestnut.

"The man who ran Carrickduff then, the Master Cosgrove"—Peader told me—"ran her as a wheat farm. Those tenants that turned his land—over 800 acres then—paid rents that would shock a spendthrift. They'd be out there breakin' their backs." He pointed to our barley fields.

I learned that Mr. Cosgrove was not a benevolent man. He was a terrible counterpart to the Crawfords and the kindness of many of the other landlords in Bray. His wife, it was said, had tried to curb her husband's recklessness, but her work brought forth a fruitless end. It must have been a darkness on her soul to watch as her great family fell.

"The ol' Cosgrove liked his drop, and he liked the gamin' table after his drop. And every year, he'd raise the rents to cover all his losses. He was nearly bankrupt, you see. Livin' like a lord with a di'vil of a hole in his pocket." He stopped to catch my wide and eager stare and then adjusted his manner to play my interest.

"Now," Peader continued, "one fall the wheat prices fell, and when the spring came, the tenants were feelin' the hardship with the first crop of their own food not ready for months. With little for them to eat and with nothin' for them to sell, the rents weren't going to be paid. There were evictions, and the tenants were put to the roads; but that didn't pay the man's debts any faster. It didn't stop him from makin' them either—he gambled away the carriage, he wagered one hundred acres of the land, and he even put up the stable. He was known as a senseless man when the drink had a hold of him. The master, Richard, wagered his way to ruin, and the ruin of his new family, and the entire legacy of the Crawford house."

"Mr. Cosgrove sold the house and returned to England alone, though some said he had one son, and that boy was with him. The wife stayed from then on in the county of Kildare with Mrs. Cosgrove's sister, or so it was said. No one ever heard from her husband again. She never mentioned any child. And that was how Carrickduff fell. Don't be askin' anymore about it." He pointed at me. "These things aren't for a young lady." He freed his trowel from the earth and opened a wet hole for the next plant. I watched as he quickly broke the brown leaves from the geranium's base, leaving only the sharply toothed green ones behind.

It was strange to think that my family had come to Carrickduff thirty-four years ago, even though that was a long time. It seemed as though we had been there forever. I had been there forever anyway, and I could not think of being anywhere else. One could envy the cleverness of the itinerant sellers who took their homes with them upon the roads. Most houses, I think, would not move so well.

"Is there anybody left?" I placed a geranium into a hole. It wasn't ladylike to dirty your hands, but I didn't care. I didn't have to because I was too young to be a lady.

"Anybody who?" Peader shrugged. He pressed the dirt about the roots and slapped the grit from his tough, work-dried hands. A pair of magpies waddled before the boxwoods in search of their dinner. Only the birds' white shoulders and breasts announced their presence in the bush's shadows.

"Well, is that nasty Cosgrove still livin'?" I said above the bird's chatterings. "What about Mrs. Cosgrove's sisters?"

"Now," he sighed, "didn't I ask you to cease questionin' about those people?"

"You should be nice since I'm helpin'." I crossed my arms as he moaned. "And I don't care about what I shouldn't hear."

"I don't know a thing about the sisters. But your Mr. Cosgrove died about three years ago. He was an old man—the blaggard—e'en God didn't want him. The son must be still around though, if there was one. Although you never know with those kind that live by the sword. He might've got smarter than his old man, married a wealthy Sasanach woman, and made a fine life for himself. Ah, girl, don't you be wipin' the dirt on your apron so, your mother'll be after me for gettin' you into a mess and not keepin' you right." He pulled a handkerchief from his coat pocket and pushed it at me. The magpies chortled their agreement on the matter.

"Do you know then, Peader"—I wiped my stained fingers—"I don't like that young Cosgrove, if there was or is one."

"Why is that, Ms. Anne?" He took back the soiled cloth.

"I don't like his father for what he did to Carrickduff and the Crawfords, and I don't like the son."

"Well, how can you know the son in that way when you've not met him?"

"Who else would he be like?" I shrugged. "All he knew was his father's ways—as the mother was gone you said—so he learned all that wickedness and nothin' else." I struck my trowel into the wet dirt.

"What if I didn't like your mother, huh? Then I wouldn't be spendin' any time with the likes of yourself."

"That's different, and it doesn't work." I shook my head. Peader leaned back with his knees bent beneath him.

"Well, how can it be different, you tell me?"

"It can be different, and it is," I explained. "You can't pretend to not like someone when you do. You like my mother, and you can't not like me. It's like pretendin' that you enjoy eatin' onions when you don't. You can't make yourself change your mind. It doesn't work, and you'd be lyin'."

"Ah girl, I just want to show you that you can't be sure of hatin' someone by the looks of who's around them. You may hate the father and take a fancy to his child, so." Peader raised an eyebrow.

"But Mrs. Cosgrove was wronged, and it wasn't just her; it was a wrong on her old family and on Carrickduff. It is a sad thing to be told, and you must feel bad from it." I poked the earth from my trowel.

"You must have strong feelin's on it, Ms. Anne"—he ran his gritty fingers through the light coppery hair—"you must, indeed. Only a blaggard or a stone wouldn't, that's to be truthful. It's a fierce-thinkin' world, girl . . . hard and oblivious to other's needs. If you're out without your hat, the rain gives not a care to drippin' on your head."

"'Tis true, Peader." I sent him a thoughtful gaze. "And you must go out prepared for the world. Mrs. Cosgrove had forgotten to bring her coverin', didn't she? And the rain fell all over her."

"So it did, girl, so it did." He pushed up from the ground with a slow but graceful motion.

"Let us take a break from the world and its ruthless ways, for the softer one of the dinner table." He rubbed the dirt from his knees. "And not a word of what I told you. It's for us and only between us. Ceart go leor, Ms. Anne?"

"Ceart go leor." I nodded. "Only between *us*."

We placed the garden tools in the wheelbarrow, and I followed Peader as he pushed the rusty-wheeled cart home. A thin stretch of lemony sky sparkled in the direction from where the cone silhouette of the Sugarloaf Mountain thrust upward from the earth. It was going to be a grand afternoon.

Carrickduff had been abandoned for four years before my grandfather, Mr. Gerald O'Hayden, from the town of Glendalough, brought her back from despair. The rest of the property, the two gardens, the neglected fields, the stone fences, and the stables did not age so well. I had been told that the boxwood had four and more seasons of untamed growth, and they had formed a frenzied border about the once-formatted gardens. It took several years to set them right. The wheat fields were blossoming with weeds, and the land lay fallow. The stables were cobwebbed and broken and worst of all, by the looks of my grandfather's sketches, were the tumbled down tenant cottages laying around the property's verges like rubble scratched up by quite monstrous badgers. The cottages of the deserted tenantry were almost past saving. Almost.

To pay for the extra cost of half-building new laborers' houses, my grandfather and my grandmother let their coastal home for sixty pounds to the masses of summer-season travelers seeking the benefits of the sea. Many of the fashionable and well placed would summer in Bray, and it was soon that my grandparents were able to sell their house named Violanda for a hefty profit so that the money might go to Carrickduff. Those thousands of pounds saw good use, for there was a lot of building to be done, laborers to be hired, and land to be plowed and revived.

The greatest amount of work rested in the raising of the cottages for the farm and house help, as well as the smaller dwellings for the harvest spalpeens. The cottages were low houses of whitewashed, mortared fieldstone and rubble. The bedrooms were located on the steep-ceiling second story. There were no windows as the four-sided roof sloped down and reached the walls of the first floor. The roofs themselves were thatch.

There had been much renovating going on in Bray and its environs since the early days of this century. There were new mail coach roads and turnpikes, despite the protests of the community once they were asked to open their purses. There were no disgruntled rallies following Gerald O'Haydon's improvements, but rather, there was quite the opposite reception. My grandfather did such a commendable job with the laborers' cottages that some of the "social reformers" of the time used them as models.

The O'Haydens spent another fair amount reconstructing the carriage house which was attached to the stable. On the top floor were found eight well-placed rooms that were converted into living spaces for any future stable hands. Although they took their meals with us, Daniel and Peader now occupied those rooms. All the field hands, the dairy workers, and the spalpeens—the seasonal harvest boys—lived in the cottages. There was also a two-story farmhouse that my grandfather purchased a few years later. The house sat across from our flax field and had ten acres of land to it. We now rent the property to the Hutchesons and have done so for the past seven years. My father mentioned that if the family had designs on buying it, he would ask them a fair and reasonable price by taking the rents that they had paid into consideration. I told my father that Sheridan, Dan, and I had spent a lot of time riding and making adventures all about the edges and fields of the Hutcheson's land, and that Mr. Hutcheson never minded once as we were always mindful of his crops and livestock. He was a kind man, and his wife was quite a pleasure as well; and it was too bad that their new baby was stolen by the fairies. My father said that he wished to see them happy. I expected that he would have.

Chapter 4

There was an endless amount of things that you could think up to do in the Hutcheson's fields. There were three plots altogether of two and four acres, each marked off with low stonewalls which weren't high enough in some patches so that the sheep would jump to freedom and wander about. And each evening, those ranging sheep would bounce right back into their respective pastures for the night.

In one of those fields, the one that was used for hay, there was a lone island of fieldstone and moss, where some young oaks had sprung up around an ancient whitethorn tree growing right in the center. The little mound looked like an altar with the whitethorn standing in the middle like an ancient priest of the pagans. The first time that you saw the rocky island and its tree-shaded bower, you couldn't help having the hair on you bristle up. And at haymaking time, when all the harvesters were done and the dozens of haycocks dotted the shaven pasture like golden beehive huts out of *Gulliver's Travels*, there wasn't a place more secluded in the world. We would spend all day there reading, talking, and fashioning wild games. You had the place to yourself with the tall palisade of trees that edged the land and the towering haycocks standing sentry inside our "Norman castle" walls.

At the corner of the northeast side of the land spired upward an ancient standing stone. I always hoped that it marked the tomb of some gold-belted warrior. There was writing on the weathered obelisk carved in short horizontals along the wobbling edge. I was withering with curiosity to decipher those simple lines chipped down its side. My father vowed to go to the college on his next trip to Dublin. That was twenty trips ago. My mother wrote to her horticulturist friend, and he went off looking to find another professor to help us. There were a scarce number of lines on that stone, so I eased my anxiety by figuring that you couldn't fit an abundance of words into so few slashes. It may have held only the name of that warrior, but that would have been enough.

Down by that chosen place was where Daniel wrote and wondered about things. He would even go there in the rain, for he would be sheltered by the thousands of flat green umbrellas made by the trees' leaves.

When my father first brought Dan from the fair two years ago, the boy was the most unsettled worker, as well as the youngest worker, that was ever brought to Carrickduff. Peader seemed worried with the boy, and he marked with a troubled voice on how my father "was cursed with the lovespot for litter runts, and if you scrubbed charcoal hard enough, you might end up with a diamond instead of ash and blackened hands. There's a lovespot for attractin' the fair sex, and a lovespot for pullin' you toward the ne'er do wells. And Mr. O'Hayden's got the second, and I know as I've got the same thing myself."

Well, Daniel was brought in to greet Sheridan, me, our mother, Ms. Farrell, the two housemaids, the two kitchen maids, and our laundry girl. It was the first time any of us had seen him since he first came on the day before. I can say that we were expecting the worst from him, and the crowd of us stood in a little bundle waiting for my father to lead him in. It didn't occur to me at the time, as I knew that they were all good natured and charitable, but it must have been a terrible shadow to have left your home for an unknown thing. Dan may have had an uncertain air about him when my father led him in. He was tall and not too thin; he had mahogany hair and gloomy green eyes that took over his whole face. I felt embarrassed to look at him, but I had to give him a welcome, and so I stared at his top waistcoat button with a smile on my face. Instantly, I knew what Peader had been warning me about with his discourse on the lovespot and its durable draw. No one else in our blank-smiling-greeting crowd seemed to have it, but I could feel the curse coming over me. I knew I had inherited it from my father; that was confirmed. I had inherited the attraction for runts.

The only thing that worried us after our first meeting with Daniel was the boy's handling of language. And you'll soon see what was to become of that thought.

Whenever any of the maids asked of him a welcome question, he would answer briefly, but generally the only words that came from him were simply "yes, sir" and "no, ma'am."

"Did you have an untroubled trip, Dan?" my mother asked.

"Yes, ma'am," the boy bowed.

"Are you comfortable in your quarters?" the older maid asked.

"Yes, ma'am." he nodded. I thought that I was going to fold up like a water lily at night with the strain of the action.

"Can you read?" Ms. Farrell asked with an eager look on her face. I looked to her.

"Yes, ma'am." The voice's suddenness snatched my ears as a frog snatches a fly.

Sure he can read, I thought, *but I don't know that he can talk. And would I own a care? I should think not, for I had the curse to like ne'er do wells.*

One peculiar situation that I had noted was that my brother Sheridan was at ease around our new groom even though Dan was still economic with his own words, as if he was afraid of using them all up. I figured that he must have had an allotted amount of words, and was now coming very near to the end of his store of them. But more strange than Dan's use or rather un-use of speech, was that Sheridan, remained wholly untouched by the affliction that I was weighed down with. Apparently, my brother had not inherited the lovespot for ne'er do wells, but this was of no true surprise.

Eventually Daniel got used to talking, and through our daily meetings, I came to know that Dan saw the things in nature that no one else was able to perceive. But he didn't see them with the bewilderment of a child. He saw them as they were—as nature saw them. He showed me how a tree would bend and twist to catch its needed light, how the stream had flowed forever down our pasture's edge lashing the water stones on its endless roll to the sea, and how the twilight would come to turn the land into a time of half-light and clarity. He said that it was the time when ghosts walked and fairies tempted wanderers, but Peader said he was daft to talk of such things.

I knew why Dan had not spoken so freely. Each word was to him a gift—a gift to be opened carefully, as carefully as one would open books from Dublin. He told me that to waste emotion and to spread it about like seed was a distasteful sight of wantonness and a harbinger of uncertainty. For to see someone who is always happy leaves the watcher to guess if and when it is that they truly are. Those were grand thoughts to come from a ne'er do well.

Daniel Whelan was born in Blesinton, in the county Wicklow. Blesinton is just a little west of Bray. His family lived on the lands of the Marquis of Downshire. Daniel wasn't interested in farming a tenant's land, as the inescapable muse of literature was hopping inside his head. He had the romantic habit about him with just the same piercing comeliness, as you would have expected of Keats or Shelley when those two were alive and writing. You were supposed to look like that if you were a poet. I don't think you could write if you weren't as showy as a pheasant. Dan was a true poet, spending all his free time moving over the hills and writing about things in that bower in

Mr. Hutcheson's hayfield. My literary nature was starving for the knowledge of one who could do those sorts of things. It wasn't long before I came to learn of Daniel's preference for the writer Alfred Lord Tennyson, and so with that, it was a rightful occurrence for me to become a friend of Dan's.

Last Wednesday, Daniel, Sheridan, and I were wasting away an evening after lessons and after Dan's stable work was seen to. We were reciting Tennyson in the middle of Mr. Hutcheson's rocky bower. We were talking over "The Lady of Shalott," and there was a good amount of reflecting to be had over such a work as that. If you are not familiar with that poem, it is a grand thing to waste an evening with, as it has just the right amount of everything. It is not maudlin, nor wanting for interest, and I am free to say that it is the finest portrayal of a fairy by an Englishman—whose creatures are often quite fanciful—that I have ever read. And that is because Mr. Tennyson undoubtedly has the soul of an Irishman, or he never could have written it.

The night we sat to talk over the poem, there was only a wisp of a wind languishing about the young oaks and making their broad leaves quiver. I sat on the rock beneath the whitethorn tree, and I could feel the rough face of it scratching through my dress and my petticoat. My hands picked senselessly at the tiny peels of lichen that grew all over the large fieldstones in the sprinkled light of the bower. Sheridan sat on the ground with his legs crossed under him. There was an abundance of moss and leaves for a carpet so he wouldn't be getting his stockings dirty, and mother would be happy, but not as happy as Ms. Shea, the laundry girl. Daniel reclined on his usual whitethorn branch. The limb had grown beneath the lip of a boulder and then stuck out in a *U* shape from the other side of the stone as it continued reaching toward the light. The boy straddled the limb with a boot resting against the rock, and his head dropped back against the body of the tree. He had just finished his turn reciting "The Lady of Shalott," and had set to brooding over it such as the hens on their clutches.

We had gotten to the part where the lady sat long and lonesomely, weaving a brightly colored web. She worked alone amidst the stones of a walled castle that rose from within the isolated island named Shalott. The island was surrounded by a river that rolled past the medieval town that was widely known, as it was Camelot, the home of King Arthur and his exalted knights. As we were sitting in the whitethorn island of Mr. Hutcheson, we were trying to figure out why that lady worked with such industry upon that enchanted loom.

"What sort of thread would she be weaving with?" Sheridan asked.

"She used dyed spider's silk," Dan said, scraping his boot against the tree.

I didn't believe it.

"How could she have used dyed spider's silk?" I asked. "Wouldn't it have stuck to the loom? And then you would need the patience of Job for dying it, and then all that you would get is a lump of colored gossamer for all of your troubles. Unless," I added before Dan opened his mouth, "if she had been a fairy like that reaper said that she was, then she would have been free to weave the sticky thread as any tiny spider. 'And by the moon the reaper weary . . . listening whispers, 'tis the fairy lady of Shalott.'"

"If that indeed she was a fairy," Daniel agreed, "then naturally the thread wouldn't have tangled onto the loom, just as it is tangle free for the spider that fashioned it."

Those words were reasonable until Sheridan mentioned that if this woman was a fairy, then why was she so unhappy doing what she had occupied herself with since fairies would only do what they wanted anyway.

"She was cursed though," Daniel explained, leaning over the book and searching for the needed section. "See—'she had heard a whisper say, a curse is on her if she stay to look down to Camelot'!" He moved his finger over the verse, and we pressed round the tree to study what he was motioning at.

"Who would curse a fairy?" Sheridan asked cynically. "Sure, if there were fairies, you couldn't curse 'em. Everybody says so."

"I don't know." I shrugged. "No one can charm a fairy, not without suffering after. And who would care if that lady stared at the town? She had the magic mirror put by her loom as it was, and through the looking glass, she could see the town as clear as from a window. There it is in the sixth verse." I leaned over the book. "'And moving through a mirror clear that hangs before her all the year, shadows of the world appear.'"

"Aye, that's true." Daniel nodded taking care not to strike his head against the tree's unyielding trunk. "But it wasn't the same as being there. She was lonely."

"Fairies don't get lonely," Sheridan corrected.

"I don't think that they do," I added.

"This is an English fairy," Daniel reminded quickly. "They're not like the kind over here. They can even die."

Sheridan and I nodded with surprise.

There was no comparing the two. An Irish fairy, worth his dignity, is in a class by himself. I didn't like English fairies. There was something naive and ineffective about them. I didn't dislike them all, as I have known only of a few, and I did like Tennyson's lady. But it is true to say that I do find it difficult to think of an English fairy chopping your head off or stealing you off to dance for a night worth fifty human years. I don't think those Sasanach fairies had it in them.

"English fairies can charm each other too." I remembered the last verse I had pointed to. "It must have been a powerful one to put that hard spell over another of their kind."

"I would hardly believe it," Sheridan said, "if I didn't see it put down on paper." He tapped the book's tooled leather cover.

And there was a curse upon the lady of Shalott, for once she was tempted to move from the web she was weaving by the handsome figure of the noble Sir Lancelot on his daring charger. As soon as the lady stepped from the loom to gaze toward Camelot, the mirror through which passed those illusions of the world, cracked and burst, and the web over which she toiled glided from the room to float upon the rolling river. The lady received the curse, and with the last of her will, she moved from her prison; and finding a boat by the shore, she wrote her name across its bow so that the world might, at last, have knowledge of her vacant days. The boat was then loosed, and it bore her stilled body past the troubled revellers of Camelot and past the fair Lancelot, who stood apart, as he marked the name upon the bow, The Lady of Shalott.

"That was a hard and morbid curse." Daniel closed the book and sighed. "It was a beautiful thing; I can imagine seein' that woman lyin' dead in that small boat, floatin' past the people of Camelot." He slowly swept his hand over the air to illustrate the boat passing over the water. "Ah, and there was himself bein' the only one to stand to her passin'; what a beautiful and sorrowful thing." He sighed again.

"How can somethin' be beautiful and sorrowful?" I leaned against the rock. "That's like bein' hot and cold." I stared at the darkening sky.

"You can be hot and cold," my brother added. "Like when you drink tea and its cold out. Your head gets hot, but your feet stay icy."

"Ah, I wasn't questionin'," I added, "just sayin' it to say it. How queer a thing it is, that's all. Havin' a hot head and cold feet is a queer thing too."

We sat in the twilight's silence.

"Do you wonder what the others were thinkin'?" I asked.

"What others?" Sheridan lay on the leaves.

"It was only Lancelot that saluted the lady. What were the others standin' there thinkin'?"

"They weren't thinkin' anythin'." Dan slipped from his perch, and sat on the ground before the rock. "That's what sets Lancelot apart. He's the only one that feels anythin'! The others don't care; they're only thinkin' of themselves."

"Ah, I don't like those kind o' people." I plucked some grass blades. "They only like themselves and money and . . . and to hell with anyone that stands in their way!"

"Hey!" Sheridan snapped.

"Oh, I didn't mean you," I returned.

"Hey! I wasn't thinkin' that either," he huffed. "I was sayin' if mother only heard you say hell."

"Father says it," I returned, "and so does Peader."

"I say it," Daniel added, with his arms folded behind his head.

"And *I* say it too!" Sheridan affirmed boldly. "Just not a bunch, 'cause I don't think of it." He shrugged. "I think it's lovely. It's as lovely as the poem." He placed his arms behind his head just as Daniel had done.

My brother left as the light faded to a dark purple, as he had forgotten his marble bag outside of the stable, and Peader was wont to fall over them. It was getting past the shadowy side of twilight, and Daniel and I left the dark bower for home. He marked the page of the book where the poem was printed with a small iron bookmark. It was in the form of an ancient-looking key, although Daniel had struck it himself, well forward of those dark ages, where its black metal form would have been most comfortable.

Three years ago, Daniel was apprenticed to the shop of a Blesinton blacksmith. When Dan turned thirteen, that promising position fell through with the passing of the shopkeeper. Both Mr. and Mrs. Whelan were dead, and the boy had been living under the care of his aunt, leaving Dan with no familial labor connections. That left the freed apprentice with two choices—the hiring fair or the farm, and the farm was not the place for a lad with aspirations. He went to the fair that was held along Bray's Main Street, where my father Mícheál O'Hayden always went to hire the grooms and field hands, the spalpeens. The story that my father brought back to us on that night was a curious piece, something that was worth recalling from those two years ago.

We had the same number of horses then as now. There was Niamh, the grey; Canon, the bay gelding; Padraic, the promising hunter, who was only three years on the earth then; and the two ponies, Ashlyn and Gavin. We needed a young groom who would work for small wages and board.

My father set off from town early on the Thursday market-mornings, and he set off before daylight on that day two years ago. He spent the day amidst the crowds—which he hated even though they weren't so nearly terrible as the ones at the Tinehaly horse fairs—searching out prospective workers. At harvest time, he didn't have a hard job of it as most of last year's spalpeens would be waiting for Mícheál O'Hayden to take them on for the barley and flax seasons. This day was different. We needed a permanent man, and my father would spend hard hours looking for the right young fellow to care for our steeds. He was to find his man, and their meeting was designed by a fine grey mare.

My father was driving his trap through the fair that day when he stopped for a chat and a talk of government things and "shouldn't Jimmy Daly run for the next term" with Mr. Sayers. Mr. Sayers ran a fish stall in town. There weren't any fish stores; everyone sold their wares in carts and baskets. Mr. Sayers sold the freshest of oysters; he even threw in a few extra. The two of them were talking along like robins, and Niamh, as they called her because of her golden forelock, was standing there in the front of the trap, getting bored with the situation. Because the fair was on Main Street, there was no grass to nibble, so she cocked a hind leg and closed her eyes for a nap. The mare had just settled in for a snooze when a shopper's dog broke his tether and tore down the street as if all the ghosts of the dead were behind him. Apparently, he deemed Mr. Sayer's fish stall an aromatic and secure place to hide, for the dog crossed the street, barrelled beneath Niamh's legs, and cowered behind the stall. I can't think of nothing like a frantic, restless mound of fur hurling by your legs to shatter a purifying nap. Niamh snapped to attention, and when the dog stumbled over her cocked hind fetlock, she didn't wait about for a pardon, but gathered her feet below her and shied in a flurry of dusty hoof steps. My father struck out for her right rein and just as he caught the leather, Niamh lunged forward. My father was thrown against the dash of the passing trap as the mare pushed into the crowd. She only went a few yards forward when she slipped and went down in the traces. She was right in the middle of Main Street, panicking where she lay. Niamh twisted herself to get up and caught those pretty grey legs in the harness. A certain boy was the first on the scene, and he held down her head to keep her from rising until my bruised father loosened her from the tangled leather. And when she rose, Niamh was standing there as quiet as if nothing happened. It was thinking like that which sealed a groom's job for a blacksmith's apprentice at Carrickduff. Although Dan was to have yet another position at the house, which had nothing to do with ponies but everything to do with literature.

It was my father who first noticed the "muse of stories" inside Daniel. He encouraged it too. Mícheál O'Hayden could detect talent in a stone and was then able to dig it out. My father hated to come across misapplied and squandered talent; he believed in making use of what you were good at. It wasn't a surprise when I came to understand that my mother was an amateur pianist.

Each time my father came back from town, a copy of the *Freeman's Journal* paper, which came out weekly, or a book of prose or poetry was waiting in the car for the boy.

Every Saturday night Daniel was asked to read for us either from print, his own words, and even sometimes from my foolscaps of poetry. At the end of each session, my mother would always say that "the boy had the voice of a poet." Dan spoke so nobly, feeling the words instead of only speaking them. In his round hazel-green eyes, ruins of legends would dance when he spoke of old Ireland where the sidhe were plentiful and the warriors bold.

Peader Hayes, our gardener, had a liking for the boy since Daniel had arrived from the fair. In his own becalmed fashion, Peader showed Dan the way that things were done even though he had no taste for the old stories, which he called a bunch of something that I am not supposed to say. Although Mr. Hayes would never tell you that he was fond of you, he would show you with his actions. He was the sort of fellow that just looked after things. I now know why he took Dan, and it wasn't because of the runt lovespot. It was because of something that happened years before my birth and Dan's as well, and that was an even stranger story than the one of my father and Niamh at the Main Street fair.

Chapter 5

Peader Doran Hayes came to the house through the workings of fate and circumstance, just as Daniel Whelan did. Peader didn't come as a gardener with a craft for planting geraniums, just as Daniel didn't come with a bridle and a brush. The two of them were brought by Carrickduff, for the house had a craving for setting matters straight. I was never supposed to know of Peader's history. I was never supposed to repeat it, but I think that I should, and so I am to write it down now.

Mr. Hayes arrived thirteen winters ago during the famine year of 1847. Indeed, I had no knowledge of the particulars of Peader's arrival anyway, and it was in those *particulars* that the curiosity rested. I was born after those times, and it was only from the dairy women and the older house staff that I learned anything much about it. Even my father and mother shied away from words about that time, and I was given to the assumption that I wasn't old enough to ask, and that they were equally unwilling to tell. This was what I had learned from visits with the lady workers. The best of the stories came from old Mrs. Byrne, the head of the dairy, and this was what she told me of those terrible years.

Bray did not fall beneath the terrible want and suffering that brought other towns to the edge of wretchedness, although she was not spared either. I didn't know the reason as to why we were favored, but I did believe that it was Bray's location along a rich sea and the goodness and sensibility of her people that saved so many of the less fortunate from dissolution.

The terror began in October of 1845 when the first of the potatoes started to blacken as if struck by a wet fire. The first year continued rather uneventfully until the winter of 1846. From what I was told, it was a hard, stormy winter with the sea lashing the coast and stopping the fishermen from bringing in their catch. The people were relying on the fish then when their own crops were failing.

"It was as if a scourge from the Bible was sweepin' o'er us," described Mrs. Byrne to me one day while I was helping with the butter making. I liked to work in the dairy shed. It was fresh with the smells of the sweet cream, the wooden buckets, and the perfumes that Mrs. Byrne carried on her from the plants in the kitchen garden. Sometimes it was rosemary or chives, or geranium and lavender. And that was the one thing I liked the most about old Mrs. Byrne. It was grand to see her handiness at growing flowers and fancy greenery. Many of the women planted flowers on their yards. They grew lavender to scent their linens, and hollyhocks, damask roses, and all sorts of kitchen herbs, but Mrs. Byrne's scotch broom would call in the spring with the biggest fountain of yellow blooms before the other plants were even thinking of flowering.

Mr. Byrne, the now-deceased husband, was once our field man; and his wife was no less the gardener, and she often helped Peader in the greenhouse, as he wasn't as good at "tendin' to the exotics." But Mrs. Byrne was as grand a talker as an "exotics" grower, and a better teacher of history I have yet to discover with any formal calling.

"It was your grandfather," she explained to me that day while I was sitting in the milk scented dairy barn, "Gerald O'Hayden—bless him—that helped so many o' those poor ones." She shook her head and started turning the barrel churn's handle.

I waited for her to continue. Nothing but the sound of the churning. I waited some more, looking into her sun-beaten face and tiny brown eyes. I began to wonder if everyone's eyes turned beady when they got old and if their faces took over more space. Peader had small eyes too, but they weren't beady, and he didn't have any extra "face" at all. The sight of Mrs. Byrne's inadequately sized eyes made me want to open mine as wide as they would go without sliding out as if I could give her a more substantial gaze.

"What did my grandfather do?" I finally asked as I squeezed my eyes back to normal. I had to blink to get the dried-out things back to their proper state.

"This isn't the sort o' talk for a young miss to be mindin' with, but I'm going to tell you seein' as we're by ourselves." She stared at me. "Is there somethin' in your eye child?"

I shook my head.

"We didn't find things too bad until that winter '46. There were hard years before and more to come and such as things like that, but the poor ones find their way through. I always believed that God's poor had more lives to 'em than yer father's cat. Always lookin' after those he is." And she turned her head to the wooden ceiling of the dairy. "It was as if the plagues were comin' that winter, as if the di'vil himself was walkin' over the land. Your father was in Italy, and his ol' man forbids the young sir to come home but to stay there with his schoolin'. 'A young man's thoughts must be shackled to his future,' I heard your grandfather saying; sure he was not a man to be takin' up a quarrel with. Your father stayed in Italy. I remember Mr. Gerald O'Hayden in the armchair before the sittin' room that winter. The room was dark, and the evenin' settin' in, and there was no lamp lit, and the two flickerin's in the room was comin' from the hearth and yer grandfather's pipe. He was smokin' that pipe as if the only pleasures in the world were smolderin' away in that bowl. It seemed as though the mountain fog had rolled down the miles into that room with all that amber smellin' smoke.

"'There's no future in Ireland,' he condemned to yer father. 'The boy's not coming back here, if I have to drive him out myself. He's got the world opening up to him; he's not coming back here!'"

"Did he not like my father?" I was baffled at these disclosures. I didn't want to think of anyone in my family turning me away. The anxiety caused my sleeves to slip down, and I had to reroll them up my arms.

"He would risk ne'er seein' the boy again!" She spoke as if she was checking each word. "And with the age comin' o'er him, yer grandfather wasn't a well man then, he thought more for the well-being of his son than for his own happiness. It was an odd manner of reasonin', some would say, but that was Gerald O'Hayden's manner. And that man loved this place too." Mrs. Byrne kept churning the butter.

"With yer father bein' the only survivin' little one out of four children, and now that one off in the world, and his own wife gone for over fourteen years, this place was like a child to him."

She let me have a turn at the handle.

"When the bad times came down in '46, it was as if despair had walked into the house. These weren't things that he wanted yer father Mícheál to see. It was the villas of Italy, the statues too beautiful to set yer eyes upon, the cathedrals of Paris . . . those were the things that he wanted his only boy to gaze on, to know. A boy should be off makin' a path for himself. Mícheál wasn't about much then. Ah, but he was startin' to court the young Carolyn after their meetin' in France. She was in the school there." She paused from the churning and swallowed the memories. She startled her thoughts back to the present and smiled slowly after studying my somber face. "Would you hand me some of them butter forms, Anne, and don't be lookin' like a hen that's lost her eggs." I readied the forms as Mrs. Byrne took over the hard finishing work when the thickened cream began to set.

"Ah, there weren't much statues and paintings to be found around here. The winter only brought more and longer sufferings on the people. The workhouses were full, the public works were not hiring, and the Board was turnin' 'em away. They were tellin' us, 'Do you have any work?' The poor things were in rags, and the answer to that question was always the same, always no. We didn't have any work for them; the harvest was months off. All that we could do was to feed them and give what clothes we had to give. At first, there were only a few, but soon more and more started comin' in a worse state than the ones before. Your grandfather went off to the other landholder's places, and he went to the town to those relief committee meetings with the other landlords to see what could be done, and the answer that met his eyes along those streets was a far worse thing than the want that we had been seein' at our own doorstep. The hunger was runnin' free in all the country, as if it had a life given to it! And the terrible part of it all was learnin' that we weren't the worse of the sufferin'. The horror was brought upon us. How could there be more than what was testin' us at Carrickduff?"

"What happened to the people?" I asked solemnly.

She nodded.

"What was goin' to happen when the spring came? That was the time between the harvests you see, same as now. But there had been no fall potato harvest, and it was a lean enough time when those things were sound. And didn't the Carrickduff crop fail as well. There was still the barley, which the distilleries gave a fair price for, and we still had the flax brought to the Putland's mill. Your grandfather was supportin' myself, and the others more so then that we had less of our own. There were the laborers that stayed on with nowhere else to go, but the shame of the workhouse, and Mr. O'Hayden kept 'em, God bless him. I knew he sold some of the silver to do it. Oh, he'd ne'er tell you that, but I saw him. I noticed the empty drawers and that big teapot I hated to clean was gone too. That was the kind of man he was. And to make livin' worse, the prices were risin' in town. Your Gerald raised our wages to eleven shillin's a week, plus the other provisions he gave us. The 'Board' was only payin' six to eight pence a day for hard labor with pickaxes and wheelbarrows, and the men havin' barely enough strength to stand. There was ne'er a fairer, kinder man. There was enough for us. But how many more could we ease the sufferin' of that came down the path?

"One mornin' in the month of April, your grandfather was settin' off early for Lord Plunkett's house, for the Lord and his wife were themselves clothin' and feedin' those that were wantin' as well as helpin' his own tenants. That man was beset on all sides. Yer grandfather had gone 'round to the stable to take to his horse, and that horse wasn't readied, but Joe—God rest him—was standin' by the door. 'Come with you to the back Mr. O'Hayden, there's somethin' for you to see.'

"I can still lay eyes on Joe's white face; I ne'er saw a more faded count'nance, and his hands were in his pockets as he tried to hide their shakin'. I had followed Mr.O'Hayden out to give him his readin' glasses; he was as blind as a stone for readin' if he was without those glasses. 'Mrs. Byrne,' Joe called, 'I think that you shouldn't follow us.' Well, I followed anyway and forgive me what I'm goin' to tell you, but it is as well as you should know for her sake." Mrs. Byrne stopped her butter work and pointed to the stable.

"We were like ghosts walkin' by the horse stalls, and the beasts themselves was turnin' in their rooms frettin' as if they knew what I didn't. In the tack room, Joe stopped and asked me again to stay, but I followed till he opened the back door." Mrs. Byrne nodded her head.

"Don't I still see all this in dreams and as clear as the day before my own head now. A woman was lyin' on the stone before the tack room door. Her clothes were poor and road soiled, worse than you'd see now in any parts 'round here. The mornin' wet was coverin' her in beads of mist; she had been dead for hours. No more than twenty she was, the poor thing. It was the hunger that brought her, and the roads that stole her life; and there she didn't even make it to the door. And that big iron knocker hung a witness to it all; and it was there then, as it is now, that bein' the only way into the carriage house where Peader and young Daniel sleep. 'I would've heard the knocker.' I remember Joe sayin' o'er and o'er again as if the words were gonna change somethin'. Your grandfather eased the man. 'She never reached the knocker,' he said. That was a sorry thing to see first thing in the mornin'. A devil of a thing to see at any time."

"What did you do?" I asked. Neither of us were working now, and the barrel churn could have gotten up and walked away, and I don't think we would have noticed. I tried to imagine what a dew-covered dead woman looked like. I was thinking about all of those times that I had run over the tack room's doorstep without ever feeling that someone had given over their life there, and maybe left a ghost. "Did you bring the woman to her family?" I wondered.

Mrs. Byrne shook her head. "And who was she?" the old woman added. "We couldn't even begin to look, and from what we had seen from her, they were probably already dead. The famine leavin's were buried anywhere. We didn't want that for her. Who was gonna care to handle another body? You know that place behind the alder and the peach-apple with the dead top branch near the wild hazel bushes?"

"The one with the low iron fence and the field rock in the middle?" I wondered. It was a small, circular garden sitting about ten feet behind the stable. The stones were ringed by the thin mushroom-shaped leaves of the pennywort plants. I liked to pick the tall bells of flowers that rose from the fleshy bases as tiny rusty-white foxgloves. Some even grew from the cracks in the stones.

"That's the place," answered Mrs. Byrne. "We put her there with a Christian burial, as near as we could get to one. There was little point for a stone, for what were we gonna put upon its face. By the end of May, there were ten more lyin' by that woman. Strange how you can grow used to seein' death in that kind of indifferent form and not grow used to it at the same time. Well, all o' them are restin' beneath the field stone now." Mrs. Byrne turned to get the salt that would be tossed into the butter.

"It's a strange thing though," she said, walking stiffly back to where I was sitting. "Just as God closes one door, He goes off and opens another. Wasn't it at the end of August of that terrible year when they started the railroad at Bray Head. That was salvation. It's ne'er been the same since."

"It brought work," I said sitting on a dairy stool, "didn't it Mrs. Byrne?"

"Hundreds of jobs." She eased herself painfully down upon another low stool. "Don't be after gettin' old, Anne, there's nothin' in it for anybody. They'll tell ya' there is, but it's only rotten eggs they're sellin', grand from the outside but holdin' a staunch smell when ya get near the inside. I'm not any wiser either. You'll promise me to stay young, Anne?"

"Aye, I'll do me best Mrs. Byrne, but I don't believe I can truly promise you anythin'. I'd be lyin' if I did."

"I knew you'd think of it like that." She smiled. "There's a fine head on ya'. You've got the wit of yer father and mother both. You should've seen the two o' them courtin'; I thought the sky would soon split open with the quarrelin' between 'em." She sent me a knowing glance.

"You should've seen your grandfather scutchin' my own daughter's suitors like flax as if she was of his own." She rubbed the memories over her small roughened hands. "Ah well, you ne'er would've believed how the town was gonna flower like a daisy patch with the comin' of those rails. These are fine days, Anne."

I never knew the Bray that Mrs. Byrne talked of in those "ancient days", over twelve years ago, when the famine struck. I only knew of the fashionable Bray, the coast of pebble beaches, grassy cliffs, caves, hotels, and sea homes. The most famous of the lodgings was Quinn's Hotel with the exotic Turkish baths that looked like a Moroccan palace, where you would sit and steam in a heated room like a kettle of black tea. And all this, along with the neighboring luxury homes, had a grand view of the smooth, grassy bluffs of Bray Head. I had told Dan that his own favorite writer, Mr. William Makepeace Thackeray, had stayed at Quinn's. I wondered if he had used the Turkish baths.

I did not know of Mr. Thackeray's business, but I certainly would not have enjoyed being left to steam like table linens, whatever the benefits. I did know that there were very few indulgences that one could compare with the joy of soaking in a cold sea to freeze away what ailed you. And the seawater was even better for the horses. You would never believe the swarms of bathers and sightseers tumbling off the trains like marbles out of a box. It was a pleasing sight for a businessman, which was what my brother said about the herds of sea-goers. He was the most peculiar-thinking boy. Sheridan was right though. With over twenty trains coming daily, there was a lot of money to be had. I was thinking then as I sat with Mrs. Byrne in the milk barn about the fortunes that rolled in along with those iron rails. We were the Italian coast, the English Brighton, without the overused tarnish of a city. That train didn't come any too soon.

"The track building would've saved all those burdened people. It was better'n the 'Board' just diggin' up the roads and causin' a mess," I reasoned. "That woman wouldn't have starved, nor any of the other ones with all the work comin' in."

"Aye, child, there's nothin' like fixin' what's behind you." She nodded slowly. "But it wouldn't have saved 'em, and we can't change what was just as we can't choose our given family." A thought came over her then, and she rubbed her hands as if it would squeeze out between the pale fingers. "But one was saved though. Saved by yer grandfather." Mrs. Byrne rose and walked away from me as she spoke the last words.

Chapter 6

"I don't understand, Mrs. Byrne." I tilted my head like a confused farm dog. "Which one was saved?"

My new "history tutor" turned on her low seat and brought her warm eyes over my face. The butter churning was hard work, and she needed to rest her legs after standing. But nobody else could work in the dairy without Mrs. Byrne's eyes on them; she made sure of that.

"There was a mornin' in late April, I remember the day as well as my own day of marriage, it was the twenty-third of April. I was just risin' to get the fires blazin' again; we kept 'em smoored as we do now. They were left to glow overnight like everybody else in the house and prodded awake in the mornin'. A fire was ne'er left to go out, lest the life of the house go out with it."

This was a revered custom amongst the old people that my father allowed them to continue. Mícheál O'Hayden did not believe in country traditions or fabulous superstitions, but he didn't see anything wicked in them either, so long as they were of an innocent nature. My mother felt the same way although she would never start anything new on a Tuesday because she said it was then sure to falter, but she didn't know why. I asked if you could finish a thing on a Tuesday. I liked the idea of keeping the fire anyway. You could imagine such a magical thing in the orient. There would be a fire crackling in the dark desert as the camels slept, and the air drowned in the spices from the caravan.

"There I was," Mrs. Byrne continued, "down in the dinin' room, puttin' the life back into the hearth when a knockin' sounded at the front door. Fear spread across me for a moment, it bein' only half five in the mornin'. I said it would be one o' the farm workers askin' for somethin' as I knew they started early, so I went to open the door. The knockin' continued as if a swarm o' honeybees was behind whoever was out there, and he was desperate for gettin' in. 'Hold yer bangin'!' I yelled, runnin'. I could still move like a rabbit then. 'Hold yer bangin', I'm goin' as fast as I can,' I said, thinkin' it was one o' those rash field boys. I didn't know where your grandfather found the likes of 'em. Well, I freed the latch and threw open the door hard like to show some mettle. Just as I was gettin' ready to curse that lad out, a shock bristled o'er me worse than the first. There was Lord Plunkett standin' before the threshold with me starin' back at him. I don't know if I was embarrassed after talkin' to the gentry like that, or worried as to what would bring the poor man here at such an hour. The combination of the two froze me to the spot, and both of us were like sculptures left on the doorstep.

"'Is Mr. O'Hayden in?' Lord Plunkett broke the enchantment o'er us. And it was then that I noticed the concern on his face, and the disturbance in his voice."

"What did he want?" I asked curiously. "He came all the way from the place of Old Connaught House at such an hour as that." I raised my eyes. "Was somebody else dyin'?" I thought of the dead woman on the carriage house step.

"You're gettin' ahead of me there, and you almost said the truth. I brought the man in, and you could feel the agitation on 'im. 'Would Your Lordship come into the sittin' room,' I said bowin' courtly and tryin' not to seem as nervous as himself. Nervous servants are a bad thing, makes you wonder what they're up to. 'I'll go and wake the master for you.' And just as I said those words, your grandfather came down the stairs buttonin' the shirt on him still; he was in such a hurry to see what the commotion was.

"'What's all the noise down there, Clara?' came his voice from the top o' the stairs. 'Who was banging at this . . . Lord Plunkett!' The same look of embarrassment and worry fell across his face. I started to dismiss myself, but our guest bade me stay, so I did."

"'Do you speak the Irish language, Clara?' He asked me graciously, and I told him that I did not. He then asked Mr. O'Hayden if any of the workers spoke it, and Mr. O'Hayden said that they did not to his knowledge. Your grandfather then asked Lord Plunkett what caused him to possess such a pressing need for an Irish translator. And he regretted that we could not be of any assistance in the matter. Lord Plunkett ran the back of his hand o'er his thin mouth so hard; I was afraid he'd wipe his lips off. In the most somber tone I e'er heard, the man asked if we would be so kind as to journey back to Old Connaught House with him."

"Did you go?" I asked excitedly, drowning in the suspense. *How could you not go?* I was thinking. I pulled up a shipping box, and sat down to listen.

"We went straight away." She nodded fervently. "Nobody said a word the whole distance. To see us goin' down the road, you'd o' thought we were all on a trip to the grave with no return tickets. Well, Lord Plunkett drove us through the gates, and it was no sight o' heaven—beggars linin' both sides o' the drive; you'd swear that you were goin' to a workhouse, that's how crowded with 'em it was there." Horror seemed to flicker in her face as she relived that time for me—the days when people were seen to walk with the look of the death that tarried for them. A moment longer, a day to come, and he would have his pick. I could not believe that such a thing could have been visited upon my country.

"The Lord and his wife had fashioned a relief station for the starvin'. The Savior only knows how many they succoured each day. They were good people, Anne, just like your grandfather. Didn't they raise their own laborer's wages to help their workers through as well. That sort o' kindness ran in the family as if it was bred into 'em. The Lord Plunkett brought us into the back o' the house where the kitchen was. You didn't even notice the splendor o' the place with all the sufferin' and worryin'. We continued down a hall, and a maid brushed past without sayin' a word and with a face as leaden as her lips, and we said nothin' ourselves. I've ne'er gone such a stretch without talkin' in me life, ne'er before, ne'er since. I think it was even makin' me dizzy, but I said in my head this was no time to be causin' a disturbance o' my own. I repeated that as we walked along, and then we stopped before a thick oak door. Lord Plunkett opened it, but neither I nor your grandfather made a move to go inside the darkened room.

"The curtains were drawn, and it took me a moment to accustom the eyes to the low light. And when I did, I could see that it was a sort o' private sittin' room with only a few chairs, a small bookcase, and a writin' desk of uncommon craftsmanship. The room was a beauty to look at despite the gloomy air. The lord bade us go into the room, and he pointed toward a corner away from the heavy-curtained window. I peered in at that corner, and there I saw an old daybed from the early part o' the century, with a fella sleepin' upon it. He was havin' a restless sleep though, for the bedclothes that had been laid on him were scuffled onto the floor. He had brown hair of a light color, tusseled and wild lookin' with the stylin' gone out of it and the ends curlin' up. His features were hard and regular as if they were carved like those Italian garden things o' your father. This man had seen bad days o' the worse sort, and he looked as though some fever were on 'im. But it was the dress that he wore that stole my attention. I was but in my sixties then, and I wager that sounds ancient to you. The eyes weren't so good as they used to be nor so bad as they are now, but I could still see that those road-worn clothes had come from a fine make. And they weren't castoffs either. The man had a fine woollen frock coat restin' on the chair by the bed. I knew it was his by the dried mud on the coat's skirt, and the wool it was cut from matched the plaid waistcoat still on 'im.

"It seemed I wasn't the only one impressed. 'The fellow came in last night,' Lord Plunkett explained. 'He was found on the side of the drive just outside of the gate,' he whispered. 'It was my steward who went out for my wife's dog, and he found Smithy barking by the hedge. My man thought him dead there, but soon we were able to rouse him and bring him in.'

"Your grandfather was noddin' his head slow like and gazin' at the unfortunate man on the daybed. 'The strange gentleman,' Lord Plunkett kept on, 'was in a frightful state, and we did what we could to ease him. My wife fetched some beef broth and bread, and after that, he said not a word more in any language. It was as if the fare had stolen his tongue. So we brought over a bit of that brandy there to rouse him into speaking. The opposite of our aspirations materialized, and our mute soon let go of his senses completely and had to be carried to where you see him now.' The lord stepped away from us and said, 'See the clothes he wears?' Mr. O'Hayden nodded again and said, 'They seem to be well made.' That was the same thing that I thought." Mrs. Byrne raised her eyes.

"'So they are.' the lord said. 'And we wished to find his family or any acquaintances, but the only words that came from his tongue have been in Irish only.'"

"He was only speakin' in Irish?" I asked Mrs. Byrne. I was astonished. Nobody on the eastern side of Wicklow spoke much Irish, if any at all. Although I was aware that there were some mountain people that did. I asked where the man was from.

"Sure at the time I didn't know." Mrs. Byrne straightened on the stool. "No, none of us did. We were startin' to wonder if our newcomer e'en spoke any English. Your grandfather inquired after the man's present health.

"'Time will tell if it is of the mortal kind.' The lord rubbed his cheek as he pondered the situation. 'From the state of things, it seems as though the fellow's gone an appreciable distance on very little sustenance before coming to this door. That coat's been away from a brush for a good deal of days.' He gestured to the article draped o'er the chair. 'And those shoes are worn past saving. But'—he went and grabbed one o' them—'see here'—he turned it o'er—'the sole's rubbed through but the leather does not show the same kind of wear. These are new shoes, and they must have fetched over four pounds.' Mr. O'Hayden held the shoe and studied its make. It was a fine article.

"'Oh!' Lord Plunkett continued, 'there was some five pounds found in the inside coat pocket.' He continued with disclosing the investigations. 'I searched the pockets on him to see if there was some identifying papers upon him, but there was only the five pounds.'"

"He could've found food with the money," I concluded. "Maybe he was holdin' it to bring to somebody?" I rubbed my palms on the side of the rough crate. "Was he a highwayman?"

"No child, but we were thinkin' that he might have some kindred in the area or that he might be on the run from somethin'. For who would risk themselves to hand-carry such a small debt; surely the man was mad if that were the case. But no, from the state of the wanderer, we knew that wasn't true. Hungry and worn near to death he was, but not mad. That man had seen better days, and those days weren't far off either from the look o' things. Fortunes were dyin' as well as men. Famine is not benevolent to the prosperous wants of a country, so it wasn't hard to believe that a fellow such as our man could fall so swiftly. It was just a matter now for the wanderer to sleep the brandy off and to give us some English talk."

I had developed a certain curiosity for the mysterious traveler. You had to admire someone who held such a yearning for something that they'd risk life and safety to see that thing done. He was like a book character brought to life. I hoped that Mrs. Byrne would tell me that he would see some fortune, or be a highwayman. I did not want my admiration dashed.

"Did he wake up?" I asked curiously.

"Aye." Mrs. Byrne's eyes smiled.

I became confused over such an amiable emotion considering the solemnity of the situation, or so I thought.

"Our talk stirred the poor fellow to awareness despite the whisperin'. It was almost noon, and he had slept since the late afternoon of the day before; but to be sure, considerin' Lord Plunkett's earlier description, I ne'er saw a bit o' brandy and a sleep do that much for a man. Oh, he was still not himself, that's for sure, that transformation'd take months. But they weren't the first words out o' his mouth in the English language." Mrs. Byrne rose from the stool and started for the barrel churn. I waited on my own seat for her to come back. I couldn't believe my cheated eyes. She started working at removing the soft butter. How could a woman leave a story like that? It was like washing a shirt before throwing it away. I got up from my stool and started helping with the butter, not to be useful, but with hopes that it might get her talking again. I never would have entertained the notion that one day I would be craving for Mrs. Byrne to be long-winded. It only took a body with working ears to get her talking.

"Did the stranger tell you, my grandfather, and Lord Plunkett anything about who he was?" Ask the question and get it over with, there's no sense in watering a flower bed with a spoon. Sure you would get the job done, but it would take you all day.

"Oh, of course he did!" She scooped out a big slop of fresh butter, and threw it on the table to be salted. "As I told you, after the meal and a sleep, that fella spoke English right off."

And that was it, the last word of it. She started scraping out the churn, and I was standing there waiting for the moon to fall. It was like climbing up the face of Bray Head.

"Who was the fella, Mrs. Bryne?" I asked feeling as if I were training for a newspaper.

"You mean to say you don't know?" She looked surprised.

"I'm sure, I don't," I answered plainly.

"Well, I can't believe it." She wiped the butter off on her apron. "That was your Peader!"

I thought my eyes were going to fall out, and I could feel all the hairs on my head. I wanted to know more of the biography. I couldn't stop thinking about Peader. I was feeling proud for him. Several days later, I caught Mrs. Byrne in my father's greenhouse, tending to the limes and pineapples. This is what she told me.

Peader came to Lord Plunkett's house inadvertently from a town in the south by the name of Timoleague in the County Cork. There he had worked a small farm on Lord Stevenson's estate. It was the same farm that was run by his grandfather and great-grandfather before him. He had a successful plot of land, and on it he raised a few milch cows, grew some kitchen vegetables, tended a stand of apples, and harvested a field of wheat with its take used to pay the rent. He wasn't alone in the two-story house that was built in the seventeenth century. There was his wife and one surviving son who stood to inherit the lot.

But as for everyone something happened to the potato crop. In no time did the stalks turn from lush, two-feet-tall bushes to withered, black stems. Underneath the swift destruction, and to everyone's relief, the potatoes rested fat and happy. Those round and lumpy roots were hastily routed from their beds and moved to a large storage pit in the field behind the kitchen garden. Soon those potatoes started to rot, right under the bright green leaves of the smartly growing carrots and cabbage. Those potatoes that were still sound were scurried off to a straw-padded barn. Despite the strict precautions, they too began to spoil. Even the ones in the kitchen baskets started to blacken and turn fowl, with the smell alone enough to kill you.

That year, Peader's family had enough money for food, and they secured a fair price on the wheat crop to meet the rent. In the early spring of '47, they put in a second potato crop; and by early summer, that one got the blight and rotted just as the ones from before. Peader was forced to sell the cash crop of wheat in order to feed his wife and only son. It fetched such a low price at market that he was lucky to be able to pay the rent with it. There wasn't enough money left to feed the family for long. Even the apple trees did not earn their keep. Lord Stevenson, the owner of the property, assured Peader and his wife that he would not take the land from them as long as he was on the earth. Daniel had once said how queer it was "when straight, sensible thinkin' sat as rare and praised as a glass egg. And then I'd expect them to eat the hen that laid it!" But Lord Stevenson would not have eaten the gift bird. I knew that that would have been so.

There was a widely employed and profitable practice among property holders to remove by eviction the tenants of the estate, and to replace the unfortunate with livestock, which brought a better price at market than did grain. I had learned from Mrs. Byrne that Lord Stevenson labored to feed the hungry on his land and even those poor from other properties as well. And that was how the man caught the road fever that the starving carried to his door. He even tended to the dying, and soon it was himself that lay dead with the promise he had made to Peader buried in the grave alongside him.

The Lord had one wife who died several years before, and with her, he had been given three children of adult age, who believed in the principle of gainful business practices. The estate was converted into grazing land, and Peader and his family were informed of their impending eviction. The 150-year-old house mastered by three generations of Hayes was to be demolished by the month's end.

To be told that your home of three generations was soon to stand no longer is a terrible enough thing to take. But to be informed of your eviction by a callous note nailed upon your door is a far worse thing, to be sure, and a thing that is still known by many in my land.

Peader was forced to sell any of the valuable furnishings to expand the amount of their savings, for there were no jobs to be had. The Hayes were one of the better-off in that part of Cork, being favored with a fair landlord like Mr. Stevenson for so many years, a suitable house and productive lands. But now, they were seeing their neighbors forced upon the roads, nature was adding her own manner of persecution, and the potato failure was taking a lamentable toll of the poorer population. Mrs. Byrne told me a frightful account of the bodies of man and beast lying unburied upon the roads, of the hungry grazing as sheep to fill themselves but dying in the lush verges. Small cottages held the dead, and the half-living were too consumed by want and sickness to pull themselves from those house tombs.

It was the consuming march of adversity which followed my country and which had sent Peader blindly to the gates of Old Connaught House. In less than two months, he had been plundered of his farm, his wife, his last heir, his future, and his past.

"It was the death of the wife and the boy—so sudden by the fever—that broke the man," Mrs. Byrne mused. "He had the money and the vigor of his remaining youth to start again. But without his wife, he had not the yearnin' in him, and without the boy—well, he and the woman worked for that boy, you see. Everything—the house, the land that they rented—was to go to him. I don't remember the boy's name, but I think it was Éamon; the poor thing ne'er had a chance at life before it was taken. Barely older than yourself he was. Well," the old woman continued, "your Peader saw no more reason to toil, and so he was after lookin' to die upon the roads. Ah, but"—she pointed a finger at me—"the Lord in heaven wouldn't have it. And so your grandfather brought the unfortunate man to Carrickduff, and what I've told you now is all that I know. You'll ne'er be gettin' anythin' out o' your Peader, as sure as I'm sittin' here. For not a word of what I've just told you e'er came out of his mouth again. God blessed me with a fine memory—so He did—for me to hold onto so much."

"Peader's not unfortunate anymore?" I asked, fearful that my old friend was unhappy still.

"Of course, he isn't!" Mrs. Byrne proclaimed although she really couldn't know. "He's got a fine, sharp miss with a worthy brother, and young Daniel is as close a boy to him now as his own. I wouldn't be frettin' about your Peader, that's the last thing he'd be wantin' anyone to do, and he bein' so proud. Now, you promise me, Anne," she whispered solemnly to me, and I bent close to catch the words, "that you'll not mention a word o' what I told you, not to anyone, nor go askin' Peader about it."

"No, I wouldn't think of doin' anything of the sort," I said earnestly, "under pains of torture and death."

"You needn't go as far as that"—she picked up—"this isn't the war o' '98," and then she rose slowly and started to unpack the butter from its home in the churn.

Mrs. Byrne was right for Peader never again spoke about his past since that trial of a day at Lord Plunkett's house over thirteen years ago. He never talked about his dead wife or about his dead son, and nobody ever asked.

One night I was out walking with Daniel and Sheridan. We were reciting Tennyson and talking over something by Dickens. Sheridan had become unimpressed with where the conversation was heading, and alone he walked ahead toward the house shadowed by the tail end of the dark twilight. When we came across by the pond, there was Peader sitting by the bank under the willow, and I wondered why the man was shedding tears over the water.

"Isn't Peader happy?" I had asked, thinking Dan was privy to information unknown to any other.

"Aye, he's happy." Daniel turned his eyes from me and tilted his head. "It's just that he's got a new future, and when you liked the path the old one was takin', the new one's a hard thing to acquire a taste for." The boy looked down toward the dark pond where the moon's reflection sliced across the water's polished face. "He's weepin' for the old dreams, you see; the ones that died those many winters ago."

Those old dreams had a habit of coming back. They rode in with the wet clouds in the spring. Thirteen years ago, Peader worked his way east with a barren mind and an unknown path awaiting him. He had seen success, he had been near to destruction, and he had tasted from all the levels in between. Peader was the most naturally self-satisfied man I have known. Sheridan was after money, my mother was always after doing things, my father always seemed to be looking for something but he didn't know what it was he was searching for, and Dan was too much given to dreams, like a book that had too many things. Everybody learned something from Peader, but Peader was attended by ghosts such as those that Dan conjured for his stories. Those past ghosts are so deeply locked within Mr. Hayes that no matter how many times you wanted to fish them out, you never could; they were so far down. I think that he keeps them coffined even from his own thoughts. Something inside me begs me not to question those ways. It's a terrible thing to lose an old life and a harder thing to cast a new one when the "old dreams" won't die.

Chapter 7

Peader and I finished planting those geraniums before dinner despite his protestations predicting the contrary. I never knew that planting flowers could be prompted into becoming a disagreeable duty, but after hearing a one-sided string of complaints about the damp ground, the clods of uncooperative mud, the aching knees, and the "condemnable weather," I was glad to see the end of the job. Peader went off for his meal, and after all the objecting in the flower patch, I was surprised to hear that he still had the stomach for it.

I met Sheridan in the nursery, and he had a terrible face on him, as if he'd been made to recite the Bible twice. We always took our dinners in the nursery.

"Where were you all mornin', Anne?" asked Sheridan, sitting on a low ottoman which looked something like a hard, stuffed pillow that had tried to eat a creepie but couldn't. You could see the tips of the stool's legs sticking out grotesquely from the bottom.

"I was out plantin' geraniums with Peader," I answered, sitting down and taking a glass of milk. "How come you didn't come out?"

He looked at me as if he'd missed seeing the moon turn purple and melt. "It was Ma caught me coming down with my boots, and she asked me if I'd help her with her lacemakin'." I made a crooked face for sympathy and he groaned me an understanding answer.

"Lace rots," he concluded.

I looked curiously at the earthy stains beneath my fingernails. Mrs. Kelly in the kitchen wouldn't let me make bread when my hands were stained like that. I liked being with Peader because I always ended up with some dirt on me, and dirt had a way of making you feel warm, as if you'd been sitting before the fire. Chickens know this as they are always cleaning themselves with the dirt.

"I hate lace," My brother moaned. "Why does she think I like it?" He rested his hand in his chin.

"Well ya' didn't like photographin', did ya'?"

He grimaced at me.

"Maybe she thinks you'll be sellin' the finest of all lace from your merchant ships—like a pirate gentleman." I nodded, and Sheridan looked as though he was to be sick.

Our mother, Mrs. Carolyn O'Hayden, was an orchid fancier, a pianist, and a photography enthusiast, and had now decided to try a hand at lacemaking. She's not terribly good at it. I don't know much about lace, but I do know that what you buy looks rather different than what my mother's been ending up with. It is a difficult and tedious undertaking, and if you enjoy sitting about with rolls of linen thread, there's a grand hobby for you. Working with my mother usually involved winding the thread on the bobbins and chasing after the ones that she'd dropped and rerolling all the thread that had wound off.

"I could've gone riding." My brother sighed at the missed opportunity. "And with us being free from lessons and all, I shouldn't have been stuck in the house. Why didn't she hire father's cat?"

"But you still can ride," I commented encouragingly. "Ashlyn's been in the barn, so she won't be wet."

My brother nodded, the spirit coming back into him. I never thought that chasing thread could do that to somebody. Generally, it only made father's cat want to sleep.

Sheridan was ten, one year less than me, but ages apart in other ways. He was a realist and not much of a dreamer. He was the opposite of Daniel, who was a true romantic, and the half-opposite of me. My brother was as straight and unadorned in manner as a black Wicklow pebble, the kind that you would find on the beaches of Bray. He read very little that interested me although he did like Tennyson, and sometimes he liked Thackeray. He didn't even really like the French Revolution. No swords hung from his chamber wall. No Chinese vase sat on his desk. He didn't care to trade his new pistol for the old pocked flintlock that Peader taught me how to shoot, and he didn't like the absurd, crooked knife that father kept in his office curio. Sheridan rarely read anything out of the old *Nation* although he said that "patriots were good for business because armies needed lots of things and that was where you could make money." Peader said that patriots were good for the undertakers too. I thought it a shame that my brother could be so much like a Wicklow pebble, as he was so fine to look at. And highwaymen and poets were always good-looking and neat. They were like peaches,—glorious and blushing on the outside, and sweet and pleasing within. Sheridan was like a bad hazelnut—shiny, mahogany and beige on the exterior, as pretty as nature could be, but once you cracked inside, you only got a handful of bitter dust. I do not wish to keep bringing up bad thoughts over the boy and his plain nature. He rode exceptionally well, and was enchanting to go on adventures with, but he would never be a romantic.

"There is a fine young man you're bringing up, Mrs. O'Hayden," people would tell my mother. They apparently were unaware that inside that looker of a boy sat a poof of dry hazel dust. They were right about the façade, though I cannot find fault with that. Sheridan had smooth black hair and blue eyes of no less a color depth than Persian lapis stone. He was a shorter forgery of our father, and it gave you a funny feeling to see them both together. My father was a farmer, and my mother had said that, "even Notre Dame couldn't tease that out of the man." Sheridan, however, was a businessman since birth. It had been bred into him, like speed into a horse. And that was where the shame lay, since Sheridan looked as though he could have been a poet even though he couldn't write anything as well as our Daniel.

"If there were no realists," Dan had said, "there could be no romantic types to bounce their thoughts off." Daniel would remind me of that each time I "bounced thoughts" with my beloved brother, whose single purpose in life was to be a philosopher's adversary. I would sit in the stables with Dan. He would have his head bent over a soapy bridle leather and he'd say, "If you wanted to be a singular creature, then adversity would be walkin' right along with you. And that was good because"—he explained with his head bent down—"if everyone was the same as you, then you couldn't be different." And he would keep on scrubbing the leather. He was right, for even Wolfe Tone and Washington had different minds.

After having our dinner, we tried to decide how to spend the rest of our long, carefree afternoon. With the sky on our side, the possibilities were endless. Daniel would be all done with the stable cleaning by now, so we'd try to find him and of course, he'd be off as soon as he could before Peader found something else for him to do. Mr. Hayes' hearing wasn't so sharp, so that was a mark in Dan's favor. My brother and I just sat back in the nursery, eating the oranges that father had bought in Dublin. We thought it best to just go out, find the young groom, and let the day plan itself.

As we were sitting finishing the fruit and milk, our governess ran into the room. Her hair was astray, and she looked a bit more ragged than usual. She reminded you of frayed linen; no matter how much you trimmed it, it kept on fraying. My father said that "the poor woman was ruffled from following the two of you about." I never thought Ms. Farrell's ruffling came from my brother and me. I was always given the impression that she was rather fond of our company and that the disordered appearance was wholly natural and certainly pleasing to the present company, at least to me anyway.

"Have you finished with your dinner?" She asked breathlessly. I never knew that packing for a short trip could cause such a stir in a person.

"I'm done," I said.

"I'm done too," Sheridan said. "And we're goin' out now and for all afternoon," he added directly like a magician telling his tricks to work.

"I'll send Norah up to gather the plates," she said sprightly, "and I'll have her pack your tea basket then. But, be sure to be back by five-thirty, I'm not going to have time to chase after you."

We nodded.

"I have my shoes to pack yet"—she pushed a stray brown hair from her forehead—"and that'll be the end of it. Thank the Lord that your mother kept an idea of what I am going to need." Suddenly, her eyes popped wide so sharply that my brother and I were roused to do the same. I readied myself to catch one of them should it fall from her head. "I didn't pack my blue hat! I didn't pack any hats! I'll have to do that. I can't just take one hat. They'll be saying that I only have one hat." She shook her brown hair, and more of it came loose from the silk mesh of her snood.

"You've got a lot of nice ones," I said.

"Have," she corrected. "Use whole words."

"You have a lot of nice hats," I said

"Thank you, Anne." She seemed to relax.

"I think you've . . . you have . . . fine shoes," my brother said, that she might be eased even further.

"Those are the words of a gentleman, Sheridan." She curtsied theatrically. "Oh, do any of you know if Norah's all packed?"

"She finished last night," I told her, and then a peculiar slanted look fell across Ms. Farrell's face.

"But she was working in the kitchen until after eight? And she always retires at ten."

"Norah says it's . . . it is good for your comp'exion to sleep at the same early hour each night. And the night air has something in it that makes you look funny, and that you are not at all as mad as the people say," my brother recalled with a smile.

Ms. Farrell listened to it with astonishment.

"Well then"—she was perplexed—"Norah only would have had two hours to pack."

"I sat with her," I said. "She packed in an hour." Ms. Farrell's eyes got big again.

That is the first time that I ever saw travel case stuffing causes anyone to fall into distractions as it did for Ms. Farrell. And this was only a two-and-a-half-day trip, from this Friday afternoon to early Monday morning. You would think that she was going to see the king of Spain, and all that she was doing was going to Dublin to see her mother for the poor woman's birthday.

Our governess was twenty years of age, twelve years younger than my mother and better by far than all the tutors that had darkened Carrickduff's door. She was born in Dublin, and she was of the Protestant faith because her family traveled over from Birmingham in the old days when the weavers lost their work.

Ms. Farrell was well travelled despite her packing affliction, and had even managed to settle the contents of her shipping trunks in order to sail off for a French education. She was a cultured woman; she knew all sorts of stories, had seen all manner of plays and operas, and no one but Peader could match her in telling a joke. She had even spent time teaching in Paris. Ms. Farrell was a grand woman, and she didn't talk to you as other adults always did, saying things such as "you're a fine young lady" or "there's a promising boy." How do you start a conversation using those statements, blathering nonsense as if they were talking to a beast who couldn't answer you back because of the way God made them. I really don't think that they wanted an answer from you much beyond the "thank you, sir" and the "thank you, ma'am." And from the sound of most of the visitors here, save a few like Mr. and Mrs. Hutcheson and their ugly fairy baby, you would probably get better wit from Mrs. O'Toole's myna bird. Well, that's what my father said, and Celie was a smart bird. My mother said that you might get a better response chatting with the wheel bellows, or at least you would get the same effect.

My parents valued fine parlaying rather highly, and that was probably the reason that they took Ms. Farrell on, as I'm sure it wasn't for the travel packing. When our governess spoke to you, she expected a conversation, and sure a conversation is what you gave her. From the two years that she's been here, my brother and I felt like we were learning about everything that you could set your mind into. We learned how to speak the right kind of English. We read about the days of antiquity in Rome, we read Shakespeare, we memorized sonnets, we even learned how to write the funny Greek letters. Sheridan and I had a bet going about five months ago over whose head was going to blow first like a teakettle from too much information. Nothing happened as of yet, but I'm still having dreams where words and steam spout from my ears. Despite the threat of our heads exploding, Ms. Farrell was a fine governess. So things should have been so easy, you were thinking? Well, they were, save one matter. Our governess had a small aversion to one particular family member. That member lived in the nursery.

The nursery was our playroom, library, and schoolroom. Sheridan and I did not attend the national school because father disliked the way that the classes were run. So at home we stayed, and at home we learned. We could find no fault with the situation, and we were happy with our tutor. There were plenty of others to play with even though most were not of my age. Even in the nursery, we were not alone. There were two other boarders in that second-floor room.

The loudest was a raven named Donovan, from the Irish for "dark brown." That was because he had a small triangular patch of ruddy feathers that ran from his chin to the end of his neck. Otherwise, he was as dark as a pair of boots rubbed smart with lampblack. Donovan slept in the nursery on an elaborate T-shaped stand. The pole was carved from mahogany brought from the East Indies, and the perch a tasselled pillow of plush velvet. Donovan required the best.

First thing in the morning, the raven groomed himself. Just a quick shuffling of feathers and a little oil on the tail was enough. After a strenuous trip, he gave himself a cursory grooming by running his feathers through his thick beak, and then finished with a bit of scratching about his ears with his feet. At night, he received a thorough rubbing, oiling all those shiny feathers from the oil spot at the base of his tail and flaring out each long wing with enough ease of movement to rival any stepper out from Kelly's dancing school. As it is common for ravens to think highly of themselves, Donovan is a believer in the keeping up of tradition. His roommate, however, did not feel the same way, and that was a common tradition if you happened to be a small well-furred stoat.

Stoats are holders of the opinion that play in itself takes precedence over grooming although they are not inclined toward slovenliness. Rowan—from Ruadhan, the "little red one", as Peader told me—was as steadfast in respecting weasel tradition as Donovan was concerning raven ones.

Rowan slept in a small basket made from willow, or sally branches, as we called them. The basket had a wool blanket stuffed inside, and Rowan found it an accommodating bed although it did not possess the elegance of materials and cleverness of workmanship as did Donovan's perch, but stoats are unconcerned with those things. Under the wool blanket, in the corner of the basket, was a small collection of Rowan's findings and acquisitions. There was a bobbin from mother's lace makings, a bone button, a halfpenny that he found amongst the hollyhocks (so it was probably Peader's), one jack, and a toy wagon wheel. Besides collecting, the little stoat loved to run about and explore everything in and out of reach, much to Donovan's vexation. One morning, the raven discovered a furry partner perched beside him on the roost. But Rowan's favorite hobby was, undoubtedly, tunnelling in the out-of-doors. He was as unhampered as a free spirit could ever be and the preposterous, or more rightfully, the most wasteful notion of it all was that although Donovan had the wings, Rowan would have gotten the most use out of those appendages for flight.

There was one last note to remark upon and that concerned the relationship betwixt the little stoat and our governess. Rowan was the member of the nursery for whose easily won affections Ms. Eaven Farrell had little interest in obtaining. From Rowan's side, this desired estrangement of Ms. Farrell was fully perplexing. He held no bad feelings for her at any point in their relationship. He just wasn't that kind of a creature. To be truthful, he held her in very high regards.

The funny part about it was that Ms. Farrell had never been bothered, nor nipped, nor had any articles of property stolen by the stoat. She had never been insulted, disgraced, vexed, or otherwise badgered by any stoats. Now my brother Sheridan, Donovan, Rowan, and I found this part of Ms. Farrell's otherwise impeccable behavior singularly peculiar. Rowan was a kind fellow, if only a little high-strung at times, especially after all those days of rain. He hadn't been out in a week. Even Donovan thought that he was getting mold under those black feathers; and each night on his mahogany perch, I saw him feverishly check under his wings for any signs of green.

And that is where things stood on that rainy afternoon which had forced my brother into the disagreeable lacemaking business. Finally after the delay, and after some paw and beak cleaning, the two boys, Sheridan, and I rattled down the staircase for the back door. If you had seen the four of us running down the hard oak stairs, you would have thought a box of croquet balls complete with the mallets and players were released down the stairs. On top of that, my brother led me into a recital of Tennyson's "Of Old Sat Freedom on the Heights."

Of old sat Freedom on the heights,
The thunders breaking at her feet;
Above her shook the starry lights;
She heard the torrents meet.

We had four hours of playtime before supper, and we weren't going to be wasting a minute of it. It was sinful to waste things anyway. We always made the odd tool shed our first stop, and I'll tell you why we called it that later. But that decision or necessity had everything to do with my brother, Ms. Farrell, and me.

Chapter 8

Our governess insisted that my brother and I wear hats in the out-of-doors, and even with the packing frenzy on her head, she still found time to fetch some for the two of us. Nobody knew whether this was intended to keep us warm, smart looking, or draft free because Ms. Farrell never explained herself, and it wasn't easy arguing with the woman. I believe that she had a peculiar liking for hats.

I disliked to wear a hat for play during fair and clear weather, nor could I see any use for one. To appear well dressed and proper in public is one thing, but to adorn oneself for the trees and the cows and the weeds is another thing altogether. I found it difficult to see with my head strapped into cloth and wire, and I found it frustrating to hold my agility over logs and streams as well. Sheridan felt the same. We found a way in which to solve this problem without involving the perpetrator. And this is where the *odd tool* shed comes in.

The shed was a small outbuilding about ten-by-twelve feet or so and made of mortared stone. It was a handsomely weathered structure. My grandfather had built it in a fashionable Gothic style after the recommendation of Lord Plunkett. And it was a gorgeous building still, as stuffy as a church. The shed had six arched windows, a ridiculously heavy oak door, some ironwork placed under the four corners of the eaves, and a circle of Italian stained glass over the lintel. It did, however, have a few problems. In wet weather, the building released a smell rather like the shallows of a pond. Even during dry weather, that fieldstone floor was as damp as a dishtowel. My father had a skylight cut into the slate roof so that the sun might shine some dryness in there, but he only succeeded in lighting the inside, which allowed a handsome blanket of green moss to spread over the cool walls. Beside the moss, on the wall opposite the door, leaned a broken potting bench. Near the bench was a barrel churn with a missing handle. On the wall with the window rested a rusty turf slane, a wheel bellows used to fan the fire that was made in Wexford with the words Original Blower cast on the body, a broken kitchen trivet, a ragged edged scythe, a flail, and underneath these lay a dust covered cart brake, now home to half a dozen spiders. Across the room were strips of leather harness, broken clay pots, and small trowels for masonry and gardening in various states of physical distress.

The shed solved our distasteful hat business, or more truly, the shed's floor solved it. Some of the fieldstones that lined the floor had come loose, and the large one before the barrel churn was now the lid to our secret vault. About one year ago, my brother and I removed the stone, dug out the loam beneath it, and propped the thing's walls up with old wood panels so that the stone would have something to rest on. You would never know, if you looked there now, that anyone was digging there. Now the crate in that hole was our hatbox. Every day that we went out to play, Ms. Farrell bid us to tie the hats about our heads and as soon as we are out of sight off came those hats and down into the hole they went like buried treasure—ribbons and all. This was usually an uneventful business, as few of the house workers ever ventured into the odd tool shed. It was a most convenient and perfect situation.

On that Friday, after the rains, we performed the same hat-smuggling ritual. My brother and I were near to death with the urge for some outdoor play. I was standing near the handleless barrel churn, wiping the moss from my hands with an old piece of sacking, when suddenly Rowan barked with fright. Sheridan motioned for us to be quiet, and we all fell silent as the even crushing sound heightened.

"Someone's coming up the peastone path," I whispered cautiously.

Donovan flew to the window to scout for us while I unlatched the back door, should we soon need a speedy escape. Rowan, hair bristled, cowered in one of the potting drawers. We all waited for the inevitable discovery of our underground hatbox. Donovan raised the feathers on his neck, and slowly waved his licorice-black wings.

The *crunch*, *crunch*, *crunch* sounded ever stronger beneath the window, matching the growth of our worry. Rowan borrowed into the potting loam, my brother squeezed behind the wheel bellows, while I cautiously crawled beneath the potting bench, being ever wary of spiders. Oh god! This was going to be the end of our secret business, but I wasn't going cheap.

"Why is Donovan at the window in broad view, as if he's lookin' at flowers?" I whispered anxiously to Sheridan. "They'll know we're here. How would Donny be here if someone didn't let him in?"

The bird was as big as a hen chicken and not readily overlooked.

"I don't know," he hissed back. "He's gonna give us up, that sneak."

"Ah, he's not that kind of bird," I added. Just as I said it, the raven looked out the window and croaked a hello.

I crawled out from beneath the bench to see what the game was about.

"Are you mad then!" my disturbed brother hissed.

"I'm just seein' what's happenin', that's all." I slithered toward the window.

It was then that I saw the reason for the raven's ease of manner, and the end of our mislead concerns. It was only Daniel on the path, bent over with his brooding, passing by with Niamh's lathered bridle on his way to the stables. His lips were moving in a measured manner, and I figured that he was reciting some verses. Shafts of daylight dripped from the clouds and down through the fat oak leaves, where a few of them stopped to pool atop the boy's head, turning the thick hair a gold-brushed mahogany. I let my demeanor ease as I waited for Donovan to release one of my shoulder tassels from his heavy beak. It seemed that our sunken hatbox would find its use for yet another day.

"What's out there?' Sheridan's voice was still hushed.

"Nothing!" I yelled.

Quickly, I left the others, running from my hiding place with Rowan jumping from the potting drawer with enthusiastic knickerings and dirt scattering into the air as he bounced to catch up to me. I pushed at the door but it didn't budge as it was still latched. I fumbled hurriedly with the iron lever and threw open the door.

"Dan!" I called out before the boy disappeared around the path. I did not believe that he expected to see anyone come out from the old shed, for he started like a spooked robin and danced about until he realized, by the jingling of the collar, that it was Rowan biting at his trouser leg. Wild stoats of the sort that you found in the woods around here didn't think tinkly belled collars fashionable. For a jangling neckpiece was only a hindrance when you were after sneaking up on a rabbit.

"Anne!" Dan started. He looked down at the little stoat and snatched him up. "Where'd this one get dusted like a mud cake?" he asked, brushing fidgety Rowan while trying to keep his fingers out of nipping distance. The stoat wriggled about like a worm.

"Oh, he was in the pottin' drawer." I answered as if that was one of the most natural things in the world, and for us it was. "Sheridan and Donovan are still in there." I pointed back toward the shed.

"In the pottin' drawer?" Dan's face looked befuddled. "There's not enough room in there?"

"No," I raised my eyes, "they're waitin' there in the shed. We're all goin' off for fun. Can you come?"

He nodded. "I'm just gonna hang this bridle up."

"Is he comin', Anne?" Sheridan yelled from the window.

"Aye!" Dan yelled back. "I'll meet ya'!" He turned his words to me. "Where're you goin?"

"We're goin' to Crawford's," I answered. "Oh, Sheridan! Don't *leave* the tea basket! Come on Rowan."

The tiny collar jingled and tinkled as its wearer bounded and snuffed after me. I trotted down the dirt path until it turned to free-growing lawn. I waited there for my brother to shut the old door, and then the four of us ran, flapped, and bounded for the wild fields. Everywhere stretched those wild, rolling, soft-rising fields. And everywhere inside, there was a forever amount of everything; and over the top of them all watched Carrickduff, as she had done for 130 years.

Down by the shallow brook that tumbled from the low hills lay a quiet spot that couldn't be seen from the house. We ran through the overgrown garden where Peader and I had put the geraniums, a place that my father had told me was planted in the last century and still hadn't seen a gardener until well into this one. The garden was perfect, with its long geometric paths and tall quieting brick walls. It was in that place that Rowan chased rabbits under the too big oak, and also where my brother and I liked to ride our ponies. But we weren't stopping this time, as we were headed for the old cemetery that lay one hundred yards behind.

There was once a house on the grounds that had been dismantled to make way for Carrickduff. But the cemetery was never touched, and so the dead of that former family still rests where they were first placed.

Near that cemetery, the past owners of Carrickduff were buried. Most of the stones belonged to the Crawfords, but none were Cosgroves, except for the one belonging to Mrs. Cosgrove who had changed her name back to Crawford upon her death. And so for the cause of accuracy, there still weren't any Cosgroves in there. I guess that she didn't desire to have the name that caused her family's destruction carved for eternity over the face of her grave. Most of the headstones were now weather-scoured beyond readability, with the oldest ones dating from the 1600s barely discernible at all. The last grave dug in there dated from 1837. My grandfather owned the place then, and that grave was Mrs. Cosgrove's, now changed back to Crawford, who at her death desired to rest forever beneath the stones of Carrickduff. And that was the last of the "Blackrock" Crawfords and the last bit of funerary earth to be lifted, for the O'Haydens were buried in Kilmacanogue.

I liked the old Crawford cemetery better with its weeds and tall grasses, unvisited stones, and rusty iron gate. The blank faces of the markers rubbed out with Nature's intention looked like so many stone hermits. Within its walls, I could dream of that part of history where the old kings of Ireland waited for her call and the willow trees sang as they walked the dark roads. I wondered what sort of music a tree would sing.

Behind the tall trees of oak and pine that lined the fenced cemetery stood our barley fields. In the early spring, you could hear the farmworkers with the ploughs turning the rain heavy earth into straight furrows for planting. Even though you could hear the men and horses, you couldn't see them, and we would pretend that they were ghosts of Celtic warriors running their battle chariots over muddy ancient plains. There weren't any warriors out today, or plowmen either, for it was too wet for a battle, and the barley was up and growing.

My brother and I waited alone by the rusty gate for Dan while Donovan and Rowan went inside the graveyard. Donovan flew to the highest obelisk and croaked and cawed before setting off to look for insects. You couldn't see Rowan for the tall grass, but you could hear him rustling about with the ringing from his collar.

We sat and waited for Dan, and by my watch, it was fifteen minutes since we first arrived at the cemetery's gate.

"Maybe Dan's had to do something?" Sheridan sighed from boredom.

"He's usually good at avoiding work," I noted. "I think that he'll be here yet."

"Ah trash! I hate waitin'. You might think we had all day, and it bein' the afternoon already." My brother pitched a lump of grass skyward.

"We still have all day. He'll be here." I nodded. "I've not seen him lose a chance at freedom," I added with determination.

"I've ne'er known him to be late either, are you sure . . ."

"Hush! Do you listen then." I rose to my knees.

Before I finished the words, a heavy and jangling disturbance sounded from the side path, which led to the stables. The ground shuddered faintly beneath the soles of my shoes.

"You brought horses!' I called to our late and mislaid partner.

Dan was riding the tall five-year-old black Padraic, and he was leading the two ponies. Gavin was my brown gelding, and Ashlyn was Sheridan's chestnut mare with the four white stockings. Our ponies, large as they were, looked small next to Padraic's almost seventeen hands.

"Your mother's makin' lace"—Dan jumped from the tall horse's narrow, unsaddled back—"and this mornin' she asked me to take him out for her when the rain let up. Now is a good time to mix tasks and pleasure. Peader helped me with 'em all." He scratched the horse's neck, and the gelding dropped his head in happiness.

"Hardly a moment misplaced." Sheridan jumped upon Ashlyn, forgetting his former lack of patience.

"Hardly at all," I mocked, standing where Paddy could nuzzle my hair.

Mother's black hunter was given to much playfulness and joking, and Daniel was his favorite playmate. He liked to bump the boy with his muzzle and to pick Dan up by grabbing him by the collar. That was Padraic's way of showing affection. Another thing that the gelding liked was the company of cows. We used to pasture him with the other horses, but he wouldn't have it, and over the fence he'd go to be with the cows. He was gentle even though he was rather impressive to the sight; and with that big stride and those dessert-plate feet, the gelding simply floated over the ground. He was the smartest hack you could choose to ride. Mother called him Paddy, and she looked fine on his back dressed in her wool-riding habit with the skirt that reached past the ground. All in black they were, and the only sparkle was shown by the white stock at her neck and the hardware on Paddy's bridle. You could do anything without shying him, and we usually did.

"What've you two got planned?" The older boy asked with the look of someone drowning in the spirit of free time.

"Why don't we ride down to the back of the flax field?" I suggested.

"Sure, Mr. Hutcheson's land's got all o' those low walls for jumping. It's all right sure as we close the gates, he says." My brother swung onto Ashlyn's back, who had been taking the opportunity to stuff her mouth with rain-fresh grass, and the green froth was slobbering from her lips.

"Aye"—I scratched Gavin's nose—"there's nobody in those fields now, and the sheep are up in the back ones."

Many of the landowners didn't like you on their property because they figured that you were not going to be up to any good. Others were just plain surly. One lady on Mr. Barrand's land caught me going home with Dan after we had gone bird watching, and she pulled me aside saying how unseemly it was for me to be off with a young man. She called up all sorts of reasons that neither Dan nor I understood, and Dan wasn't even a young man, he was only fourteen, and I certainly had no intention of shaming my family in the future. I was wondering if she had found out that I liked photography, and maybe that was how I was going to shame my parents. My mother had a camera, which had had no such effect upon any of us at all. Dan and I were sure to never go by that road again.

But Mr. Hutcheson was different. I never heard him say a bad word about a camera. He even had my mother photograph his prized bull "George". Instead of terrible thoughts, he raised cattle and sheep, and he didn't mind anyone in his empty pastures, as long as you didn't worry the beasts, and you shut all the gates behind you.

Before mounting Gavin, I put the tea basket inside the cemetery gate for safekeeping, and then I called for Rowan. Soon the low tinkling sounds grew louder, and a little burst of brown fur squeezed under the lowest bar of the cast iron fence. I picked up the snuffling, squirming stoat and jumped into the saddle. He stuffed himself between my leg and the pommel, and off we all rode, with Donovan flapping and rolling along overhead.

Down we travelled in single file along the edge of the barley field, where our brewery stock matured. I felt like one of the trooping fairies who traversed the countryside in grand numbers on their way to splendid festivals of enchanted merrymaking.

Just as we turned down the bohereen, which was the narrow road that ran between our barley and our flax field; we overtook a boy with tussled hair walking eastward down the lane. He was dressed in a grey frieze jacket and a pair of patched corduroy trousers that would've seemed more proper on a larger boy. He stopped and turned to see where the horses were coming from, and then he saw the familiar big black gelding leading the way. He drew his hand from his pocket and waved.

I squeezed Ashlyn forward, and we trotted toward our lone friend. Rowan bobbed jarringly on the saddle, and I kept him from bouncing off, while his collar bell marked each stride with a jingle. I waved to the boy, and he started walking toward us to lessen the distance.

That boy's name was Thomas, and he lived down at the end of the bohereen that ran past our flax field. They were tenants of the Barrands'. Thomas had four brothers and eight sisters, and very little else. They were awfully poor. My father would shake his narrow head whenever anyone mentioned the Timoneys, and he said that it was a sinful thing for a family to have more young ones than they could care for in a proper way. The English government brought trouble, but "they didn't bring babies." But we cared for Thomas, and we wanted to have him stay under our roof, and he would have if his family thought better of us.

Thomas's family never came to our door for work, food, or linens. We had many "unlucky beggars"—as Peader called them—but never the Timoneys, and it wasn't for lack of want either. One night at our sitting room hearth, my father and Peader were having a smoke and a glass of Jameson's finest. They were talking politics while my mother had dismissed her lacemaking for a book about the orchids in Siam, and Daniel was reading geography to me and Sheridan. We were having a hard time concentrating on the lesson over the talk of worldly things, the "new man" trying to get into the government, and my mother adding her two bits from the back of the flower book.

The Timoneys didn't like us—all save Thomas, that was. They weren't even tenants of ours, but we've never had any complaints from renters. Actually, we had hardly ever met, not properly anyway. It seemed that we could never get near enough to talk. I was thinking that maybe Mr. Timoney had heard of my mother's photographing interests and he had the same poor feelings toward the art as that woman who had stopped me on the Barrand estate. I told my father that, but he sent me a confused look, and he said that it was an unlikely reason.

It was then that I figured that maybe it was Carrickduff that they hated, because she was big and grey and black when it rained. Maybe they knew about her past, the way that the tenants were evicted, and how the precious land was left to waste. But we weren't that kind of people, and now she was our Carrickduff. All of our workers had been given notice to be civil and courteous should, in a rare incident, a Timoney come to the door. That has yet to play itself out, but none of the servants would ever cross their kind master's wishes, at least not in a manner where he was likely to hear about it anyway. But as far as our contact with the Barrand's tenants was concerned, the cats were envious at our skill at never crossing each other's paths. Ours was a singular, artful relationship of avoidance.

Chapter 9

The Timoney's house was a small two-room cottage with an "upstairs" loft that was so low ceilinged that you couldn't stand up in it unless you were a fairy. In that loft was where Thomas and his brothers and sisters retired for the night. In good weather, Thomas slept in the barn with the cows, goats, and the few chickens that also declined their allotted quarters in the main house by the fire. He said that you'd be surprised at how warm a few cows could keep a barn. The roof was thatched on the barn, on the cottage, and on the turf lean-to; but the thatch on the house was sprouting a crop of something, and the goats would go up there to graze upon it. I didn't blame them. It was the cleanest place in the yard, which was otherwise filled with various sorts of muck, and the walls of the housefront were little cleaner. It looked as though it was waiting for a good washing rain. My parents always told me that your eyes should be blind in the home of another, especially when the "others" were less fortunate than you. And my mother would then remind me that "it wasn't so long ago that your own grandfather on your father's side came from nothing." She always would stress the *on your father's side*, because her family were always well-off or well-seen-to since when their smuggling business on the Kerry coast took off somewhere in the seventeenth century. But that was all right because those were desperate times, and if the English could steal and plunder all over our country, then the Irish could also do whatever was necessary. "What's good for the goose is good for the gander," she said. Apparently, the seventeenth century Timoneys never took advantage of those great Bray seaside caves, or they could've made their fortune in pirating as well. Sheridan called those things *lost opportunities*, and you couldn't succeed in business with too many of them. That was too bad because Thomas's family were very good at missing opportunities, even the ones that we gave to them.

Once, my father and I went down to the cottage to offer Mr. Timoney a job on our farm. He was even going to take them off the Barrand's estate, if Mr. Timoney wished, before the Barrands forcibly did it as their rents were in arrears anyway. This was toward the dying edge of summer, and our money crop was to be brought in. Something must have come forth in an uncomfortably wrong way, for our offer was declined.

Mr. Timoney was standing there outside of the door, and the door was open enough that I could see the cottage's dirt floor. Inside there was almost no furniture compared to our stuffed and cluttered rooms. Mr. Timoney was not pleased to see us there, since we were greeted with a pitchfork and the owner saying that he didn't want any traitors on his land. My father told him that his information, from wherever it had come, was mistaken. Then my father gestured for me to move behind him. The man wasn't interested in hearing Mícheál O'Hayden explain himself. He said that there were no worse scoundrels on this land. We were "wolves in the fold," and because of people like us, the land would never prosper, and that was why we were "still in bondage after all of those hundreds of years."

I remembered people talking about the soup bowls that were put out by some relief stations during the famine, but in order to get the food, you had to forsake the Catholic religion for the Protestant one. It was better to die than to *turn over* because if you died a Catholic, you wouldn't be shamed and you would go to heaven. But if you "turned," you would be doomed forever all for a bowl of soup. I told my father about it. And he asked me if I thought Ms. Farrell was doomed because she was a Protestant and George Washington and Lord Edward Fitzgerald, the hero of '98, and anybody else I could think of? I said no. He couldn't believe that there was anyone could pass on such nonsense; but this was Ireland, and he had heard worse: "It was too bad that we couldn't sell nonsense, or we'd be the richest country," and, "if you could eat it, we would be feeding the world. And to think somebody had figured that if you ate the American corn meal, you'd turn into a heathen. God save us."

I don't think that Mr. Timoney mused over things in the same color of thought as my father. He said that he "didn't want any traitors on his land," and my father removed his hat and bid Mr. Timoney a good day. But before he left, my father said that he had "no interest in your rented land, and neither do you—I think—as you are so near to losing it and are taking no pains to address the matter. I do, however, sir, take affront to your licentious use of my family's name. The O'Haydens have given their share to the cause of national interest and have wished to mend the injustices, if that be so asked."

I had never heard my father talk about politics in that way. Despite the stiffening effects of this extraordinary chaos, I managed to note that the intimidating Mr. Timoney was not accepting my father's words, and I noticed that my father was not at all unsteadied by any of these events. He looked as though he had just come from a hunt with Mr. Hutcheson. Later at home, I asked my father what all that Mr. Timoney had said meant. Why did having money and living at Carrickduff make us bad Catholics? Weren't Catholics supposed to have money? He said sure Catholics could have money, "look at the church, look at Rome, huh!"

"Well, why did he say we weren't good Irishmen?" We read the old *Nation,* and Peader told stories of the War of '98, and told us about the poems of Thomas Moore and about the other writers in the *Nation* that he didn't like. Now I wasn't so sure I had the right to those things anymore.

My father took me to his study that was full of his business things, and his books, and the statues from India of elephants in costume, and people with four arms that looked like they were dancing. He took me over to his desk; and he opened the center drawer, pulled from it a linen cloth, and from that cloth he unwrapped an old tarnished knife, and he handed it to me. It looked like a big pocketknife with a strange narrow blade. He told me that my great grandfather, the one that was exiled to France, had fought in the war of 1798, which was the Irish version of the American and French revolutions. At the time, our family were still tenant farmers, living beneath the Wicklow Mountains in the town of Tinahely. In that spring and summer, the Irish people rose to change the injustices of the government. My great-grandfather belonged to the United Irishmen along with those men with the names of William Drennan and Lord Edward Fitzgerald. My father told me that it was how you governed your life, like Lord Edward, that made you a good person of any religion. Having money didn't make you bad, but the way that you had procured it and the way that you used it were what really counted.

I didn't always believe my father's words—which was a sinful thing to do—but I couldn't change the way that I felt, not honestly anyway. This time, however, as in the times when he spoke of the old stories, I believed him entirely. I was proud to be a part of him. I wanted to be an O'Hayden even though I was only eleven.

I didn't feel so wretched after that, but the scratch was still there too; that was the first time I had been set upon by the outside world. It was the queerest moment of my entire life or of those eight or so years I could actually remember. I had never seen that sort of heedless passion in a person before

I met Mr. Timoney. It was a terrible circumstance to find yourself facing reasonless anger, and any reason that you place before you is eaten up, cast aside, and rendered powerless. And I was angry too. It was a strange, dark anger. An anger that was rich and fearless and seemed to live from me. But my hate was not meant for Mr. Timoney; it was for all things wrong. And I knew that wasn't going to be the last experience of that nature that I was going to see.

One day, I was walking back from the narrow lane that ran past the back of the Timoney's few acres. I was returning home from playing along the stream with Thomas and had worked my way down to where the big grey farmhouse of the Hutchesons stood. I ran along the stonewall and then down into their hayfield, dotted with the big haycocks. Scrambling over the boundary wall, I landed on the quiet bohereen that ran along our flax field. I started my way back up the lane, and who should I meet but a friend of Thomas's older sister, Mina. Her name was Sara, and she spotted me before I could make fast my escape behind the hedges. Mina was fourteen and not bad to look at except that she had the character of a dying thistle. I was hoping for her to pass me, but I could see that she was after something.

She was looking at me as if I had just done something wrong or I had a squirrel on my head. *Send them to live in the devil's house*, I thought, *and in a way that they would be looking forward to the trip*; but the argument didn't last long save some more well-placed insults.

How can you have a quarrel with people you have never exchanged opinions with? I never understood that kind of natural hate. My father said that when Thomas was old enough, he could come and stay with us. Of course, if his da ever found out that his son spent time in the house of the O'Haydens, it wouldn't be a picture worth hanging.

After hearing my father recount to me the patriotic past of my near ancestors, it was terribly presumptuous of Mr. Timoney to take such liberties in the manner in which he had treated my father and my entire family. It was an entirely disagreeable situation, and one I hope to never encounter again. Although that small ember of temper that resides inside me is, I fear, present to forewarn me that I will one day be privileged to such an attack again.

I had intended to reveal the entire incident to Daniel and Sheridan, but I spoke to my mother first; and she said that it "was best not to spread such animosity about, unless some noble end should come of it. Because"—she consoled me brushing the loose hair from my face—"if you light one reed, it burns to ash; but touch the flaming piece to a roof of thatch, and the entire house is alight." My mother was from a long line of patriots, and she knew what she was talking about. I wasn't completely sure of what she meant, but it sounded bad. I found it best to not linger on a thing that I could not change. Although there was one gain that arose out of the unfortunate encounter, and he was eleven, the same age as me—the boy that we were meeting on the bohereen that Friday.

Thomas was a romantic; although he didn't like to write or tell stories like Dan, he loved to read them. He loved Tennyson, Defoe, and Dickens, and all the grand writers. He liked Mary and Percy Shelley, Keats and Lord Byron, and even the Irish poet Thomas Moore. I asked once if he had been named after Moore, but he said no, and so Daniel rechristened him after the poet in a solemn but speedy ceremony beneath the whitethorn tree in the Hutcheson bower.

We gave Thomas our books from the library because his family couldn't afford such things. My father would buy him books, and Thomas would put them in the barn so his mother wouldn't throw them away because she said that reading would make your eyes bad. Tom didn't believe his mother because both of my parents read, and so did Peader and none of them were blind. Thomas said that the books were good because they stuffed you full of pictures of wild lands, exotic honeydew, thunderstorms, and frightening visions like Frankenstein's monster and all such grand things; and so I was glad to see Thomas on this, our first endless day of freedom.

"Where are ya' goin', Thomas?" I asked, letting Gavin walk up to the small brown-haired boy. Rowan stretched out his long neck and sniffed a vigorous welcome, and he got a scratch behind the ears in return.

"I'm returnin' your Frankenstein." He shrugged his shoulders and almost stepped back upon Donovan's feet. "What are you doin' waddlin' up behind people like that?" The large bird cocked his head and rattled a greeting.

"We're goin' ridin' through Hutcheson's sheep fields," my brother divulged. "Do you want to come?"

"Sit behind me," Daniel brushed his hand over Padraic's long back.

"You've no saddle," Thomas added. He rubbed his spirited hair.

Dan shrugged.

"I'll come," Thomas answered, "but I have to give you this book." He stood holding out the encumbering object.

"Put it behind the haycock over there, the third one in," my brother said brazenly.

I thought my eyes were going to pop out of my head.

"How did you know that, who told ya!" I was astonished.

"Your captain told me." Sheridan pointed to the condemned boy.

"Daniel, you're an informer!" I was even more astonished. "You took the oath under penalty of death." My admiration for the boy hissed away like teakettle smoke. I hadn't expected such sorry behavior from a gifted poet and a reader of the *Nation*. "Is there a shadow of purity in the world?" I moaned.

"It wasn't like that, Anne!" Dan was trying to offer a weak justification. Padraic snorted with scepticism, "I'm still as straight as an arrow."

"You weren't supposed to tell the places where the messages were put." Thomas poked Daniel's shoulder. "Not to anyone."

"It was only Sheridan." Dan tried to cover his slip.

"Only Sheridan?" My brother huffed indignantly, "the *Wicklow pebble*."

He tried to mimic me. I squinted at him.

"It was Monday mornin', and I had to get Niamh tacked for your father." Dan spun Paddy around so that he could face me. "I knew that you had sent a message the night before, Anne, and I wouldn't have had time to gather it up, and the clouds were comin' fast with the rain. So would you two have rather lost the message with the wet, or have it neatly delivered by the hands of Sheridan?" Daniel squinted a purposeful look at me and elbowed Thomas behind him. "Did you read the message, Sheridan?"

"I did not, sir." My brother answered straightening in the saddle with mock respect.

"Even if you didn't believe us"—Dan continued, and Sheridan huffed again—"I had another reason why I had considered it safe to send this fellow." He pointed to my brother. I could see in Dan's face that he was holding on to some significant point.

"Why?" I asked, knowing something was coming. "Will it rekindle my faith, Mr. Whelan?"

"Because," Sheridan added, "I'm a fine fellow."

"No," Dan looked at Sheridan blankly. "The letters are written in lemon juice, so nobody without a flame could ever hastily read them." He smiled handsomely.

He was right.

"Your sentence is commuted, Mr. Whelan," I called up those jagged words. "To the glory of France!" I raised my hand in a phantom toast. I was glad that I was never able to blush.

"To the glory of France!" was my threefold echo. "Liberté, equalité, fraternité!"

Daniel, Thomas, and myself were three *citoyens* of old France. We belonged to a group named Les Hirondelles, the "swallows," and we were fighting the French Revolution. We used swallows because if you were to steal or damage their nests, they would remember your actions and punish you for the wrongdoing. And that was what the citizens of France were doing then, punishing their bad leaders for stealing and "damaging the nests" of their people. Citoyens Daniel, Thomas, and I were the only members. My brother wasn't interested, Rowan was too distracted to be a patriot, and Donovan made too much noise. Donovan could have been a perfect message carrier like a big black carrier pigeon, but you couldn't have a spy that crowed and croaked away the minute he reached his secret destination.

The messages that we sent were rolled up and bound with a red, white, and blue ribbon. A tiny token of a liberty branch in the form of a boxwood twig was stuck under the ribbon. Now, if you had unrolled the paper, you wouldn't have seen a thing on it, not a word, not a scribble. But there were words written on it with lemon juice, and if you were to put that paper over a candle, the message would come out. So you see Dan was right, Sheridan could never had read the letter. The messages were invisible because they carried the words of our secret society, specifically the plans for the rebellion.

The message that I had hid behind the haycock was for Daniel. For security reasons,

I didn't know what the letter said because it was sent from Thomas. If by treachery the message was to be stolen, or if I were to be captured and tortured, I would have nothing to say. All of us took an oath that we would be as straight as a rush, and that "I—would die first, for the glory of France before anyone could force a betrayal out of me."

We all had our own spot into which our messages were to be placed. Mine was the haycock, the third from the left, by the side of the stonewall with the notch in it that was made from a fallen stone. The haycock was just before the break in the wall. Thomas's notes were placed in the Crawfords' cemetery, under a slate below Mrs. Crawford's headstone, and Daniel's were tucked inside a book, Thomas Paine's *Rights of Man*, that lay inside a tack box in the stable. The spying and note sending filled the days with many a suspenseful hour, but only when Sheridan wasn't around because he said it was "too made up and had to it no real danger at all." He was right in a real sense, but for a romantic there was plenty of danger if you just imagined hard enough. But my brother was with us today, and so there could be no uprising against the traitorous Duke de Meule de Foin, who lived in the tree-fortressed stronghold of the hayfield. *Le jour de Gloire*, "the day of glory," would have to wait.

Chapter 10

"I didn't know that you were goin' to storm the nobleman's castle." My brother's eyes widened after I revealed the plans of Les Hirondelles, the citizen fighters of Chantilly. As he'd already been made privy to our note running from Citoyen Daniel, there wasn't much point in taking secrecy any further.

"Aye"—Dan straightened on the horse—"the messages were sent to rally the town into comin' to join us. They have, you see, and we've got weapons from the Bastille, and we've freed Thomas from the torments of that terrible prison, and now we're ready to fight. And so you, Mr. Sheridan O'Hayden, have come to know our plans." The boy's voice turned dark and serious. My brother's expression widened with concern.

"Dan, you got me involved, you remember that!" Sheridan pointed an angry finger at the boy.

"Citoyen Whelan, not Dan," I corrected.

"Citoyen Whelan got me involved! We've proved that already."

"This is war." Dan shrugged. "The quarrel has already begun, and corruption is rotting the land."

"No one can walk away after knowin' the plans of Les Hirondelles," I warned.

"You kill 'em, don't ya?" Sheridan said knowingly. "That's why they don't walk away."

"Y've got two choices." Thomas leaned forward from his high furry seat and brandished two fingers. "Join and fight for freedom or meet your death."

"That's a grand choice your given' to me Citoyen Timoney. Sure I'll join; death sounds boring."

"And you couldn't stay still long enough," I added. "Have you somethin' to say, Citoyen Timoney?"

"First," Thomas raised a finger, "were you in Paris on May the fourteenth?"

"I've ne'er been in Paris at all," my brother quickly added.

"So, you say to me now that you had nothin' to do with my arrest then?" Thomas narrowed his eyes in doubt. "You had no knowledge that I was rottin' away in the Bastille?"

"I had absolutely nothin' to do with it; I ne'er knew that you'd been held in the Bastille e'er." Sheridan answered. "I don't e'en know where the place is."

"Do you know the Duke de Meule de Foin?" I asked.

"No, I swear to you that I don't. I can't e'en say it."

"So, do you wish to join us and fight for the glory of France?" Daniel asked with the solemnity of a statue and the hard stare of a highwayman. He looked like a Bray pirate. The sun slashed through the afternoon clouds to warm his high, pale forehead.

"I believe that would be better'n dyin', Citoyen Whelan." Daniel grinned coldly.

"Then take the oath Citoyen Sheridan Gerald O'Hayden," I asserted, dismounting from my horse with Rowan still in my arms. Everyone did the same, and we all stood in a little circle to give credit to the solemnity of the occasion.

"In the awful presence of God, I, Sheridan O'Hayden, declare that I will dedicate myself to bring justice and prosperity to the nation of France." I nodded to my brother, and he sent a dead stare back at me.

"Yer supposed to repeat it," Thomas nudged him, whispering the prompt, as if we, standing right near them, couldn't see it.

"Well," I said.

"You'll have to section it up," he said. "I can't say all that and think about what's comin' next."

I "sectioned" it all up so that my brother's short memory could work unhindered, and we soon had four instead of three Hirondelles.

"Now"—Daniel pulled himself up onto Paddy's bare back—"let us ride to our store of weapons so that we may give this day to *liberté*!"

"To *liberté*!" We echoed the glorious battle cry and mounted our horses. This time Thomas scrambled up behind Sheridan. Ashlyn had a lower back than the black gelding, and the boy now had a saddle cantle to hold onto. Even here though, Thomas's attempts were not looking very gallant, and revolutionaries and highwaymen were supposed to look gallant. Sheridan tried to pull the boy up, but it didn't work, save to cause Ashlyn to dance away from the tugging by her side. Sheridan almost slipped from the saddle himself, but soon everything was made right. I just hoped we weren't going to face any fast escapes during the battle.

We took off at a canter down the narrow road. The wet dirt stuck onto and flew out from the horses' hooves as the iron shoes clattered over the loose stones. I had one hand on the rein leather and the other gripped around Rowan who didn't seem to be enjoying the rattling and bouncing he was getting from Gavin's rocking gait. His black winged friend had taken to the air above us flapping far ahead toward the Hutcheson hayfield. Donovan had an incredible ability to know wherever it was that you were going.

The hayfield didn't look anything like it did in the fall when the haycocks were up. Now it was just a green lay of pasture, growing and waiting for the scythe. Mr. Hutcheson would always leave us five stacks from the past year because we liked to use them so. He left us the one by the notch in the stonewall and the four behind it. I had to use the gate to enter the place since I had Rowan, and he was already shaken up just by the cantering. The others jumped the low wall. Sheridan and Ashlyn bounced over quite well. Daniel took it easily with Paddy squaring his knees off perfectly as they sailed over the stones. But it was Thomas who had the unlucky fortune of sitting close to the gelding's haunches, and he was given a good jar when the horse lurched from the ground. It was only from great luck and exceptional balance that the boy managed to keep his seat.

We let the horses loose, and then made our way through the tall grass toward the last haycock that rose from the far left corner of the field. The bough of an oak hung low and leafy over the stack's head, giving it a shaded, brooding look. Donovan was perched on the top, picking over the dried grass for insects.

"Where're we goin'?" Sheridan trudged slowly behind me with Rowan in my arms. And Daniel and Thomas followed too.

"Up to the first haycock, there." I pointed at the one by the broken section of the wall with my free hand, the other wrapped close around the narrow stoat. Rowan was wiggling in my grasp, and his little bell was tinkling with the excitement of its furry owner. "Ease your squirmin', Rowan. I'll let yourself down when were a little farther up."

I dropped my active bundle by the side of the tall stack, and he took off, hair bristled, snickering and bouncing round and round the hay's base like a hairy inchworm. There was no problem with letting the little fellow off in strange places, for he stayed about the area without straying, and you always knew where he was with the ringing from his collar.

Rowan climbed the haycock to snap at and badger Donovan. Daniel went around to a ruffed and tossed up area of the hay and started moving flakes of it out of the way. He looked like a dog digging himself a hole.

"It's all hid in here, you see—the weapons, the sashes, the colors, everything." He was halfway inside the haycock. "All right, I got 'em. Anne, could ya stand by my legs and catch."

I walked over to the kneeling and straw-strewn figure, and I waited for the first of the lot to come forth. And the first was a sword—two feet long with a flat wooden blade pushed into a carved oak hilt. A second such "sword" came next and then a third. I handed these to Thomas, and he to my brother who then set them in a pile. There was a pause and then a long, narrow box of maple wood with a brass latch was handed back. I passed the box to the rest of the waiting line. When this was finished, we had the three swords; the maple box; a three-foot-long red, white, and blue banner that was to be flown as our colors; and three sashes of red, white, and blue cloth sewn together by young Norah, the maid travelling with Ms. Farrell, who was also fond of the French cause. All we needed now was a pole to set the banner onto, but first we had to divvy up the weapons. Sheridan took hold of the maple wood box, and he flipped open the small latch.

"Oh, Anne, sure da'll not be pleased with ya' takin' the firelock and shovin' it in there! What if it rusted?" He took the old gun from the velvet-lined box and turned the heavy curiosity over in his hand.

"It was in the case"—I gestured toward the shuffled hay—"and inside there is as dry as can be."

"It's as dry as Mrs. O'Toole's conversation," Daniel added.

"Do you see any spot of rust on it?" I asked with a slight bit of sarcasm.

"No." My brother turned the pistol over. He was desperate for finding a spot of tarnish.

"So," I said.

"So?" Sheridan cocked an eye at me.

"So, Da won't care a squirrel's hair about it," I said.

"We had to have it," Thomas confirmed.

"It makes the thing seem more natural." The groom brushed the straw from his thick hair.

"Aye, your right," Sheridan nodded. He was a stickler for authenticity. "You need the firelock for things to look proper." He lifted and tilted the gun as if he was going to fire it. "It's too bad you can't shoot sweet, Anne, or you'd be a credit to us." He squinted down the barrel.

"At least I didn't go over backward with the kick from father's rifle." I sneered. "And you don't talk to officers like that. 'Tis a floggin' offence, Citoyen O'Hayden."

"All right," Dan stepped to the pile. A few bits of hay fell from his clothes. "All right, who wants what?"

We divided the weapons. Everybody grabbed a sash. Daniel took the flag and a wooden sword. My brother and Thomas tied their swords onto their tricolored waist belts. I wore one of the sashes around my waist and stuck the gun highwayman-like into the cloth belt. The old weapon was heavy and too big for me, and whenever I moved quickly, the butt stuck me in the side. As much as I liked the 1750's gun, I could never get used to shooting it. I couldn't aim it right, and the recoil hurt my hand as if someone had struck me with a flat, round stick. The gun was a rare "sweet" shooter too, as accurate as a pistol could be. Peader was a wonder with it, as if he was one of those American riflemen like Daniel Boone. He said it was from all those years of poaching, and if you could shoot straight under the moon, "you're a miracle in the light of day, but don't you tell your mother anythin'." I couldn't understand why he was shy of bragging about that to an ancestor of a pack of pirates.

I tried my father's shotgun, but I couldn't hit anything smaller than a haycock at fifty paces, and the kick was enough to knock my arm off, and almost send me over backward. My mother was almost as good a shot as Peader, but then she was a full patriot and part-pirate. My father wouldn't use the firelock. He only used his new percussion cap for bird shooting, or for any other larder-stuffing purpose. Carolyn O'Hayden didn't like for anyone to go off destroying birds. She felt sorry for the "wee things" as they were so pretty and darted about like singing flowers adding life to the grounds as goldfish do to a still pool. "The land would be stiff and stagnant if it wasn't for the birds," she said. My father reminded her that he didn't shoot songbirds, and she told him that she was aware of that. Mícheál O'Hayden did agree with her, and he deplored any man who found pleasure in causing someone else's death no matter how small or uncomely as the creature happened to be. He would always tell my brother and I that it didn't matter if you didn't hold any regard for some beast's life, for all creatures loved the life that God gave them, and that was what counted in His eyes.

My father then subsequently found himself in rather a quandary. As much as he hated to hunt to fill our table, he hated even more to take any of the livestock for the same purpose even though he would have some sold, and you had to know where they were eventually going. He couldn't kill anything that he raised because "there's something deceitful in winning over the trust of an animal, and then making a meal of it for the thing has no thoughts of getting away, for it had been thinking that you were a friend. I give the wild ones a sporting chance to secure their escape, and those that don't mind their chances were destined to grace the O'Hayden's table."

If it wasn't for Mr. Huston's butcher shop, we never would have tasted chicken besides an old stewing bird, or any other form of roasted or boiled (and that would have disappointed Donovan who was terribly fond of beefsteak), shell or finned fish, or anything that tread or swam on the earth.

Peader didn't understand Mr. O'Hayden's method of thought on the subject of nonvegetable-food procurement, but he lived under it nonetheless. "When my own mother was livin' and seekin' a bird for the table, it was out the back she went for the henyard." He then made plucking motions that would have made Donovan grimace. "Well, we don't live like we used to anymore. You're a lucky young thing, and don't you think otherwise, anois." Luckier than the Hayes' chickens, I could safely say. And luckier than the ill-destined Duke de Meule de Foin, who if things went as planned, wouldn't be seeing the end of today.

We were armed in the name of liberty; we had the people of France behind us and the will of justice before. We left the horses to graze and to spend some time together, talking and scratching each other's withers. I took Rowan from the top of the haycock where he had been biting the raven's tail, and I stuck the squirming fellow under my arm. Donovan bobbed his head in relief, jumped from the haycock, and followed me in his awkward, stiff-legged gait. If you have ever seen a raven walk, you knew why God gave them a pair of wings. He gave them intelligence, proper taste, and a gentle person's manner, but their skill in the skies was the crown on it all.

"Are we all ready then?" Daniel took the flag and held the cloth aloft, the pole resting on the ground. He looked like the lead fellow in that painting by Scheffer, *Allons, Enfants de la Patrie*! There was no wind, and if there had been, that limp flag would have waved gallantly in the boy's grasp.

"I'm ready," I nodded. I could feel Rowan's back legs kicking at the gun's grip.

"What's himself gonna fight with?" My brother addressed Rowan with a tic of his head.

"He's gonna run up their trouser legs," Dan said mockingly.

"They didn't wear trousers then. I saw pictures of them in books." Thomas rubbed his chin. "Weren't they in knee-britches?"

"Sure, they were in them," I agreed. "Hey, Rowan"—I scratched his tiny chin—you're gonna bite their ankles." He looked up at me and licked my fingers. I smiled back at the others.

"All right, now that Citoyen Rowan has his orders, we've only got one left." Dan kneeled and clicked for the raven to come over. "Come here, come on, Donovan. Now, what're we gonna have you do?" Donovan wiped his beak on the boy's leg for an answer. He had been snacking on pasture flies and beetles, and there was now a tiny black wing sticking to the trouser cloth. Daniel ignored being used as a napkin. The boy was always the gentleman. "You, Citoyen Donovan, who has the ability to fly without a balloon, is commissioned to carry information from the siege to the villagers and from Les Hirondelle's headquarters to us in the tyrant duke's castle. Donovan rattled an answer and hopped up onto Daniel's bent knee and then onto his shoulder. Dan raised himself with his new passenger, and he held the tricolor before him.

"Are we all ready?" Dan put the question to us and put his right hand to the hilt of the sword at his belt. From the edge of his thin shoulder, the raven bobbed his dark, silky head.

We were off to save France.

Chapter 11

"Avançons pour justice!"

Down the hill, we ran through the waist high grass. The cows wouldn't mind us running over their dinner when it was for freedom that we were doing it. It was hard to run at full speed with grass that high, lashing against your dress. Each time the firelock bounced off my waist, I shifted to the left; and each time Rowan squirmed, I shifted to the right. My brother stumbled ungraciously over the point of his sword at every other stride. Thomas hitched his sword up with his left hand like a lady, cocking up her skirt before stepping over some horse's business in the street. Daniel was the only one who fared well, being a good five to ten inches taller than the rest of us. But with each patriot finding his way, we made it to the Duke's rocky door with the clearing figure of war swirling through our minds.

"Go to the rear, Thomas and Sheridan!" Daniel thrust out his arm toward the back of the manor, and he stood there with the stout fearlessness of Wolfe Tone on the deck of the *Indomptable* as it tossed over the storm-crushed shores of Bantry Bay.

"Go, Donovan! Téigh ar aghaidh! Follow them and bring us news of freedom!"

The raven didn't leave the ground to follow the disappearing figures of Citoyens Sheridan and Thomas, so I picked him up and gave him a boost for inspiration. Some people needed more rallying than others, and it was my job to rally, as I was second in command. I also had the pleasure of shooting deserters, and should Daniel fall in battle, I was to directly take his place. I didn't want to be the commander because it's always on the head of the leader when something goes askew. The commander is supposed to know things, and when you are at the top, there is no one higher than you to point the finger at. I saw myself in the best possible position. I had people below me and a scapegoat above me, whom I could safely say made a neat, grand figure in that position. Romantics always made the best leaders.

Daniel took the wooden sword from his sash. "We're goin' through those front gates. It's a hard lot to be cast, but the men are brave."

"God save all of us, Daniel! We must watch the ramparts. That's where they'll have the most of their men. They're too cowardly for a direct fight. This'll be siege warfare like Cromwell. We'll be takin' this place at a great cost to ourselves. It's them in there that's got the advantage, shootin' down at us like hittin' at sheep in a fold."

"True"—Daniel moved the loose hair from his face—"but they're gonna pay for each man. All we need is to get enough through the front and into the house. Send your best marksmen about as skirmishers, tell 'em to lay hidden and keep after the murderers on the roof. That's our best chance."

I nodded. "The men at the rear will be ready now. There's Donovan at the top of the dying oak back there." I pointed over the trees. "He's tellin' us they're ready. The men have spirit; it's time to go." I took the gun from my belt, and Citoyen Rowan sniffed the oiled barrel.

Daniel raised his banner, and it waved for an instant as he held it high. The black silhouette of the swallow flashed from its center as the colors unfurled.

"Avonçons!" Daniel brandished the sword before him and pointed the blade at arm's length like a storming cavalrymen, and we charged the castle.

I released Rowan about one hundred yards from the enemy, and he took off at full bounce toward the castle gates.

"There's a brave one," I yelled gathering up my skirt. I could gallop as fast as Daniel when I wasn't in a crinoline. "Look, it's Rowan. Right into the hands of death he's goin'! He'll show our skirmishers where to put themselves!" I could just see the little stoat skimming over the grass like a short-legged rabbit.

"I've ne'er seen a braver man"—Daniel observed as we ran along—"or a narrower one. No one'll note his coming. If Rowan can shoot like he hides, we've won the day for *liberté*!"

The boy broke a smile, and that struck me odd. I feared then, that he might have been going daft with the horror of battle. I hurried along, nonetheless, preparing myself to take Dan's place should he fall to the enemy. We took off at a faster gallop, and Rowan disappeared into the oaks surrounding "the manor." He dove beneath a rock-propped ledge and shot into the underbrush.

Daniel leaped over the rock and bolted through the narrow opening. I followed with my pistol drawn, the hammer pulled back, and both hands on the awkward maple grip. I stepped over the thick ledge, and there I stopped by slamming into Daniel's back.

"What'd you stop for?" I asked with chafed tone. "We'll all be shot for sure now."

I rubbed the place where the gun had slammed into my waist.

"There's nobody here," the boy whispered. "They've all gone, the cowards," he hissed. Dan stiffened and then struck the end of the tricolored banner into a rare soft spot of ground.

"Maybe it's a trick. Traitors and tyrants always have tricks."

"No, look." He pointed to the higher outcropping of stones and hollows. "Citoyen Rowen's searched the place." The stoat was snickering and slithering over the "manor's" walls. His collar bell echoed hollowly as he padded through the hollow fissures. The place had the trappings of emptiness. The air was silent and cool and untouched.

"The yellow bastards." Daniel threw his sword on the ground. "It's a grand day for freedom, and it was poured into our hands like water." He grabbed my waist and lifted me from the earth, then set me down. "We are lying in the stream of liberty, and the thirst is on us. We have won! Let us drink." He sat on the rock and folded his arms about his knees.

"I'm wonderin' if Thomas and Sheridan saw them flee. If anyone did, it'd be Donovan." I sat down on a mossy ledge. "You can't get dust past him."

We sat in silence for a few minutes on the ledge. I ran my fingers over the soft, damp moss, and Daniel weaved some grass blades into a plait. It was a perfect time to just waste some moments, say nothing, and adore the silence. This could not be—this ideal state—because of two problems.

"Do you think we should tell the rearguard somewhere in the grass o'er there?" I squinted through the oak's young trunks set thickly about the green island's perimeter. "Tell 'em about what's happened?"

"It would be a good thing, I suppose." Dan put down the grass braid but made no effort for anything else.

I went over the side of the ledge where the rocks were staggered outward enough to serve as stepping-stones. I made my way over the flat top of the island, and it was there that I met up with Rowan, who then followed me down the other side past the oaks and into the clear. I sent my eyes over the hayfield while the stoat ran circles round my legs.

"Are ya there!" I yelled over the grass. A dark-haired head popped up from the grassy wilderness. The head belonged to my brother. He looked around warily before sending his eyes my way. "Is it done?"

"Is it done?" he asks. I don't think George Washington said "is it done" after the battle of Yorktown.

"Done?" I called back. "Do you think that we were baking a penny cake? This is war, Citoyen O'Hayden. You should be flogged for such a devil-may-care choice of words!" Rowan bounded off over the field to meet the figure with the familiar voice.

"It wasn't a devil-may-care attitude!" He called back over the field. "That's what came to my head, and I'm as solemn and steadfast in spirit as yourself. I didn't know there was such a thing as proper battle words." A second tussled head popped up from the grass, and words were exchanged between my brother and Thomas beyond the range of my ears.

"What's goin' on?" Thomas yelled. "We didn't hear any noises, no yellin', no shootin', no cries of death. Battles are supposed to have those things. So is it over?"

I could see Sheridan shrug his shoulders.

"Aye, it's over! It never started. We advanced the men over and through the manor's gates, and the brave men had their hearts set for a tough and valiant fight. A more steady band of men I have never seen, so willing to offer their lives for the cause of liberty. But you heard no noise—that is true my comrades—for there was none to be heard. Lives were spared today, for the Duke de Meule de Foin has taken flight!"

"There's a good thing for that."

I jumped sideways with a start after the voice sounded from behind my back.

"Peader!" I looked at the weather-molded face.

"I see that I wasn't invited." He ran his long hand against his chin. "I'm not so old as to not have any fight in me yet. I've still got a fair share of vigor," he huffed.

"I didn't know that you would've wanted to play." But to be more truthful, I had never thought to ask him, and it was a secret operation. Sheridan wasn't even supposed to be here, but of course, now he was a true Hirondelle. "I didn't think you were interested."

Thomas and Sheridan walked up to where we were standing. Rowan squirmed in Thomas's arms.

"I'm always interested in you young ones." He nodded. "Someone's got to be sure that none of ya's are up to doin' mischief." He rubbed his chin again, raised an eyebrow, and cocked his head. I screwed up a crooked face toward him for an answer, and he smiled. You could never get through too many moments with Peader before he started a slagging match.

"Good afternoon, Masters Sheridan and Thomas," he tilted his hat in a greeting to the two boys. "Hello, Your Honor." He scratched Rowan's flat little head. "And where's yer feathered mate?"

"Ah, he's gone off somewhere, leavin' us stranded." Daniel sat down on the rock behind me. He was right; Donovan had left his post. The bird was a deserter if you brought it down to proper military conventions. But Donovan's self-contained disposition would be impossible to correct. He was somewhere about the countryside, and nobody knew where, for no one had ever taken the inclination, or had the ability, to follow him. But the raven had a clock in his head, for once the hour of four was struck, he would come back for his tea.

"Well, I suppose that I should be off then, and leave you all to yer play." Peader lifted his hat and smoothed the flattened hair beneath it. "I'm off to Hutchesons to see if the man's got a filin' rasp. I broke the handle off me spade, splintered the bugger half down the pole, and now I've got to file down a new one. That handle had the rot in it, must've been as old as King James."

Daniel smiled as if something great was said; he pulled his knees toward him and clasped his arms around them. "Probably O'Carolan's shovel." His eyes sparkled with a devious light.

"What would a musician be doin' with a spade?" Peader turned to the boy. "How would he go o'er the land with both the instrument and the shovel, and he bein' blind too. What'd he do at the manor gates—'a two-fold offer for yer gracious hospitality, a song played on this harp, and a nice hole for a rose dug out from the garden with this shovel?'" Peader removed his hat again and bowed like a jester.

I smiled, and Thomas laughed. Peader liked Thomas, and he'd always give him a shilling at the week's end or sweets from the town.

"But who would you rather have to speak about?" Daniel rose and tossed his head. Peader rolled his eyes with anticipation for he could sense the boy was readying for a resplendent soliloquy. "Who would you care to speak about," the boy began, "a dead king or a harper? A musician that was held in the esteem of the noblest muse, walkin' the land like Homer was O'Carolan. An Odyssey in song, the Illiad in a ballad. The strings of his harp singing as if the wind was playin' o'er 'em. The gods of old are speakin' through his touch. All the feelings in you are stolen' by those airs and driven through storms of despair, the rain tearin' the veil of thought from your eyes, and the next moment, the laughter of sunlight, and the teasin' breath of a zephyr lifts you from the gale, and your soul is tossed like a shell from the cloaking waters of the sea for the sharpness of the rocky shore. Ah, now what would a king give ya' of an evenin'?" He crossed his arms and raised an eyebrow.

"He might give you land or maybe money if he liked you well enough." Sheridan was painfully serious. "The king would be the smarter one to take because then if you caught the man's favor, he'd have you on as one of his court, and then you could buy as many harpers and bards as you liked."

Peader shook his head in amazement. "You're a rare one, young Mr. O'Hayden."

"Ah, and what about me?" Daniel cocked his comely head.

"You boy, are as odd as a corncrake."

"I'd like the harper," Thomas lowered the wriggling stoat to the ground. Rowan had been giving off some terribly uneasy motions that if he was to be held any longer, he was going to explode like a fur-wrapped ball of gunpowder. Upon touching earth, he dashed into the rocky island at full speed.

"Why the harper, Thomas?" I asked. "The harper would fill yer mind with peacocks and bazaars and desert nights, but the king could send you there, mind and body."

"Sure, go against my thoughts then." Daniel sulked.

"Well," Thomas explained, "whenever a king gets tired of ya' they always throw you in a gaol or chop off your head. I wouldn't ever trust a king, Catholic king like James, or any king. You ever hear of anyone losin' their heads to a harper, in the literal sense?"

We shook our heads. There was no arguing with that.

"Don't we always end up with the strangest conversations," Peader observed. "Now how did this broken shovel bring forth such a discourse o'er dead Catholic kings and weather-changing harpers?"

"Daniel started it all." Sheridan pointed at the boy.

"It's a gem, that shovel." Daniel bit his lip and gestured to the spade with the shattered remnants of a handle sticking from its top.

"So what was all this rantin' and rallyin'?" Peader asked. "Sounded as though the hounds of hell were after ye's."

"We were pretendin' that we were fightin' in the French Revolution." Thomas took the sash from his waist and brandished it before Peader. Then the boy looked about the ground for a moment and next toward me. "I left my sword in the grass o'er there." He pointed behind him.

"Aye," I said, "I'm second in command and Dan's our leader, and we're called Les Hirondelles, and we're rightin' the wrongs of our land." Peader raised his eyes with understanding. "The evil Duke de Meule de Foin needed to be overthrown," I continued. "But he must've gotten word of us comin' because he's gone."

"Well, it's better than soapin' saddles," Dan added after the older man shot him an odd stare. "Did you see anything on the road, Peader?" The boy squinted one eye in mock gravity.

"Diabhal scéal." Peader shook his head. "From the looks o' things yer Duke's been gone for days. Ten shillings says he's crossed the water to see Queen Victoria, and he's on his keepin' somewhere's in England. Rest easy, he'll not be back soon *mes* patriots."

"I didn't know that you spoke French!" I was exhilarated with finding this new quality in my old friend.

"When I was a young man before any of ye's were born, there was a Frenchman moved down the road from our place. About two miles or so it was."

Here we were given a rare selected passage from Mr. Hayes's youth, and that always caused you to freeze in your business. They popped up sporadically like mushrooms after a rain. You didn't know when they'd come, what made them, or how long it was that they were planning to stay. We were as quiet as secreted grouse.

"I used to sell that man apples in the fall. My English wasn't so abundant then and neither was his, so there was one thing that we had in common. I liked the sound of him, and we started gettin' along well enough. He had for himself an Irish wife, and she had English that was as grand as her French; and even though she didn't have any Irish, soon I could understand her well enough. I got to know some of the French words, you see, when those two bought a drivin' pony that had never been backed or put into the harness. They got a rot of a deal. He was a fine animal, but he couldn't be drivin', and he was skittish as well. They needed him for the work. He wasn't worth what they'd paid for 'im. I was over there with some eggs one day, and they told me they were thinkin' of takin' a loss and sellin' the gelding; but that was a hard decision for 'em for I could see that they had grown to like the horse. They didn't want to spend any more on the poor animal for they didn't have money go leor. So I said 'I'll train 'im for ya. I'll not ask any fee.' I assured them, as I liked the two of them, you see. But I could see that they were after wantin' to give me somethin', and they insisted on me takin' all sorts o' different reparations. After about a dozen 'no, ma'ams' and 'I'll not take that, sir,' I was desperate for peace. 'Give me some o' those French words in exchange for the work and that'll be a fair deal.' And so I learned 'em that way. He was a gentleman, that husband. Ah, well." He broke a shard of wood from the spade's handle and let it fall. "Does any of ye's have the hour on you?"

I snapped my watch's lid open. It was a silver-cased hunter that my father had given to me at my birth. It was a match to the one he gave my mother after they had wed. "Almost half four," I said.

"Ah, Hutcheson'll definitely be home now. He went to town before noon, he told me he was goin' yesterday, and barrin' him missin' Mrs. O'Toole's mouth on the way, he should be home or his woman'll get the file for me."

"I'm sure that she will." Daniel smiled strangely, and Peader was taken aback slightly with his partner's unusually charming and bright behavior.

"I can't find my watch?" Sheridan shrugged. "I don't know where 'tis."

"Oh," I said looking away from Dan, "that's 'cuz Rowan's got it." I explained, "I saw him goin' downstairs to the dinin' room with it. It's in father's tea box, I'll bet ya. That's where he puts things downstairs."

"Why didn't he just leave it upstairs in his basket?" Daniel asked.

I shrugged. "Probably he thought we'd look there first."

"Why didn't he just leave it on the dresser by my bed where he found it," Sheridan groaned. I smiled. "Sure!" His eyes widened as if somebody was squeezing him. "He's gonna get me in trouble. Ma'll kill me. She spent a fortune on that watch! Rowan"—he yelled into the tree-lined island—"you'd better give it back!"

"Ah, he's a thief, that stoat. Is gadaí é, a natural filcher? You can ne'er get that out o' anybody." Mr. Hayes clutched his woeful spade, and clambered back over the rocks, and started for the road. All four of us followed in single file, and as I passed the tree-dotted ridge, Rowan popped out from below the whitethorn and made a low snickering sound. Sheridan caught sight of him, and his eyes narrowed as they seized a look at the furry antagonist.

"Thief!" he yelled. The little weasel stopped in his tracks and sniffed. "You were seen doin' it, and when we get home, your givin' the watch over!"

Rowan twitched and spun around for the hole in the ledge. The black tip of his tail flicked and disappeared into the darkness. A new battle was on.

Peader said his farewell at the turn of the road where the stonewall broke off into a spill of collapsed rubble. A tall oak grew there, and its roots and trunk heaved and pushed against the old stack of stones until they toppled from the slow expansion of their woody neighbor.

I leaned against the rough-shingled body of the tree and watched the gardener amble down the muddy lane. Peader's "rheumatics" were always awakened after a spell of damp weather, and the aches made him look lopsided when he moved at a steady gait.

Daniel and Thomas had gone to get the horses, and Sheridan was hunting down Rowan, who was in hiding in the island. The call to the chase was sounded by a crashing in the hedges and the tinkling of a bell.

"Come back here, Rowan!" The disembodied voice of my brother sounded from the island, while a small brown animal bounced and dingled into the clearing, past my legs, and into the unkempt stonewall. A bell sounded somewhere inside the stones, and they seemed to be the retainer of a ghost.

My brother panted past me. "Where'd he go?" he snapped.

"In there." I pointed to the stones.

"Get out o' there and face me, you rogue!" My brother started picking up the heavy stones that he could manage to budge.

"He'll not come to you, I don't think," I said with the smile of sarcasm on my lips.

Sheridan scowled, "It's not your watch he's got."

I moved from the oak and knelt down by the broken wall. I started clicking for Rowan.

"He's not gonna come now. You have him scared." I said crawling over the stones. I could hear the tinkling bell moving farther from me. "Look, Sheridan." And before I could get over the stones, I was struck with a shock that sent me scrambling over the wall completely. The lane was muddy, rutted, and poorly travelled, and I doubt that it had ever seen the likes of what was to happen to my brother and me on that day.

A green brougham of the finest order with black and yellow edging hurdled round the walled corner at such a speed that should have sent it tipping over. And if the gaping rut on the far side of the road had moved five steps to the right, the thing would have. It was drawn by a heavy chestnut in black harness that was so well kept that the leather seemed to have melted to liquid licorice. The coach rushed around the sharp corner of the narrow lane as if it was after trying to take flight like a black swan. The edge of my eye caught sight of the flash of motion, and I jumped recklessly away from the hastening coach with no time for the thought of doing so, and I ended up on top of my brother with the both of us on the ground.

The big feet of the chestnut carved into the soft road sending cups of mud into the air while others slapped hollowly against the front panel of the Brougham. The carriage rocked from the speed. The earth rumbled with the passing weight, and my brother and I were spattered with mud and horse lather as the private coach passed. The driver cut the corner too close, and the metal hob on the rear wheel sparked and screeched across the wall where I had been standing. My teeth gritted at the sound of it. The hob would have taken my leg off. When I checked later, there was a four-foot white bar of powdered stone where the wall had been gashed. Better the hard stones than me.

My hands flushed with the chill of fright, and they shivered as I tried to rub the grit from my face. Sheridan wriggled beneath me, and I rolled over to free his legs.

"God, there's a madman!" he gasped.

I didn't have anything to say. I was glad to just have my legs.

My brother and I pushed ourselves from the rocky ground to watch the carriage rumble over the road, and we watched it overtake Peader and the broken spade on the slow rise of the next hill. The gardener had moved to the road's edge, and he stood and stared at the crazed devils as we did until they could be seen no more.

Daniel and Thomas rode at a fast canter down the backfield. Dan had to constantly check Paddy to keep him from outpacing the smaller ponies. They had seen the whole thing from the clear view at the top of the Hutcheson's hayfield where the horses had been grazing.

"Have ya' ever seen the likes?" Daniel slowed the black gelding. "You were near kil't!" I set my shaken gaze upon his steady, pale eyes.

"I was near made legless." I tried to wipe the mud from my skirt, but I only seemed to be spreading it around. "I've never been near kil't before!" I would not think of large carriages in the same trifling way again. I couldn't think why my hands were still light and jittery.

"My uncle was backed over by a dray." Thomas leaned from his high seat on Paddy's back. "They took off his leg, they did. Now he's only one, and the other is wood."

I looked at the boy. I didn't like the idea of losing a piece of my body. You didn't realize how fond you were for those four extremities that you were given at birth, until one was being removed. For myself, I wanted to leave the world with all of the pieces I had come in with, whether I needed them or not. "I think it inconsiderate to tear about a place like that carriage did." I rubbed my battered knees.

"I wonder who that was." Dan shifted in his seat.

"I don't know," Sheridan grumbled. "But I don't like 'em, and I don't care to see 'em again, ever." He crossed his arms with determination.

All of us agreed, and none of us could say that they recognized the coach. I figured that they were lost and not too pleased about it, but they shouldn't have freed their anger on such as ourselves. Indeed, all they had to do was slow up and give us their question, and maybe we could've had the answer. We could have saved our scraped legs, and we could have saved their time, their scratched hob, and their lathered horse.

They didn't have a sound mind between them, however many there were. Peader says that that's the way the people were today. He said that if it wasn't for putting the hatmakers out of business, you could pop off people's heads for all of the use they got out of them, and none would note the difference. I thought that you might have to stick their eyes somewhere else, or they couldn't see where they were tearing off to, and they would be bumping into things. But those in that green carriage had eyes, and look what good those eyes were doing them.

Sheridan and I hopped onto our ponies, and all of us headed back to Carrickduff for tea. I think that we all wanted to get within her walls. I had Rowan in my arms, and the little stoat stared warily at his dark-haired enemy. My brother had, during the commotion, momentarily forgotten their row. But as soon as the distress wore off, he remembered, and he sent the antagonist a fermenting stare.

"Should we wait for your Peader?" Thomas leaned from Gavin's back. He was again riding double with my brother.

"Oh, and is he at the Hutchesons on a Friday night?" Dan scratched the black gelding's shoulders. "Huh, you'll grow a beard before he gets back."

"Why on a Friday?" Thomas asked with an odd look on his face.

"He forgot, you see,"—Dan raised a finger—"and I didn't remind him either. I've been waitin' for this day when I could get even with himself." A narrow grin spread across the boy's mouth. "Last Thursday, Peader made me shoe old Hewson's plowin' mare."

"What's wrong with that?" I wondered. "Old Hewson always pays ya." I was glad to talk about something, so that I could stop thinking about my interrupted meeting with death, and being almost dispatched to heaven without all of the parts I had been sent in with.

"Oh, the man pays ya," Daniel squirmed on Paddy's back. "And he stands there while ya work. Right o'er your shoulder like a sack o' bricks. 'Oh no, no, boy,'"—Daniel shook his head in imitation of the old farmer—"'sure Mr. Hayes doesn't do it like that. He pulls the shoe a different way than that. No! She likes the left fore shorter'n the right, or she won't plow straight for me. Rasp the near foot a little more'n that or she'll o'er-reach in the boggy ground. Ah, when I was a boy, I could shoe ten horses a day, but now I've got the pains in my right hand, and I can't stand for more'n an hour at a time or my left leg cripples o'er.'" Daniel closed his eyes and groaned. "And!"—his eyes popped open—"that horse is a leaner. My back was breakin' holdin' that mare's leg up. That's why Peader gave the job o'er to me. He was sick of the business, and he left me holdin' the dirty reins. I told him about it too, and he laughed, he did. It was a lovely trick, it was. And today I'm gettin' him back."

"How're you gettin' him back, Dan?' Thomas asked.

"Yeah, how?" my brother and I chorused in.

"On Friday nights, Mrs. O'Toole goes o'er to the Hutcheson's for supper and cards. And nobody gets away from Mrs. Hutcheson and Mrs. O'Toole—"

"Is it Mrs. Hutcheson with the baby that was switched by the fairies?" Thomas interrupted Daniel.

"The same. And those two—not the baby, mind you—could talk a dead man out o' the earth; and if you weren't dead when you were sittin' with 'em, in an hour you'd be wishin' for God to take you in his mercy. That's why Mr. Hutcheson's gone to town. And that confirms it, those women are havin' an evenin' all right with our Peader walkin' straight into the lair. The two o' them'll grab him—'won't you come in for some tea, Mr. Hayes?'" Dan twittered like a woman and gestured like a child playing fancy teatime. "'Come in, Mr. Hayes, and we'll not take no for an answer. Don't you be shy there, no, we'd love to have you.'" A broad grin sizzled on the boy's face and warmed the always cold eyes.

"Peader's gonna kill you," Sheridan said flatly, and the words reminded him to send another dirty look over to Rowan posthaste. The stoat pushed closer against me.

"Ah"—Dan waved the words of warning away—"I'm doin' the fella a favor. He's to learn not to play such tricks on people, and if I don't do it, then who will?" He shook his brown hair. "Are ya' comin' for tea, Thomas?"

"He always comes for Friday tea," I said blandly.

"Well, I was wonderin', Tom, that maybe your folks were after having visitors with that coach that went by, you know?" Dan asked.

Tom shook his head. "My father's not so fond o' visitors. Besides we'd ne'er know anybody that owns a fine coach like that one—oh, save the Barrands. But they ne'er come to the house, so." He shrugged.

"Well, I don't know," Dan continued, "the lanes dead end after the oak tree. There's just you and then just us, and I've ne'er seen a green coach at the house before. Have you, Anne?"

"No," I said.

"No," my brother said. "And they almost had us dead. You don't drive like that on a nowhere-goin' road."

"They had to go to yours then Tom, huh?" Dan figured. "They didn't look happy either, tearin' around and half aimin' for any soul in their path."

"Unless"—I pushed Gavin forward to meet up with Paddy—"unless they had come from Carrickduff?"

Chapter 12

We sat down for a hasty tea in the Crawford cemetery where I had left the picnic basket. That was our usual tea place when we were out playing on fair days. And a grand spot it was too, with the mouldy stones and the concealing grass for the horses to graze on. I thought it pleasing to give the dead a taste of life again as I was sure that Mr. Crawford and his silent fellows were watching while we took our midday repast. I hoped that Mrs. Cosgrove, changed back to Crawford, was watching so that she could know that we were taking care of her house.

The promise of ginger beer and cake was enough to remove all ghosts of the dreadful mad-carriage incident, and we sat on the grass in a tight circle around the hallowed picnic basket, like the pagans in the old days, around the May Eve bonfires lit to the great god Baal. We were giving our bests to the makers of ginger beer even though we did not have a bonfire to consecrate the toast.

The drink was a lovely and rare treat. It was favored, along with the peppermint and lemonade, by the followers of Father Theobald Mathew. Those were the temperance men, the teetotallers, the men and women who refrained from all manner of spirits but the medicinal. Mr. Kelly, who worked on the farm, had taken "the pledge," and he wore the round pewter temperance medal with pride. On the side of his hearth, you'd see displayed the accompanying certificate that he received for joining the abstainers.

My father had not "taken the pledge," but he went to the town to purchase the bottles, and while there, he also procured the licorice pieces that my mother was fond of, as well as a variety of candies for us. Mr. Timoney never went to town for confections, and my father always saved a special bag of sweets for Thomas, and we always saved for him an extra bottle of ginger beer.

Thomas had never had the drink until he came to Carrickduff. He took to the sweet stuff swiftly despite choking on the astonishing bite of the ginger juice that struck your throat soon after the first sip. Rowan got over the first bracing swallow by sneezing and sticking his tongue out. Donovan was immune and drank with apathetic abandon. Sheridan liked ginger beer better than tea, and Thomas and I were inclined to agree. But it was fair to say that old Father Mathew would've found the next hard men a difficult pair to break over. Daniel and Peader "swore" that there was nothing finer than ale, but nobody agreed with them except Donovan who was even partial to Jameson's.

The raven rolled down from the sky as sure as clockwork at a little after half four. He settled down near Daniel and bobbed his head and clicked his beak in eagerness for the forthcoming food. He had yet to miss a tea. Although when we were away, his snack ended up being a bit of bread, potato pieces, and a dish of water, with no ginger beer and not a drop of the malt to be found to enliven the bird's spirits. He looked forward to us being around.

Inside our basket rested potato rolls and the ginger cake, which married so well with the bottled sweet beer. These were doled out between us, and out from the corner of the basket, I removed a small jar of potted eels for Rowan; Eels, because it was Friday, and you couldn't eat meat on Friday. Potting was one of the best ways for keeping fresh meat, fish, and fowl. You cooked it in spices like nutmeg and pepper and then scooped it into jars sealed with clear butter. In the larder, we had two shelves of tiny sealed jars filled with potted treats for Rowan.

The little stoat had been curled up behind me waiting impatiently for the coming food. He would have been scrambling all over the basket, but for his dread of my brother who continued sending vile looks toward the little fellow's way. I passed some ginger beer into a tin cup and placed it on the ground near me. Rowan scampered quickly out, took the tin's rim into his mouth, and set it down in a safe place behind my back. I opened the potted eels and dumped the greasy chunks of fish into another tin. Rowan struck out from behind and snatched the food back toward his place of refuge. Every now and then, he poked his small head around my skirt to satisfy himself that his enemy was still sitting and taking tea next to Thomas.

The food reminded me of poor Peader, left to wither over a supper with Mrs. O'Toole and Mrs. Hutcheson, the mother of the ugly fairy baby. But the yoke was placed by his own hands after playing that trick upon Daniel. And that thought struck a match in my head.

"Oh!" I exclaimed. "Dan, you know that Peader can't stay for supper at the Hutchesons'? He's got to drive Ms. Farrell and Norah to the train."

The boy squeezed the potato roll in his hand.

"That man would find his way off a scaffold," he mumbled. "A few hours with Mrs. Hutcheson and Mrs. O'Toole is punishment enough. I shouldn't have wanted to push it into the realms of torture." He stretched himself upon the grass and rested his head in his hands.

"They say it's not right to seek revenge on people." My brother sent a burning glance toward the furry head peeking around my skirt. "But it's a sweet thing even though it's not worth goin' to hell for."

"You're not supposed to say *hell*," Thomas added. "And they do say revenge is sweet, too. I agree with that."

"Anything that you're not supposed to do is sweet," I confirmed. "And sure it can't be all that bad, because then everybody'd be in hell with no room left, and then God'd be in heaven all lonely."

"Ah, grand thoughts." Daniel grasped Donovan off the ground.

The boy rolled onto his back and held the large bird aloft over himself before calling up some lines from Tom Moore.

"I'd mourn the hopes that leave me, if thy smiles had left me too; I'd weep when friends deceive me, if thou wert, like them, untrue. But while I've thee before me, with heart so warm and eyes so bright, no clouds can linger o'er me, that smile turns them all to light." He dropped a befuddled Donovan, who went back to picking at his own potato roll, dipping each piece into the ginger beer.

By five, the sun returned, and I made a note of recognizing its yellow, glowing finery. We spent the time talking about Shelley's *Frankenstein*, seeing as we were in a cemetery. Daniel said that he could dig up a body and that it wouldn't bother him. Sheridan said he'd do it, but only if he didn't know the corpse, and somebody offered him a lot of money. I said I'd do it if the thing was made up of bleached bones, but never otherwise, because dead things smelled and looked terrible, and I knew that as Rowan had stowed a herring under the sideboard in the kitchen, and the whole place smouldered with the foulness of it. Although I would bury something, and I mentioned the day that Rowan caught a field mouse. He had the poor thing by the scruff of its neck. You couldn't hold them by the tail because the tail would snap off in your grip like a horse bean. But Rowan had that mouse, and the wee animal had met an early demise. He put the mouse in the jackstone bag with the jacks and the ball for keeping, and that bag was then left in the nursery. It was our governess that had accidentally upturned it while she was cleaning, and out fell the jacks with a clang, out bounced the tiny ball, and out came the mouse with a thump. I learned that day that Ms. Farrell's aversion to stoats expanded to include field mice as well. She wouldn't go into the nursery for a week after. I was beholden to lay out the poor beast and to say an "ave" over the grave.

"You could've made a Frankenstein mouse," Sheridan added. "A mouse that eats watch-nickin' stoats"—he turned toward Rowan—"after torturin' them to confess what they did, in a long and horrible way!"

Rowan didn't answer.

"No, I'd ne'er touch a dead thing." Thomas made a crooked face to show his repugnance. "I wouldn't touch it for money or anythin'. I'd ne'er be a Doctor Frankenstein. Dead bodies are disgustin'. We had our grandfather lyin' out in our house when he died. I had to go and see him there, right under my bed, stiff and cold he was. Everyone was there for the wake celebrations and hangin' about the body. He was a good man, and it was not right to have my grandfather gone, but I couldn't stand the sight of him dead like that. I slept in the cow barn until he was taken to be buried, and I got a hidin' fer bein' 'disrespectful.' But I wasn't sleepin' o'er a body. Death's a terrible awful way for you to get to your reward or punishment; wherever you're headed."

"I ne'er saw a body," Sheridan said.

"Our grandparents died before we were born," I added.

"Ah, you get used to seein' 'em," Daniel reassured with a lazy air and a languishing flick of his hand. "We e'en waked our neighbors as they had nobody else. I lost my own father when I was four. It wasn't till I was near five and a half before I realized that he wasn't comin' back. I thought they'd just brought him down to the cemetery 'cause there was too many people in the house, and he was gonna live in a little box inside the ground so that we'd have more room. The things that you think of when you're not grown up. My sister died the following year, and then mother two years after. That's why we were livin' with my aunt. Sister Sarah was too young to marry, and the older brother was still with us too. He's the one in America now."

"Is that the newspaperman that writes to ya?" I asked.

"That's James," he nodded.

"Oh," I yawned. The afternoon was turning lazy. I glanced around to see if Rowan was still behind me. He was curled up by his food tin and fast asleep. You could never wake him. He slept like a statue. You could even pick him up and move him, and he wouldn't wake. My mother liked to use him for a model because nobody else wanted to sit and stare and pose for her camera. We've got an album full of Rowan as Dante, Cuchulainn strapped to the stone so that he would die whilst standing up, Mariana of the Moated Grange, and various other suitable subjects. Of course, we didn't display that album to amuse our dinner guests, lest they were to think us any more peculiar than they already did at present. Once, she had Peader all dressed up as King Arthur with a heavy sword hanging from his waist. She left to ready the plate, and something must've happened in the other room for she forgot him there, standing against the cold stonewall with the big, heavy sword dragging at his side and his knees killing him, he said. Peader was very difficult to procure for pictures after that. But Rowan was the best model when he was sleeping. He only moved in two ways, fast and slow. He was either scuttling up our big stairway or draped like a rag, sleeping on the wide handrail. Although there was that time when he was full out in a slumber on Donovan's roost, and the raven came in to preen without a concern for his neighbor's whereabouts. The bird just landed as usual, pinning Rowan to the roost as if he was no more than a furred doily. He woke up at that time with a nightmare to beat any from before.

"What's the time?" I wondered.

"Don't ask me." Sheridan glowered. "Why don't you ask Rowan."

"Half five." Daniel held his watch above his face. "When's your Ms. Farrell leavin' for the Dublin train?"

"About an hour," Sheridan answered.

"Supper's at half six, so we've got to change before Ms. Farrell goes." I rose up from the grass. "She'll have our heads if we make her late." I took Rowan's leash from my pocket.

"My parents'll have my head," Thomas stood too, "they'll be wonderin' where the fourth one's gone off too. And I'll have stale tea."

"Come back tomorrow mornin'," I said. "We're schoolin' the horses down by the flax field at nine."

He nodded a yes before running home. You could hear Thomas's hard shoes clicking over the stones as he went.

I clipped the leash onto a sleepy Rowan. Daniel took hold of the horses and Sheridan the picnic basket. Donovan perched upon Padraic's back, and we all made off for Carrickduff.

We usually ate "workman" style because my father was out with the field help most of the year, and it was convenient to take meals as they did. The kitchen staff took their meals after us. We had a large dinner at half twelve, or one, as the farmers. Tea was at half four and at seven came a supper of lighter fare before studying, play, and bed. This only changed on Wednesdays when the dancing master came, and then we would have a large supper at eight to accommodate him.

Mr. O'Malley was a rather small man with a moustache that was black and not the color of his red-brown hair. He had a quick and nervous manner which made him seem even smaller. Peader said that he looked like a squirrel, and on Wednesday when Mr. O'Malley was to arrive, Peader would go about making little, fidgety squirrel motions that made us laugh and my mother frown admonishingly.

"You are a nasty influence on the children, Mr. Hayes," she would say. "You must know that they follow your example." There was a bit of humor in her voice, nonetheless.

"Indeed, ma'am," he would answer, touching his hand to his breast. "You must know that I try my best."

But my favorite night of the week was Friday. We would dine by six or half past six, and Peader and Daniel would join us at the table. Friday was story night, or céilí night, and that was an evening of music and fun, where the workers would come to our sitting room to dance and take refreshments.

On special occasions, we would hire musicians to play a concert, or for the rare ball that our parents held for their fellows. It was on those nights that my brother, Norah, and I would look in the windows when it turned dark or listen to the grand waltzes and reels. The men were in their fancy waistcoats; and the ladies, with their big, flounced skirts in cake-icing colors, floated around the floor like upturned parasols. I hoped that I never would have to look like that, and I prayed that I would have my parents on my side. My mother had the smallest crinoline in the room because my father said that the fashion was ridiculous, and he wouldn't have any number of the family who couldn't fit through doorways while parading around in whimsical excess, thank you. My mother said that such a large skirt made you look like an umbrella with a head instead of a blooming lily, and she didn't want any ungainly umbrellas knocking over her orchids.

God save you if you touched her orchids, especially the ones she hand-carried from India. My father said that she wouldn't let him touch, nor so much as look, at those orchids for the long weeks of their return to Ireland. In retribution, he wouldn't let her near the myna bird that he was carrying back. But didn't the poor, wee creature take ill and succumb along the way. "There," she had said, "that's why your not touching my orchids, although it would've been better to lose the plants than have the bird give up it's little soul." But so went the workings of fate. Tonight was story night, and what that tale would be was known only to Daniel and destiny.

Sheridan had been giving Rowan hair-bristling glances all the way to the house.

"Give me the little fellow," he said as we walked into the empty hall; and he made a grab for the leash.

Rowan dashed between my legs.

"He's afraid of you now, see. We'll look for the watch ourselves."

"But he knows where it is."

"He's not gonna show you. He won't let you near him, never mind show you."

"Oh," Sheridan pleaded, "let's try. Come Rowan," he said pleasantly, as if he was going to give the fellow a treat.

Rowan wasn't won over.

"He thinks you a terrible actor," I said. I handed the leash over to my brother. Donovan flew to the stair's newel post and bobbed his head.

Oh god above! As soon as my brother touched the thin leather, Rowan went mad. You would have thought there was the ghost of Cromwell holding on to the other end. He twisted like a hooked salmon, and I couldn't get a hold of him. I told my brother not to let go of the leash with Rowan bucking fiercely on the tether. And then with a sharp backward tug, his head slipped from the collar itself, and he scampered under the free-standing part of the stairs.

Sheridan and I stepped gingerly to the back of the stairway. I clicked for the stoat, but nobody answered. We searched around the back, but there was only dust. Rowan was gone.

"What're we gonna do?" Sheridan turned to me with a sickly gaze.

"Find him!" I said harshly. "If Ma and Da get to him first, we're gonna be gettin' it after."

"*Caw, caw, caw!*" Donovan's shrill call echoed awfully loud in the open entranceway.

"Hush," I warned.

"Do you think that he squeezed into the kitchen?" My brother's eyes glared anxiously.

"We'll go there first."

After almost getting killed by a raving-wild coach, and after losing a day of glory because of the yellow Duke de Meule de Foin, this was a very successful day for disagreeable affairs. And now I had to hunt about for a collarless weasel.

Rowan was very small and flexibly narrow. He could get under furniture, under pillows, into bins, and everywhere he shouldn't have been. He could even squeeze under the scullery door. Once, he even landed in the laundry. It was his fierce luck that Ms. Shea, the young wash girl, handled the linens one by one, and when she came across the soft, hairy one, her singing of "Siuil A Ruin" altered to a scream, saving himself a right hot bath. It was only after

Rowan ended up shut in the sugar bin that he no longer enjoyed the run of the house, lest the boy be sat on, boiled or gaoled with the oatmeal. Indoors, Rowan was bade to wear his collar and bell.

To cover more ground, the two of us split up. I ran into the kitchen and said hello to Mrs. Kelly, the wife of our kindly temperance man, and to Mrs. O'Leary. They asked me what I was needing, and I answered as plain as white turf that I was looking for beetles for Donovan's supper. A pair of revolted looks were my answers, and I knew that I was free to rummage about. They were fine, talkative women and that was the only way I could keep them off my trail as I plundered about the sink and bins.

Mrs. O'Leary peered at me every so often to see if I had caught anything. I hadn't as a matter of course, since it wasn't for bugs I was hunting. I heard her sneezing away behind me, so I knew where she was, and I knew when to keep up the bug search act.

Mrs. O'Leary took snuff from a pretty cloisonné tin. She took it to clear her head and to ward off colds. I never understood how the snuff was supposed to work since it caused her to take little fits of sneezing now and again.

I wasn't so sure that I would take snuff to chase away a cold. It seemed better to suffer a week of snivelling and be done with it, rather than a forever amount of sneezing. I figured that maybe the fits were a symptom of old age—like Mrs. Byrne's beady eyes—rather than an effect from the snuff. But Peader didn't have beady eyes, and I never heard Mrs. Byrne sneeze, and she was eight years older than Mrs. O'Leary. I came to hope that our old cook never suffered a fit directly over my dinner; but if the soup ever tasted of tobacco, I would know why.

I watched young Mrs. Kelly to see if she bore any peculiar physical reactions. She didn't; but then her husband was a teetotaller, so that made sense, I suppose. Unfortunately, I couldn't tell if Mrs. Kelly was coming up close behind me, but I didn't have to wonder about snuff-tasting soup either.

"Do you like artichoke pie, Ms. Anne?"

"I do Mrs. Kelly. And did you make some?" Underneath the cupboard, I moved a pot out of my way. I was on my knees and half squeezed inside the area. My hand suddenly slipped off an edge, and I pitched sideward until my head caught my fall by slamming against a pot shelf. Nobody noticed.

"I . . . ahh-tch, ahh-tch, ahh-tch . . . oh my!" Mrs. Byrne had another fit.

"God bless you, Mirah." Mrs. Kelly spoke as I removed my stinging head from the cupboard.

"God bless you," I said. I figured that from all of the sneeze blessings that she received, Mrs. O'Leary was holier than the pope.

"You won't have any knees left there crawlin' around like that," Mrs. Kelly warned. She wiped her hands on her apron. "You'll be lame before you're old. I'm sure Mrs. Carolyn doesn't want to see her daughter's pretty knees all rubbed."

"No, Mrs. Kelly"—I called from under the sink—"I'll not rub my knees." I moved some brushes and a box of something out of the way. The under sink smelled of old towels and stale soap. I found some dried bits and a lost knife all sticky with layers of dust. But there was no Rowan to be seen. He just wasn't in the kitchen. *The ladies would've seen him coming in anyway*, I thought.

At quarter to six, my brother and I met at the base of the staircase, neither of us was accompanied by a small brown stoat. Ms. Farrell stood at the top of the stairs with a look more dismal than the ones that we were wearing. A raucous croak rang hollowly from the brass chandelier. Donovan was here anyway. We had no choice now but to run upstairs and change for supper. We were late too, and that made Ms. Farrell late and unhappy. It was a rare thing to see her unhappy, but she was going to Dublin, and the northbound train was not in the habit of waiting for delayed tutors. I think that it was an unspoken decision between Sheridan and me not to mention the missing stoat. We had left the hats in the "odd tool" shed. I was trying to invoke another unholy lie, but apparently, Ms. Farrell was in such a flitter that the woman never noticed our bare heads. It was a good thing that my family was not strongly religious like so many others, or I'd be keeping Father Doyle in the confessional—well past his supper.

Chapter 13

By six, travel plans turned to a frenzy. Down the stairs came Daniel with Norah's travel bag. I didn't know why, but Donovan would always follow you whenever you had a bag, and down he hopped behind Dan one step at a time.

Some cursing came from Ms. Farrell's bedroom. It seemed Donovan had left his calling card on top of her cloth travel bag. The bag had been expensive, and the "little gift" had set there for a while. Peader had tried to rub it away, but the stain had held fast; and he then remarked to the wide-eyed woman how "the dropping sat very well with the rest of your pattern, Miss. Now, you should bless your luck that he wasn't eatin' those elderberries instead of the strawberry paste the lady put up." Ms. Farrell had said something, but it wasn't ladylike, and it wasn't a blessing in any religion I knew.

Down the stairs went Peader with the travel bag and a huge grin. Apparently, he was not aware that Daniel had unleashed his revenge by neglecting to warn him about Mrs. O'Toole and Mrs. Hutcheson, and that the boy had relished the few hours of fatal boredom that Peader had spent at the Hutcheson table. I was relieved to note Peader's blessed ignorance in the matter, but there was suspense in the air, as if one was waiting for a new Pompeii to erupt. There was an eruption of a different sort, and that active volcano was on her way to Dublin. Down came Ms. Farrell with the present for her mother's birthday and a tight, exasperated look on her face. Peader wiped the tears of laughter from the corners of his eyes. Donovan was now nowhere to be seen. I wondered if he was hiding out with Rowan.

Peader and Dan weren't eating with us that night. They were driving the ladies to the train. A small sick feeling had run through me as I heard the carriage rattle down the drive. What if Rowan had gotten into the bags? But that he couldn't have done, as they were packed in the morning, and I had seen them shut and placed in the hall before we had gone out to play. With any remaining hope, he would still be somewhere in the house. It was too bad that poor Mrs. Cosgrove, buried as Crawford, wasn't a ghost. I would've liked to have had the honor of her acquaintance, even if she was dead. She could find Rowan. Ghosts could find things, and she'd find him even though he'd just been washed, and he didn't have the weasel smell that offended Mrs. Hutcheson with the ugly baby. Maybe, if after supper I lit a candle for her, she'd come and help. She would never come now as it wasn't dark enough yet, and ghosts never came at supper.

I didn't feel like eating and neither did Sheridan, but we would have to keep up appearances at the table. We met Donovan in the nursery, and he was on his roost, looking pleased with himself. He was probably thinking of the travel-bag prank he had played on Ms. Farrell. My brother and I made a quick once over of the room. I looked in the space behind the bookcase, I looked behind each row of books, and I looked behind the bookends. I looked inside the toy chest. We both looked around the curtains and inside the writing desk. We looked under the pillows of the daybed and under the bed itself. Rowan wasn't in the nursery. Donovan began to cackle, so I picked him up and we headed down to the dining room. At least someone was hungry anyway.

The table was set when we arrived, and I put the raven on his oak dining perch. It was just high enough for him to eat off the table. Daniel had spent many hours training the bird to pick his meal off a plate without jumping onto the tabletop. My mother was so impressed with the result that she had asked the boy if he would next train her husband to do the same. My father had inserted that he had, up until then, "assumed his manners at table had won her fancy." I didn't understand his meaning, as I had never seen him atop any table at dinner, or otherwise. I did know that any such table acrobatics would not secure my favors for any suitor at all.

I kept hoping that the smell of the food would lure the little stoat into the dining room. I put his dish on the floor in the front of the sideboard. I didn't think my parents would mark his absence as Rowan usually ate rather quickly.

I smeared the bowl with some of the butter pattie that had been set out onto the table to warm, to make the dish look as if it had been eaten out of. The butter was from our dairy, where I would go to talk to Mrs. Byrne. We had our own particular butter stamp that was carved out of wood, and we would put a mark on the butter with it. That way people would know that the produce was ours. Our stamp had a barley sheaf ringed round with holly leaves and berries. Sometimes I would help in the dairy, making the butter by taking a turn at the barrel churn. Mrs. Byrne was the head of the dairy, and because of that, she always wore three rings. Each ring was blessed from the Trinity. One was worn toward off the tricks of women, another for the tricks of men, and the third was to repel the acts of witches, whom she feared would steal or sour the milk. The rings seemed to be working, for we have not yet had a witch or a fairy come near the place.

There were dairy girls besides our Mrs. Byrne, and they would sing as they worked, and after "The Wearing of the Green," they would always burst into the "Marseillaise," the French anthem that they learned from Dan and me, even though they didn't know they had been learning it from Les Hirondelles, the French patriots. It always made me laugh to hear them singing in French, but I liked it too. We would all pretend that we were churning away at the palace of the Sun King in a grand stone dairy. We would talk about living in such a magnificent palace even though I was actually fighting against members of the evil aristocracy. I had said that the house was so big that you would need a map to find your way about. We laughed after the youngest girl said,

"How the milk would've spoiled by the time you got it from the dairy to the grand table." We chanted, "Louis the Great drank spoiled milk!"

One thing that we found uncanny was the persecution of the French Protestants called the Huguenots in the 1680s, and how it was just like the persecution of the Irish Catholics. The French government wanted the Huguenots to turn Catholic, just like the English government tried to force the Catholics in this country to turn Protestant by using fowl laws. This was a solemn dairy room discussion, because people shouldn't be telling others what to do.

Mother came to supper first in her brown silk dinner dress. She asked how we had spent our day and said that she had seen us while on her afternoon walk. We made no mention of the fumbling siege of the Duke's demesne.

My mother poured our tea from the old thin silver pitcher as we waited for Father.

"Where's Father?" Sheridan asked. I could see him casting nervous glances around the room. I knew who he was really looking for even though it was odd for my father to be late.

"He'll be down soon." She placed the pot back on the table. "He had some unexpected business this afternoon. I was just leaving for a walk when I met this older gentleman at the door. He was pleasant enough but not chatty, and he asked directly for your father. I asked for him to leave a card if he had not come a long way, for Mr. O'Hayden had presently just returned from business and was rather weary. He asked to whom he was speaking, and I told him 'the wife of the man of whose attentions he wished.' The matter was pressing, he said, and he had come a long way. I sent for your father and the two of them met. I went for my walk, and that man was a gentleman, truly. He had a gorgeous coach drawn by a handsome bay."

"Aw, was it green and shiny?" My brother received a silencing kick in the leg.

"Yes, dark green. Did you two see it?"

"We did," I said. "Down on the bohereen," I added, "it was lovely." I smiled. I didn't mention a quip about nearly being killed by it although I knew that Sheridan was bursting to. Mother would never let us ride down the road again after a story like that. Even if that was the only coach that the tiny, dead-end road had ever seen, was ever likely to see, she wouldn't let you go there. The possibility of lightning striking twice was too great. That's the way she thought. If there was a 1 percent chance of the moon falling on your head next Thursday, she would keep you in. Whenever we went somewhere with father alone for fun, the day always ended with "now don't tell your mother, I let you jump Daly's ditch" or, "don't tell your mother I let you race to the post road." That sort of caution didn't run in her family of smugglers though.

O'Donoghue was my mother's maiden name. She was raised in an Irish-speaking house in the county of Kerry, and we learned some of the language from her as much as from Peader. Her family were Catholics, and they came from Cahirciveen, where "the Liberator" Daniel O'Connell was born. That man had been a friend of her father's; and both of their families had been in the smuggling business, sending wool, fabric, butter, seaweed called *claucan*, and even Irish students to the rest of Europe. So the O'Donoghues had money unlike the O'Haydens. Her family was fond of learning and escaped the shadow of the Penal Laws. Young Carolyn studied in a fine boarding school in France. I was to go to that place of study when I turned fifteen, but I cared not for the thought of leaving Carrickduff. I suppose that the desire for travel must seize one when they grew older. I would like to think that to be so.

My mother would always dress for dinner, as she used to do in her own home, and as she learned to do while in France. In that boarding school, the girls learned about dancing and about how to conduct themselves as proper ladies, all this on top of their regular lessons. They had to perform exercises with sticks and such things so that they might walk with a fine carriage and not slouch or stomp about. They also learned about the art of music, and my mother caught on very well as she could play the piano better than some of the musicians that would come to our door. She could play Mozart as well as the come-all-ye's that the maids and workers loved to dance to.

My father could play the violin, but he wasn't so nearly as accomplished as his wife; but Mícheál was a grand singer though, and every so often after we had dined, he would perform for us as my mother accompanied on the piano.

At times, Peader would pick up his fiddle that he had "learned by listening and trying his hand," and he would join them at our Saturday céilís that were held in the sitting room. The furniture was moved out of the way for the spirited reels and waltzes. You would find very little to compare my parents' grand parties with the céilís. Needless to say, Sheridan and I and Daniel much preferred the keen cheerfulness of the latter, and that had a lot to do with the fact that we were actually invited and didn't have to spend any of the evening outside peering through windows while praying that Ms. Farrell would continue not to note our absence. One night she caught us and a bargain was made; she wouldn't tell on us, and we wouldn't mention the odd glances she was sending through the window as well. But it wasn't just the people that enjoyed the merrymaking; the boys loved the music too. Rowan would climb onto Daniel's lap, and the groom would catch him under the arms for a dance. Donovan would sit on father's armchair and cackle hoping for a drop of the whiskey. But Friday night was storytelling night, and Dan was our favorite seanachie. Tonight though, my brother and I could only think about Rowan, and how long the stoat was planning to remain on his keeping.

My father arrived as the meal came from the kitchen. Mrs. O'Leary said that she couldn't have kept the fare any longer on the hob, or it would not have been hitting the table in a proper state. Mícheál O'Hayden looked grand in the black frock coat with the velvet collar and thick velvet buttons. The coat was as black as his hair. And all the darkness made his small face all the paler, and his eyes became the strangest cold blue. He was tall, especially to me, but his narrowness made him seem taller. He always reminded me of someone that you'd see in a painting from long ago. Helen said that he looked like Dierdre's fated lover Naoise, with the deep black hair and the skin of white frost. It was a great old tale of sorrow from the storytelling days of old. "But Mr. O'Hayden was no Naoise," I told her. "He was never connected with royalty, and he couldn't even play chess." Although he was teaching Daniel how to become a poet, my father was a born farmer, and he'd rather be on a horse in the flax rows than a warrior on old Ireland's hills. My mother said that it was fine for Mícheál to be a farmer so long as he kept looking the part of the wild Naoise. One way or the other, he put fine clothes on our backs, money in the worker's pockets, and food on our table.

Today was Friday, and as we were Catholic there was no meat on our plates. The quality and the preparation of the Friday table was far from dull, and the lack of roasts or boils inspired a sense of creativity from the cooks, and I thought the meals the best of the week. Everybody liked the frequent dish of steaming pasta for which my father had acquired a taste while he was studying in Italy. He said that it was an extremely popular side dish there, and after you've had a taste of it, you would soon know why. It was rather like boiled bread dough, but far better than could be imagined. The boys were very fond of it, and I think that Donovan thought that they were little, flat worms as he always grasped each strand in his beak and slapped it upon the plate before swallowing it.

It was said that when young Mícheál O'Hayden first returned from Italy, he had a large portion of the doughy stuff made up for the workers at Carrickduff. Needless to say, it was the first time that any of them had been introduced to slimy strips of "God knows what" and would have declined a taste had they not been overseen by "the young master."

"It was an acquired taste, sir," they had said. But soon in came a young field worker's wife on a mission from her husband. He had apparently been thinking about the "slippery bread," and even though it had disagreed with him at first, he had been craving since and would like for his wife to try some for herself. A lesson in pasta making was conducted by Mícheál himself, and soon the recipe spread from house to house along the properties of Carrickduff.

Tonight, instead of pasta, we had the baker's bread that my father had carried from Dublin. Donovan was tapping the table with his beak as I took a piece of the bread and put it into his bowl. On top of the "trencher," I scooped some rice and poured a gravy of the *anraith glé*, as my mother called the clear soup of fish stock, and passed the sopping repast in front of the raven.

"Where's old Rowan, Anne?" my mother asked, laying a slice of artichoke pie into my dish. I almost choked on the Dublin bread.

"The little fella's all stuffed and gone?" My father had come to an inadvertent rescue. I watched as he hid a yawn with his napkin.

"Yes, he is," Sheridan had piped up like one of the fanciest stage actors in London. "He came in before you and ate up a slice of the artichoke pie." My brother had pointed to the empty bowl that I had neatly greased up. "There you see it's all eaten' up."

I grew a little nervous and then I found it rather odd that nobody had noticed what I had done. For wouldn't it seem rather strange for Rowan to have received a slice of pie when my mother was the first to cut into the perfect tart? I started to simmer with unpleasantness.

"Oh no!" My mother raised a napkin and wiped the corner of her lip. I went as hot as coal. I was thinking now that she must have noticed it. "Rowan doesn't like artichokes, Sheridan."

I was relieved, but this was not going to be an enjoyable meal. I smiled at her. Even when she was upset, my mother's voice was soft and punctuated. The only thing that would tell you that she was mad was the slight raise in her voice's pitch, but she didn't start speaking in Irish as Peader did. And I was very glad about that because when someone is displeased with you, it sounds terribly grave when you are informed of the grievance through the use of the Irish language. Everyone felt sorry for Daniel. My father never yelled; he spoke in a very distinct, quiet voice decorated with his singular accent that made it seem as though you were about to be executed. But tonight he was unconcerned with the artichoke business.

"Did you give him a slice with a whole lot of them?" my mother continued, haunted by the fear that she might find a greasy vegetable in her jewelry box.

Sheridan was wide-eyed, and his mouth was full of white-sauced eggs. There was a boy who couldn't produce enough of a lie to make soap. I almost choked on the Dublin bread again.

"We'll be looking for those artichokes for weeks." My father smiled. "Maybe they'll be in the tea box again."

"Oh, Mícheál," my mother moaned, "don't remind me."

We smiled. My cheeks were aching with it.

"And what did that gentleman want that called on you today?' She brightened as she recalled the question she had wished to ask before the artichoke discussion. "The children saw the carriage too, and marked its good looks. It was rather fine." Caroline O'Hayden enjoyed nice things. If you put her in a museum, she'd starve to death looking at everything unless someone went in to drag her out.

My father shrugged. He never liked business talk at the table; he'd rather hear about music and literature, and don't ever start on politics or he'd change the subject on you. And although I never mentioned it, I was inclined to agree with him. There was no place for tedious talk at the table. Sheridan, as it could be guessed, would have found a discussion of economic theory rather stimulating, but then a Wicklow pebble would.

"Ah, that man"—he spoke with bland detachment, never putting his eyes on the questioner—"he wished to know if the home was for sale. I believe he was acting on another's behalf."

Sheridan and I looked at each other. We usually didn't get involved in our parents' conversations unless summoned directly.

"For sale, huh." My mother released the 'huh' with surprise. "Wherever did he hear of Carrickduff being up for sale?" She was baiting him. "Of all the places to pick at that." You could see that she didn't have much faith in his answers. You couldn't sneak anything past her. It wasn't worth trying. She was like Peader. She knew what you were going to say before you said it, and so there wasn't much use in lying to a mind reader. They both spoke Irish, and I knew that had something to do with the sorcery, but I didn't know exactly what the secret was as of yet.

My father shrugged again and let a thin smile spread across his face. He knew he was losing the war. His small grins always looked like sneers because of the sharpness of his features, and if he squinted, it looked entirely derisive.

"I don't know where he found the idea"—he rubbed his eyes—"might've been out shooting and caught sight of the place. He wouldn't give me his name though, or the one for whom he was working. Ah, but I didn't press it, embarrassed he was, probably. Somebody might have told him we were looking to sell as a joke. Very abrupt he was"—he tapped a finger on the table—"and it was I who should've been, with him taking me away from thoughts of a nap." He let the thin smile come again, as he hurriedly altered the tension by changing the subject. "Shouldn't I be awake when I'm spending time with the likes of you?" He played an edged stare over my brother and me. "You two know where Rowan is, I doubt not?"

I smiled despite not knowing what was going on. Nobody could alter the course of a story like my father, and henceforth the meal finished dutifully. I even managed to finish the bread without choking completely. It was a very good supper considering the foggy air about the table.

After supper, my brother and I continued to root about for Rowan. Daniel and Peader had returned a half hour ago from the train. All stoat searching ceased for the evening when my brother and I were commanded hastily into the sitting room for stories.

Chapter 14

Rowan hadn't shown up for stories. My brother and I were lost as to where else to scratch about for him. He could have been anywhere—in any drawer that had been left open, in any of the many parts and holes in our cellar, in any cupboard, and even under the braces of chair seats. One place we could tick off were the seat bottoms in the sitting room where we were gathered, as there had been no squeaks following the sitter who had placed himself on the chair. There was always the hope that the little stoat had simply settled back into the nursery during the quiet hours; but wherever he was, Rowan was still on his keeping.

My father had the Jameson's poured out for himself and Peader. My mother and Daniel had some claret wine, and Sheridan and I, had cups of tea. Donovan sat in my father's armchair and was running his beak over his feathers. Daniel sat on a low creepie beside the peat fire. He poked the stacks of sweet-smoking turf blocks and a burst of orange embers sparkled in the hearth.

"Tell us a good one, Dan." My brother leaned forward in his chair.

"True," I said, "look, you're boring old Donovan with this waiting." I pointed to the raven.

"Well," Daniel leaned back on the stool, and he looked sleepily at the ceiling, "I'm not sure I can think of any." That was the way he always made us wait for a story. Peader smiled as he watched us get anxious. My father yawned.

We had drawn a few of the curtains so that the room would be darker. It was almost June, so the night would stay away until after ten. There was no need to close the many curtains for the sitting room was a dim place, even in midday, with all the dark panelling and such. Stories were always better without too much raucous light intruding on the play of the words.

"Liar!" my brother and I teased.

"It's 'cause he thinks too much," my brother added.

"What do you two fancy this evening?" my father asked before sipping the amber whiskey.

"I want to read a poem from the *Nation*," answered Dan, who had not been addressed. "A poem that is touched down from the very mists in the morning air, words that read like music out of the black-bordered pages. Words carved for these shores, pages that lay bare their white leaves to sing of those that have lined her path with their lives." The boy raised his goblet with respect.

"I want to hear a ghost story!" my brother called out.

"I don't know any of them." Daniel shook his head as if it would slip off his shoulders.

"Sure you do, Dan," I added, "you know you do."

"I think our Dan starting to lose his memory," my mother teased.

"Well"—Daniel shifted on the creepie—"seein' as I'm not wanted to read from this paper so, I'm going to tell a quiet tale."

Sheridan and I groaned.

"There was a small farm just south of here in the shadow of the mountains in a neat and pretty glen. Low stonewalls marked each share of field, and on the first field's byre sang a hen robin with a voice as fine and clear as the stream that rushed from the hills." Daniel stopped and looked at our blank faces.

"Now," he continued, staring at our bland eyes, "a black-faced ewe had just dropped her lamb, and the young farm wife had come out to gaze upon the fine creature, but . . . ,"—he sent his eyes toward the window—"she hadn't long to spend with the young one, as it was the night of Samhain, Hallow Eve, and she had to be home before the darkness came down the hills."

We began to grow excited, and we knew that we were going to be getting the story that we wanted.

"Hallow Eve"—Daniel continued to stare past us out the window—"was in the old times the beginnin' of the dry season of winter. On every hillside across the land, the great bonfires were lit, and the island glowed as if she burned. It was on this night that those who had died could wake and work their will upon the living. No mortal was safe upon the roads in the darkness and to stay about a graveyard would be no less than courtin' death yourself.

"And the dead made good use of their power on that night. 'Oh, that woeful mortal men did not know of the gift that they waste,' cried the wraiths. But mark this, gentle listener, for the dead would make good use of their freedom to play once again with the style of the livin', and many would hastily return to that cottage and manor where they had squandered their earthly days. That is why you would not be walkin' the night-covered lanes, for even though you had left alone from your door, alone you would not be on the return. The steps of the dead would sound at your back, and should you turn to see their phantom kind, then surely and quickly would you join those fearful ranks.

"On the bells of midnight, all of the hoary host gather in their white grave clothes, like droplets from the moon and drink of the fairy liquor to the joys of life, however short-lived its stay. Their revels could be heard by all fearful mortals in their houses and by all of the unlucky who found themselves upon the roads. The dead danced to the fairy music until the first glimpse of the day cast them back into the dark realm, and mortals once again gained control of life.

"It was in the season of death that a young girl and a young man made their way into the mountains by the town of Glendalough. They walked together in the trees until they came to a clearin', where the pine boughs broke the daylight softly upon the ground. And there on the moss, those lovers sat.

"And on that day, they pledged that they would wed no other man or woman. The lovers know that those words were not simply spoken, for the girl was finely bred, and he was the son of a weaver. Their love they kept between them only, with the pine and the fir trees standin' witness.

"On the day of the elopement, she was to go and take the silver from her house, and that wealth itself reaped from the pain of others, so that they might live without need. And you see, as her power to choose her love was stolen by the manor at her birth, then she would take her rightful dowry. With it, their engagement was sealed, without her family's blessing; and on the seventh day of October, she was to wait for him, silver in hand, beneath the tower and amidst the headstones of the monastery's ruins.

"The eve of the seventh fell upon the churchyard, and there the girl sat at the round tower's base, and there sat the silver at her feet. There she waited until the black of night, at the bottom of the doorless tower. She waited as the moon stood guard before heaven. And so as each hour moved on, her once bright soul flickered and dimmed with despair.

"The dark sky paled slowly with the first mark of light, but her lover never came.

It was known those few days before, that the two had not shared their vows with the pine trees alone. When the girl had left the manor gates, a servant had been set upon her heels, and there he followed her all the way up into the hills, where he took cover beneath a pine bough. And it was not her lover, but the same servant that waited that night amongst the silent graves with a pistol in his belt."

Daniel stopped and shifted in his seat. He searched our absorbent faces, and he knew we were swallowing the words. Even my father didn't move, but he always preferred a scary story. Daniel took a sip from the glass of dark claret at his feet.

"The eve of the seventh," he continued, "had found her lover faithfully on the road to the ruins at Glendalough. But the road turned sharply where two blackthorns twisted about an aged elder tree, and there waited the men from the manor. The weaver's son had not passed the spot when his loyal eyes were darkened by a swath of leather, and his mind blinded by the swift strike of a pistol's hilt. He never knew where his place of holdin' had been, for it was not until the new dawn that the poor weaver found himself dazed at his own cottage's gate.

"On the morning of the eighth, the men from the manor went down to the monastery to see why their young lady and servant had not returned. At the tower's base, a spot of grass had been pressed, but the sitter was no longer there. They searched about the graves and about the ruins until they came to the monastery's door. And down among the toppled graves was found the body of their fair miss, who found her death in the grief-filled dawn. The bag of silver no longer lay at her side, and the traitorous servant never again was seen."

"Did the bad servant shoot her?" my brother asked.

"No," I interrupted, "I bet that she fell on the rocks. Didn't she fall on the gravestones, Dan?"

Dan turned to me. "The scoundrel didn't shoot her. He waited till she died before stealin' the wealth of the dowry from his mistress's side. She fell on the broken stones in the darkness, and she was so full of despair thinkin' then that her man had betrayed her. But that he didn't. He was faithful, so he was.

"When the young man learned of his lady's death," Daniel explained, "he grieved alone for no one knew of their plans to wed. He worked each day upon his father's loom, and he worked with the silence upon him. No one knew why the life had gone from the fourth son of the weaver, or when if ever it would return. He only spoke to the shopkeeper's wife, and only when he went to buy the family's goods. And, it was then she would take him to sit with her behind the shop to speak of weather and business.

"One afternoon, he stayed with the old couple to a supper of porridge and a piggin of milk, and it wasn't until darkness fell that he left the shopkeeper's cottage. The road was empty of man and of beast, and a chill wet wind kept one step before him as he shivered slowly home. He turned up the lonely path that crossed the hill, so that the trees would keep the wind from him. He could feel the loose, full skirt of his coat blowin' against his back. And as he crossed the top of that hill, the wind picked itself through the trees to dampen the high road. He stopped then to bring the collar closer about his neck, and as he again looked forward to the walk before him, there stood his fated bride. He stepped back, stiffinin' from fright, for he knew that she had been found dead. His lady was dressed in the palest blue with a white haze clouding over it all and settlin' like fog into the folds. The fabric glowed like backlit candle wax. Gold embroidery burned bright upon the stiff stomacher and against the ghostly cast of the garment, the lady's flesh appeared whole.

"The young man came forward and she spoke to him to come by her side, but that he mustn't touch her as yet, for then she would have to go back to the dead. And he came to her side, and they walked down the hill together."

"Oh," my mother said, "I don't think I'd be near anything like that! She wouldn't have any fear of me touching her, I'd promise that."

"They were lovers, Mrs. O'Hayden," Daniel mused.

"Wouldn't you walk by my side if I were to come back to you"—my father asked, tucked back in his chair—"your faithful husband?"

"No, I would not," she faked a shiver.

"Not even if it was me?" Peader asked. "I've been faithful too. And I'll be faithful as a taibhse."

I listened flatly. The playful banter was breaking the shadowy mood.

"I would not," my mother stated, "but maybe I might consider it if you promised to nip back my roses with your ghostly pruners while you were visiting."

"Well," Daniel continued with the grave face that he had managed to hold, "there wasn't any ghostly prunin' going on that night, but the two lovers walked over the hills until the spirit girl had to go back to the dead.

"All of the nights after, he would meet her in the cemetery at Glendalough with the mountains risin' all around them. Each night she would come to him in the gossamer, blue dress. And each day, he spent alone at the loom longin' for those visits with each pass of the yarn-threaded shuttle. He spoke now to no one, not even the shopkeeper's wife. No one knew why the young man pined so stoically. But one night he waited for his love under the lintel of the ruin's door, and it was not 'till after midnight that she appeared. She stood at the fore of an arching window at the ruin's far wall. The blue dress absorbed the light from the low set moon, and she glowed like lantern glass. A frost rose on his skin as he noted the change in her demeanor. And he did no longer desire to approach her.

"'My love,' she said, "'I can come to you for one night more.' She turned pale and wavered as she spoke and the rocks on the wall showed through her waning form. 'I will come to the weaving-room, when the night is full grown; it is then when I will come.' And promptly she disappeared.

"The next night he returned to the old shop woman, and after supper they sat by the fire as he told her of the ghostly visits and of what was to follow on that future October night. The old woman feared for the boy, and she told him to place a burning coal at the door and with that, he would be safe from harm. By his bed, she said he should trace a circle with a hazel stick for no ghost or fairy could pass that place. She gave him a hazel branch kept in her dresser, for only those cut on May morning were useful against danger.

"On the eve of October 31, the young man placed the heated coal by the door, and he went to his bed by the light of the turf fire. He thought to himself that maybe she would not come, and soon he began to fall asleep. In the cool, dark house, there came a rattlin' at the door, and he was shaken from his sleep. The coal still burned hot before the front of the threshold despite the passed hours. The door rattled in its casin', and a sigh like the voice of no earthly breeze sounded from outside.

"The young man's nerves began to ease, and he was relieved to see that the old woman was right about the hot coal. He lit the rush light by the side of his bed and just as the flame took, a strange rattlin' came from the eaves and just as the rattlin' ended, a flurry of air gust into the room. He leaned over to keep the rush light from blowin' out and as he looked up there at the foot of the bed stood his love as she had promised. Her dress was of the same pale blue, and the gold swirled upon her bodice and her flesh was whole. For the first time he feared her entirely, even more than on the night in the monastery.

"'Why have you placed the coal by the door?' she asked. He did not answer."

"'Why have you tried to shut me away?' she pleaded. And again he did not answer, but he did see the sadness in her face.

"'Now, I must leave,' she said softly walkin' toward where he sat upon the bed. 'Tonight was the last night I could stand in this world at my will. And that, my love,' she sat next to him now on the bed, 'is why you could never touch me. For if you had, then at that instant, I would have had to leave you. But you didn't, and I was free to walk the earth once again so that we may walk it together.' It was then that she leaned toward his forehead, and placed her kiss as frost upon his face before she flashed away in a tall, blue flame.

"The frost-kiss was the last that he felt in life. The next mornin' the young weaver was found dead by his bed. On his forehead was a strange, pale mark as if the flesh had been frozen. By the door was found a cold, blue coal that after would never take heat. And on the dresser by the fire lay a hazel wand covered in the ash of the burned down rush light."

"He forgot the hazel stick," my brother observed.

"He had to draw a circle around himself with it," I added, "to keep her away."

Our storyteller said, "Yes."

"He was so busy lightin' the rush," Dan explained, "that he forgot about the second charm. But you know," he leaned forward on the creepie, "I think it was for the better. The young weaver was still taken with the young lady and herself was comin' for him too. Don't you think it was for the better, Mrs. O'Hayden?"

"Yes, I do, Mr. Whelan," my mother answered.

"Well, I'm glad," my father sat back in his chair with mock relief. "I'll be looking forward to being a ghost now."

"We have ourselves some happy ghosts," Peader stroked Donovan's head, as during the story the raven had jumped upon the gardener's lap for a sip of the Jameson's.

"We do have some happy ghosts," Daniel added. "Because if you wait in the monastery in Glendalough till well after midnight when the air is quiet, then you'll know what I'm sayin'. If you wait by the back of the ruins for when the moon of October shines full upon the floor, so will you see a pale young man with a girl in a dress of polished blue, talkin' in the moon's glow. The two now had what they could not catch in life; for only in death could they be wed. We must hold the pleasure of such things."

Chapter 15

It was after ten before we all headed to bed. My brother and I still hadn't found Rowan. We had gone into the nursery to shut Donovan's light, after he had fluffed and preened himself upon his roost. Rowan's sally basket, however, was empty. And it wasn't an overstatement to say that we now were quite worried. In the morning, we had agreed that we would have to tell about the little stoat, whether we wanted to, or not. There was still the chance that he might show up, and then we wouldn't have to say anything. I prayed for that.

My brother turned down the lamp and we both went solemnly into our rooms. I changed into my nightclothes, and I slid into bed hoping that after I had turned down the lamp, there would be no ghosts with cold lips sitting anywhere near my bed. My arms started to ache in the quiet of bedtime when all worries and pains worsened and pestered more than they did during the day. My left knee rubbed painfully against the bedclothes, and I realized I had gained yet another wound from the coach scrap of the afternoon. You didn't tumble over a stonewall, even a broken one, without inheriting bruises and other such ornaments. I picked up my copy of *Little Women*, and I hoped that it would take my mind off Dan's story and the wild coach incident. I didn't really care for the dullness of *Little Women*, but it was written in Massachusetts, in America, and I liked American stories, especially those with settlers and Indians. I liked adventurous stories, but I had given my *Gulliver's Travels* to Thomas along with *Robinson Crusoe*, so I had nothing much left in my room. I had left my new book in the sitting room, and I certainly wasn't going down to the first floor alone tonight. The maids that I had deceived earlier, Mrs. Kelly and Mrs. O'Leary, had finished cleaning hours ago, and the rooms would now be ominously dark. Mrs. Kelly was upstairs helping my mother get undressed. A quiet story like *Little Women* was a good choice for someone with a mind full of ghosts, and the lack of adventure would certainly help me sleep.

I started getting pretty drowsy by the time I had arrived at chapter two. I laid the book upon the bed table before I reached over to dim the lamp. I tried to fall asleep in the coolness of the bedsheets, but thoughts of Rowan kept badgering my head. I worried about forcing myself to sleep because I knew that it wouldn't work. You could never make yourself sleep. I would be exhausted tomorrow, and there could be no changing that. And I soon started thinking of ghosts again because I had put out the lamp, and ghosts never came to you on a blazingly sunny afternoon like macabre butterflies, they always came to you at night and then especially when you were in bed. You would never hear of anyone being visited by ghosts while they were on the lawn playing croquet. Sure enough, as soon as I had shut all sources of light from my room, there came a terrible yell hurtling down the hall. I jumped up in my bed as the tap of running steps sounded past my door, and then continued down the stairs. Somehow, the sound of the footsteps going by fortified me with curiosity, and the knowledge that, hitherto, there had been no ghost sightings, even with the dead famine woman, at Carrickduff fed my courage. I got out of bed and threw a wrap about my shoulders. Apparently, my brother had done the same, for I soon met him on the balcony—with Rowan.

Mother went to her room when the others had left for their beds. I went to the nursery with Sheridan, and we lit one dim lamp and put Rowan into his bed. He was very rattled from his daylong ordeal just as we were from ours, but we were happy to have him back. Mrs. Kelly came in with some Bishop for Rowan's nightcap, as he had had no supper. The stoat lapped the warmed spice wine without lemon because he didn't like it, but with plenty of ginger as he liked that above all the other spices.

While Rowan drank, we sat on the floor so that Mary Kelly could tell us what had happened on the stairs. She crossed her legs beneath her skirts as she sat, so we knew that we would be getting all the details. Here was what she told us:

Our mother had been in the bedroom, brushing out her ripe-straw-colored hair before the mirror. She then stood to remove the dress. Her back was to Mrs. Kelly who was filling a washbowl for my mother to freshen her face. My mother unbuttoned the front and wiggled out of the garment. When the dress fell to the floor, Mary let out a thunderclap of a scream while pointing to my mother's back. Then the maid promptly jumped upon the dressing table chair and yelled, "Mrs. O'Hayden, there's a rat upon ya'!"

Well, Mary grabbed a poker from the hearth, and she jumped from the chair to give the "rat" one for the road. My mother twisted round to see what she was fussing about. After one short glance at the small, brown, furry animal clinging to her hoop, she didn't hang about for chatting.

My mother shot out of the bedroom as if the devil was behind her. Mary was coming too, brandishing that poker like Queen Maeve. The stoat had been hiding out in the bedroom, and at some point had decided the great, upside-down bowl of a dress would be a fantastic destination for exploring. It was a good thing that my mother was a formidable sprinter, or Rowan would have gotten himself a screamer of a headache.

It was the kind of story that you wouldn't believe if somebody was to tell it to you. You would say that they were a rotten liar. I would have said that, had I not seen the thing for myself.

Mrs. Kelly went to her room, and I didn't think that she'd be getting much sleep with the state that she had been in. My brother sulked off too, a bit more at ease than he had been a half hour before. I heard him laughing to himself. Donovan was all puffed up and sitting on his roost. The bird had missed the whole thing. He croaked sleepily as everyone left the room. I told the others that I would stay behind to close the lamp.

Rowan was curled up in his bed, licking his painful paw and chattering, while I scratched his furry head with my good arm. Tomorrow, I told Rowan, we were all going to be bawled out for what had happened. Rowan snickered and licked my fingers. I stood up and closed the lamp before going to my room.

Chapter 16

Mother asked if I wanted to go riding. She said that we could go down past the Hutcheson field and as far as the police barracks that sat atop a slow-rising hill. We wouldn't be back for lunch, so we could pack some bread with ham and bring some wedges of shortbread.

"How would you like that, Anne?" She pushed a curl of amber hair from the side of her forehead.

I liked it very much. We were to go after breakfast. Strangely, there was no mention of last night's bizarre events, and I wasn't going to bring it up. I was much relieved over escaping a scolding.

"Go and have your riding wools ready, and I'll come and dress you then." She smiled. I could tell that she needed to go somewhere. Every so often she would get the urge to run like father's tomcat. Sitting around with books filled her with unused energy that apparently had not been tapped by a fall over an Indian rug.

Carolyn O'Hayden had the face of one of those old paintings of the Madonna, the really pretty ones, with all of the perfect features. Two of her other sisters were uncommonly plain. One had dull hair, the other a turned up nose, and the youngest had the disposition of an old billy goat even though she was finely made. But you couldn't be beautiful with that unpersonable behavior, because people were bound to talk to you, and only statues and paintings could only be beautiful. My father said that she acted like a hard minister, the kind that hated everything, and that went about with their heads up as if they couldn't even stand the smell of air. But Cathleen was a Catholic, and with her looks she easily married, although it was said that her husband had taken a second vow with the bottle that was stronger than his first when he took a wife. I felt sorry for Cathleen, even though she was not of the liking sort. It was the sorry that you felt for a seven legged spider.

There was a fourth sister named Ellen who married a rich Protestant man from Tipperary who was as sociable as a sunny day. He was an old man when she married him and she was only twenty-three, which isn't really young, but he was fifty. I couldn't imagine doing a thing like that. I was fond of Aunt Ellen and her old husband, and I was pleased when they came to visit. What I liked the best about her was her affection for walking out, and we would go for many a grand and wild romp when she came. At the first stream we'd meet, she'd drop upon a rock and remove her shoes, stockings, and garters and splash right in. She would tread all the way to the middle and lift her skirt without a care until you could see the lace edge of her knickers. Her husband, James, would not go in the water as the chill bothered his legs, so he'd just sit by the side and smoke.

Peader would come on most of our walks and he, James, and Ellen would have a grand time of storytelling and joking with each other. She didn't care if

Peader saw her knickers; she didn't care if the whole world did. Her husband didn't care either. I thought that was grand and romantic, feeling so free and wild as they did out with all the natural things. Byron would have done it, and our Daniel would have too—if he were a woman and wore knickers. I would be free when I grew older than eleven, but only in nature, not in town. My uncle said that God made the women and the men all the same respectively. James was old; he would know about such things. I suppose that it was worth believing, although I had nothing much to go on save those Renaissance paintings and statues, which did seem to support the theory rather well.

But in that framework flowered a garden of variation. Ellen's husband, James, was as tall as Peader, but that was all the similarity there was. Our Peader's legs were too long and he was tough and wiry, but James was soft and almost portly. It was a strange shape, regular-sized arms and legs, but then he looked as though he had a bit of ticking stuffed in the middle under his waistcoat. I liked James. I sinfully envied the way he reasoned over things and confessed it in church to Father Daly. I liked the way he bantered frivolously with his wife.

On one walk we were down by the edge of the barley field that we had once used to pasture cattle. There was still a fence and wall there and a rickety wooden slatted gate where the wrens sat and bickered. Through the center of the field ran a small stream that the cattle used to drink from. My aunt saw that stream from the other side of the gate. "Oh, let's be game," she said with the purest enthusiasm, "and cross over the next hill by way of that stream over there." She went for the gate, and I was expecting her to open it, but she started over the top of it, using each slat as a ladder. My eyes were starting from out of my head. It was a five-foot rickety gate, and Mrs. Ellen wasn't a small woman like my mother and the other sisters. My aunt had substantial legs and a well-built frame. They said she came from their father's side, the O'Donoghue's part of the family. I feared that the slats wouldn't hold, but it seemed she had no such fear for she started over like a gigantic costumed squirrel. The evicted wrens were perched along the stonewall; and there they sat, gaping with amazement. She had made it to the top, whereupon she waved us to follow gleefully. We did as bade—perplexed but playful—and stood in queue, waiting our turn.

She swung her leg over the top in a most comical *Punch* cartoon fashion; but just as she made to raise the other, some part of her got caught up on the gate, and the momentum from her action sent her hanging downside up in a most embarrassing manner. My aunt could move neither earthward nor skyward as she was fully suspended from the gate like a big blue moth on a window. The two men went to her side, stopping short with confusion as to how to best save the woman. James grabbed my shoulders and held me back as if he feared his wife was about to explode.

"Oh!" she said this in a somewhat calm manner, considering her circumstance, with her face flushed, and the whole world seeing the entirety of her lace-edged unmentionables.

"I think it's the back of the petticoat hung up!"

That must have been one well-made piece of cloth to support its owner like that. It was a strange thought to creep into your head in a moment such as that, but it crept into mine, as I was always being permeated with queer notions, and I had no control over them at all. I had a predisposition for them. I believe that it had some connections with the inherited curse for *ne'er-do-wells*. With that thought in my head, I tried to find where and what cloth had stuck, as I was the smallest and most nimble. But I could not find it. There was too much fabric. It was like trying to find a barleycorn in the oatmeal bin.

"Hold on, Ellen!" James called out, as if his wife was being eaten by tigers. "I'll try and pull you over." He made for the fence with the staggering apprehension of a man preparing to jump into a cold sea.

"No, man!" Peader snatched my uncle backward. "You'll not be able to do it. The situation's not callin' for that. The fence is too high, *anois*."

"So then, what do we do?"

"Well, do you mind me, beggin' your pardon, Mr. James?" Peader ran his fingers through his hair. "Do you mind me liftin' your wife?"

"No!" came the voice from the other side of the gate. "I don't mind. Just get me off!" My aunt's voice was now uncharacteristically strained.

"Do what you must, sir." Her husband agreed with over-dire solemnity, as if the tigers were closing in.

Peader climbed over the stonewall. I watched him through the slats in the gate. He crawled daringly beneath the dangling woman. It looked dangerous. She was sure to crush him if she ever came loose. Silently, I pleaded for the cotton petticoat to hold.

"You grab my shoulders, Mrs. Ellen and I'll push you up. Just like liftin' a stuck carriage, so." The familiar voice came from somewhere beneath my aunt.

"I've got you," she said restlessly. The gate creaked ominously.

"James, there! You grab your wife when I've heaved her to the top."

"I'm waitin' on you, Mr. Hayes."

I went up next to my uncle to help him pull. I stood on the third rung, and I grabbed my aunt's arm. With a rustling of grass and a stomping of earth, Peader put his weight into the job and heaved the woman up. I pulled her arm, and James had her waist; but Peader had almost the full weight of the formidable woman atop his narrow back.

Once we had pulled her up, my aunt was able to steady herself upon the wide top slat, free her petticoat, and jump down. To the great shock of us rescuers, the woman jumped down upon the opposite side, just missing the exhausted Peader. She thanked him profusely for the lending of his back in the daring rescue.

"Tá fáilte romhat, ma'am," he panted, his voice cracking by the last word. "It was an honor for me, be sure of it. But if you don't take this wrongly, ma'am, for I've enjoyed your company, I must be goin' for there's a tiredness on me from all o' the walkin' about."

I continued on with the walk, and on our return I went into the kitchen to tell Mrs. Kelly about it. But I saw Peader at the scullery table, and I found that he had beaten me to it.

The whole kitchen was smelling of lemons. The brisk air tickled your nose, and caused you to tighten your lips with the imagined bitterness.

"You're a wicked man, Mr. Hayes—wicked!" Mrs. Kelly poured out a glass of lemonade, plunking it on the table before him. He smiled impishly. "Anne, come and sit for a drink." I was gestured over to the table. "You shouldn't have helped the woman, if you were just gonna run off and make comments after and behind Mrs. Ellen's back. You scoundrel!"

He smiled again. I smiled too, and Peader nodded at me.

"Shouldn't I?" Peader leaned back in the chair. "It was my duty to help the woman and to save her husband from breakin' his back by liftin' her over the top of the fence." He gestured, describing the motion. "It was any man's duty that knew which way to turn and that was me. Ba liomsa é! That James didn't know to turn which way. I said to her it was an honor for me to help, and it was. Did I not say that Ms. Anne, who helped so bravely as well?"

"You did. He did. I heard him." The lemonade was fresh and bright like chilled moonlight. "Peader bent under her and lifted her up like a stuck carriage."

"See there. Now all I said to you was that our Mrs. Ellen was a healthy-sized woman. And so she is, everybody knows it, and there's nothin' wrong with that." He crossed his arms.

"You said she'd a weighty arse." Mrs. Kelly set her fists on her hips.

"Hush, not in front of the miss here!" He gestured nervously. "I didn't say it like that. You make it sound all wrong."

"Oh, I didn't know that there was a right way. And besides how'd you know that when she'd her arms on your shoulders?"

"Ah, I figured that when I was heavin' her up with all the strength in me. And then it struck me queer that as she was light in the top half, where could all the weight I was feelin' be? And the weight was uneven, unbalanced, like liftin' a stick with a rock on the end. So I thought to myself 'God she must have a solid arse, for where else could all the weight be."

Mrs. Kelly rolled her eyes, and turned to the sink to toss the drained lemon halves into the clippings basket.

I liked the word *arse*. It made you laugh to hear it, and you didn't hear it very often. It wasn't a nice word, but Peader said it perfectly. I don't think anyone else could say it like that, just right. The other bad words like *hell* or *damn* never made you laugh like *arse* did. I smiled while I drank my lemonade.

"Don't you be goin' around with that about to be sayin' it." Peader looked at me. It was frightful to wonder if that man had the gift to read minds. "Your mother'll have me head."

"Sayin' what, Peader?" I pretended that I didn't know he was talking about the *arse* word. Of course, it was a dying plan.

"You know 'sayin' what'. Don't say the word, and don't say that I said it. They'll think I'm teachin' ya odd things." He was trying not to smirk. "I'll have to say your Daniel did it, as a scapegoat."

I smiled. "No, I won't. It isn't ladylike. And I don't want you to hafta blame Daniel."

"No, it isn't gentlemanlike either," Mrs. Kelly said.

Peader nodded that he was satisfied.

"*Anois*," he raised from the chair, "that's our secret then, the whole story, especially the word." He bent and kissed my head before going out the back door.

Chapter 17

My mother was a grand rider, the best of her family. Her sister Ellen was too well-built to sit a saddle comfortably, and Cathleen didn't like horses. This morning she wore the black riding dress with the braid trim jacket. The whole dress was black—the braid, the buttons, and the band of ribbon on the skirt that reached past the ground. The white flashed only from the cuffs of her cambric shirt. To top it off she placed a tall felt hat on her head, just like one that father would wear.

Daniel brought Paddy and Gavin out. Paddy was trying to get the brown gelding to play with him but Gavin ignored all the nipping and frivolity. Dan wasn't able to ride out with us for he had the stable work still to do. He held the black horse's head while my mother mounted, but the gelding's back legs were free, and they danced about as if under a separate will.

"He'll be a handful today, ma'am." The boy received a swift nudge in the shoulder, and the horse grabbed the loose collar of the coat. "I'll be pleased to see the back of him." He let go of the reins and stepped back to study the slobber left on his frock.

"I don't believe that Daniel," my mother laughed. "You two are of the same mold."

Paddy settled down and snorted when he felt his mistress's weight.

"There. If I was a horse I'd be as wild as the hills, but gentle as the lambs for the lady on my back." He cocked his head like a rooster and nodded. He always spoke scholarly around my parents, as opposed to the "free" bad speech he used around us. I watched him turn and run for the stable.

We rode at a walk down to the main road that passed Carrickduff. The drive followed a long low slope from the house and on both verges flourished haphazard stands of trees that bent their heads towards the road to catch the best of the light. They were so thick in the summer as to shade you on your travels from both the sun and the rain. There was always the same smell there as you passed. It was the smell of moss and leaves and bark: tree smells. The air seemed to be filled with green and brown, and the crush of the road stones seemed to bring those scents to life. The canopy veiled the larks from your eyes so that only through your ears could you see them singing above. My eyes squinted with the thought of searching the birds out as they flapped in silhouette beneath the glaring sun. When you reached the drive's end the world opened before you with the sky on your head, and if you turned to check from where you had come there would be nothing save lines of those bark-skinned soldiers, for Carrickduff was obscured by the trees. But should you know to look just above the top of the central canopy, there would you see a stone chimney rising over the green to greet your eyes.

"When did you first sit a horse?" I asked my mother as we made our way down the road. The measured crush of the hooves was the best sound in the world, and their big soft bodies, the most comforting friend. I had to keep squeezing my lazy Gavin so that he would match up alongside Paddy. He didn't like to be too near the dark horse's head, lest a nip be sent his way.

"Oh," she said, "I first sat a horse before I could remember. Your grandfather O'Donoghue was a proud horseman, and he wasn't about to leave any daughter or son of his name not fond of the most honored creature on earth."

"But Cathleen doesn't like horses."

"No, she does not, then. But I didn't say that my father succeeded, for all of his trying. I couldn't get her to ride either, even when I offered her young Mr. Joshua's favor in exchange." She grinned. "It just wasn't in her. She was for the drawing room only. It was a shame to see her sewing, and her house managing was worse. At least she could dance like a peacock. But anyway . . . I would say though that her husband is rather too fond of the track horses." Her eyes widened.

I nodded, and received her approval. Cathleen's husband raised a poor stable of thoroughbreds. Only a handful took any winnings worth mentioning. I felt sorry for the horses, as I felt sorry for Cathleen, for as they said, her man had taken a second vow with the bottle. "When did you really learn to ride?"

"Well?" She touched her chin with the small, gloved hand.

"Well."

"When I was young, just your age then. My father taught me, as yours taught you."

"You showed me too." I corrected. She agreed.

"I rode every day if the weather held, and if I could. I rode all of the horses we had. I raced my brothers on the beaches, and the sons of Mr. Barrett."

"Was that the Mr. Barrett who had held your grandfather's land, when we couldn't have any by the laws?"

"That was the man, his grandfather was the first. My family went hunting with them, danced with them, dined with them . . . It's funny to hear that last name, as if it wasn't proper at all. I always felt that we were part of them, and they part of us—wholly joined beyond the rules of breeding and society. I cannot think of them any other way. Cousins, and aunts, and uncles of no blood relation, but we were bound by the gift of salvation. They had saved my family. The deed was never thought about, never mentioned. Our future waited under that name." The memories put a warmth in her face. I knew that this wasn't the first time that she thought about that. It was the first time that she spoke it.

My ancestors had placed their property into the Barrett's hands during those dark ages when many Catholics were forbidden to have all but the most woeful amounts of property. The Barretts saved the O'Donoghue fortune from the greedy. England could not collect what would not fall.

The warmth stayed on her face. "That sounds lovely," I said.

"It was." She said the last words with determination, and reached from her seat to brush a hair from my cheek.

We took a side lane and left the ruled paths of man for the unbounded fields, where the road followed you like a lap dog. I loved the fields and hills. It seemed, in their silence, that none had ever gone before you, but you knew that they had, even though there was not a trace to find. My mother and I cantered the happy horses across the living grass that was young and green. The bees mumbled over the white clover heads. We slowed to pass plowed fields or to greet the faces about the small, weathered cabins that broke the wildness of the country. I knew that we could have dwelt in a small, rubble half house, with only earth or stone beneath our feet. I thanked the long-dead Mr. Barrett, who left this world unbeknownst to all but those around him like the Lady of Shalott. I wanted the world to know that he had saved the O'Donoghues. He had saved Sheridan and me. "Our future waited under that name."

I never wanted to be poor. Thomas was poor, not really so, but he didn't have the food and the clothes that we had. They never bought ginger beer. The house wasn't his father's; it was the possession of the Barrands. I knew it was bad to take things for granted, but it was easing to know that you could. I did not want money or did I long to gain it. I only wanted the safety that it brought. I could see that safety in my mother's face. Her skin was pale and seemed as if it had never been touched, like the cream that rose to the milk's top. She had never worked like those women in the cabins with the oldness on them before the time. Her duties were self-imposed, her meals forthright and luxurious. Only her mind knew the tiredness of work. She had known pain but had never suffered. There was a difference. And all of this came to be, solely because of which roof she was born under. There was such difference. That was the world that was meant to stay hidden from me . . . that world of want that was all around me.

We rode on; jumping a low stone wall to enter the wild space of a low-climbing hill. Paddy loved to jump, and Gavin pricked his ears with resolution as he studied the stacked stone obstacle. We pulled up on the opposite side. Paddy rattled and chewed his bit, as my mother roughly scratched his withers.

"Is Paul to be home this year, do you think?" I released my hold on the reins so that Gavin could sneeze properly.

"Paul?" Her eyes went quiet. "My brother?"

I smiled.

"How strange . . . no, not strange . . . but you have never met him." She seemed to be talking to herself. I wished I hadn't mentioned it.

"Oh, I know that I would like to meet him," I said eagerly. "I never met him, but I feel as though I have, and I would know him when I do. He is tall like father, with green eyes. He is brown like Gavin, and he has a thin, sharp nose like a hawk's. That's what your painting says."

"So, it does." She seemed impressed with my description. She looked at the ground, and Paddy sidestepped as her weight shifted. "And I think that you two would get along grand." She smiled at me, but there was a sadness behind her eyes.

"He is a patriot," I said. I wanted to cheer her spirits, make her happy like she was before. I didn't like it when she wasn't happy.

"One of the best. And do you know why?"

"No."

"Because he wasn't afraid, and all of his hate lay with injustice so that there was not any left to go anywhere else. He wasn't afraid to serve his thoughts, to act. That is what a patriot does." She looked as if she was to cry. I didn't like to think that she would. She smiled to cast off the tears. I learned from her that you couldn't smile and cry. I wanted to be like her and father. I would never cry. It was a matter of will. Peader could cry, because he had to. He had a new life, and the "old dreams" made him.

"My friend Thomas is like that too."

"Is he?"

"I think so."

"Do so encourage him, Anne." She seemed to think about her words. "He is very much like you then. What a perfect match for a friend." She rubbed her eye, but I knew there was a tear crawling out. "Do you know then what my brother did before you were born?" She released a sniffled laugh.

"In Kerry?" I asked. I smiled unconsciously, and I squeezed my lips to stop, but she had caught it and grinned softly. We laughed at each other even though you couldn't see it.

"In Kerry," she said. "You see, I was gone then, in Paris, at school. But I wrote home constantly. I was in a class with your father then, and he said I had a share in the French post office with the stamps I was buying." She tried to mimic his voice.

I laughed. My father couldn't write a letter to save him from starvation. He wrote to newspapers, and he wrote for business, but nothing could come to his head for a letter.

"Paul's letters were beautiful," she continued. "Just to see his hand on the envelope gave me the freedom to be happy. They were pages long . . . all about the new calves, the drip from the roof, and then fixing the slates, building the loose boxes into the stable, and tearing out the stalls. He wrote about the balls, and the dinners, and the day the house was opened for the steward's and ladies-maid's wedding. He made me pine for home when I had forgotten to. I wanted to ride the wind home like a leaf in a gale, to the life that was mine, not the shadow that I was living in Paris."

"What about father?" I couldn't imagine the two separate. They seemed to be as one person even though that was silly. They were a door and a doorknob, two separate pieces that were part of one thing. You couldn't work a door without a knob, and a knob was useless without a door.

"Oh, I didn't know your father then as I do now. He was just another friend. But strangely enough we were to be wed in two years." Her voice was distant.

I wondered if she was glad that she married him, the man that would bring her across the land to Bray, and the man that would take her away from Kerry. I wondered if she regretted that. Did she still want to go west like that leaf on the wind? She seemed happy, so I did not think so. I think it was too late for that.

We rode down a small rut-pocked road. The holes and unkempt roughness reminded me of old Mrs. Byrne's Famine roads, what the traveler in those days faced when he came upon the Relief Works that dug up highways and cut down hills to add to the road's impassability. But those half-dead men, barely standing to the job, needed to work for gain, lest they be idly dependent on charity. I was eleven, and I knew better. I would go to England and be the youngest politician. I would show them how to run my country and order them to give us back what was ours anyway. And then we would be like America, rich and happy, with all manner of persons coming to see us. I would go to Australia and bring back my mother's brother. That would make her very happy.

"I hadn't noticed the changes in the letters. I was married then. We had remained in France." She let Paddy have his head, and he dropped his nose down to see the ruts better. "They were just small mentionings in the beginning, side-thoughts. That's how I saw them, but I was wrong. He did not wish to trouble his sister's mind." She smiled at me. "He had penned things as . . . 'had trouble with old Mr. Lewis over the building of the relief corn-mill. Lewis said it was on his land. It was not, indeed. I had the papers to show his ridiculous fabrication. Well, he did not like to see it from his garden, he said. Rubbish! We did not like to see his garden from the mill, I said'."

The mill was for the relief of the tenants, when the potatoes they grew had failed. There were shipments of corn coming, but the grains were in their natural form. There was no way to grind them and the people didn't know how to make the course yellow meal eatable. It took nearly forever to cook.

"One day coming Anne, I will take you west, and you can see the mill, and the house, and my childhood." Her eyes brightened.

"Who was old Mr. Lewis?" I asked. She was talking of the Famine days. She never talked of them. She thought that I didn't know.

"He was a neighbor. His holding did not bring the same yearly gain as ours. I think that he was jealous in knowing that an old family was making out so well. The O'Donoghues were an older family . . . centuries older." She raised her proud head. "Paul carried on with the mill. Mr. Lewis tried to stop the work, but he could have no say, for there was no legal reason to stop the building of it. And on one meeting Mr. Lewis informed my brother that he would bring the mill down should it ever be finished. My brother was unmoved by the threat. He said he would bring the law should another such attack be made. But that did not end the feud. Paul knew that our neighbor had been compensating the sheriff and the magistrate for their troubles. You could say it was a hired threesome."

'Paul went on with his business, anyway?" I asked, not fully understanding what she said, but knowing from her voice that it was bad. Gavin snorted even though the road wasn't dusty.

"He went on. The mill was built and working. Mr. Lewis was not happy and the law passed our house rather too frequently. Our neighbor had evicted several of his tenants who could not pay their debts. He paid the passages to America for some. We were doubly burdened by the extra orphans, and I believe that was part of his strategy, for even our own tenants were suffering. And that was the last letter Paul sent me, the last letter from anyone at home."

I knew the rest of the story; father told me. One day I had asked mother why I didn't have an older brother like Daniel to play with, because Sheridan couldn't do anything right, he couldn't keep up. He was only one year younger than me, but that apparently was enough to weigh upon the situation. My mother started to cry. I couldn't believe it, she had never cried in her life, not before me anyway. I thought that maybe she wanted an older son more than I wanted another brother. I knew she was pleased to have Sheridan. She had to, because he was her child, but maybe he wasn't enough. Father told me why she had cried even though I didn't ask. He saw what had happened; he was in the room. It had everything to do with all those years ago in Cahirciveen. It had everything to do with Paul, and Mr. Lewis, and the Famine times, even though he hadn't mentioned the last part.

In the fall of 1846 Paul had received a request by a horseboy it seemed, to go and attend to a difficult foaling at the Lewis stable. Paul was good with horses, he had learned from his father. Despite his dislike for that scoundrel of a neighbor, he was not to let the mare suffer. Indeed, he found it rather odd that Lewis would have even asked him. The situation must have been desperate, and the darkness was beginning to come. Upon his arrival, the horse-boy swiftly disappeared with the coming of his master. It was a strained meeting, but there was business to be done, if it could be.

Mr. Lewis was in high spirits, for he tut-tutted over Paul's pains at coming the distance. The mare had foaled by herself, wasn't that grand. My uncle said nothing as he looked at the days old foal, and anyone but a fool would see that there was no recent birth. He was crossed by fear then, for he now knew that he had fallen into a trap. He never made it home for some "peelers" and a hired sheriff were waiting on the dark road to grab "their man". The Coercion Act was cited. No man was to be found out of his own house from the time of sunset to the time of sunrise. The sentence was fourteen years transportation to Australia. That was why there were no more letters to my mother in France. Nothing could be done. Mr. Lewis had won.

My father had told me that my mother received no notice of this from her family so that she would not be startled. My father said that was partly the reason, for everyone knew that Mrs. Carolyn O'Hayden was not a wilting violet of a woman even though she looked it. The real reason, he had said, was a very delicate matter and not proper for a child to know. He said that was why my mother had found her tears when I had mentioned an older brother. She was seven months with child when she had made the trip to Kerry. There were strong admonitions offered, but she would not hear them. Upon the receipt of the news of Paul's transportation, she had lost the child. I did not understand him then, but I knew what he was trying to tell me. It took four years for her to give me a small part of that story. I believed that we were too proud of Paul to think of anything else.

"Where shall we take our lunch, Anne?" She pushed Paddy into a trot." We need a suitable place to toast our hero."

"We will go where nobody can see us but the trees." Gavin cantered to keep up. "We will stop in a wild place, and we can pretend it's Australia."

We found a stand of old oaks and horse chestnuts that blocked the sight of the road. After loosing the horses from their corseting girths, we spread the hasty picnic upon the ground. We raised a shortbread to the rebel of Cahirciveen.

"Good day to you, ma'am and miss. I never expected to meet such singular blossoms in such a place." The tall man removed his hat, revealing a stylish mass of light thatch-brown hair. He seemed a few years older than my father, I figured, but only just. He had a narrow squarish face, with a sharply hewed linear nose that had it been a trifle more pronounced would have been an ill-favored addition to his countenance. I put my shortbread politely down on the napkin.

"And a good day to you, sir. You are too kind," My mother answered. "Can we be of any help to you?"

"Is it that noticeable?" He cocked his head amiably.

"Oh, your accent," she said, "not like that. But it is rather that most folk this far into the country tend to have mislaid their paths. I thought I might try readin' your mind. Has my boldness proven right?"

"Remarkably, ma'am." He rubbed his chin with curiosity. His eyes hardened with inborn intelligence. He seemed the kind of man fond of keen wit. "I believe that I am an hour out of my way. I was out searching for native Irish perennial flora—"

"And you happened upon specimens of native Irish perennial fauna," My mother interrupted with mischief on her face. I liked the sound of his accent, it was fresh and seemed as though it could never be coarse.

"So the day has been an unintended success." He straightened. "You see, I noticed the side-saddled horses by the road, a black and a dun, and I have left my own there so that I might search out the owners."

"You have found the owners. I hope that we can get you back on your path, so that you would never again regret the hour that you lost. Where is your way?"

The man was hesitant for a moment, which struck me queer. It was as if he was asked what the cost of boots were in Switzerland. Maybe he wasn't as quick-minded as I had thought.

"Oh yes!" He started as one who was sleeping. "I was headed for Kilmacanogue. I have still to get my tongue used to the lavishness of such words."

"Má thugann tú maithiúnas dhom, a dhuine uasail, tá rud níos measa ná é sin," My mother answered.

"I hope I have not just been ill used?" he said slyly.

"That would've be an insult to my country should I have done such a thing to a guest." My mother was earnest. "My daughter and I have not the pleasure of your name."

"It is Cosgrove, ma'am." The man's voice grew strangely precise. My mother's welcoming expression remained the same, but there was now a glow of interest there.

"Do you know then, that is familiar. My husband knew of such a family, but I doubt you would know of them, although they were from England. I'll bet that there are plenty of Cosgroves in your country, eh?"

"To be sure, ma'am. I'd be a lifetime finding my own family of them." He tilted his head to show the absurdity of the overwhelming task. "Apparently, there is such a plethora of Cosgroves that we've spread across the sea to Ireland, for want of space." He smiled. It was a tired, burdened smile. I was beginning to grow uncomfortable, as if this man was going to explode, or turn into a fox, or any such queer, supernatural thing. "Ah but," he sighed, "I would bore you. I, too, have not the honor of your dynasty."

"I am Mrs. O'Hayden, and this is my daughter, Anne."

"I should have known the connection, when two such ladies appear so equally fair. Again, it is a pleasure." He bowed to me, and instinctively I wanted to cringe. How strange. Peader said that it was not right to dislike someone whom you didn't even know, but I did. That was a bad thing.

"Is it business that brings you to Bray, sir?" My mother's question broke my unfriendly thoughts.

"Business?" The question pushed the man in what seemed to be another awkward position. It was as if he needed space to think of what was an obvious answer. I wondered if all Englishmen were like this one? Their fairies were inferior, anyway.

"Business." She said the word again, as one would to someone unfamiliar with the language.

"In some ways"—he seemed to drift and then return to us—"old family business." His voice grew tempered and restrained. "Old family business and a property dispute. Maybe all will turn out well."

"I hope it will finish in your favor." My mother's tone softened.

"Indeed." The word was almost a question, as if he hadn't expected us to sympathize with him. "I hope so too, ma'am. Thank you, it is a trying time . . . the property part especially."

"Is the holding near?"

"In Bray, actually"—he smiled restrainedly as he set his eyes on her—"in Bray. But I find the country suits me. There's no more room for another Cosgrove in England." A satirical friendliness aired from him again. He wanted to change the tone. I felt that he may have told us more than he wished. I could have eased his mind, for I was not about to send the story about. I was hardly interested, and he had interrupted our lunch.

"Well, we have been uncivil," my mother chirped, "would you take a drink with us? You must have been traveling long." She gestured to a bottle of peppermint peeping from the saddlebag.

"It would be an honor, ma'am"—he seemed strangely nervous, as if he had seen or heard something unnatural—"but I must be on my way. I have quite a journey yet, especially if I was to mislay myself again. Even with your gracious directions, my ill-formed sense of location remains a shameful attribute to my character." He smiled.

"Then," she nodded, "I will give you my gracious directions. Kilmacanogue is south of here. But it is quite a ways truly, although it is not a hard ride. No doubt, you have already traveled the road? Go down to the end here by the stream, take a left and another sharp left at the end of that road. Go south then, toward the barracks on the hill, and soon you will meet the main road to Kilmacanogue."

"I thank you, ma'am, for your help." He bowed and turned from us. We followed him to the horses, to show him which way to set off. He seemed anxious.

"Your horse is hardly in a lather from such a trip as you've had." My mother was amused. The mare's hooves were wide like Paddy's, but her coat was roan.

"She is a treasure, this mare. If it wasn't for the time, I believe you could go to China on her." He smiled and touched his hat before riding toward the stream.

We packed up our linens and set off for Carrickduff. I was glad to see the back of the Englishman. I was eased to hear my mother speak of his unique manner. I didn't want to think of myself as one who passed hasty judgments. Peader would have been disappointed with me.

As we rode along we retraced our steps in several places. The roads were soft from the past days of rain, and I could hear the mud sucking at Gavin's feet and slapping onto his lower legs. When we hit higher ground I could see the imprints we had left when riding in.

I loved the mark of hoofs, and I stared down at them as we rode along: Gavin's small and narrow, Paddy's wide and deeply pressed . . . and then another's—another's? The prints were deep and newly left, from a heavy horse, but not as large as the gelding's. They followed ours too closely, but I had never noticed anyone riding behind us. My curiosity heightened as I watched the hoof marks appear in places where we had even left the road. The marks would have matched those made by the roan mare. It was too strange to think, though, that the Englishman had followed us. What would he have cared for two riders from Carrickduff? He would have had no interest in that.

Chapter 18

The next days passed uneventfully. The sun was happy that he was being acknowledged, and he shone down upon Carrickduff until she turned back to her silver grey. They were days that you had to spend outside.

"Where's Dan?" I asked, leaning over the edge of the high stall partition.

"Out behind the carriage house," Peader answered, "where I sent him, an rógaire beag . . ." And then he started talking in Irish so I knew that he wasn't in a fine manner. He sent a rakeful of bedding straw into the wheelbarrow. He was not in his usual humor, and I figured that he was warming over the lasting impression of Dan's prank. I didn't know how he'd found out about it, but it had to be sometime after story-night. Peader seemed in an irritated temper; the volcano had erupted. I truly wasn't sure whether he was angry at being allowed to walk into an evening with Mrs. Hutcheson and Mrs. O'Toole, or if he was in a huff, because he fell for the prank with heedless abandon.

"Do you want your pony, Ms. Anne?" He said flatly.

"We're goin' schoolin'," I smiled and said it in a terribly obvious "cheer up" kind of voice that sounded so awful to the person you were addressing. I hated being "cheered up". And now I wished I hadn't done it to Peader.

"I'll bring him out to you then." Another rakeful of straw swished into the wheelbarrow. He wasn't "cheered up".

Dan was picking clean Paddy's feet out in front of the small iron-fenced island where the woman and all of those other people were buried so many years ago. The boy was bent over with the black gelding's forefoot wedged between his legs. While the horse munched the spring grass, Dan scraped the hoof quickly, and the small lumps of dirt flicked out from the hoof pick's end.

"What're you doin' out here?" I asked.

"Ah, himself doesn't want me cleanin' hoofs out in the stable," Daniel mumbled with his back to me. "He just sweeped the aisle and doesn't want to be cleaning it ten times a day, go raibh maith agat."

"He's still mad at you, isn't he?"

"Well"—Daniel lowered Paddy's foot and straightened up—"why should he be mad? I'm the one who should be mad. He played the trick on me first"—he pointed at himself—"didn't he?" His waistcoat was open, and his shirt was decorated with short black horse hairs. "If you play a trick like that on someone, shouldn't you be expectin' one comin' back at you in return?"

"That is the way it usually goes," I said.

It was terrible to have the two of them quarreling, and over something ridiculous at that. And even though I was an outsider in the feud, I felt as though I was in the middle of it; and it was a gray and taut feeling. The only thing I could think to do was to get their minds onto something else. But it was sort of like cleaning a greasy spot with water. The mess was still there, and all you did was spread it around. If Dan went riding with us, the little grey cloud would float along too and unfurl over all of us.

"Are you comin' ridin'?" I asked anyway.

He shrugged. "We'll see. Does your mother want me to take the freshness out of this one?"

"I don't know, she might." I leaned against the iron fence, and Daniel went back to hoof picking. There was a bitter air in the stable today.

"Do you know what this is?" He looked up at me as I spoke, and I tapped on the iron fence.

"Do you know why there's this gardeny thing here?"

"I don't," he answered, "never thought of it, though it could use cleaning in there I suppose."

"Under that stone there, they've put a dead woman."

He dropped Paddy's hoof and came over to me. "You're playin' me . . . that big stone there?" He leaned over the fence. "Was she dead before they put her there, or after?"

"Before, funny that." I humored him. "It's what Mrs. Byrne told me. She said that there is a woman there and some others too. But I only know about the woman. It was my grandfather that built this island, but not as a garden. They didn't know who the people were, but they wanted to see them buried in a Christian manner, and so they fenced around this garden here. It's a cemetery."

"Where'd these dead people come from?" Dan asked.

"During the Famine."

"Ah, well there you go. What is it about the woman you know?"

"She was the first dead and about thirty she was, I think Mrs. Byrne said. She must've come during the night and that's when she died. One of the old grooms found her on the carriage house step." I pointed to the building behind me.

"On the step there, right where I live?"

I nodded. "There you are walking over the spot where somebody passed on and whistling and running and not thinking anything because you didn't know."

"Aye"—he rubbed his cheek—"and me sleepin' o'er the place. She was dead on top of the step there?"

"Right on top of it, and all dew covered like the bluebells on the grave there now."

"Ah, all dew covered," Daniel repeated slowly. "And nobody knowin' who she was. She was like the Lady of Shalott but without a boat to carve her name on. And then it was only one man that took the time to read it, and that was Lancelot. And we shall muse on our lady who lay upon the stones of Carrickduff with only the tears of the dew weeping for her memory. *Oh! make her a grave where the sunbeams rest, when they promise a glorious morrow; they'll shine o'er her sleep, like a smile from the West, from her own lov'd island of sorrow.*"

"Thomas Moore is fitting," I said.

"So he is."

I helped Daniel saddle Paddy. The gelding called up a spirited manner as soon as he saw the tack, and he danced about in anticipation for the coming ride. Gavin and Ashlyn were saddled and waiting in their stalls, and Niamh was getting another pleasing day off after her Dublin trip. Peader was nowhere to be found now, and it wasn't difficult to see that he was avoiding his younger rooming partner.

"Hey!" a voice called from down the end of the side, "are ya not goin' today?"

"We are, Thomas," I answered, "we're just waitin' for father and Sheridan."

"Ah," he said. "Is Mr. O'Hayden meeting with somebody?"

"What do you mean?" That took me by surprise. I didn't know what he was talking about.

"Oh, well there's a big green coach out in your drive, so I thought you might be having guests. And it looks so much like the one you were near kil't with!"

It was the one I was nearly "kil't with". And it was my mother that came out to us. Father was talking to that older gentleman again, and I was getting tired of seeing that man interrupting our plans. My mother told us that he was an Englishman, and that was all that she knew. "The man was not taken to talking much," she said.

The coachman gave me a funny look. I didn't like that man. He had a flat small-featured face and a small flat-bottomed nose. He had tried to run us down and on top of that he gave me the funny look. He'd have to work hard to win my favors now. And besides that, he brought the man that ruined our day of schooling. There would be no jumping Daly's ditch today. Daniel took Paddy out for a gallop seeing as the horse was full of himself and ready for a ride. I didn't feel up to schooling anymore. I asked Thomas if he wanted to come up to the nursery to see my new Dublin books.

Thomas and I galloped up the stairs. My shoes clapped on the wooden steps with the sound of pony hooves. I loved stomping on the stairs, it was the grandest way to pretend that you were a horse. Thomas's unshod feet made a flat thump. His brother was wearing his shoes because he was going to town and Thomas wasn't going anywhere. We struck swiftly past Mrs. Kelly, who was polishing the steps for Norah as the girl was still in Dublin. The sudden violence of our appearance tipped her half-over, and we excused ourselves with inadequate haste, before dashing off to the nursery.

"Why is your father leavin' his room open like that?" Thomas was still standing outside the playroom's door.

"I don't know," I shrugged. I stopped and listened. There was talking coming from the study. My father was meeting with the older man from the green brougham. Their tone was unfriendly, but polite.

"All right. Let's see those books, then." Thomas left me in the hall. I didn't follow. I walked nearer to my father's study.

"Anne?" Thomas noted my absence. He came back out with one of the new books in his hand.

I went back into the nursery, but with the door left open, so that the voices from the study could be heard. Thomas sat crossed-legged on the floor with his chosen book. I sat down near to him, but I could not keep my mind from the voices.

"I do not know, sir, from where the news of this holding being offered for sale has come to meet you or your client's ears." I heard my father speak. "Carrickduff is not for sale—to anyone. That was the answer I gave to you when you last called, that is the answer that I give to you now. It will not change. I fail to see the nature of this game, but I have removed my pieces, and that is that. I do not care how much is offered, I do not care if you work for Her Majesty, I do not care if your client is homeless, or if he simply fancies the dandelions in my gravel approach—my home is not for sale."

There was a passion in my father's voice that I had never heard. It was controlled, and barely noticeable, but I knew.

"Is that it, then? I feared it would come to this." The older man spoke. "My client said it would come to this, but I had hoped you would be reasonable. Unfortunately, Mr. O'Hayden, you are not the one who will decide when the game, as you call it, has ended."

"Come to this? Come to what? Are you threatening me?" My father's chair creaked. I could almost see him leaning on the desk, the glaze leaving his pale eyes for the clearness of his anger. The peculiar accent was gone from his speech, and he spoke each word with dictionary precision. Thomas stopped his reading now, and he came nearer to me.

"No, this is not a threat, sir, no." The older man was not angry. His voice was dry and cold, as if he was merely acting in a play, as if he had proofed his lines. He sounded the sort of man that got annoyed but never angry. "I will show you what my client had wished me to produce earlier. The document that my good-nature, nay . . . my faith in yourself, sir, your sense of reason, has witheld 'til now. I see that I have judged you wrongly. Apparently I had a different notion of you Mr. O'Hayden."

"What is this document, sir." My father was growing tired and impatient. There was a rustling of paper, and then silence.

"God, what's all this about, then?" Thomas spoke. He crawled closer to me. "It's that man from the green coach that almost kilt ya'?"

"It is. I don't know what's goin' on, but ma is gettin' mad too. She wanted to send for the lawyer. Someone wants us to sell the house, but we're not sellin' 'cause it's our house. I don't like it."

"And why should ya?!" Thomas said indignantly. "It's your house. They can only take it if you don't own it like us." I stared at the lock of hair that curled from his head in the odd manner. I turned my ear to the silence. There was the hush of moving paper.

"My God," My father sighed. He must have read over the document. I didn't like the mood of his voice. I was frightened, and I was glad Thomas was there. There were footsteps on the stairs, quiet and soft. I could tell it was my mother coming up.

"Hey, there's your mother," Thomas whispered.

"Hush, I know."

"She's off to her room, eh?"

She stopped short for the voices. She had passed right by us in the nursery without noticing, and she always noticed everything. She stayed in the hall though, just outside of the study. I prayed that she wouldn't go in the study with the men, not now. I didn't know why. I just didn't want her to go.

"My God." My father repeated the words softly, as if he wanted to hear them again. "Mr. William Cosgrove." He cursed the name as it passed his lips.

"You wanted to know my client, and so there you have it. He knew that you were not going to be pleased with the circumstances. It is an unfortunate business, and I daresay that I regret the task. I want you to know that. Mr. Cosgrove has spoken of how much Carrickduff has meant to your family . . ."

"Meant to my family? Means to my family. Mr. Cosgrove does not know me. His father had darkened the name of Carrickduff forever, darkened the name of the Crawford family, and broken the lives of the tenantry. We have changed what could be saved. I was born in this house, and I have bound myself to care for her. The claim you have handed to me is ridiculous, as ridiculous as this outline of Richard Cosgrove's will."

"It is not ridiculous, I assure you . . ."

"Sir, I cannot believe that you have even taken the pains to show it to me!" The chair slid back, and I could hear my father walking inside the room. I could almost see him raking his hand through the black hair. "I cannot believe that you could have taken this on without researching the document's history. You . . . a solicitor!" The paper rustled, and I heard it struck down upon the desk. "I am sorry for you, sir, but Mr. William Cosgrove has led you down a counterfeit path. I can say this plainly now, because I can see the act before me. He is a known liar, as his father was before him. Shamed out of England was the swindling rake of his father, and God strike me down if I am wrong, sir"—his voice softened with a sorrowful tenderness—"but be this will original, its claims, its bequeaths are groundless."

"I will ignore the slandering of my client's name, for I can see you are under the effects of a heated mind. I assure you, Mr. O'Hayden, the will is genuine."

"I am sure that it is genuine. And as genuine as it is, so true is its pitiful state. I will give you, sir, the history that you are so obviously lacking." My father's voice was calm, almost mechanical. "The only thing that your client, Mr. William Cosgrove can claim as his rightful inheritence are bills, sir, bills. Mr. Richard Cosgrove, whose hand no doubt is on those papers, died debt-ridden in England. He left his wife and the name of her family shamed in Ireland; and his son, your client, God knows where in England, with this house languishing in ruin. My father bought her from the bank. A half-penniless man"—his words were slow and weary—"cannot leave a will listing a property he did no longer own. I am sorry, sir, you have wasted your time with this . . . William Cosgrove."

There was silence.

"I regret to hear that." The other man said with half apathy, as if he had asked my father a question and was now disappointed with the answer.

"And I regret to say it, sir." The words fainted on my father's lips.

My mother turned and hurried back down the stairs. I was afraid to think, but I was glad that Thomas had heard it. Things weren't so bad sometimes after Thomas knew of them. I did not want to hear about losing the house again. I wanted it to be over.

That afternoon I took Rowan for a walk near the brook that ran past the old garden that nobody tended to. I sat on a damp rock while Rowan snickered with curiosity and sniffed along the water's edge snapping at flies and pouncing fruitlessly after frogs. I was glad that he couldn't ever catch one. I would think that being eaten by a sharp-toothed stoat was an unpleasant way like that before God. Dying like the Lady of Shalott sounded rather acceptable. You went and reclined in a boat with your name carved on the front so that people would know what to write on you headstone, and then as the boat floated along you simply died, and if you went to heaven you looked wonderful and peaceful, and you would be all set. I wondered how Daniel wanted to die. I would have put a wager on him, wanting to hang in Dublin like Robert Emmet the patriot. Because if you died a patriot's death like that, then people wrote stories and songs about you because you were a hero. You didn't die for yourself like most people; you died for your country, for Ireland, and that was a big thing to die for. Maybe it was worth the few minutes, or however long it took to hang, so that you could be remembered and sung about forever. But people read about the Lady of Shalott, as well, and she wasn't a patriot, and her way was a much more leisurely way to die. I could ask Peader, but he'd just scold me for talking about "such things," and then he'd probably say something in Irish. He had lost a son and a wife, and you shouldn't talk about dying to people who have lost, because they said it was a terrible thing to go through, and I didn't want to do that to him. I could never do anything that would wrong Peader.

I wasn't going to ask my parents because it wasn't a proper thing to talk to your elders about. They would think that you were filling your head with decadent thoughts and that meant that you were given too much free time. As a result, Ms. Farrell would be contacted, and then you would be bestowed with more schoolwork. I didn't want to meddle with that either.

I snapped Rowan's leash back onto his collar, and we walked on to the cemetery where he could play in the tall grass. I wished that I had brought my black book to sketch in so that I wouldn't be thinking and conjuring up things and getting in trouble with idle hands. I sat in the grass with my hands placed beneath me.

I wondered what it was like to live in the old times in the dark ages with King Arthur and the Lady of Shalott. But they lived in England, and I would probably be stuck in Ireland since that was where I had been placed. The land was full of Celts then, and there were fairies, better looking than Mrs. Hutcheson's baby, all over the hills and mountains and fields. That's what my father told me, and he said that I should know about the history of my country. Rowan bounded over to where I was sitting. I put the leash on him, and he snickered and sniffed the air that blew about us.

"Excuse me, young miss."

I turned and startled upright. My hand gripped tight onto the leather leash. I tried to listen for the men in the fields behind the trees, but it was the second week of May, and the land was silent. I looked dumbfounded at the dark-haired man leaning on the bowed iron gate. There was the look of recognition on my face.

"Oh my!"—he bowed, removing his hat—"what a singular pleasure that we meet again. And again, in such a dreary place." The eccentric fellow referred to the hasty introduction on the day he had fallen upon our picnic. "Do you know," he continued with a cheerful air oblivious to my now open and wary expression, "I've been searching for the burial places of a few people on this note I have here." He tapped a thick paper that was rested from a pocket. "I have been informed, whether in good faith told or not, I cannot say, but it has been offered to my attention that this"—he tapped the gate—"might be the place where my journey could end."

"What are the names of those for whom you search, sir?" I answered somewhat stiffly. Rowan snickered and bounced to safety behind my legs.

"Ah, there's a most curious pet you have, miss." He smiled. "Oh, the names, well there are only two; the first and the oldest is Crawford, and the second, more current, is Cosgrove. Do you know of those names?"

"I do, sir," I said, and then not knowing whether I should have or not for I preferred the strange man to remain on the opposite side of the fence from me, and I felt that I had unwittingly opened an invitation for him to cross to my side.

"Oh, that is wonderful news. I have come a rather long and obstacled distance and that is the really best news." He folded the paper and jittered with enthusiasm. It was as if a river had dried up around a drowning man, he was that pleased. "Do you know on whose property this lone, sad graveyard rests?"

"It is my father's land, sir, and I'm sure he would not mind for you to see your stones if you were to ask. The house is but a short walk down that path. You would face the back when you come upon it." I was hoping that was enough of a suggestion to influence him to leave. "My father is in presently."

"Ah, lovely." He fumbled through another pocket and drew out a pencil and leather-cased notebook. "Might I have the gentleman's name? I'm awful forgetful; it is a curse you see." He smiled and shook his head.

"Mícheál O'Hayden."

"Ah, thank you, miss. I must say how relieved I am to find such charitable assistance."

"You are welcome, sir. I am honored to have been able to help." I was feeling at ease now that he was making notions to leave.

"Oh"—he paused with his hand brought again to the occupied coat pocket—"I know I am being a bother . . ."

"No, sir, you are not a bother at all." I answered. You are a little, I thought. It was a rare occasion for anyone to be found at this location as it was a secluded and ineffectual corner of the property. And it is somewhat uncomfortable to be in a place where you expect to see no one and then find someone there.

"You are most kind, miss, a credit to your parents' lives indeed. It has struck me that I might save your father's valuable time as I'm sure he has more pressing business than entertaining a trivial cemetery enthusiast, if any of these names I have here are familiar to you?"

"I'm sure that my father would not mind helping you, sir, as he is very fond of antiquities." If I told the man the information he needed, then he would surely go away. "I would know the names, I know all of the names in this graveyard, sir."

"Excellent!" he said and leaned upon the iron gate. "Have you seen a Crawford?"

"He is here, sir, as well as his wife and children. He had Carrickduff built, sir."

"Excellent again. I'm so very pleased. Do you know a Cosgrove?"

"I do, sir. He was the husband of one of Crawford's daughters. He is buried in England, I believe." That was all I cared to say about that man. "His wife, sir, is buried here."

"It is for the wife I was asking. And you are right there, the husband is buried in England. And that is rather an unusual circumstance, don't you think?"

"I do, sir." I wanted to clap my hand to my lips for prompting a conversation. "I'm not sure of that reason, sir."

"Ah well"—he stood away from the fence—"you have been more than helpful, young Ms. O'Hayden, is it?"

"It is, sir." Rowan walked between my legs, and I could feel his fur sticking through my stockings.

"You're probably wondering why I am after such inconsequential information?"

"No, sir. It isn't any of my business."

"But it is, this is your land." He gestured to the air around him.

"It's my father's land, in truth, sir."

"Ah, well so it is. And there is something that we do have in common, if time did not enter upon our days. For you see"—he pointed slowly to the nearest stone behind me and inclined his head for emphasis—"there is the stone that reads Crawford now, the name of my mother."

My form stiffened. He knew that I shivered for a smile showed that welcome knowledge on his lips.

"Good day, miss." A pale finger touched his hat's brim before he turned from me.

I waited for the man to go down to the bohereen, and then I picked up Rowan, squeezed through the gap in the gate and ran as fast as I dared toward

Carrickduff. I ran through the back door and released Rowan from the leash. I had to say something, but I didn't know what. What could I do? I didn't understand what I had heard. I really wanted for all of it to go away.

I found my father in the sitting room. He was in the blue chair with the golden tassels. A book was pressed open recklessly over his knee. His hand was still on the cover while his head rested against the chair's back as he was fast asleep. *So*, I thought with relief, *so now it could wait. And maybe it would go away—if one would just wait.*

Chapter 19

On Monday, Ms. Farrell and Norah returned on a morning train. Our tutor was refreshed despite her travels and the party for her mother went well. She asked me if I wanted any lessons during the afternoon after she unpacked. No, I said that I didn't want any, and I silently hoped that her unpacking would move with the same expediency enjoyed during the wretched act of packing.

My father and Sheridan had gone to town, with Gavin in the traces, to buy my mother some more photography chemicals as the weather looked promising for picture taking, and she wanted to take advantage of any light that would be available. The one individualizing point in my mother's personality was her immeasurable quantity of patience. You needed as much of it as you could hold to be a photographer with all of the things in and out of your control that could go wrong. My father's distractible temperament would never allow him success in the hobby. "The O'Haydens were naturally agitated," my mother explained, "they couldn't help it; it was in their breeding."

I went out to the barn with Rowan by my side to see Daniel and I hurried to catch him before he finished his work and went off somewhere. The barn was quiet with only a few of the hens exploring the aisle. The horses were out at pasture, and the chickens had free rein of the place without worrying about getting stepped on. They *ucked* a greeting as I passed, and I said the same back. I knew that Daniel wasn't there because the hens would've been gathered around him, especially Cecely, who was very fond of the boy. I let Rowan loose and he scampered around sniffing the chickens until an aggravated Catherine gave him a solid pick on the nose that sent him scurrying for the carriage house.

I went around toward the rear of the barn, where I found Daniel resting against the corner wall with a peculiar, occupied gaze on his face.

"What do you see?" I asked.

"Hush, listen! It's Peader round the corner talking to that old gentleman that was here talkin' to your father."

I closed in next to the boy and listened. He took me by the shoulders and inched me over to the corner of the stables. I peered around and I saw the strange man addressing our Peader. The man was in a brown frock with matching trousers and waistcoat. He wore an old-style haircut, and was handing a document over to Peader. I shivered after having studied the man's face. It was again the solicitor from the green brougham. It was the one that had argued with father the other day.

"The gentleman, Mr. O'Hayden, is not home, sir. You'd be wise to give me the papers so, he'll be sure to get it." Peader reached his hand out for the papers.

"Pardon, sir, but I truly wish to hand this to your master directly." The old gentleman stepped a pace back.

"He does not wish to speak to you, sir. I believe he's already discussed this matter with you and has given his answer, am I correct?" Peader inclined his head. I think that my mouth was open because Daniel clapped his hand to my mouth, thinking that I was daft enough to speak. I was a little insulted at his underestimating my perspicacity, for after all, I was still second in command of "Les Hirondelles". And if we weren't be secret, I would have made my views known.

"I do not discuss any matter with servants," The man said ostentatiously.

"Ah, well so I would bring out Padraic then, he's a man like yourself, sir. And if you'd pardon me for sayin' so, sir, the resemblance from behind is uncanny."

"Please, do so." The man half closed his eyes.

"Well, I'd go quickly to find him, but he's gone out, you see."

The older man was perturbed, and it seemed as though it was taking all of his will for restraint to prevent him casting torments at his clever rival.

"Against my better judgment, and I say that with the utmost certainty, I will hand over these documents to you. And I warn you, sir"—he snatched the envelope back toward himself—"if I do not hear from your master in a week's time, than I will assume that he did not receive these." He tapped the papers aggressively, "and I will have you summoned to court!" The man finally handed the papers over to our friend with such pains as if his wife was inside the envelope. Peader took the envelope with an elegant action, removed his hat with a dandy's flourish, and he bowed before the old gentleman, bidding him a good day.

My father and Sheridan returned at one with the photography chemicals. He was commandeered by Peader in the hall, and the older man presented him with the envelope. My father opened the letter and perused the text swiftly. He put the document back into the envelope and asked Peader to follow him to his office. Neither men looked pleased, and I figured that this was a bad time to tell my father about the man in the cemetery.

I met up with Sheridan, and we went up to the nursery for lunch. We ate in less than fifteen minutes in order to have a large amount of playtime without too much of it being wasted for such necessities as dining. My brother ran out before me to see if Daniel was free to go down to the stream and search for frogs with us. I stayed behind to snap Rowan's leash on. Donovan flew to the window and rapped the pane with his heavy beak. I left Rowan, but he followed anyway, trailing the leather lead behind him and waiting by my feet as I opened the stubborn, old window for the raven. I could only budge the swollen wood up half a foot. I told Donovan that he would have to squeeze and make do with the space I gave him or go through the back door like the rest of us. He bent his head, flattened his shoulders, and waddled under the sill taking some loose flakes of paint with him, before pushing off to freedom as best he could. Whenever I saw him go, I was always want to consider where it was his flight would take him, and whether or not he stopped to visit anyone along the way. He never told, or maybe he did, and we didn't quite know how to understand.

How many people, in fascination, muse over thoughts of speaking to God's creatures, wondering with scientific method whether or not those creatures could ever learn to talk? And to this the animals would answer, "*that we the beasts both wild and tame, have been speaking through all of the days present and since and it is not a matter of us talking, good scientists and assorted society, but rather it is a matter of you learning how to listen.*"

I picked up Rowan and I left the nursery, shutting the door behind me. I walked the long way toward the stairs, the way that ran past my father's study, and I stopped outside the door where the voices carried out from inside that room with the Indian statues and the rusty knife from '98. The voices belonged to my father and Peader, and they must have stayed there since I had last seen them leave the downstairs hall.

"No, they can't mean anything by it, you're right there sir?" I heard Peader say.

"An old will is an old will, and the man who wrote it was a drunk and a deserter. He can have no claim to a place that was wrongfully treated and rightfully bought."

"What kind of a fellow is that, that won't show his face, and forever sending a solicitor like that." I heard papers shuffle on my father's desk.

"Seems to run in the family then doesn't it?" Peader added.

"I'll play the same game then," my father spoke, and he must've leaned back in his chair for I heard the wooden joints creak. I envisioned him there with his long legs stretched out and his hands clasped over his chest. "I'll send for Mr. Richardson, we will play this out solicitor to solicitor. That was what Carolyn wanted."

"That's the way to do it, sir. It's queer, sir, but a wife keeps a strange gift of knowledge about those things."

"And I'll do it before the deadline so that you won't be carted off to gaol, Peader."

"Ah, that's a grand decision, sir." I heard Peader laugh, and I heard my father join in the fun.

The chairs shifted on the floor. I ran down the stairs before they left the room. So that old man and the fellow in the cemetery were allies then. What did they want with Carrickduff? It was our house, and my father already made it known that we weren't interested in selling. And what did the will have to do with the business, or did that connect with the Englishman telling me that we both had parental ties to the land. It was a strange connection of circumstances to be considering on another day off.

"Ah, there's not a lot of frogs here?" Sheridan was bent over the stream. He was perched on a rock in the middle. Rowan was on the boulder beside him sniffing wherever Sheridan dabbled in the water.

"That's because there aren't enough reeds, and rushes, and things," I said teetering on a piece of ledge that rocked whenever I shifted my weight.

"Let's go by the pond then, that's where they'll be for sure, there's lots of weeds there."

Daniel crossed over a rickety and haphazard boulder bridge that we had hastily constructed the summer before.

"Maybe there'll be some of those little black, fishy things." Thomas jumped across. "What do they call 'em?"

"Tadpoles," I said, skipping the last stone and jumping up on the bank.

"Didn't I catch one once and have it grow up," Thomas said.

"I thought that they were already grown up?" Sheridan said.

"How big do they get?" I asked.

"Oh, they don't . . . ." Daniel inserted.

"Shut up, I want to tell 'em." Thomas nudged the older boy. "Sure you wouldn't believe it to see it. And I'm glad I kept the little, fishy thing in the 'odd tool' shed, for my mother would've shot it away if she saw what became of it. She would've said there was nothin' good in a creature that could do that."

"Could do what?" I said.

"Turn into somethin' else." Thomas nodded.

"What do you mean?" Sheridan glowered, feeling taunted by his friend.

"That is what I mean. It turned into somethin' else, it was done all slow like though, so you could see everythin'. You wouldn't believe it to see it."

"Yes, you would," Daniel added. "That's what they all do."

"Shut up." Thomas nudged him again. "You'd swear it was one of the sidhe, like a selkie, the seals that become women."

"What do you mean?" Sheridan squinted a glance.

"They're never happy on the land those women. They're never happy anywhere land or water." Daniel shrugged. "They're cast a sad lot. There's a fairy seal sittin' on a sea rock and she sees for herself a handsome man, and they'd all be handsome to her anyway as Merrow men are terrible ugly with fish faces and scaled bodies. Well, she sees that human and off she goes to turn into a woman as she knows that human men aren't fond of weddin' seals, or at least she's never seen it happen anyway, and she's not interested in takin' any chances. So when she reappears to him as a beautiful human, it's not long before they wed. She's fond of her circumstances at first but then as the years pass, she spends more and more time by the sea, and her very soul yearns most desperately for the coolness of the waves. And the husband always wonders why at the warmth of his hearth she stares through the flames as if the smoke could carry her away. And so it is that one night, the sound of the sea and the fresh smell of the brine drive her from the house, and just as she pined for life as a woman, she now pined for life as a free-livin' seal. The man never sees her again, and he never knows that she waits and watches still for his boat. He sees the creature on the sea washed rock, the fine sea-grass growin' on its boat-crushin' head. He watches the grass lift and unfurl in the swells like the hair of a drowned maiden. He turns his gaze to the seal that had yet to flee from him. He looked at the whiskers and the wet, shiny hair, and he met the stare of familiar eyes before the animal returned to the sea."

"Well, that's what you get for marryin' a seal," my brother said.

"They are not just seals, they're selkies, there's a difference," Thomas explained.

"How is that," my brother taunted, "and what's it to do with tadpoles?"

"One's a fairy, and the other is a plain seal," I finished the debate. "It's got nothin' to do with tadpoles."

"Ah, the tadpole wasn't a selkie." Thomas returned to his original story. "It turned into somethin' else, and it took its time too."

"Whatever happened to that tadpole?" I asked, pushing the story along.

"The little black, fishy-thing turned into a frog." The boy nodded. "There were legs poppin' out of it as plain as day, and then the fishtail disappeared as sure as I'm standin' here."

"You really expect me to believe that!" My brother's mouth made an *O* with surprise.

"'Tis true!" Thomas confirmed.

"Aye"—Daniel came to a prosaic rescue—"tadpoles grow up into frogs. Everybody knows that."

"Not everybody," I corrected. "I wouldn't mind seein' one turn from a fish to a frog." I wondered if the tadpole knew that it was turning into something and what did it feel like to have legs popping out of your body. "Whatever did you feed it?"

"Green stuff out of the pond and beans." Daniel smiled.

"Why beans?" I asked.

"They're soft." Thomas justified the use of beans as a tadpole foodstuff.

"What happened to the frog?" Sheridan asked.

"We put him back in the pond with the others," Daniel said, pointing toward the trees where the stream poured into the large lake-pool that old Mr. Crawford had dammed over one hundred years before.

The pond was a grand place. You could see it from the top floor in the rear of the house. The croquet lawn rolled down to the front of the dammed pool, where the willow was, but we always approached it from the path that ran along the stream, because that led to the back of the pond where the reeds, and the rushes, and the cattails grew. The grass grew as tall as your waist, and you had to dodge the thistles and briars that were lying in wait to tear your socks and sting your legs. Once you passed the grassy area there was a narrow clearing of sand and stone awaiting you as your brave reward.

Daniel climbed the oak tree that bent toward the water and Rowan tried to follow, but he couldn't get past the first steep climb of too-smooth trunk. Thomas walked over toward the narrow stand of reeds and a little startled splash heralded his approach.

"I saw him!" Daniel called. He nodded and pointed to the ripple running to shore. "That was a small frog."

Rowan dashed to the source of the splash and snickered and sniffed the water's edge before gently forging the chilly main. He paddled out and tacked a left for the reeds. He liked to fish, but he was a sorry fisherman and he usually satisfied himself with a meal of water beetles.

We all removed our shoes and stockings, except Daniel who was perched in the oak, and we waded into the slimy carpeted water. The first step was frightfully cold, but once you staunchly bore the initial leg-numbing process you were free to cavort as you wished. There were boulders and small rocks galore in the mud, and each wore a coat of slime. And if you weren't careful to mind your step, you'd be down in the water before you knew that you had slipped.

Once Peader waded in with me as he was very fond of birds, and I had found a little grebe's nest down at the edge of the pond. The only way that you could get to it without disturbing the feathered setter was by way of the water. Peader had his trousers rolled up neatly round his thighs, and he rolled up his sleeves. I thought that he'd never actually get into the pond with all of the tedious preparations he was taking. He took off his left shoe, and then the right, and he set the socks over each mate of a shoe as if he wouldn't remember which foot to put which sock over, as if it would matter anyway. I started to wonder just how very long it must take for Mr. Hayes to ready himself for a bath, but that wasn't a proper thing for a young lady to think about. We finally made it into the water, taking painful precautions so as not to disturb the grebe. I rounded the patch of weeds, and I slowly motioned Peader to follow. He waded up behind me and was just about to peer over my shoulder for a view of the nest, when one of his feet must have slipped from a stone for there came a great splash behind me which sent the little grebe flapping into the water, and myself turning to find my bird-watching companion full out in the drink. It was rather a shame, since he had taken such exquisite precautions before wading in. The shoes and socks were as dry as bread upon the shore; while their owner was as thoroughly sodden as the fish in the pond, for which he had a better view than for the grebe on the bank.

Daniel had said that sometimes older people had unsatisfactory control over their legs. I was inclined to agree, as I can't say that I've ever seen an adult climb a tree or run for no reason. I suppose then that one should get all of their allotted tree climbing and nonsense running before one became an adult and inherited the unsatisfactory leg control.

We waded among the reeds for frogs, with Rowan paddling around our legs. Daniel pointed the small shiny creatures out to us from his perch. I detected a green frog under a lily leave. His head was just above the water. I stalked in from behind, and I am certain that frogs have been graced with the power to see behind them, for this one dove under as soon as I started for him. Thomas was content enough by just following tadpoles, and that seemed to be a more fulfilling hobby by far.

"I'm not catchin' any frogs, I'm not even gettin' near any frogs." I wiped the loose hairs from my face, and straightened.

"I'm not either. This rots," my brother scowled. "Why don't we go in the boat?"

Daniel jumped from the tree. "Thomas can float it over to us and pretend that he's the Lady of Shalott."

"Thomas will do no such thing, and will not be the Lady of Shalott." The young Mr. Timoney spoke up from behind the cattails. "We all will go to get the boat. It's not my boat."

"Hey, where's Rowan?" I searched the shallows to show him that we were about to leave.

"He's not likely to go under, he could swim clear across the Atlantic to Ameri-kay." Daniel clicked to him from the shore.

I climbed the bank and moved along the weeds and grass. Over by a large stone, I made out a patch of ruddy brown something of a texture rarely found in the plant kingdom. "Come here, Rowan!" I called but he didn't make any motions to answer. I called again and received a similar response. I would have to pick him up. He would acknowledge you when the mood suited him, otherwise he was as "deaf" as an acorn. He curled up tight when he heard me approach, and I reached down carefully so as not to be bit. He tried to run, but I had him firm and it was then that I noticed the reason for his misanthropic behaviour. Somebody had caught a frog that day and had invited the poor beast for dinner.

Chapter 20

I was wasting an afternoon playing chess with Sheridan. I could have been doing nothing, even if it was sinful. We were playing on the old, gate-legged side table in the carriage house. Peader was sitting by the window with his "rheumatic" legs propped upon a stool. He was nestled behind the daily paper, and every other moment the air was startled by the rustled turning of a page. Rowan was undisturbed by this, and continued to snooze away on the man's lap with the deepness of dreams only obtained by stoats.

Daniel leaned upon the playing-table with his chin resting on his arm, and his eyes drying out from their aimless staring. He was supposed to be timing our game to mark how fast Sheridan would beat me, but I was afraid that he had fallen asleep with his eyes open. Only goldfish and others of the sort could do that safely, seeing as they lived in the water. Daniel was likely to end up blinded, and all because of a chess game. I clicked my piece extra hard upon the board to startle him and save his sight. Sheridan won all of us at chess, save old Mrs. Byrne the dairy woman, and that was a miracle yet to be understood. That woman had a gift beyond the nurturing of pineapples, and tomatoes, and milk.

I hated playing chess, or ficheall, as Peader called it. My brother loved it and so out of charity, occasionally I would give him a game. I wasn't set against chess only. I disliked all table games, although I could manage to enjoy an evening game of charades. Charades was sociable, unstructured, and of a purely ridiculous, theatrical nature. Should I be granted a moment's leisure, I would rather spend it with a book, a beast, or the unbound ways of the fields. But today, I was playing chess. My mind was as far away as a mind could travel, and I lost the game with merciful speed.

"You're not even playin'!" my brother snapped. "You lost on purpose!"

I smiled. I had played three games and that was the third round. I was free. Daniel had to take my place. He wasn't all that fond of chess either, but he too had pledged three rounds.

I left Rowan on his living paper-reading seat, and I went back to the main house. I didn't know what I was going to do, but should I meet no diversions I would go for a walk. I wouldn't go far lest I see that man again. I would just stay away from the cemetery.

Donovan was poking around the house's gravel approach. The raven was moving away the rocks from the base of a flowering dandelion with the concentration of a brick layer. There was an ant's nest by the root, and he was enjoying the plundered spoils. He licked his beak and croaked as I approached. I waited for him to finish before I carried him into the house.

My father and mother were talking in the sitting room. I heard their voices. I told Donovan to stay quiet while I sneaked closer to the noise. They weren't arguing, but they weren't chatting either. It was a different form of exaggerated talking with the immediacy of a quarrel. It sounded as if it was all over the strange man that had come calling a few days before over the selling of our house which wasn't for sale. My mind saw the man in the green coach that had tried to cut my leg off, so that I couldn't go to heaven with all of the parts that I wanted to go with, and I'd be forced to go like Thomas's uncle that was hit by the dray. I became angry thinking about it. What right did anybody have to take off parts of you without telling you about it? Did they ever stop to think that maybe you had planned to meet God, or the Devil, or wherever you were going with both your arms and legs? If it wasn't for the sake of the hat-sellers, there was no need for most people to be bothered with having a head. And that saying proved that Peader was a genius, smarter than Ms. Farrell in some things.

I heard the rough edged discussion end and my mother said something about telling the solicitor just in case, and to stop "covering over" things, she had a "right to know".

She met me and Donovan in the hall and there was a wrinkle of strain on her smooth half-expressionless face. I knew that she had thought me to be playing in the carriage house, and I was now an unexpected ghost appearing at an inconvenient moment.

"Oh, Anne!" My mother seemed embarrassed. She looked over her shoulder in an agitated way. I watched as she recovered herself. I knew that she was going to lie about what had been going on, as adults always did, but that was all right. Nothing much ever involved me anyway. Unless, of course, they were planning to catch hold of the man that had almost cut off my leg, even though they didn't know about that.

"Have you just come in?" She asked smiling, trying to hide her agitation. She hoped that I was going to say "no," that I didn't hear much.

"No." I shook my head. I hadn't been long inside, and it was true, I didn't hear much save the parts about getting the solicitor and the "stop coverin' over things." But I did hear the quarrel in their voices, the soft argument. They weren't supposed to argue because they liked each other. I liked Daniel, and we never argued, we just disagreed without raising our voices.

"I played my three rounds and then I left, as Daniel had pledged three with Sheridan. Rowan was sleepin', and Peader's readin' the paper so he'll soon be sleepin' too."

Donovan croaked, and nodded for my mother to scratch his neck feathers.

"Sheridan loves to play chess, that was nice of you. Do tell him for me, I will pledge him a game after supper?" She was trying not to be angry anymore. "Will Thomas come this evenin'?"

"No, he has to go to town with his father."

"Oh, it's good to see a father and son go on so kindly. He is a soft-natured man, Mr. Timoney. I'd like to peel away the rind for the sweet parts to come out," she laughed, "like a French cheese. Carrickduff would melt it out of him, look what she did to your father. Maybe Thomas'll convince him to come someday, to see what wonders lie behind these walls."

"Maybe." I was wondering what she was talking about. I never saw any wonders around here, save that Peader was a mind-reader and he could say "arse" better than anyone, even though you weren't supposed to say it. Maybe she meant that? "I'm goin' out to play with Donovan, I think."

"All right, then." She said. "But stay by the house." She sent a dark glance toward the sitting room where my father was still.

I nodded.

My mother turned and walked past me, the mass of dress fabric rustled with her fluid steps. She was thinking, I could tell by the way she walked. She probably wanted to go away somewhere, but she couldn't. It was not the time. She would go and read her books instead. She must have been a brilliant woman, for going over piles of books was all that she did.

My father was standing in front of the wall with all of the bookshelves stuck into it. He didn't seem to be looking for any books, he just seemed to be standing and staring at the air as if one of the heavy-covered tomes was going to pop out and talk to him. I was watching and waiting. He didn't know that I had come in, but he must have heard me talking in the hall. I was going to turn quietly away, but Donovan croaked to his like-haired, and now startled, master. Our position was summarily revealed, my father seemed as one tossed from a dream.

"Ah, is the chess all over?" His eyes darted from me to Donovan, toward the door and back. He sighed. No, she's gone, I wanted to say. Yes, I heard you talking. I felt the ordeal in his voice. It was low then, almost a whisper, but one that you could hear clearly. The words were expressionless. They echoed through you like a sound in your sleep. I still didn't want to tell him about the man in the cemetery.

"I played my rounds," I answered, "and now Dan's doin' his."

"Oh, now what does your brother think about you two martyrs offering up yourselves as such dry matchmates?" He leaned on the inset bookcase with the other arm sticking out from his narrow waist. He tried to take the soft anger away by swallowing.

"He doesn't think too much of it, so long as someone plays. My rounds are the shortest." I smiled with pride.

"Are you that bad of a player?" My father acquired an amused expression of surprise. It was barely noticeable, but for him it was a lot.

"I am not. I do it on purpose, so that I can go away faster. I don't like chess. I don't like games."

"Wily, are you?" He raised an eye. His voice was warming, and I felt happy.

"Wily, the best. And Donovan's just as wily."

"I'll be wise to keep an eye out for you two, then."

"You would be, but we'll be one step ahead like highwaymen." I tried to look sneaky.

"Now what are people gonna say when they've heard I've brought up a daughter who's a highwayman? That's from your mother's pirate side," He sneered. "Have you come for a book, you rogue?"

"I think so. I was gonna go out with Donovan, but maybe I'll have a book."

"Do you know what I was readin' about?" He crossed his arms and dropped his chin. Some dark hair uncurled upon his cheek. His nose seemed angular in that position, and he looked like a hawk.

I could tell that he wanted to talk, and that was fine. I liked to be with him. I was proud to see people noting his beauty. He was my father, I would say in my head. You were given your father at birth, and no one could change that, money couldn't buy it, and he was mine. I knew that he would be valiant like uncle Paul in Australia, if he had to be.

"No, I don't know what you were readin'." I scratched Donovan's flat head.

"I was reading about a place far from here, all the way across the country, off of the western shores, and out into the Atlantic waves."

"America?"

"No, not that far, and farther still." He sat in the big armchair, and rested his chin on his hand. "I can tell you where, and how to go, and what to expect, but neither I nor you could find it, should we ever set out."

"Even with the best of sailors?" I asked.

"Even with the best. To go there is like being happy. You can say what it is to be happy, you can read about it, you can see it in others, but it must come to you because no one can tell you how to be happy. You can't even try to be so, you either are or not. And so it is with going to this place in the sea. It must come to you." He clasped his hands before him. "I suppose I shouldn't have mentioned anything." He looked at my face.

"Oh," I said with a touch of disappointment. Donovan squirmed, and I put him down.

"But"—he touched his clasped hands to his thin lips—"I would go so far, and boldly to say that I'd bet this place is fairer than Florence even. Oh, there's no Michelangelo, no Leonardo, but there's things just as grand, and to put the roof on the house of cards, I'd ne'er get a day older than I am now." He smirked like a schoolboy. There was some animation in his face, some melody in his voice.

"Not a day?"

"Well, maybe a day, but no more." He tilted his head. Donovan mimicked the tilt, and waddled over to the chair. He jumped upon its stuffed-fabric arm, and poked my father for a pet.

"Do you think it might be good if I told you? Just in case you see, should you ever find yourself being asked there, like that one man I heard of, then you'd know what you were getting into, what to expect."

"It's always good to know what you're gettin' into." I tried to hide my curiosity. I was dying to know all the strange things he was telling me.

"So, it is. I agree entirely. Test the water before the plunge." He gestured me over to him, and he sat me down upon his lap.

I had to set my weight against the chair arm now, because I was getting to heavy, not for him but for me. His leg was too narrow, and I was too big to rest there comfortably. He seemed smaller than he was when I was younger. I was thinking about the things that happened when you got older, old like Mrs. Byrne. You got the unsatisfactory leg control, the beady eyes that Peader was not old enough to have yet, and then the shrinking. You shrunk when you aged. Mrs. Byrne was short, and now father was smaller. Maybe it had something to do with having children. I was getting bigger, people always said that. It was the first thing they said, so it must have been pretty noticeable. But where was all my new height coming from? I believe it possible to think that children appropriated some of that height from their parents. Whether it was taken from the top or the bottom, I do not know. The result, as consequence, was that the parent began to shrink. And so, by the time that they grew old like Mrs. Byrne, they could be quite small, according to the size and number of their height stealing young ones. I say that because Mrs. Byrne was small, and she had quite a few children to take the height off of her. I would bet that she was once a rather tall woman, near six feet or more. Peader wasn't small because his poor son had died before the boy could take the height from him, and so now Peader wouldn't have to worry about shrinking. I am not going to have any children, so. I don't want to shrink.

I looked at my father's pale eyes and at the hard face where they lived. I hoped that my mother saw some sense when she was talking angrily at him, and I hoped that he saw that sense in her. A door shouldn't argue with a doorknob, or a doorknob with a door. They had to live together, and that was that. Even the man with the green brougham couldn't take that away, so they shouldn't have been quarreling.

"I want to know what happened to the man that you knew, who went to that place in the sea. I would know what to do then."

"Well, I really didn't know the man, but I felt as though I did from hearing the story. There were three men, actually." My father's voice was soft and punctual, the words rolled from him, one to the next, and each of the same timbre and melody.

"Tell me about the first man that your father told you about."

"Ah, the first man was Ryan, I think. But that doesn't matter. The man was fishing with his brother and neighbor. They were off the Clare coast, and it was a beautiful, calm day, so they went out a little farther than usual. They had taken quite a catch and were as happy with that as anyone would be. All three o' them were daydreaming about the money they'd be bringing home. The neighbor man said, to the agreement of all, that he was sure that was the greatest they had taken. Well, there was no rush in going home, and they settled down for a smoke and a repast."

"Was this long ago?"

"Not too long, I don't think, but before we were born."

"That's a long time."

He nodded. "When you're eleven." He smiled.

"Everythin's a long time," I sighed.

"Well, it won't always be. And that's what happened to our fishermen. Time went too quickly, and there was a fog settling in from the depths of the sea. The men set sail for the shore, and the wind was with them. It was with them, so they thought. And in came the fog like earth hugging smoke riding the sea winds, and it was circling the boat as a spider binds her prey. They didn't know which way was to shore and which to the Atlantic. They could no longer follow the wind, for it seemed to shift and turn with each deep breath of fog. It's a terribly frightening thing to be lost on the water. They were never so alone as then." He took his eyes from me, and he gazed at the door and out the open frame. He seemed to be looking for something, or someone.

"I don't like to be lost." My voice startled him back. You shouldn't have shouted, and she shouldn't have shouted. I know what you're thinking.

"Being lost wastes time, unless you're somewhere nice," I muttered.

"Indeed, and this wasn't somewhere nice. The sea was asking for their lives. So they lowered the sails and waited it out. It was best to be patient, and if the fog should break, they might spot a light or some sign off the shore. And sure, they hadn't waited an hour and the brother asked for assurance that he had spotted a light flickering in the mist. They all saw it. It was faint, and a strange white and blue. It was feeble and far off, but to the desperate men it was the star of Bethlehem leading the Magi, and so they set off toward the glow. But the closer they sailed, the farther off seemed the flicker. The fog grew heavier, and it cloaked the tiny beacon. A bell clanked and tolled with the rhythm of the waves, just like metal against tin, and then again like a cathedral's chime, and the men moved toward that. A wind sighed eastward, blowing the mist to shore, and there in the cleared space it left arose an island out of the sea. The mens' souls eased at the sight, and they made for the land, their deaths postponed."

"Was it cold on the sea?" I asked.

"I believe it was. Not really cold, but damp and salty as the early morning by the shore. It was a cold you could taste." He paused.

"Our fellows had not much of an idea what the time was, for it seemed they had been out for days. Their bodies were sickened by the seaweed-smelling fogs of brine. All they wanted was for their tired legs to feel the earth and for their noses to smell the land. They were nearing the island, and so close to it now that the neighbor marked out the lights over the hills, and he thought he was mad with fatigue, for he was hearing laughter and jovial talking from the shore. He wasn't mad, for all the men heard, and there was music coming to them over the waves. They were cautious now to clear the rocks, the low cliffs reaching out to the sea that would dash apart the boat. But just as they set to turning, the sea wind set herself against them, and the men feared they would be thrown upon the rocks. But there was nothing to fear, the wind died as fast as she came. The mist cleared to show the island with the lights and the laughter, one hundred yards off. 'We were just on the rocks!' the brother yelled. 'I could've cast a rope to 'em they were that close.'" My father pretended to throw the phantom rope, with despair in his hands.

"They sailed again for the shore, but again came the wind and the fog. On the third try the sea rose against them, the wind lifted the waves over the sides of the fishing boat, and the bells clanked and chimed with the sound of death in their desperate ears. The swells crashed upon the bow, and the tired men were dampened and weakened with the spray. So now they thought they would die now on the most splendid day of the year, with the most splendid catch of their lives. The island sat in the distance. The music still echoed despite the rage of the sea. The laughter tinkled with the bells as the darkness fell. There was no sound to the night, and the seas dropped their tantrum, lapping the boards of the boat like a cat stroking her sides. Exhausted, they slept where they fell 'til the dawn cleared the Atlantic and sparkled on the water. The sunlight rolled with the waves. The men shielded their brows from her glare. They searched the distance with their light-stung eyes, and there was nothing but the sea." He waved his hand in front of him to measure the emptiness.

"The island was gone." I reached for Donovan who had been sitting comfortably all the while.

"Gone. Not a sign of it—the mists, the bells, the cliffs, the laughter—all of it gone. The man who I think was Ryan walked to the front of the boat, and a flash of excitement bade him call out to the others. The shore from whence they had sailed that morning past spread before the bow. And when they had landed not one made a mention of the island in the ocean—not the laughter, not the music, not the bells, none of it. But one day that Ryan fellow told my father, your grandfather, and it never went further'n that 'til today. And you must tell it to your own children only, my wee girl?" He touched my hair.

"I don't want children"—*for the shrinking, of course*—"but then I will tell it to them. I will keep the secret."

"Do you know what that island is in the water, with the bells and all?"

"No."

"It is the island that few have come to know and others have died trying. It is the Land of the Young, Tir na n'Óg, where no one grows old like me." He laughed and touched my nose. "It is where nobody falls with sickness, where the trees always fruit, where there is laughter and merry-makin'—"

"And nobody quarrels."

His face froze, and his lips were parted, just. I turned away from his always-distant eyes. I knew that he was still looking at me even though the stare seemed to pass through me, as if I was no more dense than glass. I could feel his eyes move, and he locked them on the open doorway as a hawk chooses his meal.

"They do not argue, save when there is a need, but only then." He touched my cheek. The hand was cold.

"Are there céilí's and storytellin'? I would miss them." He let his arm fall about my waist.

"There's the best you've ever known. And when all the quarreling is forgot for joy, you would never know such pleasure. There graze the finest steeds to match the levity, great men to match the steeds, and women with the grace and pride of the dawn to rhyme with those men. It is the past of our country, the will inside us, the dreams of our land as she stirs in her sleep."

My country stirs in her sleep 'til the dawn rests her from her chains. That is what Daniel wrote in the newspaper poem. Carrickduff had awoke, and we had roused her. Now there is laughter and levity, and no quarreling, and no strangers who do not think, and waste their heads but for the hat-maker as they drive about wild to tear you apart. Those things cannot happen in my house.

Chapter 21

It was most remarkable to consider the changeableness of a two-week frame. Classes had again started with a vengeance. Rowan had slowly shaken his offensive reputation as one who dined on frogs. He had missed the close proximity that he had shared with members of the household and was befuddled as to why he was no longer showered with carresses and scratches. Peader and Daniel had abandoned their grievances as swiftly as they had adopted them originally. My father had contacted Mr. Richardson, Esquire, and the case had been handled in the alloted ten days time so that Peader was not carted off to gaol. I had dismissed the strange man in the cemetery from my thoughts.

Thomas's family had experienced a hard time of things lately, and their "larder" had been woefully low. They were desperately scratching up all savings and such so that they may have enough to pay the coming rent. We would have offered help, of course, but they would never have taken anything from a family at Carrickduff. Thomas had been taking dinner with us.

"Anne, now there's a sorry face to go around with." My mother stared at me from her generously built library chair. She had a book by Trollope open on her silk covered lap. "You should choose a better volume, if the present one causes such a look to fall on you."

I smiled. It was near midnight, but I was allowed to stay up on summer weekends. The days seemed to live forever and still not be long enough.

"Is it Thomas that's bothering you?" She leaned forward. Her expression begged for me to talk. "Poverty is a curse, but to dismiss opportunity is a worse thing. It's a bad thing being done for that boy. I hope he has the judgment that his father never showed." She turned to check the lamp on the high narrow table, and the light flickered across her left cheek and spilled over the dip in the bridge of her nose.

It wasn't unusual for strangers to think of Carolyn O'Hayden as my older sister, and she'd blush as she corrected the unintentional compliment. She possessed the quiet spirit so illustrated by writers—that balance of mind and beauty, desired by women and respected by men.

"Will you say that he has the judgment?" She would speak to me as though I were of adult age. Childish talk was forbidden, as it encouraged the formation of a weak mind.

"I think that he does," I said. I played uncomfortably with my book, not looking at her.

"Ah, then why are you brooding?" She tilted forward in a rustle of cloth.

"Why have we what we have, and the others have hardly what they need?"

"I could tell you that your grandfather and then my father had made their fortunes, and then that we have cultivated them wisely, but I know that is not what you are asking. I can offer the few reasons I have for such things. Your father's sire had a deliberate son, and so we are as we are. Thomas's father concerns himself with bringing in the troubles he doesn't have, and culturing them there under his own roof, and denying those access who wish to help. A man who does nothing when others are willing should have very little to say about anything. I can only answer part of your question because misfortune falls where it wishes, and it is a heavy cloth to shake."

Her green eyes were blackened by the flame, and her dried-straw hair reddened in the halo of weak light. "Don't you worry over Thomas, Anne, we'll have him soon enough." She smiled. It wasn't my father's smile, wolflike and narrow. He could never reflect the emotions of his mind through his features. I'm sure that he thought he did, as he was a tempestuous willed but compassionate man, the kind that would offer the contents of his purse to the lowest street child and be left bereft of his own dinner. We were all taught that the rich should give of themselves, because wealth was a burden unless it was made to do things for others brought low by fate. My mother matched his sympathy, but even coming from the tinderbox of a patriot family as she did, she was never tempestuous. She was straight and proud, and her stare stopped full at your eyes without searing through. They had said that Carolyn from Cahirciveen would never be married for no man could break a will like that, but they did not know that clear across the island there lived a black-haired man from the valley of Glendalough who could match it. Old widow Byrne told me that.

I stared at the pages of my book, but I wasn't reading any of the words. I was thinking of Peader. I knew why my mother didn't mention him as she assumed that

I wasn't familiar with his history. I was sure that she had planned to tell me some day, but Mrs. Byrne had taken the bit. How strange of fate to hand suffering over to a man like Mr. Hayes. A man who thought nothing for the ways of misfortune was fully dealt the wrath of it. Mr. Timoney tempted such sadness; he should have spoken to Peader, for that man down by the bohereen did not know to watch for what he wished. "It is a shaded life we are given, and the clouds and the rain wait in the distance. We all must build mountains to arrest their advance. We must cast hope, like dust, into the face of despair," so said my mother.

There was an accelerated rapping at the library's paneled door. The noise was unexpected as it was quite late in the night, and I turned to it.

"There's no need to bang"—my mother did not move from the chair—"just come straight in!"

"I usually do"—the voice was quickened—"the lock has gone all stiff again. Oscail an doras, le do thoil!"

My mother rose swiftly now incited by the voice's spirited tone. She twisted the iron knob, and a squeak ground out from the old lock. She pressed her shoulder to the door and pushed up on the knob to align the lock and twisted. The lock clumped open, and the door was pushed in from the outside. Peader bent his shoulder to match his mistress's height. He then spoke hushed and quickly in Irish, so that I could not understand. And I was sure that was the desired effect.

"Tá an scioball cló ag dó! Thug Daniel an solas faoin deara ar a bhealach abhaile, ach bhí sé aniomarca don bhuachaill. Tar tháinig sé chomh topaí agus a d'fhéadhfadh."

"Imigh leat agus fáigh Mícheál, Peader! Imigh anois!" She took the man's arm and turned him from the room. "Anne"—she turned to face me—"you and Sheridan come down to the library. See Ms. Farrell and have her stay with you, and bring your brother down, he is in his room."

She lifted her skirt and dashed from the library. Her low boots tapped over the floor, and I followed quickly from the room. I turned the hall corner too fast, and I had to catch the edge of the wall to keep from slipping. The leather on my shoe soles was a hindrance to my speed, but I slid and scampered up the stairs to my brother's room.

"Sheridan! Sheridan!" I drummed my fist on his door.

"What is it?" he asked dryly. I had hoped that he would have noted the intensity of my knocking and matched my hasty mood, but I was frustratingly disappointed.

"Come, Sheridan." I rapped the door again, and my foot started to tap. The door opened.

"What—"

"Somethin's goin' on!" I pulled him out. "Peader was talkin' Irish, so I couldn't understand. Mother ran out, and we have to catch her to find out where it is." I had dragged him halfway down the hall as I explained my haste. I let go of his arm when he started to move on his own.

"So you don't know then?" Sheridan panted as we ran out the door and down the stone steps.

"No, that's why I want to find mother before she gets too far ahead. She knows what it is!" A lantern's glow stole my gaze, and I caught sight of her turning toward the stable. I was gripped with a terrible panic, thinking that there might be something wrong with the horses.

"Where's da?" my brother called from close behind.

"Peader's gone to get him!" I lost sight of our mother in the darkness, and I stopped running. We were on our own now.

"Do ya' smell that?" Sheridan turned his nose to the air, and he looked like Rowan. "It's like *burnin'*."

I sniffed and turned to locate the source of the smell, but the air was light, and there was no breeze of strength to carry a scent. The odor seemed to seethe from everywhere. The smoke was as musty and sweet as the smell that escaped from a turf fire. The smoke thickened, and I moved my head to find a clear source of night air.

"My eyes are waterin'." Sheridan made two fists and rubbed the sting from his pale eyes.

I squinted and coughed and stared into the patch of trees behind the stable. A patch of white smoke issued from between the tall trunks, looking like a host of the sidhe, as Peadar said, raging over the land for a night of wild fairy revels. A small glow of white and orange light flickered and sparkled in the center of the shadowy gale.

"It's a fire! Sheridan, look!" I grabbed his shoulders and dragged him in front of me. He broke from my grasp and ran toward the trees. I started after him and covered my nose against the drying smoke. I tripped through the tangle of low hedges and weeds. My eyes scratched and dried so in the smoky veil that I could barely see. The atmosphere warmed as I reached the peastone path. I stood behind my brother, and the fire-singed air burned our faces. Small embers of ash twisted and cavorted in the hot draft. At every other moment a roof timber would burst open in the conflagration, and a legion of embers would race like souls from the devil's cages out from the gaping chasm that was once the "odd tool" shed's roof. The vaunting, gothic windows were gone, and only flames licked the empty frames. There was nothing left but three blackened stone walls glowing in the light like bones. The north side had crumbled into itself from the heat and the pull of the rafters.

My mother stood on the far side of the path. She stared into the fire, and the fire stared back sending its golden gaze across the front of her blue dress. Some of the workers were sitting on the ground with buckets of pond water, but apparently they had come too late. A hand touched my shoulder, and I started round to see who had set it there.

"A gharsúin! Tagaigí anseo! Come away from here." Peader pulled us toward him. "This is no place for you. Who brought you out here?"

He grasped our hands, and we followed him back to the path where my mother and father stood. Ms. Farrell was there as well. She must have heard the commotion in the house. She held the paisley shawl tight about her neck, but with the scorching heat she couldn't have been chilled.

"What are you two doing here?" Our father turned to us when he heard our approach.

"They were over on the opposite side, they were, sir." Peader let us go. "I thought they would be."

"Did your mother not tell you to stay in the house with Ms. Farrell?" His voice was flat and unnatural. I looked at my mother, and she had been crying. "Your Daniel has gone to look for you. That was a terrible thing you did, not minding, so it was."

"You shouldn't blame 'em, sir," Peader said softly. "They were curious—"

"This matter no longer concerns you!" Mícheál turned to face the older man. He stopped to reconsider the harshness of his words. He dropped his head, and sent a glazed stare toward the ground. "Go and find Daniel, Peader; he shouldn't be out alone."

Mr. Hayes walked into the cool darkness. My father rubbed his face.

"Go to Ms. Farrell, you two"—his words seemed to die in the air—"and don't leave her side." My father left us and went over to where the men with the full buckets were sitting. The fire's light glinted and reflected mockingly across the captured water.

I had done a terrible thing. I had even dragged Sheridan and Peader into it. Even Daniel was after looking for us. I should not have disobeyed my mother. I didn't know that she was going to be miserable, worrying herself like that. That was the second time I had ever seen her cry. I didn't know whether to be frightened and saddened by the violent loss of our pretty outbuilding, or ashamed for doing wrong by my mother. A bitter wave rolled through me. I chose to feel all three. When you did something wrong and the accuser couldn't face you, then you knew that it was a terrible thing indeed. I didn't feel sorry for myself. My father had sent a turbulent reprimand at Peader. Those two had never quarreled in all of the days I was able to know.

My brother and I stood by our tutor. We didn't dare move as the effects of fright and grief began to steep within us. We didn't say a word. Ms. Farrell didn't turn to look at us; she stared at the fire as if it was speaking to her.

We waited for nothing in a placid, soundless ring, watching time click forward with the punctual lashes of flame. My father took one of the buckets and poured the water on the ground. The other men around him were doing the same so that the fire would not spread. My mother and a few of the others received the empty buckets and returned to the pond to fill them again. It was like watching earth being spread over a grave.

Peader returned with Daniel and the older man was slowed with the aches in his legs. I saw them move from the shadows to where a large rock showed itself in the unnatural light. Peader sat down upon it, and he pointed the boy over to where the three of us were standing.

"What a disaster this." Daniel stopped next to me. "I should've come back earlier."

"Where were you?" I asked softly.

"Oh, I was o'er by Hutcheson's writin' a poem to send, but I was havin' a hard time callin' down the words. Must've been the will o' God though, for if I was followed by the muse and I stayed later, maybe the fire would've spread to the stable." He fussed with a sleeve that had undone itself, and he re-rolled the cuff back up to his elbow. "I was thinkin' I could've saved the place." He nudged me.

"That would've been a dangerous thing for you to do, Daniel." Ms. Farrell spoke, but did not take her eyes from the blaze.

"But how could you? You didn't know it was burnin'?" Sheridan shook his head.

Daniel shrugged. "Well, I would've got back sooner, you see. I met some men on the bohereen. They must've been lost or somethin' seein' as that's a nowhere goin' road. They were comin' back from some sort o' field work as some were messy with straw. They must've worked around here before, because they knew that I was from Carrickduff. That took me by surprise. And when the tall, dark-haired fella asked for me name, it was as if he already knew what the answer was, and that the answer just confirmed his suspicions."

My father walked over during the explanation. He stood behind the boy.

"I'm dreadful sorry, Mr. O'Hayden. Oh, I wish I could've saved the place for you." Daniel stepped back to face the man who had brought him to Carrickduff. My father again rubbed the smoke from his glass-like eyes as if he was taking the night's ruins away.

"Ms. Farrell's right, Daniel. A building is one thing, a man's security is another. And what matters is that it wasn't the stable. How's Peader? Maybe he should go to his bed."

"It's just the night damp that's set his rheumatics to aching. He won't leave here until this thing's burned down, sir."

"I know that he won't, Daniel. I know that he won't." My father placed his hand on the boy's shoulder, and guided him toward my brother and I. "You stay here with Ms. Farrell, and Anne, and Sheridan."

"I will, sir."

"Did you ask those men with the straw on them for the name of their employer?" My father raised his eyes. The fire's light carve a glowing path across his face.

"Oh, I did, sir. I think it was something like Groves? I ne'er heard the name before."

"Cosgrove?"

"Ah, sir! that is the name. I figured that you might've heard o' them."

"Oh, I have heard of him, Daniel." Hardness touched the words. "You have done more than a boy's rightful share tonight."

"I wish I could've done more, sir."

"You did more than could be asked." My father bowed his head. His face held the mark of despondent exhaustion. He left us, and went over to where Peader watched the flames from his rocky seat.

"I ne'er thought I'd see the likes o' this tonight. And there I was wonderin' only if I could get a poem into the *Freeman's Journal*. It's a rare world wouldn't you say, Anne? . . . Anne?"

I stared at the low illumination that bled from the scullery window. The submissive glow was entombed in the vast, stone case of its frame. There was just enough moonlight to distinguish Carrickduff from the rest of the land that she rested on. I looked at her, and she watched over me. She watched over everything.

Chapter 22

The ashes had been sifted through and the removal process begun. One question arose from the now deceased flames, and that was: how did such a searingly hot fire come to be in a bare, stone-rubble structure? The floor was stone, the walls were stone and mortar, and the roof was slate not thatch. Only the beams were wood. They were huge oak beams. It was not the sort of building that would set itself alight with swift facility and we had just gone through a spell of wet weather. My father ordered a search made; most of which he carried out himself.

My brother, myself, and our mother made our trip to the scene soon after. An hour earlier Sheridan and I had offered her our apologies for disregarding those orders the night before. Ms. Farrell ushered us over to Mrs. O'Hayden as if we were traitors sent before the queen, and it was a most uncomfortable situation. My brother hung his head and mumbled his regrets. We never would have done that ourselves, it was simply too disquieting, and a most awful feeling settled into my head. Our apologies were accepted and half of the awfulness went away. My mother asked if we would accompany her to the burned ruins. If all could be made fully well again, the use of that invitation was the best that could ever be got from the apothecary's wooden shelves.

Before you reached the path behind the stable, an aged smell of wood smoke floated in the air. You could not see a trace of smoke, the air was clear, but the invisible herald of the night's misfortune allowed you to remember. A scattering of ash and cinder gradually filled the pea-stone walk until it ended at its source which was still sighing with bursts of heat, and red traces of luminosity warned that the dragon still had life yet.

"This won't be cooled for hours," my mother said tapping some freed ashes with her boot. Mícheál walked over when he heard his wife's voice.

"It's a blessin' only that this didn't spread to the stable," she spoke to all of us.

My father nodded.

"God, I still can't believe that this could've happened. There was nothing stored there that would've gone alight. It burned like a hearth fire. We won't be able to get near enough to search for the cause yet." She said.

"I'm thinking about where to search, and my nose is leading me in a cooler direction. There's one thing that I'm gonna sift over now though. Have you two rebels seen Daniel yet?" He asked us.

"No," was the simultaneous reply.

"He's usually in the stable or the field." I added. "We can go and find him?" I feared that our father was still displeased with us.

"Go and find him then," the tall man tossed his head. "But you two mind this," he pointed sternly to the steaming rubble, "this is still smoldering. Anne," he pointed stiffly at me, "you stay away with your frock. I don't want you any more fiery than you already are. Do you understand me then?"

I nodded. He had dropped his anger toward us. I figured that anyone who didn't want to see you set alight, harboured a certain amount of kindness for you. Whenever Mícheál O'Hayden was mad at you, you knew that the row was mended when a line of wit appeared.

Dan was in the field. He was giving all of the horses their breakfast outside at pasture. His expression was dry and grey. We had all had a night involving very little sleep. I felt as if my head was hollow and my legs were wobbly like the old people who had the "unsatisfactory leg-control". We commandeered young Mr. Whelan, and brought the yawning groom to the site of destruction.

"Oh!" Peader was sitting on the big rock. "There's a sight to cure me rheumatics. Dan you've a face on you like a chicken's bottom." He rubbed his unyielding knees.

"If I had seen you this mornin', I'd of thought you had yer trousers on yer head and yer . . ."

"There's no talkin' like that in the front of a lady! Excuse the boy's lack of manners Ms. Anne. You're as fair as a lily still this day." He gave Dan a scouring look.

"Thank you Peader." I curtsied. "Sure, I feel like Dan's face."

"Oh, thank you," Dan bowed.

"I didn't mean it to sound as you thought." I spoke the atoning words.

"I wouldn't say you look so lily-like this mornin' Anne." Sheridan observed. I gave him a sour grimace.

"Nobody likes a Wicklow pebble with a mouth," I said.

"Don't you be talkin' to your sister in such a manner! I've ne'er heard the likes of, and don't have me hearin' it again Master Sheridan." My brother got a reproachful finger. "Agus bíodh sé sin mar dheireadh!"

I smiled. My brother wanted to say that I had called him a Wicklow pebble, but he did not want to prolong the matter now that Peader was speaking Irish.

"Your father wants to see me, does he?" Daniel rubbed the soil with the side of his boot.

"He does." I said.

"Ah, I know what Mr. O'Hayden wants." Peader rested his head in his hand. His tone turned slow and reflective. "It's important Dan. Go see him. And mind yourself 'round the fire; it's still terrible hot and there's glass about."

My brother and I walked Dan over to where the men were, but we didn't follow him as he walked toward our father. We sat on the grass verge where we would be out-of-the way, but where we still could hear.

"Are you well this mornin, Dan?" My father approached the boy, his dark head inclined and a narrow greeting waited on his lips.

"I am, sir. You asked for me?"

Mr. O'Hayden nodded. "When you left last night, did you leave by way of this path?" He straightened.

"Oh, yes I did." Dan affirmed, looking down at the thousands of pea-stones.

"Can you recall the time that you left?"

"I don't know exactly," the boy rubbed the buttons on his waistcoat. He was still staring at the path. "I know that it was at least half-seven though, as I had brought the horses their evenin' feed."

"Was there all those scraps of straw on the ground when you left?" My father shifted his weight, and the pebbles crushed and protested against the pressure change upon their stony heads.

"I don't think that there was any scraps like that, no. I always go 'round the front with the soiled beddin'. Maybe Peader brought some 'round this way for the gardens?"

"And out toward the pond with a load of bedding? No, I asked him, he had not been this way. So, we have no explanation for these wisps of straw, and their being freshly strewn."

"I do not remember seein' them on my way, sir. 'Course t'was too dark for me to notice on me way back."

"But those men who approached you, you noticed them laced with straw, you said."

"That I did"—Dan nodded—"and t'was a strange sight, seein' as it's not the season, and there's no farms down the bohereen save this one. The Timoney's don't hire help like that."

"No, they don't, Dan."

There was a pause before the boy's head rose up quickly to catch my father's eyes.

"Are you sayin'—are you sayin' that the blaze was set, sir! And were those men of an odd lot to see."

"I'm not sayin' it, but I'm thinkin' it. God help me, but I'm thinkin' it." He closed his eyes.

"Who would've hired 'em to set it?" Dan looked at the remains with the smoke rising from the shell, and it appeared as the dawn did rising from the surface of the pond.

A dreadful smile etched over my father's lips, and his shoulders shook like one hiding a silent laugh. "When will Padraic be ready, Dan?" His voice was dry and it made me think of gunpowder waiting for the barrel.

The boy held back on his answer. He stared at the "odd tool" shed.

"He's had his breakfast. Ah, in an hour he'll be ready." He kept his gaze upon the rubble.

"Saddle him then, Daniel. I'll come out to get him at the stable. And this evening—No, at any time, boy—you aren't to go away like you're want to do. Stay by your duties, do you hear me, eh? Peader knows that you aren't to leave alone."

"I'm not to come any more." Thomas rested on the grass. He was bent over at the waist with his elbows on his knees.

"How'd they know?" I said.

"It was the Robinson Crusoe I hid in the loft of the turf shed. Somehow me mother found it, and she asked me father if it was his, as he's the only one who can read. Well, he opened the cover and there was your name on it and your mother's under that. And I was found out. I'm not to come anymore." The boy picked lethargically at the grass by his legs.

"So, what're you gonna do?" I asked.

"I told 'em I took work with an old lady about two miles down the road on the Plunkett's estate. I said I was gonna do errands and such. They believed it. So, they won't know I'm comin' here." He smiled.

"Who's the lady?"

"There's no lady. I made it up."

"Oh." I nodded. "But what about the pay?"

"What pay?"

"Won't your folks notice that you're off workin' and not gettin' any money?"

"I'll figure somethin' out," he said with the voice of the newly disappointed.

We sat lazily by the front of the pond. We could still be seen by the house there, and that was the rule. Peader was raking thatch and debris from the lawn, and every ten minutes he yawned over the business. You could've set your watch by the yawns.

"I thought I smelled somethin' last night. I figured someone was after burnin' scraps, I didn't know your old shed went up. Wasn't it all stone and mortared rubble, so how'd it burn?" Thomas raised his head with a different concern showing on his face. He could move from inconvenience, to calm, to sympathy in minutes. Although there was no trouble that he couldn't find his way out of. He may not have had much, but he had all of his faith invested into the workings of optimism. But that's what happened when you were bereft of all but the things in your head.

"Well"—shrugged—"my father went out on Padraic to find out. I don't know where he went or when he'll be back, but I don't feel so great about the business. My father thinks that it was set, that someone wanted it to burn to ashes."

"Had it set, do you say?!' Thomas sat up on his bent knees. His face was lit with a dismayed wonder. I felt awkward accepting condolences from my friend, whose family was about to lose their rented possession, their home.

"There was all o' this straw layin' about the path, you see. Dan was out writin'. He had left the yard 'round half-seven, and he said that he didn't see hardly a trace of straw then, and it was too dark for him to see on his return. He saw the fire first . . ." I told Thomas all of the known facts from the fiery evening; the evidence, the strange straw-covered men, everything.

"God, I can't imagine somethin' like that." Thomas seemed to be speaking the words in his head, but his mouth betrayed him by echoing those thoughts. "You own your own place, so who would be after chasin' you out like that?"

Chasin' you out. Those words exploded in my head with the terribleness of a thunderstorm. "So who would be after chasin' you out." Thomas had said the words without hooking their worth. But they were saying something to me, and they could just have been in a different language. I could not pull the meaning out of them. They were an answer to a question, but you had to find the question.

"I don't know." I shrugged and peeled a pond reed. That was all that I could say. "But father told us not to leave sight o' the house, not e'en Dan. And he's not fond of that order."

"Ah, that's a wise practice maybe, huh." Thomas twitched up his nose.

I was watching the house and she was supposed to be watching me. A small lamp flickered from the sitting room, and it wasn't just a light to me now. Fire became an entity, it had become a life, a will. The flames weren't licking at nothingness anymore. They were waiting to break free of the wick to spread about their sinister purpose.

"Thomas"—I turned my thoughts from the blazing shed—"would you really want to work for a woman, not an old woman maybe, but one who could solve the second problem in your plan?"

"Ah, I would surely." He watched the opportunity grow in his head. "But I don't know any, you see."

"Come with me." I stood up and ran down the lawn, past the yawning and startled Peader and into the back door.

Thomas and I stood in the sitting room. You could almost here the shoes on the wood and the music of the waltzes and the reels, and it was grand that you couldn't think with the clamor of it all. It was the sound of pleasure being polished to perfection. The ghosts danced weakly in the table lamp's glow.

"Mother?" I asked. The small boy with the incorrigible hair was standing to attention at my side. Carolyn was at studying her botany books, and the leaves of notes were scattered about her feet. She drank knowledge unconstrainedly, covering the thoughts of worry with the droning tones of science. But you knew that she was drunk with the image of her husband off somewhere on Padraic, to search for the "match" that struck our fire. "Mother, do you think that Thomas could have a job?"

"I think that young Mr. Timoney would be an industrious and promising workman of the highest order. He will have no trouble procuring employment." She turned to the boy. "You have my word Thomas." My mother smiled.

Thomas smiled.

There was a stretch of nothing. Thomas kept smiling. Apparently, I had failed to assemble my question properly.

"Do you think, mother . . . that Thomas might work for us?" I suggested humbly.

"Well, Anne he is rather young." She turned to the no-longer grinning boy. "Is it money you're in need of Thomas?"

"Oh no, ma'am!" His eyes expanded. My mother had a soft and confused expression on her face. She knew that the Timoney's always needed a shilling; their rent was in arrears, and they had refused all of our offers of redemption. The rope had been thrown, but the man had chosen to go under the waves.

"If you ever are in need Thomas, do remember that these doors are open always." She smiled, but my plan was not advancing. I knew what course of action to take.

"Thomas's father says that he is not to come here anymore." I elaborated. "We are all cut-up about it."

"That is a sad course of events, Thomas." Her mouth formed a downcast "O". She enjoyed the boy's company as did all of us, and she took immense pleasure at procuring him a meal and secreting him a shilling or two.

"We have a plan," I said, looking sharp.

"We do, ma'am," Thomas said, looking reserved.

"Well, what a bright relief to hear. And what is your plan?" She clapped her hands before her.

"Thomas told his father that he had taken' employment with an old woman two miles down the road, and so he is now expected to be gone for several hours doing her errands," I explained.

"Doesn't your father mind you not being in the school?" she asked.

"Ah no. Me father thinks work's better'n school, since I'm eleven. I've enough schoolin' for meself now."

"If that's the way it is then." My mother frowned slightly. "It is lovely that you can do the woman some service."

"There is a problem." I sulked.

"There is, ma'am," Thomas echoed.

"Oh?" Mrs. O'Hayden cocked her head, and her delicate brow wrinkled.

"It is the old woman, ma'am," Thomas added queasily.

"Is she not kind, then? Does she not pay you prompt?" My mother spoke plainly. Her innate sense for justice was lit. The dormant patriot was roused and resplendent.

"She does not exist," I said.

"Not exist?"

"She's made up. 'Tis a lie," Thomas murmured. "'Tis a lie, so that I can come here with none of me sisters trailin' me."

"But Thomas won't have any earnin's to show." I dropped my eyes. "I thought that he might be able to work for us, seein' as we were gonna take him on when he was big."

"It is against your parents' likings for you to come here, Thomas." My mother nodded, and Thomas did too. "We cannot interfere with that. You are their son and so are bound by their wishes. To disobey would be a sin, you know that, Thomas."

"T'would be a sin, ma'am." He thrust his hands into his coat's pocket.

She leaned back in the chair as my father did when he was going to say something valuable. "Ah, but you had said to them that you are employed?"

"That I did, ma'am. And t'was a sin to say it."

"But you cry *sin* too soon!"

Thomas raised an eye after my mother spoke. He had apparently not expected her to go against her own words. I'm sure that he feared that Mrs. O'Hayden was going daft.

"Did they tell you that you could not seek work here?" she asked.

"No, they did not." He shook his head.

"Well, then," she figured, "the kitchen staff could be relieved of some errands to and from and such; the maids could have their cleaning buckets refreshed; Daniel would love to have his duties lessened . . . would any of that please you, young Mr. Timoney?"

"It would please me very much." The boy's face appeared eager and vivacious. "You would be savin' me from sin as well, ma'am."

"Ah, but not all of the sin, Thomas." My mother waved a cautious finger. I thought that the face of her new, young worker was going to pop off like a watch lid, and fall upon the floor. I couldn't think of what she meant, but the nuances of sin were a mystery to me.

"Can you, in truth, still say that your employer is an old woman."

Thomas's eyes grew. Sure, I didn't want to be in his shoes then, and I could think of nothing to save him.

"Well . . . ," he said slowly, "no, Mrs. O'Hayden, I cannot."

"Ah, that is what I wanted to hear. But do keep that lie Thomas, it is a good one. It will be my lie, and I may still then revel in the remaining days of my youth." She smiled and offered her slender hand to the small hand of the boy.

Chapter 23

Thomas arrived for "work" at seven. I had just risen when he arrived at the back door. I dressed as fast as I could, pulling on my lace-up boots so that I wouldn't have to bother with any buttons. I ran from my room, and nodded a "good morning" to my father as I passed his private workroom where you could find him at half-six every morning except Sunday and Saturday. My mother rose at half-six or seven depending on her enthusiasm for whatever breed of curiosity she was after at the time. During bird migrations, she could be seen out-of-doors by five, along with the field hands, spalpeens, dairy workers, and her maid, Norah, who was tending to her complexion—or com-pexion, as my brother called it. Most of the house and laundry staff rose at six. Dan rose at half-six and Peader at seven, because the early dampness was "bad for me rheumatics".

My brother and I followed Thomas around as Norah took him on a tour of his possible duties. She kept him away from the scullery, where he was really needed, so that she could have his industry all to herself. Mrs. O'Leary was already wary of the young maid's strategy, and as soon as we entered the dining room the boy was swiftly commandeered. We followed the elderly Mrs. O'Leary as she shuffled gooselike into the kitchen, and we rather resembled a string of quick-footed goslings. The tour ended at eight when Ms. Farrell told us to go to the nursery for breakfast, Thomas included.

Ms. Farrell opened the door and groaned at her first sight of the room.

"Oh! What is this!" She pushed back her troublesome hair. I clasped my hand to my guilty mouth.

The floor around the old, neglected toy chest, that had once served as a traveling trunk, was strewn with shipwrecked flotsam. There were marbles, china-headed dolls, leather dolls, ivory elephants, chalk, puzzle pieces, tops, and model animals.

Donovan was standing on a small, cloth horse, from which he had plucked out the glass eye. Our tutor ran over and snatched the raven up. He was croaking with amusement.

"You didn't do this, did you?" she asked as the raven picked at the brooch on her collar. She chose her way over the toys and peered into the trunk. "Oh!" she exclaimed. And as soon as said it, a long muff of brown fur bounded over the rim and scampered beneath the low settee. Ms. Farrell screamed.

"I left the lid open last night," I confessed. "Mother needed something for to hold her photography plates off of the work table, so that they wouldn't get dusty. I went and got some blocks from the chest." I shrugged. "I never remembered to shut the lid."

We placed the toys back into their trunk before Norah appeared with the breakfast tray. She set it on the heavy table, and carefully placed down the chocolate and coffee pots. She grimaced when she lifted the lid off of the small china bowl before placing it on the ground. The moment the bowl's bottom clumped to rest on flooring wood, the brown fur muff reappeared from beneath the settee, and commenced his meal of bread in rendered fat and raw fish scraps.

"God help me, Rowan, I don't see how that you can eat such things!" Norah made another face at the stoat before leaving with Ms. Farrell, so that they might turn their attentions to their own breakfasts.

I fed Donovan his plate of oatmeal and bread ends before helping myself to tea, oatmeal stirabout, and toast points. There were also a few pickled herrings, patties of our butter, and orange marmalade that father had brought in from Dublin.

"What's that?" Thomas pointed at the jellified bits of orange in the glass cup.

"That's mar-mee-lade, but with oranges from Spain. You've got to buy it in Dublin." My brother crunched a dark toast point.

"Sure, you can buy it in Bray Town!" I corrected. "You can buy it in town, Thomas. You can probably buy it anywhere."

"Oh," the boy shook his head, "I've ne'er seen it before." He squinted at the cup and then at me.

"It is rather good. It is if you like oranges anyway," my brother encouraged. "I like it best."

After a bite for experimentation our guest concluded with utter certainty that he was indeed, very fond of orange marmalade. During breakfast

Thomas asked if Mr. O'Hayden had found anything out about the fire while he was away, or about the man who wanted to take our house. We did not know, of course, as he did not return until quite late, and we had gone to bed. When Norah came to clean away the things she took Thomas, too, and we had planned to follow but were ushered off to lessons instead.

I had to walk up from study, because I had left my Latin book on a chair in my room. I rather did it on purpose, leaving the book that is, in hopes that Ms. Farrell would overlook the language for today. If it had worked I had plans of leaving it more often in future. Why learn a language that you will not ever actually speak, just because the adult intelligentsia decided it was a necessity of good learning. They didn't decide that being able to build a temple to Zeus was a mark of a learned man, even though that would have been a spot more useful. I would have rather studied Italian, so that I could discuss with the people the cathedral of St. Peters, the Arch of Constantine, and all of those other splendid things. I told my father this once, and he was very pleased with my apparent enthusiasm. He then suggested that I learn Latin as well as Italian, and he was to teach me the latter personally. I was not pleased with the outcome of my quest to remove the ancient language from my academic pursuits. I would have been better off saying nothing to begin with. I fear that one day I will find myself saying how pleasing the ride in the rowboat was, only to be ushered off onto a full-rigged sailing vessel on a voyage around the Cape Horn.

I dragged myself to my room, passing father's study on the way. His door was not fully shut, and the two voices coming from the chamber distracted me sufficiently to stop and attend to them. I wasn't going to eavesdrop. I intended to take only that information which concerned me, and I hoped to discover something about the fire from my father's trip to somewhere. I noted that the second voice was Peader's.

"There was the half-burnt straw all about the place. Those were the one's carried out by the wind, and there was ne'er any straw in that area in such amounts." Peader spoke with loathing. "The stuff from the stable doesn't blow about back there, ne'er did. Ne'er did 'til that night, and I'll bet you fifty guineas that was foreign straw put to di'vilish use."

"I know it was put to devilish use. There was nobody in that solicitor's office. It wasn't even an office, in the true sense. I was not surprised. The door was locked. I asked the building's attendant if he knew how long the room was rented. And he knew too, for the place was just taken four months ago," my father said. "I asked for the name of the man who had taken out the lease, and for five pounds I was given leave to search the book at my leisure. As to the name, I found what I needed: William Cosgrove, his father's namesake."

"Do you think then that he hired those men that Daniel saw?" Peader raised an eye.

"I don't know. He's been the one sending the solicitor, if that man is indeed a solicitor. The man has no right to a place mentioned in a drunkard's will."

"That he does not, sir. Your own man told you that. They know about Carrickduff round here, they know old Gerald, your father. The place was abandoned so it was. God, if we could only get the proof, we'd have that man arrested, and that solicitor too, for wantin' to gaol me. He had no business threatenin' me as if I was a stock street beggar. I ne'er liked the looks o' him from the beginnin'. Walkin' in here like the prince himself, and he a common workin' man. You could buy and sell 'im yourself, sir, and not think so much as if you were buyin' a paper."

"I wish it was that man troublin' me and not the master. It seems as though this Mr. Cosgrove is takin' pains to not show himself. He has used henchmen before, Peader—the lawyer and the coachman. Does it not seem possible the five men that passed Dan were henchmen as well?"

"It does. I was thinkin' o' that meself." Peader's voice was slow and thoughtful. "After the fire, the solicitor and his employer, your Mr. Cosgrove, came into thought. But how could that be, as I had no proof or process to lay the hand of reproach onto 'em. Who else could we name who carries out his actions through another? I know none."

"God, it kills me not to understand this!" My father's chair creaked as its owner shifted with anxiety. "Does he want money, damn him! Is this extortion?" He uttered a soft groan.

"He wants somethin'," Peader sighed. "And I hate to say that I'm thinkin' it's not money. He doesn't want the grapes, he wants the vine they've seasoned on. This is startin' me to ruminate o'er Shakespeare's writin's. Are there such in this world as are called from tragedies of old?"

"I hope not, Peader," my father whispered in desperation. "Let fiction continue to sit dormant in its pages. I have enough of this world."

I ran to my room as softly as I could. I had more to tell Thomas than I had wanted to know. It might be wise to reread some Shakespeare. Of which tome Peader was talking, I could not think of. I couldn't remember any burning tool sheds in *Macbeth*.

Thomas's first day of work went along rather well. He would spend the last two hours of his day studying with us and Ms. Farrell, before going home with a boiled egg from mother. I followed him as far as the rear of the pond so that I could tell him what I had heard about the fire. Thomas asked of what we were going to do. I had no answer for him, but his question was to become more significant as the days progressed.

Thursday had the first clear sky in a three-day spell of wet weather. My father had received a post from Dublin that kept him in a brooding and shadowed mood for the entire day. A meeting had taken place in his room. Peader and my mother were in attendance. He had scheduled it for the hours between two and four, when myself, Sheridan and Thomas were taking lessons. After the meeting my mother came down to give Thomas a wrapped portion of cheese. Her face was enlivened with an awkwardly cheery expression, which still failed to mask the troubled one lurking beneath.

Later that day I had taken Rowan out for a romp by the pond. Daniel wandered over and the three of us made use of the small rowboat until supper broke our amusement.

"Come to shore!" Sheridan was waving from the lawn. He turned and seemed to be anxiously searching the area.

We rowed to where he stood, and I helped Daniel pull the boat to dry earth.

"Do you know what I heard?" my brother whispered.

"'Tis most unlikely, seein' as we've been out and you in." Dan was being cheeky. He got a dirty look from Sheridan.

"And don't call me a Wicklow pebble." My brother reproached me.

"I wasn't gonna say anythin' but what," I confessed.

He stared until he was satisfied.

"Ma and da were talkin' in the sittin'-room, and I stayed in the hall to hear 'em."

"What were they talkin' about?" Daniel wiped the wet rope fibers from his hands, and the wisps stuck to his corduroy trousers.

"It was about that letter. Mother thinks that they should get somebody to see it, but father says it wouldn't do any good because they've no dense-somethin'."

"Evidence," I said.

"That's what they don't have any of, father said."

"What did the letter say?" Daniel shrugged with bewilderment.

"I don't know. I only heard 'em talkin'."

"I'll bet it has to do with that Mr. Cosgrove, the one I saw in the cemetery. He said that we both had fathers that owned Carrickduff, and that doesn't make any sense to me." I observed.

"Ah, it might make sense though, if we could only see that letter," Daniel groaned with frustration.

"Peader read it! He must've, he was in that meetin'. He's been talkin' with father all along," I said excitedly.

"You won't get anythin' out o' him." Dan shook his head. "You'd a better chance gettin' milk out o' the bull. He barely talks to me, now. He says naught about anythin'."

"We should read it, then," Sheridan decided.

"Did you see 'em with it in the sittin' room?" Dan asked.

Sheridan thought for a moment, while Rowan sniffed cautiously in his direction. Their relationship had not been comfortably close since the watch incident. "No." He raised a finger. "They didn't have anythin', they were just talkin'. Donovan was with 'em."

"I doubt he'll be much of an informant," Daniel said cynically.

"I think Norah can read the letter. She cleans in there. We could ask her," I figured.

"Would herself be partial to our situation?" The oldest boy added some caution.

"I believe that she would. She watches the dances with us outside o' the windows and that's eavesdroppin'." I spoke in the young maid's favor, elaborating on her level of trustworthiness.

"Have her speak with us," Dan decided.

"I'll go see her after supper," I concluded. The plan was ready to be loosed.

The young woman sat on a long, flat rock by the edge of the pond. Her dark brown hair was smoothed and parted over her forehead like parlor drapes, and tucked beneath her bonnet. She was still wearing the ivory work apron.

"So there you see it!" Daniel sat cross-legged on the grass looking up at the seventeen-year-old. "Will you help us, Norah? It's for all of our benefit, even the house's. You live here. If we know what's goin' on, we can do somethin' about things."

"I'll see what I can do." She sent her eyes skyward. She wanted to be involved, but she had embarrassed herself for having such improper curiosity. "But I'll not be goin' through the master's things." She shook an admonishing finger at the groom.

"If the letter's on the desk as it was tonight, I'll flip through it. I'm not that good at readin' though."

"Don't tell me now, that you're not good at readin'!" Daniel leaned back and sighed over the unforeseen snag.

"No!" Norah was indignant. "I can read, Daniel, so I can." She poked her blouse. "I'm not good at readin' fancy words, that's all. If it's that solicitor's letter like you said it might be, I thought that there might be some o' those kinds o' words in it."

"All right," Dan sighed. "Just so as you get the ideas in the letter, that's all."

"Were you two involved in goin' through your father's things?" She accused my brother and I. We shook our heads.

"That's why we're havin' you do it. It wouldn't have been proper for Anne or Sheridan." Dan nodded and smiled.

"Oh!" She threw back her head, and narrowed her eyes. "But you're a liar Daniel."

"Thank you, ma'am." Dan bowed his head. "I was just tryin' to see how quick-witted you are."

"Quick-witted enough to know you're still lyin'!" She moved to cuff him.

There and then the scheme was thoroughly tested and ready for execution. When father left the study that night to take tea with Peader in the sitting room, Norah would be sent in to "clean" the room. We were fairly certain that the letter would still be on his desk, as it was rare for Mr. O'Hayden to shuffle things about, even though he was fidgity.

At nine the plan was launched. Norah returned to the nursery at a quarter-past, where the three of us were waiting. Rowan was anxious to see his aproned foodserver, and he bounced and arched his back in invitation for a mock-battle. Donovan was still off in the countryside, as it was summer, and the land was still lit. The window was cracked for him, but we all assumed that he would not have been terribly amused with our findings.

"So what'd it say?" Sheridan jumped from the settee, causing Rowan to run behind Norah's skirt.

"Well, it didn't make any sense, you see." She winced.

"It didn't make any sense?" Daniel shrugged. "Wasn't it the right letter, then?"

"So it was," Norah confirmed brusquely. "But what was written was almost in some kind o' code."

"So you couldn't understand then?" I assumed.

"No, it wasn't that sort o' code. I wrote it all down here on this note paper." She pulled the sheet from her apron pocket. "It's written plain, you see. I copied it over, but the words don't make sense. Listen, 'I have asked you to consider the truths delineated in my father, the late Richard Cosgrove's will. He was the true and rightful owner of the property, the estate of Carrickduff, built by his great father-in-law Arthur Crawford. This estate, upon Mr. Cosgrove's death, was to be handed down to his son, William, his sole heir. I have asked you on several occasions to consider these findings. You have denied each of my offers for the property to be taken. You have denied what was the only honorable course of action. I am then led to believe that this matter can only be settled in disagreeable form. I know not of your limits, sir, but I am willing to find them out. I am prepared to meet any price that you lay before me.' And then it is signed William Cosgrove, Surrey, England." Norah folded the note-paper. "See then, it doesn't make any sense. There's no mention o' the fire a t'all."

Daniel dropped languidly against the back of the settee. "There's the wet blanket thrown a'top our fire. I can see the steam risin' now." The boy raised his arms in discouragement.

"Well, maybe it does mean somethin'." I rose from the floor and went over to the young maid. "Can I see your notes, Norah?" She nodded and pulled the sheet from her apron.

"Before the fire," I explained, "I met a man 'round father's age. I was in the cemetery, and that man said he was after lookin' at those old gravestones."

"There's a strange place to find a fella'." Dan pointed a finger in the air. "Wouldn't you say that's an outta-the-way place Sheridan?" He tapped the head of the boy sitting on the floor before the settee.

"I would say that." Sheridan nodded.

"Indeed," I confirmed. "I was taken with distractions o'er it. You only expect to meet dead people in a cemetery, and not only that, but I met him out ridin' with ma the other day. I never expected to see the same man twice. But the thing I was tryin' to get from this letter is that the strange man was not just lookin' for any stone. He was lookin' for the Cosgrove and Crawford ones. You'd think he'd be after the ol' ones from the 1600s."

"Well, the other ones almost fill the whole place anyway. From what you said before wasn't he lookin' for the blighted ol' Cosgrove, the wee wife o' his and her family." Sheridan crossed his legs beneath him.

"Aye, he was," I continued. "And that wasn't odd, but he said somethin' when he was turnin' to go. I thought it was just a slip o' grammar, but now I believe it was wholly meant. I told him that we were standin' on father's land, and that was who he should speak to. And he said somethin, there is a thing that we do have in common. I thought he wished to use 'did', but he may very well have used 'do' with desired sincerity." I pointed to the letter. "And here it is again. If that man was William Cosgrove, and now I think that he is, then Richard Cosgrove was his father."

"Ah"—Daniel leaned forward—"then the ol' gambler must've wrote up a will givin' everythin' to his son."

"I didn't think he had anythin' to give?" Norah figured.

"He didn't." Sheridan grasped the business end. "He had not a shillin' left when he died. Carrickduff was bankrupt. He was plannin' to go to England to run away from his debts."

"The wife was livin' in Kildare," Dan added.

"But what about the child?" Norah asked, confused. "How could William be in England? Wasn't he an Englishman that you met, Anne?"

"Ah, he was," I confirmed.

Sheridan shrugged.

"Now, who would know then?" Daniel rubbed the buttons on his short jacket.

"My parents." Sheridan looked up at the figure on the settee.

"Ah, no! We can't ask them. They're tryin' to keep us from knowin' anythin'. That's why we're sneakin' around."

"Mrs. Byrne would know. She knows a lot o' things, she's old." A smile of accomplishment sat over my lips.

"Let's call on her." Daniel pressed his hands together.

"It's half-ten!" Norah pointed to the clock. She sent the boy a scowling "are you mad" look.

"We can't go now, it's too late." I said the same thing the maid's face was saying. "We'll go in the mornin'." I covered a yawn.

"All right"—Dan caught my yawn for he had one of his own—"ten o'clock by Mrs. Byrne's cottage then."

We all scattered to our beds, but I had to wait for Donovan to scramble in through the half-closed window. He flew to his perch and nodded his head. Rowan was already curled in his basket for a short nap. I stayed behind for a moment longer to put out the lamp. I waited with sleepy impatience for Donovan to finish his nightly toilet. I dreamed about lying down on the cold boards and drifting right off there. And if it wasn't for everyone to find such a thing odd, I would have. After ages past, the bird fluffed his breast feathers over his feet and settled in.

I pressed on to my room, and I didn't dare sit down to unlace my shoes, should I fall asleep in the process, and drop noisily upon the floor. The ancient bed smiled warmly. It had slept many before me, all alike. The heavy bedclothes were turned down, and you could have shown me the greatest castles in the world, but all I wanted was that linen swathed four-poster box. I hadn't slept thoroughly in days, but tonight appeared decidedly promising.

Chapter 24

It was four o'clock in the dark morning. Mrs. Kelly's husband had yet to return to his bed. I would use his bed, but I was too concerned for his wife to consider the rare luxury of a full night's sleep. I did, however, find it rather difficult to fathom such a thing as a man not wanting to be home in his room.

"It's not him to stay out so late!" The woman rubbed her hands. She spoke as if she was pleading for the circumstance to realize its own absurdity. My mother sat with her on the sitting room sofa, fiddling with the sash to her dressing gown.

"Of course, he might have had to help someone home. You know how things go at taverns, Mary." My mother endeavored to find another interpretation for the event. "The public house can be a well-spring for so many oddities of behaviour." Mrs. Kelly smiled wanly.

"I'll go and see the tavern keeper." My father passed the room in his dark, paisley robe. "He'll tell us not to worry, I'll bet, and I'll be takin' that poor man from his bed for nothin'."

My father came down shortly, dressed for the road. The look of solace on my mother's face had evolved into weak concern. There is always a shade of darkness in unknown things. We had left Mrs. Kelly in the sitting room with a spot of whiskey coffee to ease her. Her husband was a temperance man, but this was Jameson in the approved medicinal form. Peader didn't take too kindly to the ideas of the temperance movement. He said that the talk about "all the evils of drink" was utter nonsense. It was the man himself that was tarnished, drink or no drink, "it was only the liquor bringin' out what was already there. I'd tell those teetotallers that I've ne'er had trouble with a drop or a pint. You give me one, and I know exactly what to do with it. It's a strengthener for man and beast, but you need the will to know when enough's enough. Same with all things, church included." He smiled. I didn't know what he had meant about the church, but he got another terrible look from my mother.

"You won't be going alone, Mícheál?" She demanded softly.

He shifted the frock coat over his shoulders. "I'm takin' Niamh under me, and this beside me." He brought a pistol into view. My mother didn't look satisfied. I don't think that she wanted to think that the night might necessitate taking such actions.

"I know what kind of a shot you are." She said. "You're no highwayman."

He smiled. "I'll not be gone long, then." He straightened and went from the house.

My father was gone long, despite those words. Sheridan and I went back to our rooms. We both changed to our day clothes and headed back down. Daniel was there in the sitting room. Peader had gone with father. There was no need to question his use with a gun. According to Daniel, there was much to do about Mr. Hayes accompaniment. My father did not want the man to go, but Peader had said that either he was going with him or behind him, and so Gavin was saddled as well.

"I was gonna go, Mrs. O'Hayden, so I was"—Daniel burst with enthusiasm—"but Peader threatened to break me neck."

"No, Daniel." My mother shook her head.

We all waited in the room with the fire brought to life earlier than usual. Mrs. Kelly looked as though she had sat upon a chatelaine hung with nails. Young Norah started some tea. For all the action there was very little talking, until a banging at the front door struck away the silence.

Norah went to attend to the knocking, and I followed along with Daniel and my brother. Our plans to visit Mrs. Byrne had now been postponed. The maid opened the heavy, panelled door, and the man at the threshold was revealed. He was shorter than my father, and he slouched slightly at the shoulders. Dark brown hair framed a roundish face detailed with small, regular features, but the first thing that you noticed was a wave of unruly forelock that would not lay flat. His clothes were clean, but worn, and the corduroy knee-breeches had patches cleverly applied so as to prolong the garment's life. The brown waistcoat was unbuttoned, and the man had a hand in the freize coat's pocket.

"I'm surprised to see you's lookin' sharp so early."

"Good mornin', Mr. Timoney." Norah spoke with house-staff duty. She wanted to say that we had had an unusual night, but that was too friendly and intimate. And this was Mr. Timoney.

"I'm up early goin' to town with a milch cow's calf for sellin'. But I'm not here to trouble you with such things." He shrugged and tilted his head.

"Would you care to step in Mr. Timoney?" Norah said. This polite course had been delayed. House staff were informed to treat our vocal rival with care, despite the awkward feud. "Master is out, but the mistress is at home. There's been a slight disturbance; however, and she may not take visitors at the moment."

The man raised a hand. "No, miss, I'll not take your hospitality. But there you've gone and answered the question. Ah, so there's been a disturbance as you calls it. I know who you get for workin' the farm. Fine men, most. An' I'm certain as today's Thursday, that I've got one of 'em in me place as we're talkin'. Found him in the ditch half a mile from where the bohereen hits the road. From the looks of 'im, I'd say your man's not handy in a fight. Got himself a hell of a thrashin'. The wife's watchin' o'er him. I wasn't bringin' the fella, savin 'im a move. I'm here to see if he's one o' yours, and I knows he is. Now, does that sound like your disturbance, miss?" Mr. Timoney inclined his head to mark his point.

Mr. Timoney had indeed found Mrs. Kelly's husband, the temperance man. He was found senseless and less than ten minutes by foot from the tavern house door, where he had been meeting with friends. That man never touched a drop of spirits, and he would have found it easy to make his way back to the estate. It was days before the man emerged from his wretched state, and days before he was sound enough to tell the story.

Of what Mr. Kelly could recall, there was very little, but just enough. He had been approached in the darkness by several men: one an Englishman, and the other two Irish, and none were after an evening chat. Mr. Kelly told them that he had no money on him, or valuables, save the clothes on his back. And of all the words that night, he remembered the tall one's answer, "'*It's not spoils we're after, Mr. Kelly,' that's what he said. How he knew my name I don't know, I ne'er saw a one o' them in the tavern. And the next thing he said was that they had somethin' to give to Mr. O'Hayden . . . that bein' the last I knew.*"

We were indebted to Mr. Timoney. But you couldn't show that to a man who had greeted you with a pitchfork. Our thanks were loosed upon young Thomas through a piece of penny cake and a tip to his pay. The "old woman down the road" wished to show her pleasure for his industry. There was nothing so lovely as a good lie.

My father went to the Kelly's cottage. And after a few moments, he returned to meet with Peader upstairs in the study. It seemed that several days earlier Mrs. Kelly had been visited by a gentleman from England who was studying the "historical artifacts of eastern Ireland," and had heard of a most remarkable standing stone in the vicinity of the estate of Carrickduff. He had asked if she could offer some information on the subject. I knocked on the door.

"Anne." My father said the word as a question. Before waving me in, he rubbed his face with his hands as if he was wiping the world from it. A smile greeted me, but I could see the tension supporting it from beneath.

"We need a bit of sun this mornin', don't we, Mícheál? Ah, and here she comes in now." Peader rested his hand on the desk. It was a hand that spoke of years of hard labor.

"What can I do for you, then?" My father smiled and smoothed down his frock coat like a man in a shuffling hurry. He moved closer to me.

"It's about Mrs. Kelly." I said clapping my gaze to his pale face. The dark hair made his features cold and stern.

"Well, what have you to say about Mrs. Kelly?" He smiled again.

"Did she meet an Englishman?"

My father looked surprised. "She did."

"I met a tall Englishman in the cemetery. He was lookin' for the graves of Mrs. Cosgrove and the Crawfords. I told him that they were there, and then he asked if you might let him see them. But I don't think that he ever came to see you."

"Seo droch rud," Peader tapped the desk, "a bad thing."

"No." My father let the graveness rise to the surface. "He never came to see me. When . . . when did this man meet you?"

"A long time ago."

"When, a long time ago?" His voice was soft.

"About three weeks time." I tried to figure over the days.

"And is that all he asked of you?"

"It is, but he said that he had something in common with me. He said that we both had fathers who owned the estate."

"So he did, eh?" My father rubbed the round links of his watch chain.

I nodded, "yes".

"It's terrible what happened to Mr. Kelly. I am sorry for him."

"Yes." My father nodded. The word seemed to linger. Slowly he walked to the window that overlooked the lawn. It was the only window in the room.

"He does seem to be getting better, though." I faced Peader.

"Well, so he does, Ms. Anne." The older man stopped drumming his fingers on the table, and he rose from the chair. My father leaned wearily upon the casement. "Now that I've got you found," Peader walked toward the door, "I've somethin' for to show you."

It was true that he found me, for where was I to be? I could go nowhere that the house could not see. I had been rather easy to catch, seeing as there was no place that I could, in good faith, go.

I felt awkward leaving my father drooping over the casement. I felt as though I was leaving a silk wrap alone in the rain, and it would return all spotted and tattered. He seemed to watch for something that no one else could see, and he was staying himself for the terrible form. I stared softly at him for a moment before Peader took me from the room. It must have been proper for us to leave, or he would not have ushered me off to the edge of the barley field, where the young plants offered their thin leaves to the sky. He beckoned me over to a narrow strip of earth that ran between some ledge and several birches and thickets. Peader pointed to the ground.

"There, do you see it?" He stepped gingerly aside.

I looked. I walked closer to where his finger gestured. I walked carefully as he seemed to have been stepping around things, like one walking in a chicken yard. I couldn't see what he was stepping over, but I wasn't taking any liberties with my feet. He stabbed the air with his finger, but I couldn't see what he saw. I looked at his finger, I looked at the surrounding air, and then I bent and squinted toward the ground.

"What're you doin' girl, lookin' for footprints?" He teased me. Apparently, I wasn't doing this in a correct method.

"I don't know what you're showin' me?" I explained tediously.

"See there, then." He pointed to a string of small mushrooms. "Those are tellin' you that the good people have been this way, and mind that you don't step on 'em. This tiny cosán is a road of the sidhe for when they are goin' to their revels. It must ne'er be blocked you see."

I looked down at the fairy road, but I failed to see any footprints, not that I initially expected to anyway. Sheridan would never had taken this for truth, mushrooms, or no.

"There was a man that I knew down and back in Timoleague. He had built himself a new barn, so he did. There were his chickens, the cow, his horse, and his good tackle inside for plowin' and drivin'. And one night he thought that he might have left the door o' the place open. So out he went in the darkness and chill to see to it, and to ease his mind about the business." Peader raised an eyebrow and marked my level of interest. I stood as still as stone with interest, and with the fear of disturbing a mushroom. I was having a strenuous time of keeping my balance, knowing all those mushrooms were laying about my feet.

"Come back to the rocks here, girl, and take some ease."

I moved gingerly over to the fungus-free place.

"Well, now that man I was tellin' you about. He was gatherin' his top-coat to go out and check on the door, you see. He was no farther past the back of his own cottage when a staggerin' chill came o'er him, and he was stopped dead. He put out his light, and he went toward the faint talkin' comin' from the byre. He wanted to kick himself for puttin' all the new harness in there in the broad daylight, for there were thieves in that place now, as sure as he was standin' there. There was no point in gettin' the sheriff, for the rogues'd be gone before the law came. He didn't know what to do, but he thought he'd glance into that place for to see how many there were." Peader crossed his arms and leaned against the ledge. He peered down at me, and then started on.

"And what do you think that man saw?" He squinted an eye at me, as if he was looking at a flea on my nose. I know well enough that this was not your ordinary query, for indeed the questioner was Peader.

"Highwaymen?" I said. He shook his head.

"There was not a thing in that byre save the beasts. There was the cow in her standin' stall restless with fear; the hens on their roost clucked and stretched their necks in the darkness, and the horse tossed his head to see where the clamour was comin' from. There was bangin' and sawin' and the shouts o' labor. There was the creak of a nail bein' rent from wood, but there was not a scrap of sawdust or a light struck within. And then came a voice above the others, 'make haste!' it called, 'the byre must be down and carried off by the daybreak, or the man will not let us finish.' And then the voice continued, movin' o'er the air like new cream, 'we will never be able to pass this way again! The man will not find his days so easy as before.' Ah, now your fella outside the place did not like the sound of that. His hands were shakin', and he was loosin' his reason from the fear, but he called up what sense he had left. He spoke to the invisible carpenters."

"What did he say?" I didn't want to find myself in the darkness with a band of bodiless carpenters.

"'Good gentlefolk,' he did not want to offend what he couldn't see to fight. 'I beg your forgiveness, but would you tell me your honours why there's such a commotion bein' raised in this barn?' And that man got his answer. It was the good people, the sidhe, that were inside. He had built that byre in the center of a fairy road, and the good people were unable to follow their usual route to their place of revelry. With his mouth as dry as wheat straw, our man again addressed the enchanted demolishers.

'I beg your forgiveness, for I had no notion that this byre would cause such hardship for another such as yourselves. I ask your honours that I may have a few days in order to take down and move the structure as it was of a great cost for me to build.'"

"Ah, did they let him take it down?"

"Well, the sound of that fairy's voice caused that man's hair to rise on his head. 'We honour your pledge,' the leader said, 'for so long as the byre is down before May Eve, that is all we shall ask of you Mr. Quinn.' That was the fella's name, you see." Peader raised his hand to call out the point.

"What happened then, did the byre come down?" I had never heard of anyone getting a deal with the sidhe. But you weren't supposed to call them fairies, they were the "good people", and they were ever so easily offended that they demanded proper consideration.

"At the first slice of dawn, Mr. Quinn was out and at the sorrowful job. Destroyin' what had taken all those months of savin' and all those days of labor to build. It was a terrible thing to see. In the space of a-half week the place was no more, and the man was searchin' in him for the will to build again."

"That was a horrid thing for the good folk to ask of him." I moaned. "Sure, couldn't they have gone 'round the barn?"

"That's the ways o' the sidhe and there's no questions can be asked. Mr. Quinn wasn't askin' 'em, for the ancient roads are sacred to them, and he should've asked leave before he built, you see."

I nodded.

"The mornin' after the byre was down, Mr. Quinn went out to start on the new one. There were some of the neighbor men, and his own wife comin' to help with it. As our fella turned past the milk shed, he saw the most singular sight of his life. Clear across the path from where the first barn had stood, grew a rectangular patch of the queerist mushrooms he had e'er set eyes upon. The pattern they made was of the same size and shape of the old byre's floor. He sent the men and his wife home."

"The next day he went 'round to the byre again, and the sight that awaited him sent him to his knees with the shock of it. They had planned to set the stone foundation, but that foundation had already been laid and expertly so. He sent the men and his wife home again."

"Each day brought the same. Two steps of the finest white marble reached up to the back door, and the roof beams were thatched over with a skill he had ne'er seen. Inside the cow and horse stalls were marked out with mahogany planks, and the chicken roosts were carved of ash boughs with gold capping the ends. And after that day, Mr. Quinn ne'er saw the sidhe again. But there were three things that came soon and fore'er after." Peader rubbed his chin, and he cast a side-long glance at me.

"On each edge of those marble steps appeared foxgloves set in full splendour with their heads tiltin' from the weight o' the blooms. The second, there was always rows of mushrooms about the foundation o' that byre at all times o' year, e'en in draught. The third thing was the grandest of all. On each May Eve mornin', behind the biggest of the foxgloves sat a silk purse bound 'round with gold cordin'. The bottom was flattened out with the weight of its insides. And that was Mr. Quinn's gift you see, for his helpin' the sidhe as he did. Now, that there path that I showed is one o' those roads. If your walkin' past here and you see the wind blowin' the grass and leaves, then you know it is them ridin' the wind." Peader moved his hand slowly across the air.

"Ah, there's a grand lot o' mushrooms about here. Look at 'em all about the rock." He stepped gingerly toward the path so as not to damage any. I followed the example. I didn't want any fairy's wrath falling over me.

"Is that why your careful around all of them growin' here?" I asked. "Would the good people not be kindly to you for destroyin' their mushrooms, like what happened to Mr. Quinn for puttin' his byre on their road?"

Peader raised his eyes to add a question to my own. "No, girl!" He shook his head as if my concern was the strangest thing in the world. "Do you want me to be walkin' on the heads of the muisiriúim that I plan to be eatin'?" He bent over and broke the capped fungus from the earth. "What do you say we catch ourselves a basket and bring some o' these o'er to Mrs. Kelly?"

I said that it was a grand idea.

Chapter 25

Our trip to Mrs. Byrne's cottage was delayed by one week, due to the misfortune that had befallen Mr. Kelly. It was a grand thing that Thomas had been taken on for he was able to help the kitchen staff while Mrs. Kelly tended to her stricken husband. The house had progressively fallen into a position of chaotic control. We were as our own state, with all of the land about us foreign. I seemed to be expecting the boards beneath my feet to shift, and all that was now constant to fall away. I fed my chickens, and I took my lessons. I let Donovan fly out through the nursery window in the morning, I shut it each night, and I ushered Rowan out on his walks, which were now closer to home than usual. The world then, indeed, was not all that strange, and I found that I could decide how much of that strangeness to let in.

Today was Saturday. At two, I met Daniel by the stable. Thomas was released from any more duties, and he and Sheridan schooled Ashlyn and Gavin on the lawn before the pond. In earlier days this was strictly forbidden, as no amount of rolling and primping could clear the divots from the grass. But what to do, when you were forbidden to venture anywhere else? Peader watched forlornly as his green carpet was pressed down with pony hooves.

Daniel and myself went over to the low cottage by the dairy. A small, stone wall encircled the garden to keep the leafy inhabitants free from nibbling wanderers. By the door flourished a fountain of green wisps with pea-like seed pods dripping from the tough stems. The scotch broom was readying himself for next spring's cascade of blooms. Daniel tapped the lower section of the opened half-door. He anounced himself, and instantly a voice bade us to come in.

Daniel pulled at the door and stepped aside for me to pass. I had to let my eyes ease themselves to the darkness, as the sun had been shining warm over the land.

"How are you today, Mrs. Byrne?" Daniel removed his cap. I courtsied my greeting.

"Ah, I'm fine I am, young sir." She twisted on the four-legged stool by the hearth.

It always amazed me to wonder, however she could get down so low. "I've got your Peader's horns boilin' here. They're almost soft and done, and you can bring 'em o'er to him in a warm towel so that he can work 'em." She stirred the contents of the big, iron pot.

Peader carved combs and such trinkets from horns, that were then sold at market. Visitors were especially fond of hand-worked "Irish" goods, and Peader would act the devil by professing very little knowledge of English, and going on as the best stage-peasant on this side of the island. If you were to pass him in the morning in his worst work-clothes, heading off to borrow the Hutcheson donkey, you then knew he was going to town to drum up some devious trade. He would always leave early with much stealth so as not to catch mother's eye, for then he would receive a chastisement for "impersonating for gain those that are less-fortunate than you. Thank God, Peader, that you are not, as the boy who turns his eyes, left to stay that way." He would stand gloomily through the reprimand before offering as penance to give some of the ill-gained spoils to the poor house, and "to bring Mrs. Carolyn a samplin' of chocolates."

I sat happily on Mrs. Byrne's creepie, while Dan procured his favorite ladder-back, sitting upon it backwards with his arms folded over the top. The cottage gave forth the scent of stone and old wood. There too, was the smell of earth, and the sweet smoke of the peat warmed all those notes together as it drifted across the open room. Mrs. Byrne knocked the contents of her pipe out into the fire.

"Isn't it the funniest thing," she turned the pipe in the air, and eyed it as it was a rare oddity. "I could ne'er stand the old man smokin' this. And so it was, after he died, I started missin' the smell of it. Now, isn't that the most curious thing. There I am missin' the one thing of him that I couldn't stand a t'all. Ah, I don't think I'll e'er get used o' the taste of it." She looked derisively into the small bowl and placed it on the table where a carved, wooden rooster stood guard.

"That reminds me," she raised a rugged finger. "Dan, would you when you leave, bring that boiled chicken to the Kelly's?" The boy nodded. "That man'll be sooner up and about after one o' me chickens, than anythin' of that town doctor, and he'll have a heavier pocket after it, too."

"So that's true, Mrs. Byrne." The boy laughed.

"How's your friend Thomas doin' at his new work, Anne?" She removed the steaming pot from the heat.

"He's doin' well, Mrs. Byrne." And I told her a goodly amount of details.

Soon we were talking about our troubles, but not directly. It only took one mention of Mr. Richard Cosgrove, and the eyes of our old friend seemed to fill with the knowledge that their owner had left to moulder inside. We had discovered post-haste that we had started our search in the right place. Here is what was handed down to us.

It was known that my grandfather, Gerald O'Hayden from Glendalough, had acted upon his interest in the abandoned estate many decades ago. But the people in the area of Carrickduff were unwilling to talk about the house, and those who did were no less free with their answers. Mr. O'Hayden's concern as to why the house had such a silencing and mysterious affect over her neighbors was thoroughly peaked. My grandfather went straight away to the bank that held the deed to the property on the hill. He had much to ask the gentleman with whom he was planning to fashion a deal, and some of his most pressing queries were dealt with. The house was sound, and hired carpenters found that to be so. The next question pertained to the odd manner of the local population. It was known, the bank man had said, that there were evictions issued under unfortunate circumstances, that had fashioned a terrible impact upon the people in the area, and so that was why they wanted nothing more to do with the house. The explanation was plausible, and Mr. O'Hayden was not unfamiliar with the superstitions of the common classes, being from them himself. He knew of hard days, and he knew of tradition. But things had changed now, and the superstitions gave way to gentlemanly pursuits, and he signed the deed to Carrickduff. And how the bank was eager to dispose of that accursed, decaying property. With much of the former land wagered off to pay gambling debts, the remainder was too small for the majority of enterprising landlords or greedy gentry. And what was there in turn, was far beyond the means of anyone else. Land was still land, and the bank was not about to lose valued earth. The house was perfect for that peasant-gentleman who had earned that impossibility from the barley trade. My grandfather offered a fair price, and when the paperwork was finished, the bank walked free from its useless, stone dependent.

There was one family on the outskirts of the estate. They were tenants of the Lord and Lady Barrand, the same Barrands upon whose land the Timoneys now lived. The man worked those fields, and the wife tended to seven children of various ages with three off and grown. The Byrne's knew Carrickduff, and they were willing to talk.

Gerald O'Hayden spent many an evening calling on the Byrne's cottage. A friendship that was to prove enduring was soon struck up. Mr. Byrne would begin to spend his leisure hours at work on Carrickduff's buildings. Although he was not a Bray man, his wife had never strayed far from the coastal town.

Sara Byrne was born in 1781 upon the estate of Arthur Crawford, when the house on the hill was grand and flourishing. She could still remember the grand lady, the wife of the deceased gentleman, who had built a fortune in the brewery trade. The woman maintained an elegance of manner until the day of her death at the age of ninety. Mrs. Arthur Crawford would walk the unblemished grounds in fair and fowl skies. There was a garden with a boxwood border, which was flawless and classical as any of its mates in France. Each creation of nature was perfectly subdued into living objects of punctual geometry.

Outside of those idyllic greens spread the acreage of Carrickduff. She would move over the property to catch the men in the fields with a "God save you," and wait knowingly until the plow met the top of the row for the man to return the greeting. The old Mrs. Crawford was birthed in England, but Ireland would own her undividedly. And there would she stay amidst those perfect gardens.

"If I didn't tell you two, that that there place where you've set in those geraniums was the grand French jardin, you'd ne'er believe it. But it was." Mrs. Byrne raised her head in a toast to the past. "And there was where herself would sit in the farthest corner to read at three o'clock on fair afternoons. Oh, I would beg me mother, 'let me go to the carved garden as I've done all me chores.' And me mother'd say for me not to be botherin' the mistress. But she'd let me go all the same." The old woman smiled.

"I'd go then, and watch Mrs. Crawford through the bushes, as I was too ashamed to have her see my person. She'd sit quiet with some book, and she had to be over seventy-eight then, and as spry as a lamb, with the hair on her head as copper as when she was a school girl. One day she was in a frock of the finest thin cotton, not like the stuff today, for the dresses were worn close, and the waists were high. The dress was white and touched with ornaments of blue, so that she looked to be wearin' the sky. I just sat down on the grass and stared through the boxwoods. I was there for a good while, when me shoulders were grabbed hold of by a groundsman. I remember what he said too, the bla'gard, 'What're you up to there, you little devil?'" She jabbed an accusing finger in the air.

"I ne'er was so startled in me life. The fear was raised in me so that I couldn't speak a word to save meself. Well, the mistress must've heard the business, for didn't she come o'er by way of the back gate, which you've got replaced now with nothin' a t'all. 'What's the matter Holland?' she said, 'Isn't that the young Byrne girl?' Now I was witherin' with the embarrassment on me. What a grand way to meet the lady. That man was sayin' how he had found me in the bushes like a weasel, and up to no good. Well, that was not bein' shown from the look on my face, and the lady Crawford picked it up. There was a turn of events that you couldn't believe, and before I could blush, I was sittin' in Carrickduff itself havin' tea with all of 'em. That's the way the woman was. All of 'em were like that, e'en the dead master they said. I ne'er met him alive you see. If there were more as them in this land, we'd have nothin' to cry for. Ah,well . . . there were three generations I saw. It was the great-grandaughter that was the last to have the house. Mrs. Crawford was gone some twenty years by that age, and her grandson had produced no survivin' heirs. Only the youngest girl stayed, and that's how the daughter got the house when she married. It's her girl child then, that you two are askin' about. Elizabeth was her name, and that's the one who married Richard Cosgrove."

"We were wonderin' why the Mrs. Elizabeth was not the caretaker of the boy, William?" Daniel asked.

"The father was a debtor, wasn't that so?" I said

"You see, that all started 'round five years after the weddin'. Grain prices were low after Napoleon's wars, and the banks were strainin'. That sent the new master, Richard Cosgrove, lookin' for some extra income. There wasn't much known about the fella, save that the rogue came from Surrey, from the sister country. Well, he was a grand man for talk. He'd have you believe that the moon was just the sun turned around." She raised the flat of her hand and flipped it. "He was a big man back in England. He had said that his father made money in linen and shippin'—as sure as those sheep in the field did. He was a liar, he was; a courtly profiteer, but you'd ne'er know it. They knew it in England though, in the gentle classes, and he was probably driven' out! The farmer had seen the fox in the hen house, and the hounds were loosed in the field. God knows then, why the rake came to Ireland, but he brought nothin' to the marriage save the winsome di'vil of himself."

Mr. Cosgrove was well pleased with the estate of Carrickduff. He was, however, not wise to the practicalities of running it, according to Mrs. Byrne. His love for acquiring money, and his distaste for the tenantry soon rose to the top of the once carefully shaped façade. And with that eruption, the damage was about to begin.

The man had invested money in property, and those investments began to fail. Carrickduff's fields were not covering the losses, and rack-renting did nothing but foster scorn amongst the peasantry. The old families that Mrs. Elizabeth had seen since childhood, the ones that worked for her grandfather with the names that were as familiar to her as the smooth stones of the house, were leaving the land. Even the Byrnes had moved to the neighboring estate. She tried to intervene when the evictions were issued, but there was nothing she could do but hate.

Mr. Cosgrove took to the drink, and he even took his young son to the gambling table with him. William was barely five when he was brought into the world of debauchery and fraud. He never knew his mother after the age of five. The very form of him reminded Elizabeth of his father. She could not live with the sight of him, and the knowledge that he was half herself was more than she could bear.

Mrs. Elizabeth was now seen less and less upon the saddened stones of her grand family's home. She would spend the weeks in Kildare, under the roof of her cousin. She was known as Ms. Crawford, because the name of her husband, "carved my soul like acid," she said. Those words unfurled across the countryside, along the resplendent beaches, and into the sitting rooms of Dublin. Carrickduff had fallen.

Elizabeth would never again show herself beyond the lawns of her cousin's estate, until the dark caleche drew her coffin past that iron gate. The house had its new master. It was her wish to be buried on the grounds of the crumbling manor, beneath her Carrickduff. And that wish was seen to by the man from the valley of Glendalough, the self-made novelty with the name of O'Hayden. The house was beginning to live again, as they lowered her coffin into the earth.

"I was there the day they brought her." Mrs. Byrne prodded the past. "I stood with your grandfather and his wife in that small cemetery. We had it groomed of the high grass and shrub for her. It had rained for three days, and the house on the hill, she was as black as the hearse that drew her mistress home. It was an awful sad thing to see, I can still remember it. Your grandfather was a headstrong and flinty man, but wasn't he the last to leave that grave. He had it dug so that the stone would face the house. He was gonna make things right for her, wasn't he. He was the last to leave that grave, and he traced a cross onto its earth." Mrs. Byrne looked quietly at us.

"And so there's your answer and more." She took the wooden spoon and tapped at the rim of the kettle.

"Ah," she pushed up slowly from the low stool and took a basket for the boiled chicken. "That there house is a queer thing. There's somethin' dark in the way she looks at you. She's like Ireland, isn't it so. They live from death, those two. Can you ne'er set the two of 'em right? And so know that that house was born from the very stones themselves, for there rests your answer."

"We're not to leave sight o' the house!" I stressed each word as if they hurt. I let my hand skim the surface of the pond as the rowboat floated along. Daniel had stopped paddling, and we were drifting on no current.

"Ah, but we're only goin' to that cemetery. It's still on the property." The boy pleaded off-handedly. He crumbled some more bread for the goldfish that followed the boat.

"Yes, but it's not *in the sight* of the house." I played lightly with the the white goldfish nibbling my finger. Her small head was smooth, and had the texture of soft, wet glass.

"No one's after us, so!" Dan reached over the boat's rim to let an orange, buck-fish take the crumbs from his fingers. "What would they want from us anyway?"

"What'd they want from, Mr. Kelly?" I added with saucy intelligence.

"That's different, he works here."

"You work here."

"Ah," the boy waved his hand, "but nobody knows me. I don't go around where there's people."

"You're not invisible, people know you. Besides, you've got no memory on you, they could've left you like Mr. Kelly."

"But they didn't. And *you* probably met the principal player himself." Daniel retorted, calling up my story about Mr. Cosgrove in the cemetery.

"That was before all of this," I shrugged. I remembered my father leaning on the window casement. I remembered Peader ushering me off to see the fairy road. I wondered how long my father had bowed his dark head over the casement, with the distraught hardness burning in his eyes.

At four, we went to the cemetery. Sheridan came, and Thomas too, with the second boy holding a basket of rolls that must've been a gift from mother. Donovan was home for tea, and Rowan came with us as well to get himself an airing. The path that we were to take was on Thomas's way, and he tarried a moment with us, as he wasn't missed at home until after five.

"See, there it is!" Daniel pointed to the newest of the gravestones. "It's her's, and Mrs. Byrne was right." He knelt before the lichened marble. "'Elizabeth

Crawford . . . . 1799-1836'. And it's set so as to face the house. Can you imagine all the stuff of her life. I ne'er thought any of it, when I looked at the stone before. I thought it was the plainest of 'em all."

"I always liked the old one over there"—I pointed toward the broken gate—"that one with the face worn off it. But now that Ms. Crawford's one has things that'll ne'er be worn off. They're sittin' inside our heads."

"My mother would go for a story like that, the woman with her scoundrel of a husband." Thomas sat on the ground "I'll tell her I learned it from the 'old woman' I work for." He smiled. "So it's her son that Mr. O'Hayden thinks is doin' the troublin'?"

"He does. William Cosgrove says the place is his by his father's will. But sure it isn't 'cause ol' Cosgrove lost the place to the bank, and he died in debt e'en though he wrote a will. You can't give away what you don't have in the first place. Apparently, Mr. William doesn't want to understand that," my brother said.

"He's tryin' to put one o'er on ye's." Thomas understood.

"We'd have to be daft to be coerced by somethin' like that. Now, how'd he figure to get away with it?" I let Rowan free from his leash to hunt about the grounds. Donovan was sitting in Daniel's arms.

"He knows what he's doin', he does," Thomas reasoned. "Your Mr. Cosgrove figured your father'd ne'er put the place for sale, nor would that William have had the brass to buy, I'd bet ya'. He brought that will for'ard just to see if he could make things easy for himself."

"Sure, there was always the chance that Mr. O'Hayden was slow-witted, and would hand the place up." Dan placed the raven on the grass.

"There was a fair bit o' confusion with the bank's handlin' of the property on ol' Cosgrove's death anyway. That's what Mrs. Byrne said. Nobody wanted the place as if there was a curse on it, and so the bank took it." I remembered. "There was ne'er any mention of a will, nor any copies."

"That was a fine mess o' things, then." Thomas was pleased to hear that his theory was working. "So now you can see that Mr. William is after burnin' you out, as they say. You've already met the sheriff, and the batterin' ram's on the road. Don't forget the fire in the shed, and the ambush of Mr. Kelly. See, the deadline's comin', and the note's on the door."

"That's why father's been so troubled. He's been talkin' to Peader, and after he spoke with mother, she's been cold to him. They're all worried, but they won't tell us anythin'." I shrugged.

"Now, that's it." Daniel tipped his head. "That blag'gard knows your father. He knows that Mr. O'Hayden won't bend. He's talked to people about him, and William knows Mr. O'Hayden better'n us, now. And he knows that your father won't give in, so long as the punishments are on him alone. That's why Mr. Kelly was roughened o'er. If the blows are struck on others, on the things he cares about, Mr. O'Hayden'll yield."

"The mention of the 'price' in the note," I interrupted, "that's what it is. The price isn't money a t'all, nor is it father's asking."

"It's what Mr. O'Hayden is willing to pay." The last words were whispers on the boy's lips.

"Why is he doin' it to us?" Sheridan tossed a rock toward the bushes.

"It's that house." Thomas leaned against Mr. Crawford's stone.

The business was terrible to think about. We couldn't get to the law. Who would believe that we were troubled with this queer affliction? We had to fight alone against a man who would not show himself. We had to put up a barricade against a ghost. Carrickduff could not help. She was of the stones of Ireland. That's what Mrs. Byrne said. She was of those stones, and so she would just watch as her courtiers laid their lives at her feet.

Daniel wanted to see the fairy road, and so Sheridan scoffed and returned to the house without us. Thomas had to hasten home before "they missed the fourth one".

I clipped Rowan back to his leash, and he dragged along behind us. Donovan followed too, hopping and flapping in an ungainly method to keep up.

"'Tis over there, between the rock and that block of hedges." I pointed to the narrow clearing. "There was a whole scatterin' of mushrooms, but they're dryin' up now . . ." I was distracted by Rowan's fidgiting. He kept running between my legs, and pulling at the leash as if he wanted to get away. He was sniffing about, and rubbing close to the ground. I tried to pick him up, and he snapped. "So stop it then!" I scolded, "you can't go off now. We're gonna have to go in soon."

"What's eatin' him?" Daniel's voice asked from behind my back. "He's had enough roamin' today."

I kneeled down to try to catch the stoat, but the little animal barked and reared so swiftly that the leash dashed away with its owner before I could tighten my loosened grip. At that same moment, a scraping sounded at my back. It was of the character of one tripping on a rocky path and foundling to claim his footing. I turned around to note the cause, and the fear that struck my eyes burned through me like a lamp flame and I gasped.

The tall blonde man held Daniel by the waist, his left hand over the boy's mouth with vicious force. Donovan bolted into the sky, and his harsh call echoed in the tiny glade.

Daniel scrambled in the stranger's grasp, battering his way half free. The blonde man maneuvered his strength to hold the boy, and I knew that I had to win him loose. I searched deliriously for a large stone, and with the will of God, there lay one by the verge. I reached for it and prayed that I might have the skill to throw it rightly, as I would have no chance in a direct struggle with the villain. With the fear in my body, I fell on the path, but I struggled to my knees and laid hold upon the rock.

"Is that what they teach you?" I was pushed to earth, and I lay flat upon my prize, with my cheek scratching the gravel. My eyes closed as I was dashed to my feet and roughly shaken. "Stones are not the proper things, James, for a young lady." The voice was English, but unfamiliar. It wasn't Cosgrove, the man would never do his own bidding. "Not proper even for an Irish one."

The man held me fast, and I dared not move until my escape plan was fully sound. The grip on my arms was unyielding, and although the scoundrel was small, he could break me. "Here's the young miss!" He laughed. I was the prize then, the next "price".

"Tell Andrew to get ropes for this one!" The blond man struggled with Daniel as the boy seemed not to tire. The man was Irish, but not from here.

I was dragged and carried back a few steps. I kicked and twisted. The fear mixed with hate, and I fought despite my shaking. "Damn you!" The Englishman shook me. "Get rid of that one!" He tried to pick me up, but I writhed savagely. I caught sight of Daniel as he bit the man's hand. The action was in vain, as he was now losing his fight. The blond man sighed with pain, but recovered too soon for Daniel to free himself, and I froze with horror as he grasped the boy to throttle him.

All of the fight left me. I stopped struggling, because I could not think anymore. I was sick. I was watching the boy die, and I seemed not to exist anymore. He should never have come here. He should never have come to the house with the black stones.

"Leave the boy! or God help me I'll shoot ya' and bury ya' where you stand!"

Peader stood before the fairy road with the new pistol readied. It was leveled upon the murderer with a steady accuracy. The blonde man released his fatal hold, and Daniel fell to the gravel. He crawled forward before dropping senseless on the side of the path.

Peader's gun did not move as he gazed sharply over his shoulder to affirm that all of the business stood before him. "The first one of ye's to run gets my bullet." He sent a glance over to the stilled boy. The blonde man ceased his movement toward the Englishman. I made no attempts to escape, but the man still held me firm.

"Will you not hand over the girl, then." Peader motioned with the pistol. The man gripped me tighter.

"I'll have you arrested for having the gun. A man like you would never get off of the charge lawfully," my assailant threatened with the carefully chosen poison.

"You'll be doin' it as a ghost." Peader's voice was low with hate. The slanderous attack was deeply felt, but he would not be provoked. "Hand her over."

"This is my prize, and I'll not send that over." The Englishman was unaware the prowess of the hand that guided the fire-arm. "Shoot that bastard if you will," he gestured to the other man, "but you'd risk this," he shook me, "if you try here."

"I'd be riskin' nothin', save my own ease at seein' you dead." Peader affirmed.

"You may not have faith in me, but you'd better faith in God, as He's the next you'll be lookin' at when you're to open the eyes again."

The Englishman did not apparently desire to test his questionable religious standing, for I was summarily released. I found my legs instantly, and I bolted to Peader.

"If you follow me, I'll put bullets in both of you." He pulled me toward him roughly. "I know what you look like, and I'm gonna share the knowledge. Go and tell your Master Cosgrove that if any of ye's are seen here on this land you'll be dragged to gaol for trespassin'. I won't be so kind; I'll kill you and bury you in a way fittin' for the rogue's that you are."

We waited for the villains to leave. I hadn't noticed that I had been shivering despite the warm air. Peader's grip on my arm was painfully secure, as he dragged me over to the still body of the boy. After a final search of the area, he stuck the pistol under his thick belt.

"Don't you go anywhere." He commanded. I nodded, and my arm was released.

"Here's a thing for young ones to see." He shook his head. "What am I gonna tell your father; that poor woman of your mother. This is a desperate business." He leaned forward over the motionless boy. "This is enough." He moved to his knees, moaning with the effort or the trouble of it all, and bent over Daniel, as if his figure was an effigy for adoration. He rolled the boy into his arms and rose.

"He's not goin' to be dead, is he?" I stood close by the man's full arms. I was still shivering, and it was only possible to utter sounds in a whisper.

"Probably not till another sixty or so years, God willing." Peader walked beside me.

The boy was brought to the carriage house and placed in bed. I was bade to stay with Peader, while a groundsman was sent to gather father. The situation was chafingly awkward. I sat on a hard chair with my hands folded before me. Peader drummed his fingers on the common room table. He would leave every other moment to note whether or not the boy had regained his senses.

There came the sound of determined-footsteps, which caused my rescuer to rise from the table and hasten down the creaking stairs. I sent my eyes to the floor as my father's boots struck the lifted old threshold. The groan of the wood ground through me, and I pressed my teeth together. The air was starched with military precision as my father crossed the room to attend to the boy. I could have faded from the world had not Niamh whinnied from her stall downstairs.

Peader moved to my side, and I gazed up quickly to the window where my father now stood. I searched over his long, narrow shoulders. His dark head was bent over the casement. Mr. O'Hayden was somewhere else. He was as the dead are; empty, with their bodies deserted.

"Would you take Anne to the house, Peader." His voice was as one asleep. He turned to look at me. "I will stay with the boy, now." I watched him move to the back room, until Peader ushered me to the stairs.

Chapter 26

"I will not give this place to the reincarnation of the man who destroyed it!" My father's voice carried up into the common room of the carriage house breaking our game of cards.

We heard one of the horses below shy and snort in protest. Daniel had awoke, but was temporarily left without the ability to speak. He had been wallowing in boredom since being ordered by the doctor to refrain from any business until the great insult to his body wore off. Peader had whistled about the stalls as he saw to the recovering boy's duties. "Oh," he said, "isn't it grand about the place. So ciúin you can go deaf hearin' yourself think," Daniel had answered with a silent scowl. There was no *ciúin* in the stable now.

The blaze of voices sent us padding swiftly from the common room, and out onto the railed walkway that overlooked the stalls below. My father paced the dusty aisle, and Peader leaned against a stall partition.

"I dare any man to claim Carrickduff, sir." Peader spoke earnestly. "I am sayin' only that the business has gone grave. We have been lettin' that man play his figures, and we've not e'en set ours down yet. We ne'er know which square he's aimin' for. He's too close to my door, sir, and I'm gonna start to move my pieces."

Daniel shifted his weight, and I laid flat upon the gritty wood. Sheridan whispered something, and I silenced him. There was a terrible feeling settling.

"I have no chessmen." My father rubbed his cheek. "So what to do, Peader? What to do to the man that has destroyed my home and turned us into kindling; to the man who has made my children prisoners, and my wife a wilting scholar. She flowers resplendent as her stem is corrupting. I cannot stand to look upon her, Peader!" His voice was anguished, and he dropped his head with self-revulsion. "She smiles as I destroy what she has created." His voice was a whisper.

"You have done nothin'." Peader's face was sullen.

"I have done nothing!" He smiled mockingly, thrusting his fingers through his dark hair. "That is the revelation. Look at the boy, Peader—at my daughter!"

"You could not have known, sir. I was there, that was all. Don't fuss o'er a thing that's come out all right."

"You were there, Peader. I was not. I was not there for my child, I never am. You see my father contrived that I should never be there. He taught me to run, so that I may never know anything but grandness, so that I may never know pain as he had. But the world doesn't fashion itself that way." He raised his finger and shook it as one scolds a child. "I don't want the heroics. I want to be a father. I want Cosgrove to become the ghost that he is. I want our lives back!" The man's harsh eyes glowered with hate. "Can I ask for that? when God has given me more than I need?"

"Now that's an off question. It is a queer world, and we take what we are given. But I ne'er believed God to have a hand in guidin' the bad. That's man's work surely." Peader walked across the aisle. The stable fell silent. The soft shuffling of the horses was all there was to hear. It seemed to echo inside you. My father stared at Padraic as if the gelding was speaking to him.

"I could ride 'til I find Cosgrove. He is a man, and as such must procure an animal's necessities. He is not of the sidhe, but if I must wait at the base of his mystical hill 'til the moon grants me passage, so be it, I will attend."

"And kill yourself," Peader said prosaically. "That's what'd happen, and you wouldn't be much of a father then. Wait and he'll come to you, sir. That's our play. If we must hold the place as a fortress, then we shall. It is just a matter of breakin' the scoundrel. He has no patience, he'll break, damn me. He'll be flushed out before we will, because we've got everythin', don't we? We've got Carrickduff, we've got men, and it's our country here. All he has is the terror, and if we don't be taken with his bluffs, then he's got nothin'. Mark me, sir. He'll come to you." The older man nodded.

"Cosgrove has the 'terror,' Peader. So I wait for him to strike again, and what will that be? We will be rabbits in the warren, prayin' that the ferret won't be loosed at our back door! We are talkin' about my wife, my children, the safety of the tenants . . . I will not place them as game pieces! Because that is what the villain wants. Cosgrove doesn't want to face me. He knows that should he strike at my family, at my men, then the result is worse than death for me. I know he will not kill me. I am asked to gamble other's lives for those blocks of stone!" He pointed savagely at the house. "How long must the children hide?" Hate had cast itself across his narrow face. My brother and I said nothing as we lay on the wood. Daniel stared down through the thick rails. A sprinkling of movement caused me to turn my head, and I saw my mother stand at the corner of Niamh's stall. The mare knickered, but the two men did not catch her warning.

"You can keep the children safe." Peader started to raise his voice. "It won't be forever. Those children want the house, you can't deny that! You want the house."

"Can that truly be practiced? Can I keep them safe?" He turned his strangled aggression toward the older man. "The guilt sticks in my throat. I want the house, Peader . . . yes. I want the house that I could kill to protect it! It scares me to know that, but it's the truth of it. I cannot risk my family. I would to be dead then, swallow the selfish guilt, and be buried with it."

"You wouldn't die, sir, because it wouldn't be." Peader lowered his tone.

"Ah, you can see into the future then. You cannot know what I suffer." My father writhed over the words. He stared coldly at his silent companion. Peader's face turned to that which I had never seen cross his gentleness before. His mouth seemed to narrow, and he stared full into my father's hard eyes. The dark-haired man sighed and half turned from the consuming gaze. "I've gone mad, then." He pointed, but did not look. "I spoke to you like that. I indulge into my own thoughts so, I have forgotten reason."

"You can't see the reason you grasp." Peader walked closer to my father's side. "You don't know what it's like, Mícheál." Peader closed on the man's gaze. "You can think it, but you cannot know it. You don't know what it's like to lose a child and a wife. It's everywhere shadowin' you like a ghost at your side. It almost speaks to you. You have the distractions to cover o'er the pain, because nothin' can heal it. And when the loud day goes, when the twilight falls, when the clouds bring the stillness; the pain comes back again, until that time when you cannot feel pain anymore. You don't know what it's like"—he stared at the silent form of my father—"and I don't want you to." He turned and walked toward Padraic's stall.

"I'm sorry, Peader." My father's whisper stilled him.

"That is the queer nature of life, Mícheál. You can't be sorry for that."

"That's not—"

"I *know* what you meant, so," Peader silenced him. "We must wait, that is all we can do."

They did not note my mother by Niamh's stall. They did not note her until she moved into the aisle. She walked with punctual step, as if she was counting the distance in a duel. Her burgundy dress swung with her gait, and her pale hand steadied before her as if it cursed the air. Peader stepped aside.

"Do you speak of my children?" Her voice was rich with darkness. My father turned to face her. They were a pair, a flint, and a steel. Fear rolled in me as I waited, should they touch.

"Do you speak of them without me? Do you dare to take such bold liberties?"

My father did not answer as he let his eyes rest upon the woman's face. His lip twisted, and the sight of his tormented wife struck him as no blow could.

"We did not want to worry you, ma'am." Peader tried to lessen the storm, but his voice was weak, and it drowned in the taught sea.

"You did not want to worry me?' She never turned her head to the older man at her back. "Because"—her head tilted with derision—"what we do not face does not exist. If we do not speak of it, then it did not happen." She stepped forward after each decree. "Well, it is happening! And nothing is not stopping it! Are we to wait until it stops with the cost of my children? Is that what you have decided?" She let her voice reveal the resentment that lived inside her.

"I wanted for you to not know this agony." My father strained the words through anger. He seemed to snarl.

"And you thought that you could do that?" She smiled mockingly. "What arrogance! You are a fool, Mícheál. Will next you put me in a cage like those ornaments in your room? You are right. You cannot run anymore." She shook her head. He closed his eyes against her words.

"It is fitting that you close your eyes. What good are they to you? They have served you poorly. I will be your eyes, for even though you have put me in a cloche, I can still see. I can see that you are already trapped, and cursed. The house has endowed that to you at birth. What an inheritance has been got for you. What a gift that has been brought forth by the very stones that entombed your first taste of life. The house has destroyed even the man who had laid her first stone. It was then the corruption began, but she was to claim more yet, before her fall. She must have life in her walls to survive. Your grandfather gave her that life as his own children died beneath him, all but you, Mícheál. Now, she lives from us as the moss lives from her stones. She will destroy you, because you are her son. But I will not let Carrickduff destroy me or my children." She turned from him as he raised his head.

"Is that what I am?" My father's gaze lowered on her silk-covered back. "A blasphemy before your presence?"

There was silence before she faced him.

"I don't know." My mother's voice was an audible whisper. She turned again to go, and the silk and burgundy enveloped her frame as she moved from the door.

The house had become a living tomb. We all walked out of earshot, but fully within sight. There was an instinctive distance kept between all of us. Daniel had regained his ability to speak, but there was very little use for talk, and even less to say. The servants shuffled about like insects inside our unwalled gaol. Ms. Farrell had been momentarily released to her mother's home in Dublin. The unpleasant holiday had been deemed a move for the best. We were bid to read our study books, but with my cluttered mind I executed the duty with boundless difficulty. My brother seemed to fare no better. Daniel wrote at all hours, as if he was vying to be the most prolific poet of the age. Our new freedom fed our weariness. Donovan and Rowan, with animal skill, were a great source of needed ease for our spirits. There was precious little joy. Even the sun came out to spite us.

I became disturbed to note the change that lived now on my father's face. He spent most of his time with the workers, or riding out on Padraic. I didn't like to see him leave the house on horseback, for then I was filled with shadows, like the Lady of Shalott. It was disconcerting to not feel his anger at me, for going to the cemetery with Daniel. All was revealed about our trek, but no word of punishment was levied for the forbidden act. Peader had intervened. "You can tell the young ones"—he had spoke to both my parents—"you can work the spirit out o' them, you can give 'em the strap so as they won't be usin' their backsides for a spell to sit. But be sure there's no teacher like experience herself, to teach what the discipline couldn't show, so long as the child lives to swallow the lesson. Ah, it's a hard way to learn, to be sure, but the garsúin prefer it, against all sense of reason."

The fear from that event paled within me, as I watched my father suffer. He never read any books now. He never told me the "old stories." He was up before the rooks and crows, and many a night, I was sure that he slept fitfully in his study. There was a passion in his eyes that deepened as he removed himself from the lowly restraints of his body. He was waiting for the next "price" to be asked. When he rode out, he wished to tempt the villain by showing himself, but Mícheál was not the game.

My mother spent much of her day in feverish study. She catalogued plants, copied their natures in watercolor—often several of one—and avoided most of us during the course of the days. She worked well into the night, and craved the isolation that the darkness could bring. I was afraid that any prolonged sight of me would remind her too deeply of the spell under which we lived. Norah was with her most out of anyone. The young maid had said that soon Mrs. Carolyn would crack like an egg and something would come out. I worried about what that something was going to be.

No one could deny what was happening to Carrickduff. Despite the shielding of our ears and the blinders on our eyes, the cock had crowed for the third time, with a voice made stronger at each turn. Who would believe that we were tormented by a living ghost. There was still no villain to show, no goods to call missing, and no unfortunate body to be retrieved. The actions were imaginary, the threats fashioned of air, and their terror carried in the wind. But the storm was felt, and its blows were real. We were captives, and we were destroying ourselves.

I soon came to find that there was a lot to occupy oneself on the farm. I had never noticed the trivial interests that lurked about when I was free to dash off and rove the countryside. We were still forbidden to leave the grounds, but I held no desire to do so yet. The odd, unsettling dream still plagued me, and I found myself needing eyes at my back, so that my neck could be saved from repeated turning. I don't think that a mouse could have footed up behind me. I thought of the man that had visited me in the cemetery. Was I the only one, save poor Mr. Kelly, to have seen William Cosgrove? Maybe he had been enlightened of Peader's harsh forewarnings and had taken them to mind. Had he cast away his thieving desire for Carrickduff and returned to swindle fortunes from artless English gentlefolk? Such a thing, such a dream, seemed unlikely.

The sprawling summer days had a gracious space in which to play themselves out. Thomas would return after his supper and stay until the sky paled. He was asked to come later in the morning now and to take care his route. It was, however, not feared that Mr. Cosgrove would seek his "price" from the unconnected boy. The warnings were revealed out of our quickened sense for caution.

With little tasks of our own, Sheridan and I spent much of our time with Thomas and the work staff. We would venture to Mrs. Byrne's cottage, tend to her garden, or follow her to the hothouse to help with the exotics. She had started several pineapples from the spiky heads taken from the fruits that we ate. She would take the tops and put the fleshy bottoms in a glass of water, where soon enough they set to rooting. The new plants were potted up under Peader's skeptical eye, and "you'll ne'er get a spot of a thing outta 'em." Mrs. Byrne turned up her nose to him. He watched her stick an apple in the center of the rugged, green spires, fold the hard leaves in, and tie them up. "Your stone mad, woman. You could stand on yer head and sing to it, and you'll still get naught from that thing." He was there when she lifted the glass, unbound the leaves that had imprisoned the apple, and the little pineapple stared up into Peader's shocked face. "Ah, I've ne'er been fond of the taste of those things. Makes your mouth all raspy like a cat's tongue. Would've been better off eatin' the apple." Mrs. Byrne smiled victoriously.

In the summer we helped her prune and fuss over father's tomatoes. The vines were tied to poles, and the bottom leaves plucked away. The whole place would have the robust smell of the tomatoes that you would soon be getting. Thomas was exceedingly fond of the scent, and I was sure that Mr. Timoney was perplexed as to the origin of the exotic aroma rolling off his son's clothes. Thomas was fond of the red fruits, but he never brought any home to share for two reasons. The first was that he wanted them for himself. The second was that tropical delicacies did not grow freely in the Irish soil, and so questions would have been bound to materialize around the Timoney table.

"Mother says that tomatoes are potatoes too." I held the vines while Thomas tied.

"How can they be potatoes, they're nothin' alike."

"Oh yes," I insisted. "They have the same leaves and flowers, 'cept one's yellow and the other's white. They're nightshades from America."

"Well, they don't make the same things. They don't taste the same. You get potatoes in the ground."

"Ah, but that's the only difference. See, the leaves are all sticky and hairy, just like potatoes."

"Sure, but that's still not a close thing."

"You've got a mackeral"—Mrs. Byrne came over—"and you've a goldfish. They hardly look a thing alike, and one's in the salt water, and t'others in the sweet. And aren't they all fish? 'Tis the same with the tomato and the prataí. One fruits on the stem, and t'other you get the root."

Thomas didn't seem to swallow that explanation, and I cannot say that it made a good deal of sense to me either. But by some other more scientific reasoning, let it be known that tomatoes and *prataí* are of the same ilk. Mr. William Cosgrove and Mrs. Elizabeth his mother were of the same ilk, and they were similar on the outside; but when you got down to things, one fruited above as red as the rose, and the other below in the darkness of the earth.

Daniel ran into the damp hothouse where we worked. His boots sounded off of the flagstones. He slid to a stop before a patch of potted tomatoes.

"Is Thomas there?" he asked with a quickened expression. As the boy panted, I pointed around a particularly bushy clump of plants.

"I'm here." The desired party stood up into view.

"Aw, then I've got some news for you." Daniel closed his eyes to stress the power of the forthcoming tale. "Your father was havin' a pint at Keenan's last night, wasn't he?"

"So he was." Thomas shrugged. "He usually goes there."

"Mr. Wickham was there too." Daniel raised his eyes.

"Who's Mr. Wickham?" Thomas echoed the expression.

"Works in the dairy, here." Dan pointed to the ground.

"What does that have to do with Thomas?" I asked. I put down the basket of aromatic tomato clippings.

"Mr. Wickham got to talkin' with Mr. Timoney, and they must've been havin' a slow go of it, because they started talkin' about you." He pointed to the boy.

"Ah, and why wouldn't they be talkin' about me?" Thomas puffed up.

"Well, your majesty," Daniel continued, "your father knows that your workin' here. That's what Wickham told him, 'cause he saw you on the property."

"He didn't!" I said in vain.

"He did, as sure as I'm standin' here." Daniel nodded. "Wickham didn't know that you weren't supposed to be here. He thought that he was sayin' a good thing; that you were a fine lad with good prospects."

"Was my father happy?' Thomas squinted nervously. Daniel shrugged.

"I don't know. But I'm sure he wasn't gonna say anythin' in the tavern." Daniel tilted his head as a thought came into view. "Didn't your father say anythin' to you this mornin' before you left?"

"No," Thomas hung his head, "not a word. He was out milkin' when I left, as usual."

"Maybe, he followed you to see if it was true, that you were comin' here?" I deduced.

"Nobody followed me."

"So maybe your ol' man doesn't mind you here after all?" Daniel leaned languidly against a dividing beam. "You're bringin' home some brass, eh. He's grown smart for himself, your father—seen the light."

Thomas raised his eyes to the boy, but his expression belied his lack of faith in Dan's words.

"Dan might be right. 'Cause you would've been bawled out already. Look, you're here now!" I observed with gleaming hope.

"Ah, you're right, I suppose." He rubbed his shoe on a flagstone. "All's the same, but I can't say I'm too eager to get home now, though."

"Here"—I reached into my pocket—"take my watch." I handed the machine-swirled silver hunter over to the boy.

"Why are you showin' me that? Am I late for somethin'?" He cocked his head like a curious hen.

"I'm givin' it to you. It's a woman's sure, but nobody'll know as it's in your pocket. So if you can come here again, it'll keep you punctual. And if you must stay away now, then you can have somethin' to remember that when you're older you can come back here, when nobody can talk against it." I pushed the watch over and he held it before him as if it would melt away.

Chapter 27

The night had brought a light rain, and the first whisper of morning drifted through the veils of mist. Color was called back into the land with those first amber strokes of the dawn. It was going to be another grand day, just to spite us. I reached for the small table clock by my bed, and I noted that the hour was painfully early. I rolled the linens from my chin, and I sat up in my ancient bed. The distant sound of bird shooters had teased me awake, and I didn't have the desire to ease myself into sleep again.

Jumping onto the cool floorboards, I went to the window. The night shirt wrapped warmly about my draft touched legs. I listened to the faint crowing of the waking rooks, and I wondered if Donovan had roused himself. An oddity teased my eye. I searched for it over by the area of the stable. Through the trees a golden light sparkled from the second floor of the carriage house. It was early for Daniel to be greeting the day. He must have been roused by the birders too. I went for my clothes and dressed hurriedly so that I might join him in watching the night climb away.

A light flickered beneath the door of my father's study. I padded past it, and the glow licked over my shoes. I went to the nursery to release Donovan. I left his window open and then dashed out the back of the house.

The air was light and new, and the beads of the past rain glistened upon the silent grass. The bushes dried their leaves on my shoulders, rustling pleasantly as I passed. I opened the stable door and trotted down the dusty, brick aisle. I was welcomed with a chorus of sleepy knickers before I rapped on the carriage-house door.

I waited, and I heard the clatter of footsteps, but they did not come my way. I looked up at the empty second floor balcony, where once we had witnessed the argument between my father and mother. There was silence now. I rapped on the door again. There was some disgruntled mumbling coming faintly from inside. As sure as magic the footsteps started again, and a hinge creaked from above.

"Anne?!" The astonished voice called my eye upward. Daniel leaned from the balcony with his ample green eyes staring down into my face. "I didn't expect you now." His face warmed. "Why didn't you use the other door?"

"Oh, I'm not gonna stand where the dead woman lay. It's too early. There's still time for ghosts to be about." I moved out to where he could see me better.

"Ah, well if your fearful of Famine ghosts bein' out, there'd be so many around there'd be no room left for the livin'." He raised his head, and ran a finger past his cheek. "So what makes you think there aren't any ghosts along the back entrance?"

I shrugged. "I do know that there weren't any bodies ever waitin' at the foot of that threshold." He nodded, and then disappeared into the house to let me in.

Inside the common room a kettle steamed over the fire while the stoneware cups waited on the table.

"God, it's so early. I'll be dyin' for breakfast." Daniel slouched in the chair.

"Why were you up then? Is Peader up?"

He gestured, "yes". "There was a man come, said that there was some sort o' shootin' accident. So Peader dressed and followed the fella. Was better for him to go than me," he said. "So I stayed."

"I heard the guns this mornin'. Bird shooters probably."

"Don't see how much luck they're gonna get. They'd have to wait around for the birds to rise up if they were out at that hour. They succeeded in wakin' everybody anyway."

"Did you hear it was a bad accident?" I toyed with the cup on the table.

"Naw, the man didn't seem concerned. He was kinda cold really, about things." Dan smiled as he went for the steaming kettle to start the tea. "I don't know why I'm makin' this, it'll only make me hungrier." The water hissed on the iron spout as it spilled into the steeping pot, and we waited for the drink to form.

"So guess what I got in the post?" He stretched his legs under the table, and clasped his hands under his chin.

I shrugged. "Did you order somethin'?"

"No. It was a letter."

"A letter from your brother in America?"

"No. Give it another try."

"Your sister, so?"

"Not from the family." He shook his head.

"Ah, that rules out Queen Victoria, then."

"Don't be cheeky." He dropped his chin to his chest.

"I'm tired, just tell me." I leaned on the table.

"I got a letter from the editor of the *Freeman's Journal*."

"You did!" My eyes widened.

"They got my poem and they liked it, and they're gonna put it in. I got some other note that said he wanted to know if I would be interested in contributin' regularly, like."

"Oh, that's grand. And they don't know you're fifteen, only?"

"Nope. On merit." He clapped his hands together. "What they don't know, they don't need." The boy pushed up to the table. "Although, that man invited me to the Dublin office. Ah, but . . . I don't know."

"Yes, father'll give you leave absolutely, on somethin' like that. You can get away from here. That fella up there won't mind your fifteen. He'll take you on your merit, as you said. Did you tell Peader?"

"I told him. And he was relieved that I might release him early from the waitin' grasp of the mad house, if I were to leave for new employment."

"Don't let him fool you. He's proud, he is." I nodded, and poured out the tea.

We talked some of the moments away while the tea simmered down to a drinkable heat. The morning seemed to linger forever, but we found the conversation to fill it.

"Mrs. Kelly'll be up now to wake the fires. We can get some bread and things from her." I sipped the tea.

"I could use somethin' like that. I'd starve before the usual breakfast." He stood from the table. "I'll go to find Peader, if I can. Tell 'im where I am. I won't be long though. If he's gone off guidin' those shootin' fella's, I'm not goin' too far to flush him out." Daniel took his jacket from the chair, and I followed him out to the yard.

"Well, I can't believe our Daniel got into the paper, and at such an age as he did." Mrs. Kelly fluttered over to the oatmeal chest and lifted out the raw ingredients for the stirabout. She dashed over to the hearth to study the readiness of the cooking water. "I'll boil an egg for him."

"I don't know when it'll be out. They didn't say in the letter." I followed the woman around the kitchen. Her ill-lucked husband had made a hasty recovery on Mrs. Byrne's chicken-broth, and if he wasn't left with a permanently askewed nose, and a limp, you would barely have known that he had had a thorough going over all those weeks before.

"Well, we sure will keep an eye out for his writin'." She grasped the dry oats and scattered them into the boiling water. "Oh, I still can't believe it. Mr. Daniel Whelan in print, and at fifteen years, and that's all. My mother said, as God closes one door he goes and opens another. We needed to hear somethin' like that under this roof. It's like a funeral every day here these past weeks. I could feel my hair goin' grey with the gloom. I'm relieved to see a sparkle of somethin' on your own young face, Ms. Anne. You were due for it. A child's not supposed to be broodin' at your age as if the world was sittin' atop your back. T'isn't right, t'isn't a t'all. There's time a'plenty for that yet. Now, we'll get your Sheridan smilin', and then we'll start work on the master and mistress. That'll be as easy once they get a look at their happy children. Keep your spirits up, Ms. Anne, that's the only way to save 'em. God, the worry's breakin' o'er 'em somethin' awful." She mixed the stirabout, and sat down on a creepie.

"Can we make somethin' for Dan? He likes a ginger cake." I inquired. That was Thomas's favorite too. I wondered if he'd be able to come today to get it.

"And why not! That would be the proper way to celebrate." Mrs. Kelly struck her hands together, and a timed echo of gunshot clapped from out the border of the house. It seemed to come from the cemetery. The stillness of the dawn raised the sound to a bell-like order that rolled over the air with a demanding shock. It was as the moment when a storm wave crashes upon the beach.

"Well, that was near!" She dashed to the window.

"Oh, there's shooters about, I heard them this mornin'." I rose from the chair to stand behind her. "Peader went out to help them."

"What are they after shootin'? Our chickens?" She wiped her hands on her apron. "Glad to not be pickin' mushrooms on this mornin' with them about. I'd be liable to be plucked and hung, if they're shootin' that close to people's properties." She shook her head and returned to the rolling contents of the boiling pot. I stared over her shoulder as she tended the early breakfast. The stirabout was getting warm-smelling. I became hungry by it.

"Oh, now wouldn't you notice, Anne, I forgot the potholder. Would you get one for me so I can keep this from burnin' and thickenin' up."

I went to the linen pantry and searched for a suitable cloth to perform the potholding duty. As I searched, I heard the outside door to the kitchen creak. I reached for a small, thick towel that rested on the top shelf by standing on the bottom rim of the dresser. A cry of astonishment broke free in the near room. It startled me so, that I slipped from the dresser and slapped upon the floor. I managed to have kept a hold upon the towel, and I quickly scrambled for the kitchen.

By the fire Mrs. Kelly had her hand to her open lips. I followed her gaping eyes to the rough scullery table, and the towel slipped from my hand. Peader leaned heavily on the wooden edge. His back was strangely bent. He heard me come in, and with great labor he raised his head to me.

"Go get your father, girl." His voice was dark and tired. My eyes fixed upon that part of the scullery table, which grew scarlet beneath where he leaned. Mrs. Kelly grasped the towel from my feet and went to the stricken man's side.

"Daniel's out lookin' for you." My voice was stubborn and unnatural.

"Jesus wept." Peader fixed his eyes on me when I said the words. He fell against the table, and Mrs. Kelly tried to ease him into a chair. He pushed her back. I watched as she removed the man's overcoat as if he would crumble and break. He tried to rise, but she pushed him down.

I ran from the room with involuntary speed. The stairs rose before me like a wooden hill, and I choked as I dashed to the top. My fist shook as I struck my father's door so hard that my fingers ached. The door had not been shut properly, and it swung open with the force. The open room seemed to speak to me with its silence. No one dwelt inside.

"Your father's gone, Anne."

I gasped when I heard the sound behind me. The speaker straightened after seeing the reaction she had caused.

"He's gone to the stable to saddle a horse." My mother stood fully dressed, her face ashen and tired. I told her about Peader in the kitchen with the blood on the table. I told her about Daniel being outside, and I spoke with the urgency of disaster. Instantly, my hand was grasped, and she ushered me down the stairs.

At the front door we halted. My father stood at the open threshold. His presence stilled our haste, and his eyes burned as he read the distress in our faces. The door gaped menacingly behind him, showing that Padraic stood readied in the drive. The early light spilled softly about my father's shoulders, and the black cloth of his frock coat was lit golden with its touch. The waistcoat of the darkest vermillion jealously held what remained of the night in its folds. The tall man stared at my mother as he read the thoughts in her eyes. She said nothing to him. They had not been forced this near together in days.

"I must go to the kitchen." She turned from him in a rustle of cloth, and I was pulled along like a doll.

"Peader wants you father." I called back as my mother's thin grasp dragged me forward.

Mrs. Kelly's hand was clumsy with emotion as she tended to the man's wounds. Peader started and groaned. The sleeve of his shirt was flushed with red, and the terrible dye had seeped down into his waistcoat.

"Have a care woman! The bullet's still in there." He pulled away from her. "It's like me side's on fire."

Mrs. Kelly looked with overwhelming anxiety toward my mother.

"They weren't bird-shooters, Anne." Daniel stood sentry by the pantry door, and I turned with relief to see him there. "They did a job on that one." He motioned toward Peader.

My mother squeezed my hand before releasing me. "Daniel," she set her hard gaze on the boy, "take Niamh, and go for Dr. Hill. Do not stop for anyone."

"I will, ma'am." Daniel made quickly for the door.

Peader straightened in the chair. There was an unfamiliar morbid luster to his eyes. "They've loosed the ferret, sir . . . and flushed me out."

Mrs. Kelly looked up. My mother had gone for the whiskey. Behind me stood my father. His face was hardened, and the paleness of outrage chilled over the flesh as he devoured his old friend's words. He began to stroke my hair, and I tensed beneath the anguish that dwelt in his gentle hand. I could feel the hate.

"Don't worry, Peader." My father's voice was low and burdened.

"Your man was there, sir," Peader continued to speak with resolute urgency despite Mrs. Kelly's attempts to silence him. "I ne'er seen a man so pleased to see me than your Cosgrove. A fine game laid out this mornin'. Sure, I ne'er saw it comin'. God, it was that fine. Ne'er would I 'av guessed there'd be such rich cleverness as that on our William."

My mother had returned with the Jameson's, and not even a glance did she have for her husband.

"I'm flattered though, that he figured he'd need to lay such an agile trap to catch me." Peader smiled with distorted pride. He seemed to quiver as my mother pressed the wet cloth beneath his waistcoat. "He was pleased to see me though, as I've ne'er seen of anyone before. I made the day grand for him, I did. And polite, that you'd swear his hat would bend to you without a hand laid on it. I'm glad to have clapped eyes on 'im, so. Got the yellow hair of Mr. Kelly, and just taller than yourself, Mícheál. And there he was standin' by the bohereen at the back, the finest gentleman to be seen, and me own pistol on the dresser. That's what I told 'im. And to prove his merit, sir, didn't he say how it was gonna pain him to shoot an unarmed man. Now then, what a gracious thing. Didn't I feel the blag'gard, sir, for puttin' that pain on him. I told him that, and he liked it."

Peader's voice was hazy now, and my father's eyes glazed as he listened to the distress that had passed into the life of his gentle friend. "There was the shame then for lettin' your Cosgrove down so hard. Ah, he meant the mark to be fatal, but his aim wasn't sharp or the gun was a poor make. But I'll bet this to be the finest bullet e'er. The first I've taken, and what a luxury is that to have it come from him. Wouldn't surprise me to see it made of gold." He drank from the whiskey, and grimaced. "Now, Mrs. Kelly, what would you give an abstainer? You go tell your fine husband to try the drop sometime, or be sure to ne'er get himself shot." The woman tried to hush him as she wiped the blood from her hands. My mother poured her a drink as well.

"Anne"—my mother raised her head—"is Thomas returning today?"

"He wasn't sure, because Mr. Timoney heard that he was workin' here, and not for some other woman." I spoke, but my mind was on the weakening man.

"Mr. Wickham was told by old Timoney that he had his blessing, since his son was old enough to get employ where he wished." That was Mrs. Kelly's answer.

"God save us." Peader dropped his head, and grasped Mrs. Kelly's arm.

The maid's last sentence struck me as no other words could. It married with something from poor Peader's voice, and cut deep into my mind. There should have been joy where fear now reigned. How those words rose to our ears. I could feel my father standing near me. I dared not look at anyone. I could not look at the blood that darkened and drowned the table's wood. I did not want to move, should even the air touch me.

"Thomas comes on the bohereen." I let the fire in the hearth flicker in my eyes. "It's his only way." I looked at Peader, and I saw the anguish my words had placed over his pain filled eyes.

My father released his hand from my shoulder. Instantly, he struck from the scullery. I followed him down the hall as he turned for the sitting room, I stopped and stood by the wide door. His boots struck the wood with explosive measure. I stepped back as he seized the rifle from the single rack above the hearth. That action was languid and sober, and the force of his purposeful grip burdened the gun to rattle.

I ran to the front hall. Sheridan waited upon the stairs, and one look at me was enough to silence all voice in him. We watched my father as he went through the front door. I ran to the window and pressed up to the casement.

He was tall enough to mount the black gelding with reckless ease. The skirt of his coat fell loosely over the horse's back. Padraic stiffened with the weight of his determined master. The gelding leaned into the bit, he clenched his teeth as the rein touched upon his neck, and he cantered from the spot with the gravel crushing beneath the black hooves.

Sheridan came to my side. I could feel his presence, as I let my face rest against the cool window glass.

"He's come hasn't he." My brother's voice ground in my head. "Cosgrove's come for the 'price'."

My father had not returned. The house was bereft of life, yet we walked throughout it. Daniel had arrived alone with Dr. Hill. Niamh was too spent to be asked to return, and would rest out the night under the Hill's hospitality. Her favorite groom was especially exhausted from the effects of his early morning and from the lack of any breakfast, save the cup of tea. Some of that discomfort was relieved by the treatments of warmed whiskey, beef broth, and a nap by the sitting room fire. I waited with Sheridan while Daniel slept, and I tried to close my eyes against the barren gun rack above the hearth.

Daniel's friend did not fare so well. Peader had fallen quite ill after the attempt on his life. He had dropped upon Mrs. Kelly, and a field hand had to be found to lift him from the scullery floor. He was conveyed to the guest room, where he had lain stricken and senseless for quite some hours. The bullet had been recovered and was unfortunately found to be composed not of gold but of common lead. Dr. Hill called him the luckiest man to be alive for "walking away from what should have been fatal. That has to be the closest accident I've ever seen." The wounds it had caused were serious but not grave, and it was to be expected that he would not be completely sound for some time to come.

Peader had returned to us at a little after five and perfectly in time for the soup that Mrs. Byrne had concocted with her renowned alchemy. I had followed her into the guest room to relieve my mother of her sick watch, but it was the startling effect of old Mrs. Byrne and her aromatic chicken broth on the man that captured my attention. The smell of the consommé alone induced the poor fellow to turn sick again, which caused Mrs. Byrne to cluck and scold at her broths not being touched. Peader closed his eyes while she admonished him by threatening that "with one lick of it you'd be up tomorrow. But do as you like you stubborn dog and sup of that laudanum, which'll be sure to lay you low." She received a narrow look from him, and he managed to groan with the weakness of a kitten that he had "two strokes of the di'vil's luck today . . . a pesterin' woman . . . and a bullet that's come to be no more gold than my . . ."

He was interrupted by Mrs. Byrne, who managed another "see what that doctor's potion does to ya'," when she noticed the effects the laudanum and wine had produced on his slowed speech. He turned his head to look at me, and I moved closer to the bed.

"Do you tell me, Anne, that the boy was in the kitchen room and was safe?" He addressed me softly, as he struggled to stay awake.

"I do, Peader. Daniel was there, and is tired now, but safe."

"You bring Thomas to me, girl, so that I will see him safe. I don't want another buried before me, Anne. I don't want that." The last words escaped with drowsy effort—"Níl mé dhá iarraidh sin . . ."

I was startled to hear that opium inspired plea, because it was not meant to be left in a dream. A sorrow was building inside me, and I stayed awhile as he slept.

It was deep into the night. My father had not passed the threshold. The sitting room was still, and a chillness settled as the hearth glowed down. No one had set it properly to rest the night, and so it would be dead by morning. I was too tired to move from the sheepskin throws, or did I desire to lose the warmth from them. Sheridan slept in the expanse of our father's chair, and the stuffed fabric had seemed to be trying to devour him. Daniel slept by me, my head rested against his side, and I feared to wake him should I move. Rowan was curled beneath my arm, and his dark eyes glistened with the glow from the embers. My thoughts rose to the nursery. I knew that Norah had brought Donovan's supper, but that would be all. No one had shut the window there, and so the raven would have the moon's breeze to keep him company.

I closed my eyes just as my mother's steps closed on the room. Her shoes were softer to hear than the heavier boots of the maid. I could sense her stand a moment, before turning back to the hall. Mrs. Kelly's voice whispered in the darkness. "Go take some rest, ma'am. All o' the men are wary, you'd ne'er a solider group of guards at Kilmainham. No one but a ghost would reach that door tonight. There's no good in hauntin' the house yourself. Mrs. Byrne's with Peader for the night. The master'll be home by the dawn. You know 'im, ma'am. He'll come back no sooner'n his own good time." A candle flickered in the hall.

"I think too much to sleep in this house, Mary." I heard my mother speak softly. "What I think asleep is worse than what I think when awake. I'll take the lesser of the two."

"Shall I go get my husband, ma'am? To keep watch here for you?"

"I'll keep watch, Mary, of everything. I don't want to miss a shadow of it, should any of it go away. Things have a way of losing themselves, don't they."

"They do, ma'am."

The voices disappeared down the hall. The candlelight faded with the footsteps. Rowan snickered and pushed himself nearer me. My hand curled round his lavish fur, and I soon fell asleep with the soft warmth of him.

The grey light of dawn flowed through the window when I started awake. Daniel stirred as I sat upright. I looked toward the window where Rowan was perched, and the glass was flecked with the droplets from the soft rain that had fallen during some part of the night. Sheridan was still asleep, and the rest of the house was calm.

"Did you hear that?" Daniel sat at attention.

"No." I rubbed my eyes.

"It woke you. Sounded like a horse. Maybe it's Niamh brought back." He pushed to his feet.

I followed him out to the front hall where there seemed to be something passing.

"No, Anne!" Mrs. Kelly grabbed my shoulder and started round. Her face was grey with sleeplessness, and her eyes were wet from past tears. She shook my shoulders, and I stared at her as if I was cut from stone. She brushed the hair from my forehead to call some expression from me, but I had none to give. With a twist, I broke from her and continued with Daniel at my back. I could hear the woman sobbing, but I dared not turn. The sound was desperate, and it echoed in the openness of the house.

I did not go into the hall. I stood awhile at the edge. Daniel waited behind me, and he stared as I did. There was little else to do. I stared into the small, dark space. The modest chandelier was out, and the narrow light from the windows spread weakly over the heavy, panelled walls, and across the stone floor.

The rifle from the sitting room now rested on the ancient oak table. The barrel glistened from the same wet that darkened the oaken stock. By the weapon's side, my father leaned upon the console's edge. His shoulders were narrow and crumpled. His head was held limply, and the thick, black hair fell wildly at his neck. The rain dripped from the raven strands, it dripped from his coat, and it formed in sparkling pools at his feet. I walked to him, and he bent his head to me as I approached. There was a darkness in his eyes like the darkness in a pool that had known a drowning. I smelled the rain on him. I smelled leather and metal. There was a dampness that seemed to fill the hall as if the very spirit of the rain had entered. I stepped back with a strange fear before my legs denied to move any farther. My father stirred and dragged his fist across the table. There was a scraping sound that I did not expect to hear from flesh, and there was no ring to make it. His hand slid from the table, and a long chain tumbled from his fist. I stared at the glistening silver lest I look at the blood that painted his fingers and the cuff of his sleeve. He held his arm out to me. I offered my open palm as I knew he wished for it. I stiffened as the chain touched my skin; as the larger hand covered my own and opened to place the object there.

I ran to the entry window. I stopped by the casement, for there was nowhere left to go. The cold, hard object burned in my closed grasp, the chain bit into my palm. I could feel a wetness on the surface of the silver case, but all the wet did not spread to my skin like rain, because there was some rain to compare the other to. I opened my palm before Daniel reached my side. I was desperate to see it alone, I needed to know alone. And I saw the silver hunter resting in my open hand. I gazed upon the watch as if it would melt away, leaving only the blood to remain. Sheridan was at the door now. I could see his shadow there.

Daniel took the gory watch from my grasp as I knew he would do. He wiped the stains from my hand with his own before I pulled it from him. I left his side and I went to the edge of the hall from where I had earlier come. There sounded a bustle of fabric from the back of the room, and I stopped to watch my mother appear. With mechanical grace, she walked into the hall. My father turned to see her standing in the center of the room. He tried to move from the console that held him. His hand slipped heavily upon the varnished surface, and he lunged again for that four-legged crutch to steady him. She walked to him, two strides away, and there she stood. He moved for his wife as one burdened by drink, but she did not stir as he fell. My mother's eyes were empty, her head set straight. She saw the dark stains on his coat that spread so unlike the rain water. She saw the blood that married with the scarlet of his waistcoat. But those marks came not from him.

My father rose to his knees, and he reached for the hem of her dress. She could not pull him from the grief. She did not turn away. She shivered from his touch, but would not give him her eyes. He swayed with a staggered coordination. His face touched her skirt. Only then did she let her hand fall onto his shoulder.

I walked to the console. The rifle barrel seemed to sweat those beads of rain that rested on its oiled skin. I reached for the steel mouth, and I ran my finger along the inside of the cold rim. The gun was impeccable but for the barrel. The black soot now soiled my finger. I wiped it on my dress, and the small stain sat starkly against the pale cloth.

My father had collapsed on the floor, and I steadied myself on the table that had once held him. My mother closed her eyes, and she let herself down by his side. Her dress floated about her like a rolling silken sea, and she sat above those waves that would never submerge her. She gazed on him, her head tilted, and she brought her hand to rest upon the raven hair.

Chapter 28

Ms. Farrell had returned from Dublin by coach. Norah had sent for her, and Mrs. Kelly had gone in the gig to collect the woman. They thought it was best that she "would be at the house for us." I was glad that Rowan and Donovan were about, as they didn't look at me with the sorrow and the pity, wondering about how I was. They knew how I was.

The funeral was to be held on Thursday. The wake was at the Timoney cottage, and Mrs. Hutcheson, even though she was Protestant, and Mrs. O'Toole were there to do everything. They were good women. I knew what they had to do. They had to make ready the body. Mrs. Timoney was being kept at the Hutcheson house. It was said that they were afraid that her mind might take leave of her should she stay in the cottage where her son was laid out. Mrs. O'Toole had taken her away, and she had said that the poor woman was moaning something over and over about seeing the raven flying over the cabin at no later than half-ten the night before the boy's death. "The raven was heralding the death!" She had cried.

I knew that that was no dark-minded bird. That had been my Donovan going home, for it was a lone bird that she saw, and the wild ones flew in groups. Donny flew alone, and he always passed the Timoney house, Thomas had said so. Our raven would not have heralded his friend's death. He would not have wanted to set Mrs. Timoney to grieving.

The Timoney children were staying with their mother at the Hutcheson's. It was only their father at the cabin with Mrs. O'Toole, Mrs. Hutcheson, the neighbor women . . . and Thomas. I thought it strange that after Thursday, I would never see Thomas again. My mother had made the one photograph of him dressed as Alexander the Great. Paddy was Bucephalus. I was glad that she had learned how to photograph, or I would never had had his likeness—save the ghost in my head. I could not sleep for that ghost, for it came in the quiet time when there was nothing. Peader had been right. He knew about those things.

The priest stayed the night with us at Carrickduff. He was up late talking with my father. I was up with the ghost in my head, and I heard them. I went over to Sheridan's room. Daniel was sleeping in there with my brother for now, for he was not to stay in the stable alone. Up we sat, the three of us. Dan told me that the priest "was come to say the Mass over Thomas, so that his soul might hastily remove itself to heaven."

"Why can't his soul stay with us?" My brother rubbed the hem of his nightshirt.

"You can't see souls," I said, thinking of the boy's picture in my head.

"No, sure, he's to go to heaven, you see. That's how it's done. 'Tis a terrible thing to wander as a ghost. Thomas is in paradise . . . that's his reward." Daniel leaned his head against the bedpost. The candle we had lit warmed the shadows on the boy's face. We had rolled a blanket by the gap under the door so that the tiny light would not betray its presence.

"I don't want to be rewarded, not like that." Sheridan frowned.

I tried to think of Thomas being happy.

"Ah yes . . . you do," Daniel whispered. "Everybody does. The Lord suffered and died so that we'd all know that reward. 'Tis a grand thing. And you'll see Thomas again."

"Will Rowan be there, in heaven . . . when he dies?" Sheridan whispered back.

"He will," Dan answered.

"And Donovan?" my brother questioned.

"And Donovan."

"And Ashlyn, and Paddy, and the chickens—"

"Yes. All animals are blessed," Daniel interrupted. "They are without sin, so they are. They don't e'en need a priest. They go right up to heaven faster than you can think."

"Even faster than that," I added. "And Thomas went that fast too." I curled up at the foot of the bed. "I'll bet he's already talkin' to Peader's son, and Lord Edward, and Robert Emmet."

"And Daniel O'Connell and our grandparents?" Sheridan stuffed his legs beneath the bedclothes.

"And the Liberator!" Daniel blew out the tiny candle. "And your grandparents, and everybody else."

Everyone would be there for the funeral. Everyone save our Peader and our Mrs. Kelly. He was too ill, and she was to stay by his side. Nobody told Peader that my father had found the boy dead. It was a wise thing; I knew that to be so. Sorrow would wait; the spreading of the news of my friend's passing would not give him back. Mourning did not ease the sick, and I did not want my Peader to die. "How much sadness can one man take"—that was what Ms. Farrell had said. "And your Mr. Hayes was so fond of that boy . . . weren't we all though."

I took the watch to the funeral. I put it in the pocket by the hem of my skirt. Nobody knew but Donovan and Rowan. The watch did not run. It had got the wet inside and had stopped at six ten in the morning. It stopped the morning that Thomas died. I never wanted the thing to be fixed. I wanted to know when my friend had stoppped growing up.

We went to the funeral in the best carriage. Padraic and Canon were in the traces stepping high as if they were headed to the shore. They didn't know. Padraic had seen the body on that morning, but he didn't know that we were going to the funeral. The wake had lasted two days.

Thomas was laid out in the cabin's large central room. He was on his parent's bed, which was to be burned after the wake. I had thought that I wouldn't have wanted to see him clothed with the burial linen and the flowers upon him. But I did, I went to him. He looked to be resting; he looked the same as he did on that last afternoon in the hothouse. I felt separated from the others in the room, like a leaf flitting through a crowd: the leaf on its business, and the people on theirs, and the two never meeting, or noting each others' paths. I was like the Lady of Shalott, but there was no Lancelot to stand to my passing. I stood to Thomas's passing.

Sheridan and Daniel were beside me. I could smell the dish of tobacco that rested by the body. I could smell the candles that burned near it. I turned my eyes to the window where my father stood. He lifted the pipe to his lip, for he only smoked at céilís and wakes. His face was thin and staring as a hawk's. The boy's death had broken him. It had broken all of us. My mother touched my shoulder, and I followed her to the corner where there were chairs for us to sit on.

I was the last to kiss Thomas good-bye before the lid was set down. The coffin was brought outside. Mr. Timoney, his eldest son, Mr. Hutcheson, and my father carried the small coffin. It was a good distance to the churchyard, and we had arranged for a hearse to take Thomas the rest of the way. We had never spent so much time with the Timoneys, and soon they would be moving their belongings to an estate in the south.

The procession had not gone a moment's progress when the rain began to fall. Carrickduff would be black again. I wanted the rain to be at the funeral. Ms. Farrell said "it was fitting."

I knew that it was.